DOCTOR WHO

LOVING THE ALIEN

ROBERT PERRY & MIKE TUCKER

DOCTOR WHO:
LOVING THE ALIEN

Commissioning Editor: Ben Dunn
Creative Consultant: Justin Richards
Project Editor: Sarah Lavelle

Published by BBC Worldwide Ltd
Woodlands, 80 Wood Lane
London W12 0TT

First published 2003
Copyright © Robert Perry and Mike Tucker
The moral right of the authors has been asserted

Original series broadcast on the BBC
Format © BBC 1963
Doctor Who and TARDIS are trademarks of the BBC

ISBN 0 563 48604 X
Cover imaging by Black Sheep, copyright © BBC 2003
Front cover photograph by Robin Prichard

Printed and bound in Great Britain by Mackays of Chatham
Cover printed by Belmont Press Ltd, Northampton

For JNT

PART ONE

Chapter One

'This is the BBC. Here at Winnerton Flats hundreds of people have turned out to watch history being made. In the distance the elegant shape of the Blue Streak rocket dominates the skyline, and on top of it the experimental Waverider, the plane that the British Rocket Group hope will put a man into orbit and them into the record books.

'Here in the launch control room there is an air of barely concealed excitement as white-coated technicians scurry around like ants, checking and re-checking their calculations, all eyes on the clock ticking relentlessly towards zero hour.

'As for Uncle Sam, well, he's starting to look a little green with envy as our plucky chaps look like beating them to the punch. On the other side of the pond the Dyna-Soar project has run into a few problems, whilst here all systems are go, ready to make the Dyna-Soar look like a dinosaur!'

Rita Hawks raised a perfectly measured eyebrow and gave an unlady-like snort of contempt.

'If that's the best reporting you can do, then you're the only dinosaur round here, bud!'

The grey-suited BBC reporter cupped his hand over his microphone and gave her a disapproving look.

'If you don't mind, madam, we are on the air!'

'Yeah? Well, chances are that any listeners you had have probably dozed off. Still, it could be worse. They might be able to see you instead of just hear you, and you've got a face that was made for radio.'

There were guffaws from her fellow – or, rather rival – journalists. The BBC man spluttered with indignation. 'Well, really.'

There was a good-natured chuckle from the doorway. 'Hey, Rita, the war's over, remember, and even if it weren't, I think we were on the same side as the Brits.'

Rita flashed a brilliant smile at the young army major who had just entered the control room. 'Ah, I know, Bill, but these BBC guys are an easy target. They bring out the worst in me.'

'And I thought it was me that did that.'

'No, you bring out the mother in me. It's those baby cheeks of yours.'

'Flattery now?'

'You get all the flattery you need from these British girls; I've seen you prowling the officers' club.'

'But you know that I prefer older women.'

'Well, if you're going to insult me, you can let me smoke a cigarette.'

Rita pulled an elegant silver cigarette case from her handbag and snapped it open. 'Got a light?'

'Sure.' The major slipped a lighter from his jacket and flicked it into life, cupping his hands over the tip of her cigarette.

'Thanks.' Rita took a deep drag and blew a cloud of blue smoke into the air. There was a cough from the control room. One of the white-coated lab technicians was looking at her sternly over the rim of his glasses.

'Miss Hawks, must I remind you yet again about smoking in the control room?'

'All right, all right! Jeez.' She fanned her hand through the cloud of cigarette smoke, sending wispy spirals towards the ceiling.

'I'd better step out onto the terrace. Care to join me, Bill?'

The major pulled his cap onto his head and grinned. 'I don't think that the general would be too pleased to find his staff fraternising with members of the opposite sex whilst on duty.'

'Well, if the general would like to fraternise with me, I could do with a few words for the paper.'

'Well, I don't know...'

'Oh, come on Bill, what's the point of me being well connected if my connections don't get me any closer than this? All I need is five minutes with him. It'd be a helluva scoop.'

'Are you sure you wouldn't rather spend five minutes with me? I know a quiet little place...'

'Bill Collins...'

'OK! OK! I'll see what I can do.' He grinned. 'But I'll have to lie about the paper. You don't think your rag usually gets invited to these shindigs, does it? I'll say you're from the *Mirror*.'

'Why not *The Times*?'

Collins smirked.

'Say anything!' Rita blurted.

'And it's going to cost you a drink later.'

Rita sighed.

'Sure. You never give up, do you?'

'Never.'

With a wink Major Collins straightened his uniform and crossed the control room. Two privates snapped to attention as he passed and he gave a lazy salute. Rita smiled. The young major was so cocky. Cute, but not her type. She raised her cigarette again, then caught the eye of the lab technician.

'I'm going! I'm going!'

She pulled open the door of the control room and stepped out onto the terrace that overlooked the launch site. The November air was crisp and cold, and Rita pulled her cardigan tighter around her shoulders, glad of the warmth from the cigarette. She squinted through the morning glare to where the rocket sat on its launch pad. The slender shape glinted under the winter sun, like the steeple of some technological church.

Rita nodded in approval. She liked that analogy. She'd use it in her article. Show the BBC guys what real journalism was all about.

A gust of cold wind sent ash from the tip of her cigarette skittering across the terrace and she ducked behind one of the crumbling columns that lined this wing of the house.

It was typical of the Brits to set a state-of-the-art space development centre in the shell of an Edwardian manor. She craned her neck and looked back along the elegant frontage. Up to the line of the second-floor windows Winnerton Manor looked like any one of a number of crumbling British country houses that littered the countryside, but the forest of aerials sprouting from the roof, and the huge radar dish that dominated the south wing, distinguished it as something different.

Winnerton Manor must have been impressive in its day, but time and the war had taken their toll. Out in the grounds, corrugated-iron huts sat amongst the rubble that had once been stables and outbuildings, rough, tyre-worn tracks cutting ugly swathes through the remains of the gardens. One wing of the house was gone completely, blown into dust by a German bomb intended for the docks. What remained had been hurriedly shored up with scaffolding and timber by the army, holes in the stonework repaired with brick and concrete forming harsh blemishes amidst the Edwardian grandeur. The gentle sweep of the drive leading from the main road was now dotted with barriers and checkpoints, khaki-uniformed soldiers tensing whenever a car rounded the curve of the road.

Whereas the house might once have dominated the sweep of land running down to the estuary, it now paled into insignificance next to the stainless steel tower that sat at the end of the lawn, the grey concrete slabs of the launch platform showing none of the skill and care that had gone into the house.

It saddened Rita. She was from Ohio. The oldest building they had back home was only 150 years old. Here in Britain they had buildings ten times older than that – a history, an ancient history, that had been systematically blown from the face of the country, and she wasn't sure whether the rebuilding was going to be as elegant. They were entering a new era, a new age, and already she was beginning to feel hopelessly out of her depth. As the BBC guy had said… a dinosaur…

It was the rocket that both impressed and terrified Rita. A *Blue Streak* rocket. One hundred and fifty feet of stainless steel powered by two Rolls Royce RZ2 rocket engines. A rocket built with the express purpose of retaliating against a Russian nuclear strike. A rocket designed to cause maximum devastation to people and property. A weapon of Armageddon.

The devastation caused here in Britain by the Germans was like petty vandalism compared with what her fellow countrymen could now inflict on the world. The day of 9 August 1945 should have been a happy one for Rita. Her thirtieth birthday. A day that she had intended celebrating sedately with her family out on the farm, then heading into town and getting unsedately drunk with her friends. A friendly, amiable celebration. Instead, it had become a day when a city was wiped from the face of the planet in the blink of an eye. A day when conflict became unwinnable. She had never been able to celebrate her birthday with any enthusiasm since then. To mark the anniversary of her arrival into the world when that same day had seen so many lives extinguished from it always left her with a bad taste in her mouth, and so she lied, made excuses, avoided any mention of her birthday at all. It was easier here in England. Here her close friends were few and far between, and her colleagues on the paper were more interested in her stories than her age.

Who could tell? Maybe the rocket would do some good – give the Russians pause for thought. If the rumours were true, this would make England a significant nuclear player, help redress the balance.

Anyway, this was a peaceful flight. The rocket had been adapted to carry a pilot. She stared up at the delta-winged shape perched precariously on the nose of the rocket where once a warhead would have sat.

The Waverider. An experimental space plane capable of taking man into space and bringing him back down again. Rita made a mental note. If this worked, then next year – her first birthday of the new decade – she would celebrate in style, with a man on her arm. Not one of these soldier boys, with their quick quips and their fancy uniforms; a proper man, someone she could settle down with...

The harsh rasp of a match on its box caused Rita to look up. A man had stepped out onto the terrace and lit a slim, twitching cigar, his eyes fixed firmly on the rocket.

Rita started. The man was none other than the director of the BRG, Edward Drakefell. She frowned. What the hell was going on? Less than fifteen minutes before the rocket was due to launch and the director of the project was stepping out for a quiet smoke? From what she had seen of the chaos inside, she couldn't imagine he would want to take his eye off the ball for a moment.

A furtive movement behind the curtains of the French windows caught her eye. A white-coated technician hovered worriedly inside the house. Seemed that she wasn't the only one who thought that Drakefell should be indoors. Drakefell seemed oblivious to both of them. He fiddled nervously with his cigar, blowing great clouds of smoke into the November morning without seeming to enjoy it.

The roar of an engine caught his attention. Rita looked down to see an army jeep roar out across the tarmac, the figure in the passenger seat bulky in a silver pressure suit, and the technicians in the rear making endless last-minute adjustments to the controls on the figure's helmet and backpack.

At the same time a klaxon started to wail and a clipped English voice crackled from the speaker above Rita's head.

'All personnel please proceed to firing positions. I repeat, would all personnel please report to their firing positions. Fuelling procedures are commencing. We are fifteen minutes from launch.'

The announcement seemed to goad the figure loitering behind the curtains into action. Opening the French window he called nervously to Drakefell.

'Director? Sir? The final checks...'

Drakefell, still watching the jeep making its way towards the rocket, ignored him.

'Sir...'

'Yes, all right, I'm coming!' Drakefell stubbed his cigar out on the side of a pillar and pushed past the embarrassed technician.

Rita took a last drag on her own cigarette and flicked the stub carelessly into the wind.

'Showtime...'

The control room was abuzz with nervous excitement. Engineers darted between banks of machinery checking and rechecking data, flight controllers relayed a steady stream of instructions to the rocket, while the voice of Colonel Thomas Kneale echoed harsh and tinny from a dozen speakers bolted without care to the Edwardian plasterwork.

'Pre-flight checks complete. All lights green on my board. Receiving you loud and clear, Control.'

Drakefell nodded.

'Thank you, Colonel. Start final checks.'

'Wilco. Oh, and tell Jefferson to get that drink he owes me set up. I'm going to be collecting.'

A ripple of laughter ran around the control room. The wager between Thomas Kneale and Hugh Jefferson, the barman at the Winnerton Hotel (strictly off-limits), that the Waverider would never get off the ground, was apparently well known.

Rita smiled and jotted the good-natured exchange down in her notebook. She liked Thomas Kneale. Thanks to Bill Collins, she'd spent an hour with him and Davey O'Brien, his relief pilot, yesterday and found the two young astronauts refreshingly straightforward and totally unflustered by what they were about to do.

She glanced over to where O'Brien was sitting at the front of the control room. His face was unreadable. Was he relieved that he wasn't there, strapped into a seat on the top of an intercontinental ballistic missile? Disappointed that it was Kneale's name and not his that would be gracing the history books?

Irritatingly, Rita heard the BBC reporter talking along similar lines into his microphone, his constant low commentary and perfect enunciation giving the entire proceedings the air of a royal wedding – or a funeral. She made a mental note to change her piece.

A door opened and Bill Collins marched smartly into the room, winking almost imperceptibly through the glass at Rita as he passed her.

'Perimeter secure, Director.'

Drakefell nodded. 'Thank you, Major.'

Bill snapped smartly to attention and turned on his heel.

11

On the far side of the control room the American contingent stood straight-backed and straight-faced. Towering over his colleagues, the imposing figure of General Crawhammer scrutinised the proceedings, impassive behind his mirrored sunglasses. Bill saluted crisply and fell into line next to the general.

Drakefell drew his chair close into his control position; an expectant hush settled over the room. Even the BBC reporter stopped his relentless commentary.

'Right, gentlemen.' The director's voice was calm and low. 'Can you please start the final countdown? Colonel Kneale, I wish you God speed.'

"Thank you, Director."

At a nod from Drakefell, one of the technicians started a stopwatch, counting down in slow, measured tones. Rita crossed to one of the bulky periscopes set on one wall, pushing in front of the gentleman from *The Times*. She had screamed about getting a proper photograph of the launch from the terrace, but Bill had cheerfully informed her that because of the chance of explosion, all observers would have to watch from the safety of the house, via several huge periscopes in the press gallery. All the photographs were being taken by automatic cameras, and appropriate pictures would be circulated to the press later. Bill had promised to make sure that Rita got the pick of the bunch, but she was sure that that would probably involve dinner – at the very least.

Through the periscope the rocket seemed impossibly close. Behind her she could hear the countdown being monotonously maintained. How could the guy remain so calm, for God's sake? Rita's heart was hammering in her chest.

'Twelve, eleven...'

Out in the grounds a siren began to wail, a long, drawn-out howl cutting through the November air. Rita shivered. It was too much like an air-raid siren, or the early warning signal for imminent nuclear strike that the radio kept reminding them of.

'Eight, seven...'

Rita gripped the sides of the periscope. Vapour had started to vent from the sides of the rocket.

'Five, four, three...'

The rest of the countdown was lost in the roar as the engines ignited. Huge gouts of flame, impossibly bright, leapt from the concrete launch structure. Clouds of smoke billowed into the air, engulfing the launch pad. Then, agonisingly slowly, the nose of the Waverider appeared above the chaos, steadily accelerating into the clear blue sky.

A cheer went up in the control room, and Rita drew in a deep shuddering breath. She hadn't even realised that she had stopped breathing during the final moments of the countdown.

Technicians were milling about in the control room hugging each other. General Crawhammer was pounding Drakefell on the back. People were shaking both his hands. Several of the journalists and soldiers had pushed out onto the terrace. Rita followed them.

In the bright blue of the winter sky the rocket was a tiny burning speck, a white trail of smoke stretching back to the ground. Rita shielded her eyes against the sun, craning her neck back to keep the tiny dot in view.

'Quite a firework show, eh, Rita?' Bill was at her elbow.

'Yeah, Bill, quite a show.' Rita flashed him a brilliant smile and decided to start making plans for her birthday.

After the excitement of the launch the next few hours were painfully dull. The exchanges between the Waverider and the control room became increasingly technical, and Rita was getting increasingly bored.

From what she could gather, the space plane had successfully separated from the rocket and was now cruising around the planet, carrying out experiments that meant nothing to Rita but were causing a great deal of glee to the assembled scientists. Any time soon they would start to bring Colonel Kneale back down, and that was the point when things would hot up again.

In the meantime, Rita had smoked far too many cigarettes and drunk far too much cheap English coffee. The atmosphere in the control room was getting tense. As time went on, Drakefell was getting more and more irritable, snapping at the slightest provocation from his team, glowering at any journalist or soldier who got in his way and shooting anxious glances toward the press gallery. He had even shouted at Crawhammer, and Rita would have loved to have had a camera to capture the expression of surprise on the big general's face.

The speakers crackled into life again.

'Just passing the terminator, readjust for final orbit.'

'Thank you, Colonel. We should have you down in a little under twenty minutes.'

Rita checked her watch. She had been at Winnerton nearly eight hours now. In twenty minutes the Waverider would be back on the ground and the press would have a field day. She pulled a compact out of her handbag and snapped it open, looking at herself in the tiny mirror.

'You've looked better, my girl. If you're going to be plastered all over the front of tomorrow's press...'

Pushing the compact back into her handbag, she crossed to the young American guard at the door.

'I need to go to the bathroom. Freshen up a bit.'

The soldier looked embarrassed and fumbled with the door. Rita slipped out into the hallway.

Whereas the control room of Winnerton Manor was the pinnacle of scientific achievement, the rest of the house was falling a long way behind. Faded paintings in peeling frames hung alongside brusque military security notices. Elegant panelled doors had been replaced with chunky fire doors, every window was barred, and ugly locks and bolts dotted every doorjamb.

Two squaddies jumped up as the door closed behind her, pulling themselves upright from where they had been slouched against the wall. When it became obvious that she was a civilian they relaxed. One of them broke into a wolfish grin. Smoothing her skirt down, Rita flicked back her hair and sauntered past them, aware of eyes on her rear. She couldn't be looking that bad...

The army had made sure that all civilians were corralled into one portion of the house. They'd provided dining areas, a press conference room and bathroom facilities. Rita could hear the clatter of pans from the kitchen, and the waft of something savoury caught her nose. Elsewhere the house was divided up into the scientists' quarters and barracks, laboratories and lecture rooms. There was even a gym where the astronauts had been training for the last eight months. Everything was well thought out and the British were running it meticulously.

The money was American of course, at least a good part of it. Eisenhower was making damn sure that his good buddy Macmillan was going to succeed. The Russians had already had satellites in orbit, and last month they had managed to get pictures of the dark side of the moon. In the space race they were drawing ahead, and if the USA weren't going to beat them to the punch, then they'd make damn sure that the British would.

Khrushchev's visit last September had been a disaster for the American government and they were determined to have a success to shout about. Denying the Russian premier permission to visit Disneyland for security reasons, for God's sake... What did they think he was going to do? Steal the secrets of the Pirates of the Caribbean? Assassinate Mickey Mouse?

Rita pushed open the door of the ladies' washroom. Two giggling kitchen girls hurriedly stubbed out their cigarettes and scurried past, nodding at her as they passed. Rita grinned. The British were always so polite. If only her editor treated her with the same respect.

Shrugging off her coat, Rita leaned on the washbasin and scrutinised herself in the mirror. Her lipstick had smudged and the make-up wasn't doing a very good job of hiding the dark shadows under her eyes from last night's 'quick drink' with Bill Collins.

She sighed... A forty-four-year-old woman trying to make herself look like a thirty-year-old. She shook her head angrily. She was damned if she was going to get maudlin. Rita Hawks looked good. She could still turn heads, and she had dozens of men who would happily take her out, get her drunk and take her to bed... Just no one that she wanted.

She adjusted the hemline of her skirt and straightened her stockings. Maybe not what the paper expected its journalists to wear, but it did open doors. And she was damn sure that she wouldn't have got as much information out of Bill if she'd been a man. She laughed. Press liaison officer! Who was he trying to kid?

Pulling her compact out of her handbag, she leant into the mirror and started to reapply her make-up. Damage limitation.

'Got to look your best for the history books...'

When Rita came back down the corridor five minutes later she could tell that something was wrong. The security guard on the door was jumpy, checking her pass over and over instead of giving it the usual cursory glance.

Inside the control room the atmosphere was electric. Crawhammer was standing directly behind Drakefell, peering at the radar screen. Red lights were blinking all across the control board.

Rita pushed through the jostling journos, looking for Bill Collins. He was talking earnestly to several of his colleagues. Rita crossed to him.

'Hey, Bill, what gives?'

The major's eyes were cold, his usually cheerful face set firm and icy. 'Not now, Rita, there's a good girl.'

He caught her by the elbow and steered her to the back of the control room where the rest of the journalists were clustered. Rita frowned. All of them were silent. Even the BBC reporter had his microphone hanging limply by his side.

Rita nudged him with her elbow.

'What the hell is going on?' she hissed. 'What's happening?'

He shushed her irritably. 'Listen!'

Over the crackling speakers Rita could hear the voice of Colonel Kneale, faint and distorted. And something else... a roar... flames?

'When did this start?'

The BBC man's voice was shaky. 'There was an explosion, a few moments ago.'

'An explosion?'

'That's what it sounded like, then the instruments started to fail, and now... now they're not sure they can get him back down.'

Rita thought of the cheerful young pilot she had spent yesterday afternoon with, tried not to think of him orbiting the Earth for ever. 'But how? What caused it?'

'Sorry, Rita. You've all got to go. This wasn't in the script.'

'The Russians?'

Rita felt sick. All the horror that she had felt on her thirtieth birthday welled back up inside her.

'Come on...' Collins was easing her into the line of journalists shuffling around the room.

'Back to the press wing, gentlemen. I'm sorry,' Collins called after them. Two armed Tommies stood at either side of the door to their rooms.

Hoping the bustle of her colleagues would hide her, Rita skipped to one side and through an open door.

A broom closet. Typical. Frantically she caught a falling mop, eased the door shut and listened to the receding footsteps.

'Right.' She could hear Drakefell's voice. It was shaky.

Rita scanned the little room. High up in the back wall there was a window. She up-ended a bucket and clambered up. On tiptoe she could see down into the control room.

'The Waverider is on its re-entry orbit,' Drakefell continued. 'We've lost most of our monitor controls, so we're going to try to talk the colonel back down. I want silence in this room. No voices other than my technicians, is that clear?'

There was a deathly hush. Every man was concentrating on his task, making calculations with pen and paper, trying to make up for the loss of their instruments.

A broken, distorted voice spluttered from the speakers, the strain audible even above the distortion. A blip suddenly appeared on a radar screen.

'We've got him.' The technician almost jumped from his seat. 'On final approach.'

'I can see that!' Drakefell snapped. Nervously he chewed on his fingers. 'Colonel, can you hear me? You're on final glide path. Are you all right there?'

A slow, measured countdown started across the control room.

Suddenly a screeching roar burst from the speakers. Technicians snatched headphones from their heads in agony. Rita clamped her hands to her ears but the scream cut right though her.

All around her people reeled in pain. Above the noise she could hear Colonel Thomas Kneale screaming.

'It's all around me! It's tearing right open. I can't hold her, she's breaking up, she's breaking...'

Silence fell like a thunderclap as the power blew in the control room. Seconds later the house shook with a shattering roar as something passed fast and low over it.

Rita bolted from her cubbyhole to the top of the stairs, towards the massive, leaded window. Her jaw dropped. In a blaze of flame the Waverider arced towards the estuary, black smoke billowing from its rear. Almost gracefully, it curved towards the water and for a moment – a fleeting moment – Rita thought that it was all going to be all right. Then the wing of the space plane caught the crest of a wave and it started to tumble.

Tears filled Rita's eyes as the spacecraft flipped end over end, fragments of burning metal slicing into the air, and then it was gone, steam billowing from the estuary as the water boiled.

There was a moment of stunned, disbelieving silence, then she heard Crawhammer bellowing.

'Major Collins! Get a recovery squad down to the river, now!'

Crawhammer exploded from the control room, followed by Bill Collins and a hoard of soldiers.

'And get the press outta here!'

Rita was jostled and pushed as the soldiers passed her. Her head was in a spin. Officers, British and American, barked orders, ambulance bells started to sound.

A firm grip suddenly caught her arm and gently guided her back inside the control room.

'Rita! What are you still – '

She sniffed back the last of her tears.

'What happened, Bill?' she asked.

Bill shook his head. Crawhammer stomped back, pacing, chewing on a fat cigar.

'Out, Rita.'

Reluctantly she headed for the open front door, through the bustle of technicians, troops and messengers. Bill watched her every step of the way.

The last thing she heard was Crawhammer booming, 'The Red bastards actually did it. Shot the goddamn rocket down. This is it, boys! Are you through to Washington yet?'

Bill Collins watched her leave, then dismissed her from his mind.

'Captain Zimmerman!' he barked, 'get the press pack onto the coach and off the estate. Tell them we'll be releasing a statement.'

'Sir.'

He knew the damage Crawhammer's mouth could do in times of crisis.

A secretary emerged from the switchboard room. 'Washington on the line, General.'

Crawhammer turned to Collins. 'See what's happening in the control room,' he said.

'Sir.'

Collins went back inside. The room was silent.

'What's happening?' he whispered to Davey O'Brien.

'They're in contact with the ship. There's a chance Tom's still alive.'

O'Brien sounded anxious. It wasn't surprising – he knew Tom Kneale better than any of them. And it could so easily have been him up there.

'Quiet!' Drakefell snapped. 'Colonel Kneale? Can you hear me?'

There was a breaking wave of static in the speakers, and then an indistinct voice. Next to him, Collins saw O'Brien grip the edge of a desk.

'Please say again, Colonel Kneale,' Drakefell enunciated.

'O'Brien here, sir.'

A puzzled muttering around the room. All eyes turned to Davey O'Brien. He was as pale as a ghost.

'I don't understand,' said Drakefell. 'Please repeat.'

'Captain O'Brien here, sir. I didn't think I was going to make it.'

Chapter Two

Inside the fantastic multicoloured corridor of the Time Vortex, the TARDIS – a dull blue brick – twisted and spun as if thrown. Not that it was without direction. No. It knew exactly where it was going. The exact planet, the exact country, the exact year, the exact month, the exact day. The landing position programmed down to the last millimetre.

But it had been told to wait. And so it waited, its holding pattern a complex Möbius-strip path through now and then, between here and there, across possibility and actuality.

It was impossible to tell how long it had waited – how do you measure time outside time? It flickered in and out of reality, realigning itself with the space/time curve, taking readings, picking fragments of history from the ether and shunting them through to the telepathic circuits for retrieval at a later date.

Inside the ship, in the impossibly huge control room, the time rotor rose and fell, keeping the rhythm like a metronome. Complex systems constantly monitored the internal configuration, keeping the structure contiguous where its passengers were residing, reconfiguring the rest of the ship as necessary.

Lights flickered on the hexagonal control column in response to a comment by one of its occupants that it was 'bloody cold in here'. The TARDIS raised the mean temperature in the pool area by eight degrees whilst still maintaining the specific temperature requirements in the rest of the ship as instructed by its other occupant.

He was concerned. The symbiotic relationship between ship and owner was a delicately balanced thing, and the TARDIS could sense it.

Events waited to be set in motion, waited until the Doctor was ready.

Setting another nonsensical path through the vortex, the TARDIS marked time.

Ace floated in the warm waters of the TARDIS swimming pool, or the bathroom as the Doctor insisted on calling it.

It was crazy. An Olympic-sized pool, but with all the trappings of a council house bathroom. A small Formica cabinet with mirrored doors was bolted to one wall (Ace meant to check out the small, delicate glass bottles that lurked inside), a wire rack filled with bath oils and a loofah hung in the shallow end and an entire flock of bright yellow plastic ducks bobbed and swirled around her. By contrast, the poolside was littered with white plastic loungers, wicker furniture piled high with huge soft towels and plants from a dozen different planets. Ace had never been sure how they got watered. The Doctor had never struck her as the green-fingered type.

She struck out for the deep end with long powerful strokes, muscles starting to ache pleasantly from her swim. The last couple of weeks had been remarkably quiet and she was starting to get out of condition. Not that she was going to complain. The Doctor had gone out of his way to make life as stress-free as possible. No alien worlds to save, no monsters to fight. In fact the last few weeks had been everything that she had hoped travelling with the Doctor would be.

After Blini-Gaar, after everything that they had both been through with Vogol Lukos and Channel 400[1], he had been quiet and withdrawn, and Ace had begun to get seriously worried about him; even the mood of the ship had started to become sombre. Dull day followed dull day as the Doctor dragged her off to one faceless, nameless planet after another.

And then they had landed at Heritage.[2]

Ace hauled herself out of the pool and pulled a towel from one of the wicker tables. She slumped down on a lounger and started drying her hair.

When it had all started Ace had been quite looking forward to it. A mystery to solve, an adventure to have. She should have known that something was wrong, but her guard was down. She had been bored and the little signs that she might otherwise have noticed had slipped past her. The Doctor had landed there with too much knowledge, as usual, but even he had been shocked by what they found.

Mel dead.

Poor trusting Mel. A do-gooder always seeing the best in people. So trusting that she had left the Doctor and headed out into the void with

[1] See *Doctor Who: Prime Time*
[2] See *Doctor Who: Heritage*

Sabalom Glitz without a moment's hesitation. Ready to take on the universe.

Ace's room in the TARDIS still showed signs of Mel's occupancy. Childish trinkets that Ace had tucked away in the back of a cupboard. All except one. All except a battered menu from the Shangri La Holiday Camp that Ace kept pinned to her noticeboard as a reminder. A reminder that she was not the first. That she was the latest in a long line of the Doctor's travelling companions. A reminder that nothing lasts forever.

After Heritage the Doctor had been lower than Ace had ever known him. She had barely seen him, a sometimes-glimpsed figure flitting through the darkened corridors, an occasional half smile thrown at her from across the control room as his hands danced in complex rhythms across the controls.

Then one day he had bounced into the control room with his infectious crooked smile on his face and announced that they were 'having a couple of weeks off'.

Since then they had been on a delightful, magical, *impossible* switchback tour of all the good places in time and space. They'd celebrated New Year at a dozen points in a dozen planets' histories, he'd taken her to a royal wedding on a planet entirely populated by giant butterflies, they'd hidden on the moon watching as Neil Armstrong took his first steps – the Doctor keeping her in stitches as he whistled like a Clanger. For a week they'd hiked through mountains on the planet Kriss, their sherpas the gentlest, kindest, funniest aliens that Ace had ever met, he'd bought her candyfloss at the Twelve Planet Fair while he entered the juggling contest, and they'd been to Live Aid. The two of them had never got on better and Ace had loved it.

And then they had landed at Woodstock.

At first everything had been fine. Ace still had a Polaroid of the Doctor from that day – ludicrous in his long wig and ankle-length kaftan, weighed down with beads, both hands raised in peace signs. But then she'd met Gavin and his friends – hippies from Canada. They'd hit it off and one night she had slipped away from the Doctor, lost herself in the crowd and spent the night in Gavin's tent.

The following morning the Doctor had found her, and Ace had never seen him so angry. He had practically dragged her back to the TARDIS and since then they had hardly spoken.

On several nights she had woken, sure that she had heard the familiar grind of the TARDIS's materialisation, but if they ever had landed anywhere then, the Doctor never acknowledged it.

He spent much of his time in a room deep in the bowels of the ship. Ace had followed him there once, hiding in the shadows watching as the Doctor unlocked a heavy door with an ornate key, checking over his shoulder before he did so, furtive and on edge.

That had made Ace uneasy. For the Doctor to be jumpy and nervous inside his own ship... She had planned to try to sneak back to that room when the Doctor wasn't looking, to see what secrets he was keeping, but something about his manner frightened her and she wasn't sure that she wanted to see inside that room anymore.

She shivered and pulled the towel tight about her.

'I thought I told you to put some heat on!' she bellowed.

In the absence of the Doctor she had been venting her frustration on the TARDIS. Pointless, she knew, but it made her feel better. Suddenly the shadows inside the ship had started to seem a little bit darker, the echoes a little more distant.

Whatever it was that was going on, she wished that it would be over soon.

Deep in the bowels of the time ship the Doctor sat back, exhausted, and took a deep breath.

He stripped the latex surgical gloves from his hands and let them drop into a stainless steel bin, trying not to look at the blood.

It was over.

He rubbed at his forehead. He was tired and starting to feel his age, and at over 800 years old that wasn't a good thing.

Across the other side of the room the body lay under a dark green surgical sheet. Ace's body. Not the body of an old woman, not a shrivelled corpse, but young, as she was now, and if he had any thoughts that she had died of natural causes, the bullet hole in her forehead had put paid to them.

The bullet itself sat in a stainless steel tray on the trolley in front of him. The Doctor leant forward and picked it out, holding it in front of his face. Such a simple thing. Such an easy way of killing someone. The powder burns on Ace's forehead meant that the gun had been close to her head when it had been fired. She had looked her killer in the eye as he ended her life. The bullet had torn through her brain and blasted out of the back of her skull.

When he had first found the body, when he had first dug the coffin out of the graveyard in the East End, the Doctor had painfully accepted that another death lay at his feet. There was nothing that he could do. His people had laws. Time had boundaries. Ace was dead. She *would* die, and he was powerless to stop it.

He had nearly given it all up at that moment. Nearly taken her back to Iceworld and left her, a billion parsecs and a thousand years from her death. Safe in the future.

Finding Mel had changed all that. Then he had realised that just abandoning her would kill her as certainly as that gunshot.

When he had first heard the rumours of the death of one of his travelling companions he had accepted the inevitable, blind to the fact that Heritage was the wrong place in the wrong time. Mel dead. And Ace was next...

That had forced him to do something.

And so he had indulged her, as an uncle might indulge a favourite niece. He made sure that she was happy and entertained, kept her as far from the circumstances of her death as he could take her. By pushing the fact of her death to the very back of his mind he had tried to ignore the inevitable, tried to cheat death.

Losing her for nearly twelve hours at Woodstock had made him realise how powerless he was to protect her. He could ignore things no longer.

A furtive trip to the British Library had revealed the date of her death – a young girl's body fished from the Thames. The papers littered the Doctor's secret surgery. Papers, maps, police reports.

He had unlocked the room where Ace lay and made himself confront the reality of her death. He had a head start, an advantage over time.

The tag on her toe was from St Thomas's Hospital.

Cutting open the body of his friend had been hard. Slicing into her lifeless corpse when she was still moving about the ship above him, laughing and shouting and alive.

He had tried to imagine her last days. A tattoo was emblazoned across her shoulder blade – a heart and crossbones, the legend 'Ace and Jimmy, 1959' underneath.

A livid bruise, just underneath the breastbone, the shape and size of a fist.

He had opened her stomach. The last thing she had eaten appeared to be a toffee-apple.

And there was something else. Chains of small contusions on her neck, shoulders and breasts. Colloquially known as love bites.

And... other, deeper evidence. Just hours before her death, she had had sex.

Ace looked up in surprise at the knock on her door.

'Come in.'

The Doctor's tousled head appeared, his expression puckish.

'Are you decent?'

Ace tugged her towel up a bit. 'Just about.'

The Doctor pushed open the door with his foot, her bomber jacket bundled up in his arms. 'I had a few moments, so I thought that I'd do some repairs.' He held it out proudly. 'You were coming apart at the seams.'

'It has been said.' Ace took it from him and dumped it unceremoniously onto the mess of clothes on her bed. She looked at him quizzically.

'Are you OK? I've been worried about you.'

The Doctor played with his tie, looking embarrassed.

'No, no, no. I'm fine. Just busy. Things to do. Housekeeping.'

Ace nodded slowly. Housekeeping? 'Right, Professor.'

He seemed about to say something else, then seemed to think better of it and turned on his heel. At the doorway he stopped.

'I was wondering...'

'Yes?' Ace cocked her head on one side.

'Well, now that I've repaired your jacket, it seems a shame not to give it an outing. To see if it's still waterproof. Fancy a little trip?'

He was looking over his shoulder at her, his grey eyes wide and expectant.

Ace smiled. 'That would be great, Doctor.'

'Good.' He vanished back into the corridor. 'I'll see you in the console room in ten minutes.'

Ace gave a deep heartfelt sigh. The pause in their lifestyle was over; whatever it was that was going on, the Doctor had decided to involve her again. Distantly the harsh, discordant grind of the TARDIS engines started to echo around the corridors.

She hopped from the bed and started to haul on her jeans.

They were landing.

Ignoring the protests of his wife, Arthur Baulstrode shrugged himself into his grimy old army coat, pulled his knitted hat over his ears and stepped out into his garden.

Arthur was proud of his garden. Since his retirement barely a day had gone by without him potting or pruning, tending to his rockery, or cutting back his climbers. But the end of the summer had been a bad one, torrential rain and howling wind, and it hadn't let up. Not through September, not through October. Only now had the weather turned dry enough for him to get out and tend to things. He tutted to himself. The lawn was looking shabby. It had needed a last cut before winter had set in. No chance of that now. Everything was still sodden despite two dry days.

Arthur didn't like the winter. Oh, he tried to keep himself busy with house plants and his greenhouse, but it was never the same as being outside, the sun on his back, the soil under his fingers.

And it got him away from his wife.

'Don't you go catching your death now, Arthur Baulstrode.' She was watching him from the kitchen window. She'd be frowning. He knew that without looking. She was always frowning. He even had a photo taken on their wedding day when she was frowning. Some baby with chocolate all over its mouth that she thought was unsightly.

'Yes, dear.'

'And don't you come back in treading mud all over my kitchen floor!'

'No, dear.'

He hurried down the narrow path towards his shed, eager to be out of earshot.

He fumbled for the key in his pocket, clumsy in his woollen gloves. He'd take them off as soon as he was sure that his wife wasn't looking. Daft great things. A Christmas present from his sister-in-law.

The door creaked open and he vanished gratefully inside. The inside of the shed was damp and musty, the air tinged with the smell of compost and manure. Arthur drew a deep breath. He'd spent too long cooped up in the house with the smell of his wife's lavender drawer-liners.

Checking guiltily over his shoulder, he reached up and pulled a stack of flower pots from a shelf above the door. Pulling the stack apart he produced a battered packet of Rothmans and a box of Swan Vestas. Confident that his wife had returned to her housework, he lit up and took a deep lungful of tobacco smoke. Sighing with contentment, he settled back into the tatty armchair that he had hidden out here last summer. He had found it on the local dump. Pete Phillips had helped him get it home one weekend when their wives were busy at some Tupperware party. Now the shed was his own private gentlemen's club. His smoking-room.

He blew another lungful of smoke into the air, watching it billow lazily through the shaft of light streaming through the doorway. He reached for a dog-eared copy of *Whitaker's Almanack*, intent on settling back in his chair to finish his cigarette, then he noticed the hole in the side of the shed.

'What the devil?'

Wedging his cigarette butt between the prongs of a small garden fork, Arthur creaked to his knees to inspect the unwelcome damage. He pulled a hessian sack to one side, cursing as the ripped bag spilled its contents across the dirt floor.

Something had been at his bulbs!

He struggled to his feet muttering angrily under his breath, all thoughts of a leisurely smoke banished. He prodded at the hole in his shed with the toe of his wellington. The entire wall was loose, the nails ripped from the timber. He scowled. A badger most likely. Determined little beggars.

He stubbed out the remains of his cigarette and rummaged in a rusty tool box for a hammer. Might as well get the repair done right away. Who knew what might invade his space if he didn't fix it? And if the buggers had been digging in his vegetable patch... Well, he still had that sprung jaw trap, and to hell with what the local bobby said about it.

Blue smoke billowed around him as he stepped out into the garden. Arthur fanned it frantically with his hand. God, if the Dragon found him smoking indoors...!

He eased himself gently along the side of the shed, boots slipping in the slick mud. He had meant to pave this side of the garden. He had the flags put to one side, ready. In the summer perhaps.

As Arthur rounded the end of the shed his jaw dropped.

'Bloody hell!'

His vegetable patch looked like the Somme. His carefully planted rows of beanpoles were broken and scattered like matchwood, earth was piled in huge untidy mounds, and potatoes and leeks were strewn everywhere. In the middle of it all was a hole, maybe three foot wide, the lip littered with the rest of his bulbs.

Arthur cursed and threw his hammer down in disgust.

'Little bugger!'

'Arthur Baulstrode, you just watch your language.'

His wife's voice drifted from the house. Arthur ignored her. There was a rake leaning against the side of the shed. Arthur snatched it up and approached the hole.

The edge was treacherous and crumbling. Arthur moved forward and peered down into it, balancing himself with the rake. It was unlike any badger sett he had ever seen.

Icy spots of rain started to fall and Arthur looked up in irritation. Grey clouds had started to encroach on the blue of the sky. That was all he needed. What chance did he have of getting any gardening done now?

A sudden high chirruping made him start. There was something moving at the bottom of the hole.

Arthur nodded grimly. 'Got you, you bugger!'

He stabbed down with the handle of the rake.

Ivy Baulstrode heard her husband's bellow of pain and frowned. He'd probably twisted his ankle again in that blasted allotment of his and would come limping into the house any moment expecting sympathy. Well, he wouldn't get any from her.

She poured herself a mug of tea and took a noisy sip. Why he bothered with that pitiful little scrub of land when there was a perfectly good greengrocer at the end of the road...

There was another cry of pain from the garden, shriller now, a note of panic in his voice. And something else, a chittering...

Ivy turned to the window in alarm, and the china mug slipped from her fingers, exploding into fragments on the linoleum.

Her husband staggered around in the middle of the lawn, flailing his arms, screaming in pain. And around him crawled... at first she'd thought they were cats –

Ants, easily a foot long. Their jaws snapped and sliced at his clothes. The lawn was already soaked in blood.

Ivy Baulstrode started to scream.

Chapter Three

Ace stepped out of the TARDIS and wrinkled her nose in distaste. It was damp and musty. Pipes and cylinders loomed out of the gloom and there was a sharp scent of engine oil. Buckets and mops were propped up against the dark brick, stained overalls hung from hooks. It looked as if they were in a boiler-room.

The Doctor was making his way around, prodding at things with the tip of his umbrella, wiping his finger along the pipes and grimacing at the grease. He'd not been very forthcoming about where they had landed. All Ace knew is that it was London and the 1950s.

She unzipped her jacket. It was sweltering. The Doctor seemed unconcerned, wrapped up in his scarf and duffel coat, straw hat perched untidily on his head.

'Great, a cellar,' Ace whined.

'Useful things, cellars.' The Doctor fiddled with the door lock. 'Good for keeping things in.'

The door swung open.

'Things like TARDISes. Shall we?'

He vanished through the door. Grinning, Ace followed him.

The basement was cavernous. Long wide corridors stretching in all directions. The walls were lined with heavy, grey metal cabinets, the ceiling hung with clusters of arm-thick pipes. Ugly industrial light fittings, most of them empty of bulbs, hung between them. The ones that did work cast grimy pools of light onto the concrete floor.

After the warmth of the boiler-room, it was bitterly cold. The Doctor was trotting down one of the corridors towards a set of heavy double doors. Ace followed him, frowning as she passed several stainless steel trolleys, thick with dust.'

'It looks like a hospital, Professor, but it's not exactly *E.R.*'

'Perhaps they weren't expecting guests.' He pushed open the double doors revealing a gloomy stairway.

'Shall we try upstairs?'

The Doctor vanished up the stairs. Ace bounded after him.

The next floor was blinding after the grime of the basement, the walls bright white tiles, hazy sunlight streaming through the netted windows. Ace pulled the nets aside and peered out. It was London all right. She could see the Houses of Parliament on the other side of the Thames. A bright red double-decker bus chugged lazily over Westminster Bridge. The pavements were wet and glinting under the morning sun. It was remarkably devoid of people.

'It's not exactly buzzing, Professor.'

The Doctor appeared at her shoulder and pulled out his pocket watch. 'It's only just after dawn. We're early birds, I'm afraid.'

'Great, worms for breakfast.'

'Very nutritious apparently, but let's see if we can find a better choice. There's bound to be a staff canteen.'

'We're not staff.'

The Doctor pulled himself up proudly. 'I'm a Doctor, aren't I?'

As they made their way through the corridors, Ace started to get uneasy. Dawn or not, there should have been someone around. Her one memory of hospital – she'd had her appendix out when she was ten – was of nurses waking her for breakfast at some ungodly hour, the sun not even up. So far they'd not seen a soul, just empty wards and echoing corridors.

The Doctor had methodically worked his way from floor to floor, occasionally peering into wards, checking signs pinned to walls. Once, somewhere on the fourth floor, he had suddenly held his hand up, head cocked on one side, and bundled her into a storage room. The room was piled high with stainless steel trays and bowls and green plastic surgical gowns. The slightly antiseptic smell had made her queasy, but before she could protest the Doctor had held his finger to his lips.

The footfalls from the corridor had been heavy, numerous and in step. Military footfalls.

She had tugged at the Doctor's sleeve. 'Soldiers?'

The Doctor had said nothing, but eased the door of the storage room open a crack. Ace hadn't been able to see a thing, just heard the clatter of the fire doors at the end of the corridor.

That had been the only sign of life they had found. Now they were climbing the stairwell to the sixth floor. The top floor. The last floor.

Ace was now certain their landing hadn't been a random one. The Doctor's wanderings were too deliberate. He was looking for something. That had pissed her off. Ulterior motives once again.

There was something else. He kept looking at her. Not directly, not obviously, but every time she looked in his direction his head snapped away sharply.

The Doctor scampered up the last flight of stairs and pulled at the heavy double doors.

'Locked...'

Ace shrugged. 'Disused?'

The Doctor tapped his lips with the handle of his umbrella. 'The rest of the place hasn't exactly been at capacity, so why lock this floor... No, I rather think the reverse is true.'

He dropped to his knees, rummaging in the pocket of his jacket.

'Keep a look-out, would you?'

He started to pick the lock with a bent hairpin.

Ace sighed and slouched over to the window to watch the constant, sometimes heavy flow of people in the street. An army truck appeared on the other side of the river. Ace watched it trundle over the bridge and pull up in the street outside. Half a dozen armed soldiers scrambled from the back of it and vanished out of her sight.

'There's an awful lot of firepower running around here, Professor.'

The Doctor just grunted, absorbed in his lock picking.

Pulling the nets aside she craned her neck, nose pressed to the glass, trying to see what was going on outside. She frowned. The truck had an American star on its side. What were the Yanks doing in an old London hospital?

'Aha!'

With a cry of triumph, the Doctor jumped to his feet and thrust his hairpin back into his pocket. He pushed at the door and it swung silently open.

Beaming at her, he reached out his hand. 'Come on, but quietly.'

Catching her by the arm, he pushed open the door. The corridor beyond was quiet and empty. Curtains were drawn over most of the windows, giving everything a murky yellow hue. There was the same antiseptic smell as before, stronger now. Ace's stomach churned.

The Doctor padded slowly through the shadows, peering through doorways. It all looked the same as everywhere else to Ace. Empty beds, disused equipment.

She tugged at his sleeve. 'This is stupid, Professor.' she hissed. 'There's nothing here.'

The Doctor raised a finger to his lips. 'Listen.'

Ace listened. There was a beep. Regular. Mechanical.

The Doctor nodded at one of the wards. 'Through there, I think.'

He crossed to the open doorway and stopped dead. 'Wait there.' Taking his hat, off he crammed it into his pocket and vanished into the ward.

Ace flushed with anger. She was damned if she was going to be left in the dark if he had found something. 'Oh, no you don't.'

She bounded after him.

'You don't drag me round some poxy old hospital then leave me out as soon as you...'

The words dried in Ace's throat. The ward was empty except for a single bed, but there was enough medical equipment scattered around that bed for a dozen patients. Tubes and wires wound from boxy cumbersome machines, drips snaked from stainless steel supports. A tangle of wires and amidst them a figure.

Ace swallowed hard.

The man was pale – unnaturally so. His head was bandaged, only his lower jaw visible. Needles dotted his arm and his breathing was shallow and regular, keeping time with the ventilator beside him.

The Doctor gave her a disapproving look. 'I did tell you to wait outside...'

'Hello?'

Ace snatched at the Doctor's arm. The man in the bed was moving, feebly trying to lift his head from the pillow. The Doctor hurried over to his side.

'It's all right. Nothing to worry about.'

'Is that you, Mr Smith?'

Ace looked quizzically at the Doctor who shrugged back.

'Mr Dumont-Smith?' The man reached out with a pale arm, heaving tubes across the bedcovers. Ace felt sick.

'I can't read you...'

'All perfectly normal.' The Doctor pushed the man's hand back down onto the covers and patted his hand. 'Just try to rest...'

The man slumped back, shaking his head. 'Can't tell if you're Dumont-Smith or not. Something's blown. Can't read you... Can't read anyone.'

The Doctor pursed his lips, his eyes narrowing. Ace knew that look. He was worried.

Abruptly the Doctor unclipped the chart from the end of the man's bed and wandered back out into the corridor. Ace followed him.

'What's he on about?' she whispered.

'I'm not sure, Ace, I'm not sure.'

He started flicking through the papers. 'Our mysterious patient is in the Royal Navy. Fleet Air Arm... or was. A pilot. An astronaut, no less. Captain David O'Brien.'

'And he's been in some kind of accident.'

'Presumably. Certainly the injuries listed here would indicate a crash of some kind.' He paused. 'Odd...'

'What?' Ace tried to peer over his shoulder.

'Several pages relating to his treatment are missing... And what's this?' He scowled. 'Why do doctors have such poor handwriting? British... Space Agency.'

'So? You said he's an astronaut.'

The Doctor fixed her with a piercing stare. 'If there had been a British Space Agency in 1959, I would know about it.'

'Maybe they forgot to tell you.'

The Doctor was about to reply when the double doors at the end of the corridor were suddenly opened by a nurse pushing a stainless steel trolley. She looked up in surprise. Ace tensed, ready to run, but the doctor caught her arm and squeezed, ever so gently.

'Ah, there you are, nurse.'

Tucking the chart behind his back he trotted down the corridor towards her.

'Just in time. The patient was starting to get a little agitated.' He lifted the cloth draped over the trolley and sniffed. 'Ah... soup. Just what the Doctor ordered.'

The nurse looked frightened. Her gaze flicking between the Doctor and Ace.

'Excuse me, sir, but...'

'Who are we?' The Doctor beamed at her. 'Smith. Dumont-Smith. This is my secretary. I understand that the patient has been asking for me?'

'Well, yes sir, but...'

'Splendid. Well, I'm quite happy that Captain O'Brien is in expert hands. No need to trouble you any further.'

The Doctor pulled his hat from his pocket, crammed it onto his head, then doffed it politely and thrust the medical chart into the bemused nurse's hand. 'You'll be needing this. Come along, Miss Gale.'

With barely a backward glance, the Doctor marched purposefully down the corridor and through the double doors. The nurse stared after him open-mouthed.

Aware that she didn't exactly look the part of a secretary, Ace tried to stride confidently after him, nodding crisply at the nurse as she passed. In the stairwell the Doctor was poised like a greyhound. As soon as Ace was through the door, he grabbed her hand.

'Come on!'

The two of them hared down the stairs, the Doctor taking them two at a time, hopping on one leg as he skidded round the corners. Breathless the two of them burst into the basement. Ace cocked a thumb at the boiler room. 'TARDIS?'

The Doctor shook his head. 'Safe enough where it is at the moment. Fire exit.'

He scampered across the corridor and pushed open the heavy fire doors. They emerged into a yard piled with crates and metal bins. A high wall surrounded the yard, the gates chained and padlocked.

'Lock pick?' asked Ace.

'No time,' said the Doctor. 'Bunk up.'

He ran over to the wall and crouched down, hands cupped ready for Ace's foot. She climbed the wall with ease. It had been designed to keep people out, not in. The top was treacherous, though – shards of glass and broken bottles set into concrete. Quickly she shrugged off her jacket and bundled it up on top of the jagged glass. Kneeling on it she reached down and hauled the Doctor up alongside her.

'Watch yourself, Professor.'

Suddenly an alarm bell started to ring, strident in the still of the morning.

The Doctor grimaced. 'I don't think our cunning cover story worked.'

Ace grinned. 'Do surprise me.'

'Well, come on, before they realise which way we got out.'

The Doctor dropped lightly into the street. Bundling up her jacket Ace followed him and the two of them vanished into London's early morning bustle.

For about the tenth time that morning Edward Drakefell picked up the crumpled copy of the *London Inquisitor* and looked at his image, staring out at him. He'd made the front page again. 'DRAKEFELL DENIES COVER-UP OVER SPACE PLANE DISASTER.' He pulled a small silver pillbox from his jacket pocket and shook several white tablets out into the palm of his hand. Filling a tumbler with water, he gulped them down and leant forward, head in his hands.

From the other side of the room Sarah Eyles watched her employer with concern. That was the second time she'd seen him reach for the pills this morning. She was worried about him. She had been his personal assistant for six months, but although his manner was brusque, although he was inclined to snap at people when under pressure and seldom observed the pleasantries that most people might expect, she had come to like Edward Drakefell, even to admire him. But in the three weeks since the Waverider disaster he had seemed almost to shrink. His brusqueness had turned to nervousness, he had become indecisive. She wasn't used to seeing him so... vulnerable.

Her mind made up that it was time to say something to him, to find out if there was anything that she could do to help, Sarah took a deep breath. As she did so, a tall, gangly lab assistant dropped a large manila envelope onto the desk in front of her.

'More paperwork for you, Blue.'

Sarah let the air out of her lungs with a deep sigh. 'Thank you, Malcolm, and please don't call me that.'

Malcolm grinned, 'Whatever you say, Blue, whatever you say.'

Sarah stuck her tongue out at his receding back. She'd been called Blue ever since she'd joined and she hated it. Still, with a name like hers she could hardly have expected anything else. Miss Eyles, personal assistant to the Director of the British Rocket Group. It was almost too good to be true. They'd nicknamed her after the rocket, the *Blue Streak*, and she was grateful that they had decided on Blue and not Streak.

She picked up a paper knife and sliced open the envelope. More requests from army personnel. More instructions from General Crawhammer as to the 'official line' that they were taking. Several of the papers needed authorisation by the director.

Plucking a pen from her desk drawer, she pushed her chair back and crossed the control room to where Drakefell was sitting.

'Excuse me, sir.'

Drakefell looked up, bleary eyed.

'Ah, Sarah...'

'More papers I'm afraid, sir.'

Drakefell took them and leafed through half-heartedly. Sarah did her best to sound cheerful and upbeat.

'Most of them I can deal with, but the top two need your signature.'
She offered him the pen.

The frightened ghost of a smile appeared at the corner of Drakefell's
mouth.

Taking the pen, he signed with the untidy scratch that marked all his
paperwork and passed the bundle back to her.

'Why don't you go home and get some sleep, Dr Drakefell? You look
exhausted.'

'Are the press still at the gates, Sarah?'

'Uh... I'm afraid so.'

'Is that bloody woman there?'

'Miss Hawks? I think so.'

Drakefell looked grey.

'I'm a prisoner in my own compound, Sarah.'

Rita had left Winnerton Flats with the scoop of a lifetime – an
exclusive, on-the-spot quote from Abe Crawhammer – and with the
beginnings of a dilemma, which back at the office had grown with
every word she typed.

The BBC were characteristically playing down the crash. There
were tributes to the late Captain Thomas Kneale, talk of a detailed
examination of the wreckage, an assumption of technical failure. But
her colleagues were openly speculating about Soviet involvement, and
bombarding her with questions. She'd been coy with them at first, but
now they were starting to get on her nerves.

The stakes were so high. She didn't want to add to the hysteria by
quoting a senior American general proclaiming war with the Russians.

And then – perhaps mercifully – the decision had been taken out of
her hands. The door to her cubbyhole had burst open and George
Pryke, the *Inquisitor*'s editor, had rumbled in.

'Come on then, Rita,' he'd bellowed. His Yorkshire bass rattled the
glass. 'Don't keep us in suspense any longer.'

His philosophy was simple – you can't shrink from a good story,
especially if it's true.

Before she could stop him he'd whipped the paper from her type-
writer and was scanning it closely. He puffed out his ruddy cheeks.

'Bloody hell... This is dynamite, Rita!'

He was right. That was the trouble.

And so she had got her headline, and not a little fame. She had been
quoted on radio and television. It had made her uneasy at first.

That was until the calls had started.

She was sitting in her office, writing up a piece about giant ants being seen in Nine Elms, when her phone had rung.

'Miss Rita Hawks?' the voice had enquired.

'That's me.'

'I have some information about Winnerton Flats. Edward Drakefell is covering something up. The rocket wasn't destroyed, and the pilot wasn't killed.'

'Who is this?'

'A concerned member of the public.'

Then there had been a click, then nothing.

Her journalistic instincts had won out. She'd been trying unsuccessfully to contact Bill Collins ever since. He must be mad as hell with her. She'd staked out Winnerton Flats, collared Drakefell, fed George Pryke with prime copy, and become something of a celebrity. Thanks to her, the rest of the papers and even the BBC were camped outside the walls of the estate, now topped with coils of barbed wire. More than once she had been seen on the news, her head bobbing in and out of shot, generally excoriating Drakefell at his reluctant press conferences.

It was Drakefell's manner that most convinced her that the anonymous tip-off was true. He was obviously hiding something. That, and the fact that the calls had continued.

Chapter Four

'Oh, bloody hell!'

The large woman in the pillbox hat gave Ace an indignant look. 'Well, really!'

The Doctor smiled apologetically. 'Please excuse my friend. She's rather exuberant.'

'Is that what you call it?' The woman hauled herself out of her seat and rang the bell of the bus. 'Well, I can do without that kind of exuberance, thank you very much. Good day to you.'

The bus swung into its stop and the woman vanished down the stairs and out into the street. Ace grunted. 'Miserable old bat.'

The Doctor sighed wearily. 'She's from an era where young ladies don't blurt out "Oh, bloody hell" on public transport.'

'But look, Professor. I tore my jacket back there on that bl...'

'Ace.' The Doctor glared at her.

'... on that wall. And after you'd fixed it as well.'

The Doctor peered at the ragged tear. 'I'll sort that out when we get back to the TARDIS.'

'And when is that likely to be, eh? Now that we've upset those squaddies it'll be harder to break in.'

'Oh, we'll worry about that when the time comes.'

The Doctor stared absently out of the window. Ace shook her head. She wasn't going to get anything out of him at the moment. She leaned forward in her seat and peered down into the jostle of London. The bus meandered through streets only half familiar to Ace. Every now and again she caught sight of buildings that she thought she recognised, rising from the rubble of bomb sites. There were police boxes everywhere, and she kept finding herself caught out by the familiar shapes. It was weird seeing so many of them. It was if a hundred Doctors had arrived in London at the same time, all intent on solving the same problem. All ganging up to thwart some alien menace. Or all watching her. She banished the thought, determined that it was her imagination.

As they pulled into Piccadilly Circus, the Doctor suddenly bounded to his feet, rang the bell and scampered down the stairs.

'Hey, hang about, Professor!' Ace jogged after him.

The bus slowed to a halt and the two of them stepped onto the pavement.

'Hold tight, please.' The conductor rang the bell and the double-decker roared away into the traffic. The Doctor stared wistfully after it. 'Always thought I'd make a good bus conductor.'

'I thought you had a morbid fear of bus stations,' Ace teased.

'True...' The Doctor spun on his heels getting his bearings. 'Now, if I'm right, it will be just over... there.' He stabbed at the air with the tip of his umbrella.

'What will?'

The Doctor beamed at her. 'Breakfast!'

The little café on Frith Street was crowded. Suited businessmen struggling with unwieldy newspapers sat elbow to elbow with their colleagues at the tiny Formica tables, empty plates greasy with the evidence of English breakfasts in front of them. Street traders and shop owners shouted their orders for sandwiches above the babble of Italian from the kitchen.

Ace sat in the window with a cracked enamel mug full of steaming tea and the remains of a plate of sausage sandwiches. The Doctor was lost amongst the mêlée behind the counter, chattering animatedly to the owner. Apparently he'd met Luigi ten years ago, helping out in the kitchen when the place had opened. Abbott and Costello had performed the opening ceremony, apparently. It hadn't surprised Ace that the Doctor knew them. He was like an old film comedian himself.

Taking a mouthful of sandwich, she stared out into the crowds of Soho. Another old stomping ground. Once again she found herself in familiar surroundings but years before her birth. The last time she had been in central London was during the Blitz. The signs of that conflict were still visible, great scars across the city, and there was a weariness in the faces of the people. But the trappings of Christmas were starting to appear. Decorations on lampposts, paper-chains in windows. The market round the corner had been crammed with baubles and freshly cut trees. It amazed Ace that so much of life had returned to normal in a little over ten years. She tried to imagine how her life would have been affected if there had been a war in the 1970s, or the 1980s. She couldn't believe that she or her friends would have coped with as much resilience as these people had.

She was startled from her musings by the Doctor dropping into the seat next to her, a dripping egg roll grasped in one hand, his fingers yellow with yolk.

'Penny for them?'

Ace slurped her tea. 'Just daydreaming, that's all.'

The Doctor crammed the last bit of egg roll into his mouth and wiped his hands on his paisley handkerchief. 'Luigi was kind enough to lend me his phone book.' He waggled a scrap of paper at her. 'I've got the addresses of every Dumont-Smith in London. As soon as you've eaten up we can get going.'

'How many of them are there?'

'Oh, only a few dozen.'

'A few dozen!' Ace's heart sank. She had hoped that they could spend some time looking around. It was one of the perks of time travel. 'Professor, we're going to be traipsing back and forth across London all day in the rain!'

The Doctor frowned at her. 'You had something better to do?'

'Well... I thought we could wander about for a bit – you know, do some Christmas shopping or something.'

The Doctor sighed. 'We find a mysterious military hospital, a pilot from a non-existent organisation and you want to go sightseeing.'

'Oh, come on, Professor, just for a bit.'

'All right, all right, all right!' He rummaged in his pockets and produced a scuffed leather bag. 'Here.' He tossed the bag to Ace. It chinked pleasantly in her hands.

'Pocket money.'

Ace grinned. 'I get to go to the pictures while you handle all the grown-up stuff, eh, Professor?'

He tapped her gently on the nose. 'There shouldn't be too much trouble you can get into in 1950s' London. I'll sort out which of these Dumont-Smiths we need to be chasing and meet you later. Nelson's Column, seven o'clock?'

Ace stuffed the bag of coins into her pocket. 'Right, Professor. Hope you find your Mr Dumont-Smith.'

She slid from behind the table, then tousled his hair cheekily, pulled the door of the café open and bounded out into the street.

The Doctor watched through the steamed-up window as Ace vanished into the crowds. She turned and waved at him, then she was gone, lost in the swirl of shoppers.

He gave a deep sigh. This was the moment that he had been dreading. The moment that he let her go her own way. The moment he gambled with her life. The last throw of the dice before she died...

He unfolded the piece of paper. A single address was written in his scrawling hand. There was only one Dumont-Smith. A solicitor just off Regent Street.

It was inconvenient – he should be giving all his attention to Ace, but something about the pilot worried him. He wasn't sure what it was yet, but it worried him greatly. Besides, Ace's body had at some time been at the same otherwise empty hospital. It could hardly be a coincidence.

He reached into his pocket and drew out a small gunmetal shape. He looked guiltily over his shoulder to check that he wasn't being watched, but an argument had started at the counter and the staff were protesting loudly and animatedly with one of the street traders. Hunkering down over the table, the Doctor pressed a small stud on the side of the device. A screen lit up and a bright point of light started moving slowly across it. The machine bleeped softly and rhythmically, the noise drowned by the babble of Italian and cockney. The Doctor nodded gently to himself. The machine was working perfectly. He hated himself for doing it, but putting the tracker on Ace had been the only way he could ensure he knew her movements, the only way that he would be able to find her when the time came.

He just hoped that when she found out what he had done she would understand why, and forgive him.

The woman edged fearfully along the curved, wet wall of the sewer tunnel, her face streaked with tears. The elegant dress she wore was stained and torn, one sleeve hanging in tatters revealing a deep cut in her pale shoulder.

A noise rang out in the darkness and she thrust her hand to her mouth, stifling a scream.

A torch beam pierced the gloom of the tunnel.

'Gloria?' a man whispered.

'Alan?' She flung herself towards him. 'Oh, Alan, I thought I'd never get out of this terrible place!'

Cradling the sobbing woman in his arms, Professor Alan Cartwright nervously swung the torch around, playing the beam over the glistening brickwork.

'General Wells and the rest of the men are at the tunnel entrance;

they're ready to blow these sewers to dust.'

Gloria's eyes widened. 'But they know we're in here, don't they? Alan, they do know...?'

Alan shook his head, his face stern. 'The only one who knows I'm here is Billy, and he's...'

A section of tunnel wall suddenly exploded inwards in a shower of bricks and mortar. Gloria screamed as the monstrous beetle pushed through the hole, antennae thrashing.

Alan pulled a revolver from his pocket firing shot after shot into the struggling insect.

'It's no good, the radiation has made them impervious to bullets!'

'Alan, look out!'

More and more shiny giant beetles emerged into the sewer tunnel, antennae waggling frantically.

All around Ace kids were screaming, girls were burying their heads in their boyfriends' shoulders. The cinema was packed.

Coming to the pictures hadn't actually been Ace's plan, she had intended having a pleasant few hours shopping, traipsing through London, comparing the city here and now with the one that she knew. The shops were so dull, though!

At first it had been amusing, staring at ludicrous ladies' fashions and impressively engineered underwear, but when she tried to find a decent record shop she realised just how far out of time she was.

She had managed to find an HMV on Oxford Street, but it was only once she stepped inside that she realised that she was back in the days when rock 'n' roll was still a novelty. The Beatles were still several years away.

Eventually she had got bored, and started to regret letting the Doctor go off on his own. She could have kicked herself. After months without a proper adventure she had let him have all the fun. When the rain started in earnest it had been the final straw.

Looking for somewhere dry, she had ended up in Piccadilly Circus. The bustle and noise had taken her by surprise. Just as in her day, the buildings were plastered with advertisements – huge posters extolling the virtues of Bovril and the ubiquitous Coca-Cola display. The buzz of people had cheered her up no end. She passed a queue huddled outside a cinema. Squinting against the cold rain, Ace had peered up at the façade. 'They Came From Beyond Time!' announced bold letters. The posters showed a scantily dressed woman swooning in the arms of a square-jawed hero, monstrous beetles towering over them.

With the bag of the Doctor's money still heavy in her pocket, and with nothing better to do, Ace had joined the queue.

The B movie had been hugely entertaining. Ace had a sneaking suspicion that she might have caught it on telly once – a late-night season of old films on BBC2 – but here and now it was the latest thing and the audience was loving it.

By the time the movie was over and Ace was back out on the streets, it was starting to get dark and the rain was heavier than ever. Feeling a spreading patch of wetness on her back Ace ducked into the shelter of an arcade. Cursing, she shrugged her jacket off and shook the water from it. The tear where she had caught it on the glass was gaping open, the wadding beneath sodden.

'Bugger.'

She scrabbled in the small leather bag. There was still plenty of money left, so she could easily get herself a new jacket, but she was going to get soaked in the meantime.

Squatting down on a window ledge, Ace started unpinning badges from her lapels. They would do to hold the tear together whilst she found something a little more waterproof. She smiled as she unclipped her red star. The badge that Sorin had given her. It suddenly struck her that wearing a Russian Army badge might not be the wisest thing to do in 1950s' London. Tucking it into her pocket, she carried on fastening the tear together with her trophies.

Suddenly she stopped, frowning.

A badge she didn't recognise hung on the sleeve of her jacket. It was about the size of a £2 coin, but fatter, brushed gunmetal with a faint sheen. Ace unclipped it, noticing that it had got bent, cracked, probably at the same time that the rip had occurred. She still couldn't remember where she had got it.

She was about to use it for her makeshift repairs when she noticed the light glinting from inside it. Puzzled, Ace looked at it more closely. There was stuff inside it. Carefully she pulled at the edge and the badge dropped apart in her hand. Ace stared at the microscopic circuitry. A single light pulsed in steady rhythm.

It was a bug.

The Doctor had bugged her.

A sudden blinding rage welled up in Ace.

'Bastard,' she whispered under her breath. Her hands were shaking. She couldn't hold it in.

'You *bastard*!'

People were looking at her now. Mothers ushering their children away from her, shopkeepers peering at her from inside their shops. Tears blurred Ace's vision. She didn't know if she wanted to scream or cry. Snatching up her jacket, she ran out into the rain, barging through the crowds. Angry voices called after her as she pushed through the Christmas shoppers. Ace ignored them. She wanted to lash out at something, and she didn't really care what or who.

She blundered into the road. There was a blare of horns, and a taxi screeched to a halt in front of her. The driver stared incredulously at her. Passers-by were turning to look at her, pointing. Ace balled up her fist and punched the bonnet, hard.

The driver started to climb out of his cab. Ace turned and ran. Everything around her became a blur. Rain stung her face, her shirt was soaked through. She was lost in a surreal world of Christmas lights and carols. Ace pushed through the mass of people, hurt and alone. She needed somewhere to think, somewhere quiet.

She emerged into Trafalgar Square. The splash of the fountains was lost in the noise of the rain. The National Gallery loomed in front of her. Gratefully, Ace slipped inside.

After the noise of the streets the gallery was silent and calm. People stared curiously at her. She was soaked, her hair plastered to her head, her shirt almost transparent. Ignoring the suspicious glances of the staff, Ace made her way to the toilets, slipping into a cubicle and locking the door behind her.

She slumped down, her head in her hands, taking deep breaths to try and calm herself. She was shivering uncontrollably and her hand hurt like hell.

Ace looked at it. Blood oozed from her knuckles; the back of her hand was swollen and purple. God knows what sort of dent she had made in the bonnet of the cab. Wiping her eyes she gave a humourless laugh.

'Don't know your own strength.'

Wrapping a paper towel around her injured hand she pulled the Doctor's bug out of her pocket and stared at it. She could see the whole set-up now. Repairing her jacket, his suggestion of a little walk. Coming apart at the seams, he had said.

'Yeah, right, Professor. And whose fault is that?'

She felt herself flushed with anger again. Why had he felt the need to bug her? What the hell was he playing at? Why couldn't he just talk to her, for God's sake?

She stood up and lifted the toilet seat. She was damned if she was going to be used again. This time the Doctor's little plan would stop right here. She held the bug over the bowl, reaching for the handle, then she stopped, a smile curling the edge of her mouth.

She had suddenly had a much better idea.

Crowds were leaving the gate of London Zoo when Ace arrived. A sea of umbrellas, families huddled underneath, making their way back home. Ace checked her watch. It was nearly five thirty, the place would be closing soon.

Shivering, she pulled her jacket around her and hurried over to the ticket barrier.

'You haven't got long, love,' said the neatly uniformed man at the ticket window. 'We shut in half an hour.'

'It's OK.' Ace gave him a weak smile. 'I know where I'm going.'

'Well, that will be two shillings then, please, miss.'

Taking her ticket, Ace pushed through the turnstile and crunched down the neat gravel path into the zoo. She stopped at a tall white-washed pole pierced with arrows, nodding to herself.

'This will show him.'

Bugging device grasped tightly in her hand, Ace made her way through the straggling line of sodden sightseers to a large white-washed hut in the centre of the zoo. She pushed open the door and a wave of warm, musty air wafted over her. Goosebumps ran up her spine. This was the warmest she'd been all day.

The monkey house was long and narrow, cages ranged along one wall. Dozens of inquisitive eyes turned towards her as she stepped into the hut. A small boy was talking excitedly to his parents at the far end of the room; apart from them the place was deserted.

Ace pretended to read the various notices about where the different species were from and what they ate, all the time keeping an eye on the family. Eventually the boy tired of the antics of the monkeys and scurried out, pursued by his mother and father.

Checking quickly around her, Ace climbed over the low fence that bordered the cages. One of the monkeys ambled over to her, climbing the mesh of his cage and looking at her quizzically.

'Hello, matey, feeling hungry?'

Ace delved in her pocket and brought out the bag of nuts that she had bought at a sweetshop. The monkey was joined by several of his fellows all looking at her expectantly.

Ace ripped the bag open and shook the nuts into her hand. A dozen arms thrust out though the cage, grasping for the nuts, the apes chattering excitedly. Ace let them grab a few handfuls, then held the bug out. 'How about a nice toy to play with as well, hmm?'

A hairy paw snatched it from her. Ace watched as the monkey chewed experimentally on the small gunmetal shape. Finding it inedible, it threw the bug across the cage, tutting in irritation. Ace nodded in satisfaction. 'That's right, you kick the nasty old thing around the cage for a while.'

She smiled. By the time the Doctor found it, it should be covered in monkey shit, or better still swallowed. That would teach him to take the piss out of her. She stuck a handful of nuts in her mouth.

'Cheers, lads.'

'Is spending time with these boys the best offer you got this evening?'

A lazy American drawl. Ace jumped and spun. A youngish male figure was silhouetted in the doorway.

'You know, you're really meant to stay on this side of the barrier.' The figure moved forward into the light. A janitor or something, wearing a dark blue boilersuit and carrying a broom. Guiltily, Ace climbed back over the low fence.

'Just wanted to get a closer look.'

The man looked at her, eyes twinkling. 'Lucky them.' He grinned cheekily. 'A pretty face and nuts, you've made their day.'

'If I'd known it was such a big deal for them, I'd have made more of an effort.' Ace tugged at her matted hair. 'They're not catching me at my best.'

The young man grinned again and stretched out his hand. 'I'm Jimmy.'

'Ace.' Ace reached to shake his hand, then realised hers was still wrapped in its makeshift bandage, blood from her knuckles staining the tissue paper.

Jimmy frowned. 'Hey, are you OK?' He nodded at the monkeys. 'They didn't do that, did they? There's a lot you can catch from a chimp...'

'No.' Ace shook her head. 'I did this punching a taxi-cab.'

Jimmy raised a quizzical eyebrow. 'Oh?'

'It's a long story.'

'Well, there's a first aid kit over in the hut. You can tell me while I find a slightly better bandage for you.'

'No, it's all right.' Ace shook her head. 'I'm fine, really...'

'Or I could call the head keeper. It's what I'm meant to do if we find people where they shouldn't be. It's up to you.'

Ace sighed. 'Do you always blackmail women to get them back to your hut?'

Jimmy shook his head. 'Normally I just club them unconscious and drag them back by the hair. I'm making an exception in your case.'

He held the door open. 'Please?'

Ace smiled and nodded. Her hand was still throbbing, and she had nothing better to do. Besides Jimmy was cheeky, good looking and kind, and at the moment that was just what she needed.

From the window of the reptile house an old man watched as Jimmy and Ace dashed through the rain to the little keeper's hut and tumbled inside, shutting the door behind them.

Smiling to himself, the man eased open the lid of a small wooden box and plucked out a struggling locust with his finger and thumb. He brought the insect up to his face and peered at it.

'Splendid,' he said.

He blinked slowly then dropped the locust into the large cage in front of him.

It lay there for a moment as if dazed and then started to crawl towards the glass. Seconds later the lizard pounced, gulping down the locust in two sharp lunges.

The man peered happily at the lizard.

'Splendid.'

Chapter Five

The Doctor's eyes flicked up as Dumont-Smith's secretary stepped out of the front door of the elegant Georgian office block and snapped open her umbrella. As she headed off into the tide of homeward-bound office workers, the Doctor slid from the plinth on which he'd been squatting, patted the statue of Lord George Bentinck on the head and trotted to the kerb.

Ducking between buses and black cabs, he crossed to the office block and pushed at the door. The hallway was empty, but from the other offices he could hear the excited chatter of secretaries looking forward to their Friday night out or the weekend. Shrugging off his duffle coat and hanging it over his arm, the Doctor straightened the collar of his jacket and made purposefully for the lift.

He'd monitored Ace for two hours, then sat in a café, watching the news on television. A man called Edward Drakefell was being harangued by shouting newsmen. A woman – an American – was bombarding him with questions, apparently about the rocket crash. He was flannelling and evading, stammering out contradictory assertions and denials. Then another figure had loomed into shot. An American soldier, chewing on a cigar.

'You boys don't want to be lookin' in here for dirty tricks,' he had boomed. 'You want to be looking east. To Moscow.'

Then he had come here and met Lord Bentinck. He had deliberately waited until precisely locking-up time to make his move. He'd decided to walk up brazenly to Dumont-Smith's office on the fourth floor rather than try and break in later. At least in this incarnation he looked vaguely respectable. He doubted that he would get away with this in his last body, or if he still went round with a fifteen-foot woollen scarf around his neck.

The lift door slid open and several people hurried out. Looking as haughty as he could, the Doctor nodded curtly to them and stepped inside.

The lift glided to a halt on the fourth floor and the Doctor peered out into the corridor. Most of the doors on the floor were closed, the offices visible behind the glass dark and empty. Light spilled out from a window at the distant end of the hallway and he could hear a muffled male voice, a man dictating a letter.

Taking a deep breath, the Doctor marched across to the door marked Miles Dumont-Smith and reached for the handle. It would be locked, of course, this was the one bit of his plan that was risky; being caught picking the lock of a London solicitor did tend to look a little suspicious. With a quick glance around him the Doctor turned the handle.

To his surprise the door clicked open. Unable to believe his luck, the Doctor slipped inside.

Long shadows stretched across the floor of Dumont-Smith's office, cast by the streetlights outside. Closing the door gently, the Doctor pulled the blinds and crossed to the window. He stared down into the hubbub for a moment, the wet pavements crammed with people, umbrellas, and bags and boxes, a sea of humanity. A smile played across his face. London at Christmas. There really wasn't anywhere else quite like it. When all this was over, when he knew once and for all that Ace was safe again, they'd have to take some time and enjoy it properly.

He was about to draw the curtains and start his search of Dumont-Smith's offices when he felt the gun barrel press against his neck.

'Okay, bub, let's take it nice and slow. Raise your hands and turn around.'

The Doctor turned slowly. A huge grin spread across his face.

'Cody McBride, what a delightful surprise!'

Cody McBride's jaw dropped. 'Oh, no...'

Ace flexed her fist, rubbing at the clean new bandage.

'Too tight?' Jimmy was watching her.

Ace shook her head. 'No. It's fine.'

'Good.' He started to pack things back into the small wooden first aid box. 'You're going to have quite a bruise for the next few days, so I'd try and avoid punching any more vehicles if you can.'

Ace grinned. 'Really?'

'Yeah, doctor's orders.'

The smile faded from Ace's face. She said nothing.

Aware of the sudden silence, Jimmy turned. 'OK, I've said something I shouldn't. Whatever it was, I'm sorry.'

'No, it's me who should be sorry.' Ace shook her head. 'It's my problem. I didn't mean to take it out on you.'

'Good. I hate evenings of awkward silence.'

Ace folded her arms. 'Oh, so we're spending the evening together, are we?'

Jimmy lit up a cigarette and nodded. 'Yeah. I had plans, of course, but I don't mind giving them up so's you don't have to start looking for some more monkeys to hang out with.'

'That's very kind of you.'

Jimmy shrugged. 'I'm that kind of guy. There's a couple of decent American bars in town. The burgers are hot and the beers are cold. And if you can avoid punching the passing traffic...'

'That sounds great.'

'Good.' Jimmy took a battered leather jacket out of his locker and slipped it on. 'I've got a delivery to make on the way, if that's all right. An errand for a friend.'

'Sure.' Ace looked at her watch. Nearly half past six. The Doctor would be at Trafalgar Square in an hour, waiting for her.

'I'm in no rush at all.'

McBride slumped down onto one of the office chairs, gun held limply in his hand.

'I don't believe it.'

The Doctor was shaking his hand vigorously, looking no different from when McBride had met him, nineteen years ago.[3]

'This really is an unexpected pleasure: always nice to catch up with old friends.'

'Doc, what the hell are you doing here?'

The Doctor looked hurt. 'I would have thought that it was obvious. Breaking and entering.' He suddenly looked concerned. 'Oh dear, you're not protecting Mr Dumont-Smith's interests are you?'

McBride shook his head. 'No, Doc, I'm here for the same reason as you. Casing the joint.'

'Excellent!' The Doctor beamed at him. 'Always nice to have company on these sorts of occasion.' Pulling the curtains closed with a flourish, the Doctor seated himself behind the large mahogany desk and started opening drawers.

McBride tried to regain some focus. 'Look, Doc, really good to see you and all, but do you mind telling me what's going on? You're not telling me that the broad has hired you as well, are you?'

The Doctor frowned. 'Broad?'

[3] See *Doctor Who: Illegal Alien*

'Dame with the great legs and the hat. Mrs Dumont-Smith!'

'Ah!' The Doctor started flicking through papers. 'And she's hired you to investigate her husband, has she?'

'Right. She thinks he may be two-timing her, asked me to check him out.'

'Hmm.' The Doctor slipped the papers back into the drawer, crossed to the tall filing cabinet in the corner, and fiddled with the lock. 'No, I'm here on another matter entirely.'

'Well, ain't that great. Simple love-rat case I thought. Open and shut, and now you turn up.' He suddenly looked worried. 'Hey, there ain't big alien nasties lurking around again are there?'

'No Cody, you're quite safe.'

'And Ace?'

'– is the reason I'm here.'

The filing cabinet opened with a click and the Doctor slid open the top drawer.

'Tell me, Cody, is Mr Dumont-Smith's illicit relationship meant to be with someone local?'

McBride looked puzzled. 'Girl from Hampstead. Why?'

'Because this equipment looks as though it might reach further than Hampstead, that's why.'

McBride crossed the room and peered over the Doctor's shoulder.

Inside the filing cabinet was the most sophisticated radio transmitter McBride had ever seen.

Rita huddled awkwardly under the mass of wet bushes, clumsy with the camera. She adjusted the lens, bringing the two figures silhouetted in the bright doorway into focus.

'Gotcha.'

She started taking shot after shot. The rain had eased, but the light was limited. She just needed a couple of good shots of the woman.

With a polite nod, the woman closed the door. Rita cursed. She pushed back into the shrubbery as a man darted back up the path and into the road. As she watched, he crossed to a bus shelter. Rita frowned. There was someone else with him. A girl.

Quickly winding on the film in her camera, Rita brought the girl into focus, wishing she was a bit closer to the street light. It was no one she recognised. No one that she had seen before. The man, on the other hand… She took several more shots, then ducked down as a bus pulled into the stop.

The two got on and the bus roared off into the night. Rita struggled out of the undergrowth and shook the rain from her hair.

'You know how to spend your Friday nights, girl, you really do.'

Tucking the camera under her raincoat, Rita trudged back to her car.

McBride examined the radio carefully.

'This is one fancy jukebox.'

'Yes,' said the Doctor absently. 'What do you make of this?'

The Doctor handed him a manila folder. McBride scanned the papers. 'Looks like Russian.'

'It is Russian.'

'Oh, great. So this is... what? A spy case now? Does trouble always come hand in hand with you, Doc?'

The Doctor smiled thinly. 'I'm afraid so.'

'So what are we going to do? Tell the police?'

The Doctor pursed his lips. 'No, I don't think we'll inform the authorities just yet. I want to do a little more digging first.'

'Oh, come on, Doc! This isn't something we can clam up about. The guy's a Russkie spy. We've gotta tell someone!'

Before the Doctor could argue, there was a sharp warble from inside his jacket. McBride jumped.

'Jeez, Doc, will you keep it down! We're gonna get caught!' He scurried over to the door and peered through the blinds.

The Doctor reached inside his jacket and pulled out his pocket watch. It was seven o' clock. 'Blast.'

He snapped the folder shut, slipped it back into the filing cabinet and closed the drawer.

'I'm afraid I'm going to have to leave you, Cody. I have a prior engagement.'

'Oh, no you don't.' McBride shook his head. 'I'm going to stick to you like glue until this is sorted, Doctor. Who've you gotta meet?'

'Ace.'

'Great. I'll tag along.'

'Oh, very well, very well.' The Doctor waggled his hands impatiently. 'Come along.'

The Doctor eased the door open and the two of them peered out into the corridor. It was deserted. Quickly and quietly the two of them slipped into the hallway and down the stairs.

They stepped out into the street, the Doctor struggling back into his duffel coat. McBride slipped on a battered fedora.

'Where are you meeting her?'

'Trafalgar Square, assuming she's on time of course.' The Doctor rummaged in his pocket and brought out a small device. McBride grunted.

'More whacky gadgets, Doc?'

The Doctor peered worriedly at the screen. 'That can't be right...' He swung the device around, punching at tiny controls on its surface. 'Oh, no.'

McBride pulled up the collar of his trenchcoat. 'Come on, Doc, it's getting wet out here.'

The Doctor turned to McBride, the anguish in his eyes unexpected and disturbing. McBride felt a shiver run down his spine.

'Hey, something's up, isn't it?'

'Cody, do you own a car?' asked the Doctor quietly.

McBride sat at the wheel of his Ford Anglia peering through the rain streaming down the windscreen and lit another cigarette.

On the journey across London the Doctor had said nothing, silent and stern in the passenger seat beside him, the only sounds the steady drum of rain on the roof, the squeak of the wipers and the insistent beep from the Doctor's device.

He had explained nothing, refused to answer questions and had snapped at McBride when he tried to press him. All McBride knew was that Ace wasn't where she should be, and that the Doctor was worried about her. No, more than worried: frantic.

That had been the most disconcerting thing. In the short time that McBride had known the mysterious little man he had always appeared to be in control, always supremely confident, waltzing through the people around him as if he knew everything. Now he looked, well... vulnerable, hunched in the seat, chewing on his nails, staring at the read-out on his electronic toy.

When the gates of London Zoo had loomed into the headlights the Doctor had finally asked McBride to stop and wait. That had been fifteen minutes ago.

McBride blew another lungful of smoke into the car. Why couldn't it have been perfume-soaked letters or orders for bunches of flowers? And if Dumont-Smith was a Russian spy, then what did that make Mrs Dumont-Smith? And if she wasn't on the level, would he even get paid? It was beginning to make McBride's head ache.

'And what the hell are we doing at the zoo?' he murmured to himself.

The door opened abruptly and the Doctor slumped into the passenger seat, his face grave.

'Did you find her?' asked McBride cautiously.

The Doctor shook his head. 'No. And without this, I'm unlikely to.' He placed a small metal disk on the dashboard of the car. McBride wrinkled his nose. It smelt of shit.

The Doctor gave a deep sigh and looked at McBride, his brilliant grey eyes sombre.

'I owe you an apology, Cody, and I owe you an explanation. Ace is in a great deal of trouble and I'm going to have to ask for your help. Is there somewhere private we can talk?'

McBride placed the newspaper down on his desk, his head reeling.

'Jeez...'

The Doctor stood at the window of McBride's third floor office looking out over the lights of the city.

'So you see my problem. In less than twenty-four hours Ace is going to be dead, washed up in the river Thames, shot through the head by an unknown assailant, and I've delivered her right into his hands.'

'But, why?' McBride was still trying to get his head around the implications of it all. 'Why kill her?'

The Doctor turned. 'Oh, it's a trap for me, a trap in time, and one where there is no chance that I would ignore the bait.'

'So the person who set it...'

'Is very clever, very cunning, and very dangerous,' said the Doctor grimly.

'Someone talking about me?'

The Doctor and McBride turned. In the doorway stood a tall, elegant woman in a knee-length dress and pillbox hat. A cigarette in a slim holder hung from the fingers of one hand, smoke curling in thin wisps around her. Eyeing the Doctor curiously, she sashayed into the room. McBride scrambled up from his chair.

'Mrs Dumont-Smith, I wasn't expecting you to...'

'Oh, I was just passing, so I thought I'd drop in and see how you were getting on with my little problem.' She threw another look at the Doctor. 'Are you going to introduce me?'

'Ah, yes,' McBride flustered. 'This is the Doctor. An old friend.'

The Doctor raised his hat politely. 'Delighted.'

McBride caught his client by the arm and tried to steer her back towards the door. 'Look, this isn't a great time at the moment. We're kinda busy.'

'Oh, don't mind me.' The Doctor was perched on McBride's desk, fishing in his pocket. He pulled out a crumpled ball of paper, which he unfurled with a flourish. A page torn from a newspaper. 'If Miss Hawks has just "popped in", then I'm sure it's for a very good reason.'

The woman turned slowly, a nervous smile on her lips. 'I'm sorry?'

McBride scratched his head. 'Doc, this is...'

'Miss Rita Hawks, investigative journalist.' The Doctor passed McBride the newspaper. 'You know, Miss Hawks, undercover reporters don't usually have glamorous pictures of themselves printed alongside their articles. Particularly when it's a rather insensitive exposé of government cover-ups.'

McBride stared in disbelief at the photo on the page. 'Sonofagun.'

Rita laughed nervously. 'I really think you are mistaken.'

'I don't think so, doll.' McBride thrust the page in front of her. 'I think that you've got some explaining to do.'

Rita took it open-mouthed. 'But I'm still writing this piece...'

McBride lit a Lucky Strike, slumped back in his chair and swung his feet up on to the desk. He grinned at Rita. 'It's the day after tomorrow's newspaper, dummy.'

McBride's office was blue with cigarette smoke. Rita had dropped the pretence with the cigarette-holder and had been chain smoking for nearly an hour now. She was angry. Angry at being found out, angry at being made to look stupid in front of McBride, angry and confused about the newspaper. And especially angry with the Doctor.

The little man sat behind McBride's desk peering at her through the haze, his eyes steely grey and menacing. He'd been quizzing her about every part of her story. About her visit to the British Rocket Group, about the anonymous tip-offs, everything.

'So this... voice on the phone told you to check out Dumont-Smith,' McBride had interrupted, busting from the little darkroom that took up a corner of his office.

'Yes.'

'And you hired me to do the dirty work without telling me I was dealing with goddam reds in bed!'

'I'm sorry, Mr McBride.'

She really was. She liked Cody McBride. She'd tried her best little-girl-lost routine, but it hadn't cut any ice. McBride was angry – more, she thought, because he'd had the wool pulled over his eyes than because of the potential dangers. She'd tried to argue that she couldn't tell him the truth, not without putting him in danger. McBride hadn't believed a word of it, and had stomped back into the dark, slamming the door behind him.

He was developing the pictures that she'd taken earlier.

'So let me see if I've got this right.' The Doctor tapped on the table with his pencil. 'The British Rocket Group launched an experimental rocket, which you witnessed. Something went wrong and the rocket crashed. An anonymous informant told you the army and the government are concealing some part of the truth, and you suspect Mr Dumont-Smith is passing secrets to the Soviet Union.'

Rita drew on her cigarette. 'That about sums it up.'

'But you have yet to establish a link between Mr Dumont-Smith and the British Rocket Group.'

'Yes,' said Rita. 'There's still something missing. Something I don't know about.'

'Or someone,' said the Doctor darkly.

He rested his chin on his steepled fingers. 'So why are the American army keeping the pilot of that spacecraft – which I think we can assume he is – in a London hospital, and what is his connection with Dumont-Smith?'

Rita's jaw dropped. 'Colonel Kneale is here in London?'

The Doctor frowned. 'Kneale? No, no, no. The man I saw was called O'Brien. Captain David O'Brien.'

'Davey O'Brien?' Rita gave a harsh laugh. 'No way, sweetheart. Davey O'Brien is at Winnerton Flats, pretty much under house arrest. The pilot of that spacecraft was Thomas 'Chipper' Kneale; Davey O'Brien was the relief pilot. I should know, I interviewed them myself two days before the launch.'

'I wouldn't take too much notice of her if I were you, Doc.' McBride ambled back into the room, cigarette stub dangling from his lips. 'I imagine there's about as much truth in her spaceman story as there was in her one about the giant ant attack last week.'

Rita turned on him. 'That was from eyewitness accounts. The poor man who...'

'Yeah, yeah, whatever.' Cutting her short, McBride dropped a bundle of black-and-white photographs on the desk. 'These might interest you, Doc.'

The Doctor picked them up and started leafing through them.

Rita reached into her bag for another cigarette. 'That guy's been delivering messages from Dumont-Smith's office to that house for at least two weeks. He's a messenger boy, no one important.'

'Yeah? Well, he might be important to us.' McBride leaned over the Doctor's shoulder, handing him an eyeglass. 'Look at the last couple of pictures. See who he's with?'

The Doctor squinted though the eyeglass. Rita saw him stiffen.

'Ace,' he murmured.

'What do you know about this man, Miss Hawks?'

'Nothing much. He looks great in overalls…'

'I beg your pardon?'

'I've seen him wearing them a couple of times. He looks like a… a park-keeper or something.'

'Or someone who works at the zoo?' said the Doctor sharply.

He looked at McBride. 'How's your petrol ration holding up? '

McBride grinned. 'I've… uh… got a special source, Doc. Back to the zoo, then.'

'No…' said the Doctor thoughtfully. 'Time is against us, and we have no real idea that she's still at the zoo.'

'If it's so urgent that you find her, why don't you put out an alert on her?'

McBride and the Doctor stared at Rita.

'What?'

'An all cars alert.' She nodded at McBride. 'He's a private dick, he must know lots of policemen. Comes with the territory.'

The Doctor and McBride stared at each other, the same name on their lips.

'Mullen!'

McBride pulled the Anglia to a halt outside the mess of ruined warehouses. From behind the façade was the glare of lights, throwing huge shadows across the rain-slick brickwork of Vauxhall.

He turned to the Doctor. 'Look, there's something you'd better know. Mullen's not exactly going to be overjoyed to see me. He's liable to be a little… ratty.'

The Doctor raised an eyebrow. 'He was never exactly jovial.'

'Yeah, well that business with the Cybermen kinda took its toll, on both of us, and… well, we've barely spoken for the last few years. I don't know how the hell he's going to react when he sees you.'

'I see.' The two men sat for a moment in silence, then McBride took a deep breath and opened the door. 'Only one way to find out.'

The two of them dashed through the rain towards the warehouses. Police and soldiers scurried to and fro. A uniformed policeman watched them approach with a frown.

'Hold on, you two, where do you think you're going? There's an unexploded bomb in there. I'm afraid that I'm going to have to ask you to leave the area.'

McBride pulled an ID card from inside his coat. 'We're here to see the officer in charge, Chief Inspector Mullen.'

The policeman peered at the card. 'Private detective, eh?' McBride could hear the distaste in his voice. 'Well that's as may be, but...'

'It's very important.' The Doctor's voice was low, calm and icy, his face obscured by shadow. 'A young girl's life is at stake.'

The policeman shuffled awkwardly and handed the card back to McBride. 'Well, yes, that's different. Carry on, sir, but put the cigarette out, please.'

'Thank you, officer.' The Doctor pushed through the battered doorway. The policeman mopped his forehead with a grubby handkerchief. McBride smiled sympathetically at him. The veiled menace in the Doctor's voice had reminded him once again that, however unassuming the little Time Lord's exterior was, a very powerful and potentially dangerous alien being lay just under the surface.

He ground the stub of his cigarette under his heel and followed the Doctor through the door. The warehouse façade was all that was left of what had once been a sizeable industrial complex. Now all that remained was rubble, though from the look of the cranes the site had already started to be redeveloped. It was probably the construction workers who had found the bomb. Even now, fourteen years on, they were still finding them.

McBride hurried to catch up with the Doctor, stumbling across the uneven surface. Not far away a cluster of soldiers and plain-clothes officers stood around a rain-filled crater in the mud. One of them looked up and pointed.

McBride's heart sank as he heard Mullen curse loudly and crudely. He had been hoping that things might have improved between them with absence; it didn't look as though they had. The big Irishman walked towards them, his face crimson. 'Get the hell out of here, McBride, before I...' His gaze swung to the Doctor and the colour drained from his face.

'Oh, Christ, no...'

The Doctor doffed his hat, smiling grimly. 'Inspector.'

'*Chief* Inspector.' Mullen tried to regain some of his composure. 'I suppose you're here to tell me that we're being invaded again, that little green men from Mars are imminently landing their fleet of flying saucers in Parliament Square. Is that it?'

The Doctor shook his head. 'I'm here to ask you to help me stop a murder.'

Mullen looked startled, then flushed. 'Well, I don't deal with that sort of thing any more. The powers that be have decided that I'm only good for digging up bloody German bombs...'

'It's Ace, Inspector. You remember Ace? I need to find her, and I need to find her tonight or she is going to be shot in the head and her body dumped in the Thames.'

'And how the hell do you know that?' Mullen was dismissive.

'Because I'm a time traveller and I've seen the future.'

McBride winced at the Doctor's bluntness. His voice had acquired that edge again. Several of the soldiers were staring curiously. Mullen must have sensed something too. His voice softened.

'When did you last see her?'

'London Zoo, earlier this evening. I didn't actually see her, but I know she was there.'

Mullen scratched at his chin. 'Well, I can put a call into headquarters, get the cars looking out for her. You can provide us with a description of what she's wearing?'

The Doctor nodded.

'Right,' said Mullen. 'I'll see what I can do.'

'Thank you, Chief Inspector.'

McBride let out his breath in a rush. A showdown with Mullen hadn't been what he wanted. He gave a curt nod to his old sparring partner. 'Thanks, appreciate it.'

Mullen grunted. 'You'd better get out of here, McBride. This isn't the safest place to be at the moment. We've got a tricky one here. Three hundred-pound German bomb caught in the foundations.' He turned back towards the hole.

The Doctor started after him. 'Perhaps I – '

McBride caught him by the hood of his duffel coat. 'I think the boys can handle the situation, Doc.'

The Doctor was about to reply, then stopped, head cocked on one side. 'Do you hear that?'

McBride listened. There *was* something – a chittering, muffled, distant. He frowned. The ground was starting to tremble, to vibrate.

'What the...?' McBride struggled to stay on his feet. The mud and rubble beneath him was heaving. Soldiers and police scattered. McBride's heart leapt. The bomb!

Suddenly, ground erupted around them. He looked in disbelief as an ant as big as a dog burst from the rubble, mandibles snapping. Others followed. He could hear gunshots and Mullen bellowing his name.

Something caught him by the sleeve and he nearly screamed. He looked up to see the Doctor leaning over him.

'We've got to get everybody out of here!' the Doctor shouted. 'The bomb –'

Too late. The bomb went off.

PART TWO

Chapter Six

'Prime Minister's Question Time witnessed an angry exchange between the Prime Minister and the Leader of the Opposition, Mr Gaitskell, over the crashed Waverider rocket. Mr Macmillan confirmed that a note had been delivered to the Soviet embassy demanding to know whether or not there was any Russian involvement in the destruction of the Waverider, and that the Russians had denied any knowledge of the incident. He also confirmed that he was keeping the Americans fully abreast of developments, and that Her Majesty's armed forces were on full alert and ready to mobilise should the need arise.

'Mr Gaitskell then asked whether there was any truth in the rumour that the real intent of the mission had been to place an advanced surveillance device into orbit. The prime minister was vigorous in denial, and angrily accused the leader of the opposition of playing into the hands of Soviet propagandists.

'Prompted by one of his own backbenchers for a response to Mr Khrushchev's increasingly belligerent statements, the prime minister's response was robust. He assured the House that NATO was resolved to meet with force any further Soviet aggression…'

'Did someone sneeze back there?'

Cody McBride shuffled into Mullen's hospital room, forcing a grin. His head hurt as if someone was drilling for oil in there, and his face was cut up a bit, but apart from that he was fine. He was shocked at the sight of his old sparring partner. He looked frail, his eyes sunken, bloodshot and black-rimmed. Old. A drip was discharging a clear fluid into Mullen's arm, and McBride could see more tubes snaking out from under the bedsheets into discreet plastic bags.

'Always when you turn up, McBride,' Mullen muttered.

'Good to see it hasn't altered your mood. They treatin' you well?'

'Can't complain,' said Mullen, turning off his radio.

McBride looked furtively towards the door. He slipped a silver hip-flask from his overcoat pocket and unscrewed the lid.

'Here,' he said, passing the flask to Mullen.

Mullen took the flask and slugged heavily from it.

'Thanks,' he said quietly when he'd drunk his fill, and handed the flask back. McBride took a slug himself.

'Any chance of a smoke?'

McBride took out a packet.

'Lucky Strike,' said Mullen. 'Nice touch.'

McBride put a cigarette in Mullen's mouth, then one in his own. He lit both. The men smoked for a moment in silence.

'The Doc's fine...'

Mullen grunted. McBride smiled blandly. Why was there never enough to goddamn say in hospital rooms?

And why was there always so much you couldn't say?

'Nice room.'

Like what the nurse had just told him outside the door.

'They brought me to the Royal London,' said Mullen. 'It used to be on my beat. Years ago. Wonder if this is the room the Elephant Man had.'

McBride was slow on the uptake. 'Oh, yeah. I heard of him. Some sort of a freak, wasn't he?'

His words tailed off as he realised.

'They had to take my legs,' said Mullen quietly.

'I know.'

McBride could see Mullen was shaking.

'What the hell am I going to do without legs?' Mullen hissed, his sudden fury bringing him close to breathless tears.

McBride didn't know what to say.

'I guess you should be glad you're alive...'

Mullen didn't reply, but stared, unblinking at the far wall of the room. The silence iced over.

'The Doc couldn't stay,' ventured McBride. 'He's running about like crazy, trying to do ten things at once, just like the last time. He's one worried guy.'

Mullen didn't reply.

'Did you see that giant ant? What a monster!'

'I don't give a damn about any giant ant,' said Mullen slowly, his anger rising, 'any more than I give a damn about Cybermen down the sewers or reds under the bloody bed!' He was shouting now. 'I was right, McBride, it *is* always you. Whenever you come charging into my life I'm dropped straight in it. You put me here, McBride. You've crippled me just like you crippled my career. Well, you and the Doctor can go and chase your giant ants, but leave me alone! Just… go.'

McBride didn't know what to say. He got up to leave, then stopped and turned.

'No.'

This wasn't fair. This wasn't goddam fair.

'You know, Mullen – there was a time when you gave a shit.'

'You reckon?' Mullen sounded bitterly sarcastic. 'When was that, then?'

'Back when we first ran into each other. When the Doc and Ace showed up.'

'When my life was first screwed up by you and your lunatic friends. When your obsession with the damned Cybermen started.'

'You were the same! We had to do something. Only we really knew what they were messing around with. We had to try.'

How many times over the years had they got into this same argument?

It had all started just days after the Doc and Ace left – just when they thought it was over. Mullen had located a partially collapsed sewer full of dormant Cybermen. Not knowing what to do, and scared to go to the authorities after their recent experiences, they had dynamited what remained of the tunnel and sealed the monsters in.

As if that was going to solve anything. Inevitably, come the end of the war, the sewers were rebuilt. Nothing was made public, but he and Mullen recognised at once what was going on. The building work was held up for weeks while the area was surrounded by wooden hoardings and military vehicles came and went. The official story was an unexploded bomb. They'd tried to warn the authorities what they were dealing with, and when that failed they'd made the whole thing public.

'You didn't pay for it with your bloody career!' Mullen growled. 'I was lucky not to be charged under the Official Secrets Act. I should have been a superintendent by now.'

What was the point? Over and over again, over years.

'You've changed, Mullen. You're not the guy I knew in the war.'

'Oh, here we go! The war! Vera bloody Lynn! Well, it's me that's still cleaning up the mess from that war, and look where it's put me.'

Suddenly Mullen switched his radio back on. The guy was still going on about the Russians.

'And you know what? You might as well forget the Blitz spirit, McBride, cos there'll be no singing down the bloody tube stations next time round. Two seconds and it'll all be over. The lot.'

The two men lapsed into silence. McBride lit another cigarette.

The door opened and a middle-aged nurse bustled in.

'We don't permit smoking around the patients,' she said. 'You'll have to put that out or go outside.'

McBride lurched from his seat and headed for the door.

'Open wide.'

The nurse briskly popped a thermometer under Mullen's tongue.

'Doctor is coming to see you,' she said.

Out in the corridor McBride slumped against a wall, drumming the back of his head slowly against the dull paintwork and pulling deeply on his cigarette. He'd screwed up. Mullen's legs had been shattered by the bomb. They'd had to amputate immediately.

McBride should have known he'd be the last person Mullen wanted to see right now. A red rag to a bull.

A man in a long white coat passed him and entered Mullen's room. A moment later the nurse emerged.

'Your friend is very lucky,' she said to McBride.

Lucky, he thought. Yeah, damned lucky, getting both your legs blown off.

'Dr Hark is one of the brightest in his field. A pioneer. He's come down specially.'

A long finger of ash dropped from McBride's cigarette to the floor. The nurse tutted.

McBride had had enough. He strode across to where a stack of shallow metal kidney-dishes sat on a shelf, stubbed out his cigarette in the topmost bowl and headed for the exit.

He left the doors swinging and took the steps two at a time. Stupid to have come here.

And yet he couldn't resist a look when he passed Mullen's window. Mullen looked, if anything, worse than before. Paler, an expression of horror on his face. The man in the white coat was standing over him, talking earnestly.

Mullen was slowly shaking his head.

McBride spun round and hurried back to the entrance. He couldn't leave it like this. However much they clashed, this was still Mullen.

He passed the doctor in the corridor, chatting to another man in a white coat.

'Perhaps we should have given him more time,' the other man was saying.

'He'll come round,' the doctor replied, smiling.

McBride crashed into Mullen's room.

'What's happened?' he barked.

Mullen was silent. He looked as if he'd seen the Devil.

'They want to fit me with artificial legs,' he eventually whispered. 'State of the art. Electronically controlled by my own nervous system.'

McBride shuddered.

'They're going to turn me into…'

He couldn't finish the sentence, but McBride knew what he meant. He felt suddenly weak, and sat down.

'Don't be a jerk,' he said with painfully unconvincing lightness.

He took out his hip-flask again and offered it to Mullen. Mullen was shaking so much he couldn't hold it to his lips. McBride did it for him.

'It might be a good thing,' he said as Mullen drank. 'If it gets you on your feet again…'

Bad choice of words.

'My feet are scattered across Bermondsey. Give us a ciggy.'

McBride lit two.

'So just tell them no if that's what you want. They can't make you do anything.'

'Can't they?' asked Mullen. 'That doctor – I think he's connected with some sort of research programme. Government stuff, hush-hush. And you know what that lot are like. They're already pumping me full of God knows what drugs. They've got stuff that'll make you agree to anything.'

'I won't let them do it,' said McBride.

'When are you going to realise you can't fight these people, McBride? We're drifting closer and closer to war with the Commies. They need Cyber technology more now than they ever did.'

Mullen took a deep drag.

'No, there's only one thing you can do for me, McBride.'

'Sure, name it.'

'Give me your gun and go.'

It took a second for Mullen's words to sink in.

'What, you… No way, Mullen. You ain't gonna shoot yourself.'

'I'm not going to be turned into a monster – a freak,' Mullen spat through gritted teeth.

'I'll stop them!'

'Like you stopped the research programme? When will you grow up, McBride? Everything's too big nowadays for the likes of you and me to change anything. The stakes are too damned high! We count for bugger all!'

Mullen stubbed his cigarette angrily into the wall.

'I'm finished, McBride. The best I can look forward to is life in a wheelchair, and the worst…'

He sank into an angry silence, then. 'Well, at least leave me your whisky. I can easily half-inch some pills from the nurses' trolley. That should do the job.'

'Will you quit it with the suicide crap?' McBride snapped.

Silence again.

'There's nothing else you can do for me,' said Mullen. 'You might as well go.'

McBride hesitated for a moment, then stood up, defeated. Momentarily he rested his hand on the bed. The blankets were damp. For the first time he noticed the drip-feed had come out of Mullen's arm and was leaking its contents into the bedclothes.

'What are you doing?' McBride shouted. 'Nurse!'

'You won't stop me!' Mullen gasped, close to tears. 'I'll find a way.'

'Nurse!'

The nurse hurried in.

'What's going on in here?'

'His drip's come loose.'

The nurse made a scolding noise, took the end of the tube and loosened the bandages that had been attaching it to Mullen's upper arm. McBride averted his eyes – he didn't like this sort of thing.

'What are we going to do with you?' the nurse chided. 'You'll have to be more careful. Try not to move around too much.'

'But I'm playing football in an hour, nurse,' Mullen grunted, rolling his eyes. And then, not quite under his breath, 'Silly bitch.'

To his surprise McBride heard Mullen chuckle.

'Now that's not the attitude, is it?' the nurse chirped. 'Bright and breezy fights diseasey.'

Mullen was guffawing openly now. Suddenly, and to his surprise, so was McBride.

'And tell me, nurse, how's my "diseasey" coming along?'

'You know what I mean,' said the nurse briskly. 'How are our bowels today, Mr Mullen?'

'Mine are fine,' snapped Mullen. 'Yours seem a bit tight…'

'Mr Mullen, there's no need to be offensive.'

She finished tying off the bandage.

'Chief Inspector Mullen.' He sounded more like his old self. 'Now if you'd excuse us…'

'Yes, well please try to – '

'Get out, woman!'

The nurse bristled, gathered her affronted dignity and left the room.

'Give me your gun,' growled Mullen. 'Not for me – change of plan.'

McBride chortled, and both men started to laugh again.

'You'd better not,' grinned McBride. 'She's NHS property.'

They laughed long and hard. It was a relief.

'Anyway I'll never be able to do myself in with her breathing down my neck,' Mullen said. 'Not a chance.'

McBride broke out the hip-flask again and they drank.

'What am I going to do, McBride?' asked Mullen with a sort of sad resignation.

'The Doc's here now,' McBride replied. 'Remember what he was up against before – Lazonby, the nut from British intelligence… that sneaky old creep George Limb, not to mention our big silver buddies. And the Nazis – you remember the news from Jersey… The Doc sorted all that out.'

'He didn't though, did he?' said Mullen. 'And now it's all started up again.'

Dr Bill Hark, the white-coated surgeon in charge of the unfortunate Chief Inspector Mullen, sipped tea from a stiff paper cup that burned his fingers and listened to Matron tearing the radiographer off a strip.

He removed a birthday card from the pocket of his lab coat. His kids had slipped it into his briefcase this morning. Or probably Sue did it for them. He smiled as he read their childish, raggedy declarations of love. He was home so infrequently because of his work…

He sat at the narrow counter and unwrapped his sandwiches. Sue had slipped in a miniature bottle of brandy, with a ribbon tied around the neck. He chuckled aloud.

He set the card up next to his little meal and started to eat.

Moments later the doors swung wildly inward and a grizzled figure in a grimy mac stormed in. Dr Hark jumped to his feet, spilling tea down the front of his white coat.

'Uh, listen… you're the guy in charge of my buddy, yeah? Joe Mullen.'

'And you'd be Mr…'

'McBride. He was saying something to me about artificial legs…'

Dr Hark put his half-empty cardboard cup down and wiped crumbs from his mouth.

'Yes…'

'Well, he ain't happy about it.'

'Naturally we will give him plenty of time to decide. We will explain the procedure fully, make sure he understands what it's all about.'

'He understands! And he's already made his mind up. The answer's no.'

'Your friend won't be strong enough for the operation for some time, Mr McBride. He has ample time to think about it.'

The intruder made to interject.

'But naturally – ' Dr Hark cut him off with smooth, calming authority. '– should he decide not to go through with the operation, we shall of course abide by his wishes.'

'Well, I'll be checking in on him regular, keeping an eye on things.'

'You are, of course, free to visit your friend.' Dr Hark smiled. 'This isn't a prison, you know.'

'Just so's you know I'm watching you.'

The American turned on his heel and marched out.

Hark's assistant scuttled across from where he'd been keeping his head down.

'Who was that?' Ernie Bure asked.

'His name is Cody McBride. An American, of course. He's a detective.'

'Police?' Bure queried nervously.

'No, of course not. Private. Didn't you notice the bad Humphrey Bogart impersonation?'

'I can't see why we need to use the old man anyway. There must be younger specimens.'

'For this particular experiment,' Dr Hark lowered his voice, 'it isn't particularly important whether the subject lives or dies. And it will be interesting to see how an older body copes with the stresses of augmentation.'

He picked up his cup and drained the dregs, watching through the glass door panels as McBride's receding figure, far off down the corridor, turned and strode out into Whitechapel Road.

'And besides,' Hark said, 'Chief Inspector Mullen and our American friend have tried to cause trouble for the Programme for years. The old bastard's got it coming to him.'

* * *

Behind them, Matron had recovered from McBride's intrusion, and was resuming her barracking of Geoff Perkins, the radiographer.

'Well, you must have done something wrong! Look at these!' She waved a sheaf of X-rays in Perkins's face.

'Look, I dunno how they got like that. It's the machine.'

'A bad workman blames his tools, Perkins. How would the machine make it look as if the poor man has two hearts?'

'It must be the lens.'

'May I see those, Matron?'

Dr Hark strolled over to Matron.

'Really, it's just some silly joke, Dr Hark.'

'Then share the joke with me, Matron.'

He gently prised the X-rays from her grasp. A male thoracic cavity... with what did indeed appear to be two hearts.

'Where is this patient, Matron?' he asked urgently.

'Oh, he was discharged hours ago,' Matron replied. 'Just cuts and bruises.'

Dr Hark crossed to the ward desk in a second, snatched up the phone and began to dial. He drummed his fingers anxiously on the desk as he waited for a reply.

'Yes... This is Dr Hark calling from the London... General Crawhammer, please... Yes, very urgent.'

Chapter Seven

Several hours earlier the Doctor had left hospital with a sore head and very little time. The bomb blast had knocked him out, and left him with a concussion that might have killed a human. He knew well that his brain had already largely healed itself, but of course the hospital staff couldn't know that, and had refused to be convinced he was fine. In the end he'd lost patience and walked out, leaving McBride with his hasty good wishes for the Chief Inspector.

He shuddered at the memory of the last time he'd walked down Whitechapel Road. The year had been 1888, and the Doctor anything but himself – he'd even tried to kill Ace.[4] Ironic – now he was racing against the clock to save her life.

Pushing away the memory, he hurried onto a crowded District Line train. Seven stops to the Temple station, then up Middle Temple Lane, past the ancient Inn of Court to Fleet Street.

It took him some time to find Rita Hawks's office. The paper she worked for turned out not actually to be *on* Fleet Street (as she had implied) so much as in a narrow passageway *not all that far from* Fleet Street. The *London Inquisitor*. He pushed through the poky reception area, which was crowded with noisy men and women all talking at once.

'One at a time!' a tetchy voice shouted from somewhere in the crowd. No one took any notice.

'Me cat's got the Divil in him! He's possessed!'

'Well, kindly tell your editor that he will be hearing from my solicitor, and that I'll see him in court!'

''Ave you 'eard about that dodgy vicar down Peckham way? Scandal, it is! On the floor, staring up the contraltos' cassocks!'

The Doctor somehow managed to reach the reception desk, where a youth sat with his shirt-sleeves rolled up, scowling blackly and filling in a crossword puzzle.

[4] See *Doctor Who – Matrix*

'Rita Hawks, please,' the Doctor said brusquely.

The young man looked up from his puzzle. 'Didn't you 'ear what I said? One at a time. Someone'll see you in a bit.'

He returned his attention to his newspaper.

'Six across,' snapped the Doctor. 'Obstructive. Three down. Ill-mannered. Twenty across. Imbecile.'

'Oh, yeah…' said the youth, scribbling hurriedly.

The Doctor wasn't prepared to waste any more time here. He shot around the desk and through a door marked 'Staff Only' while the youth was still making his corrections.

He closed the door on the din and trotted down the corridor in search of Rita.

In fact she found him.

'Where the hell have you been?' Her voice blasted out from one in a line of cubbyholes that passed for offices. 'Come in! There was a bomb.'

'Yes,' said the Doctor. 'I'm afraid Chief Inspector Mullen was badly injured. Mr McBride's all right, I'm glad to say.'

'But you haven't found your friend?'

'No. I was hoping you might help me.'

'Sure. This is great stuff.'

'Ace will die soon unless I can prevent it,' the Doctor said gravely.

'I'm sorry,' Rita replied. 'Go on.'

'It seems certain that our separate problems are in fact one. For some reason Ace is involved on the fringes of espionage. And so I can only hope that my decision is the right one.'

He drew a heavy breath, then fished in his pocket and handed Rita a brown envelope.

'I want you to give this to Cody as soon as you see him. And if – heaven forbid – anything untoward should happen to him, I want you to open it yourself immediately and – though I have no right to demand this of you, and it will involve danger – carry out the instructions inside to the letter.'

'What are you going to do?' asked Rita.

'I'm going to Winnerton Flats. If things do not go well, I might find myself detained there. Locked up. I might not get back before Ace…'

He couldn't finish the sentence.

'What are you going to do out there?'

The Doctor began pacing the tiny space. It helped him think.

'Is your Major O'Brien permitted visitors at Winnerton Flats?'

'Not without clearance, no.'

'I see.'

'What can O'Brien tell you? Trust me, Doctor – he never went up in that ship.'

'Oh, I just need him to confirm a worrying theory. But I also need to know exactly what they're doing out there. I suspect it's something very dangerous.'

'Dangerous… like… war?'

'The ants were the clincher.'

'Ants?'

'One-foot-long ants, Miss Hawks.'

'So it's true…'

'Oh, yes.'

'And that's what? Radiation doing that to them?'

'No.'

'So, what are they? Like, space ants?'

'Space/time pollution. Very dangerous. Very destructive. And I must get to the bottom of it or Ace's future will be only one of billions lost.'

He suddenly turned and shook her hand. 'I thank you in advance for what you might have to do for Ace. Forgive me for putting this trust in you – I know it isn't fair.'

Rita smiled.

The Doctor smiled back.

'Do you have a car?'

An hour and a half later the Doctor was lost. Rita had drawn the way on a road map (and had even done a quick sketch of what she knew of the Winnerton Manor set-up on the back), but he'd lost it when the bubble blew open.

He had braved the City traffic, navigated round Bank and crossed London Bridge in a giant light-bulb. It was a terrifying experience. He was below the level of the rest of the traffic – they couldn't see him and he couldn't see past them. He vaguely remembered that these things were made by Messerschmitt after the war, using the machinery and design of their wartime fighter cockpits. He knew how the pilots must have felt.

His sudden emergence into fields took the Doctor by surprise. He'd forgotten how far London had still to spread before Ace's time.

It occurred to him that he might not have given Rita the best explanation of the events she was caught up in. That had been shockingly

selfish of him. She deserved the whole truth. Then it struck him
how often in the past he had done exactly the same thing. The truth
was, he hated giving explanations before he was sure he was right.
Or maybe he was just a pathological show-off. Or maybe he'd read
too much Agatha Christie. He didn't know – but it was just such
deception, he recalled with a shudder, that had possibly driven Ace to
her death.

And yet what else could he do?

He was hamstrung by his knowledge of future events. He knew
Ace's death was merely a bait for him, and he knew he was meant to
discover what was happening out at Winnerton Flats. Why otherwise
the hospital tag on Ace's toe? They were removed before burial.

He knew it was a trap, and yet what else could he do? It was already
sprung, and he was being drawn irresistibly in.

There was a vague, niggling familiarity about the situation.

The horizon was flat now – long, low heathland skirted by a lattice
of streams, low dykes and patches of waterlogged marsh.

At last he could see where he was going. He spotted the great house
with ease, on slightly raised ground, surrounded by a large, walled,
lightly wooded estate. The wall was topped with barbed wire. Signs
every fifty yards or so read 'HM Government Property – Maximum
Security. Absolutely no admittance.'

He couldn't help but smile. That should foil the Russians.

The gate, when he found it, was open. Clearly, a stern warning was
considered sufficient.

He hunched his head down, gripped the steering-wheel hard, and hit
the accelerator.

The little car roared forward, backfiring as it shot through the gate
and up the long drive towards the old house.

To the sentries in the gateside guard-boxes it looked and sounded
like a giant champagne cork popping.

The Doctor's eyes darted about frantically. Keeper's Lodge, off the main
drive, set in a beech thicket… The drive forked. The Doctor chose at
random. In his aviator's wing-mirrors he could see the two guards in
pursuit. They were on motorbikes and catching up with him.

They closed, one on each side of him. He was about level with their
knees.

And then he saw the brown stone lodge. He jammed on the brakes,
hit the handbrake and swung the wheel wildly. The little chariot spun

around in a broad arc, narrowly missing the pursuing bikes as they shot past. It teetered alarmingly on only two of its three wheels, and skidded into a narrow gap between beech trees. The sound of the bikes was suddenly swallowed by the great trees. The cottage was dead ahead at the end of a white gravel path.

He scraped to a halt at the cottage porch and flung open the windscreen-cum-door on this ghastly contraption. Why Rita had bought it he couldn't imagine. He scrambled out and rang the bell urgently and continuously until the door was answered. He pushed inside, his hand offered to a young man in cardigan and slippers.

'Hello. It's Captain O'Brien, isn't it? I'm a friend of Rita Hawks.'

An amused smile played around O'Brien's mouth. He shook the Doctor's hand.

'Pleased to meet you, uh…?'

'Oh, Doctor,' said the Doctor.

O'Brien shrugged. 'OK…'

From outside the door they could hear two motorbikes drawing up.

'I should warn you, there are some guards chasing me. I think this is them.'

'Really?' O'Brien couldn't suppress a grin. There was a hammering on the door.

'I really do need to talk to you,' the Doctor said.

O'Brien opened the door. The two guards had guns in their hands.

'What is it, boys?' O'Brien said.

'It's him, sir,' one of the guards said, gesturing past O'Brien to where the Doctor was standing. 'Do you know him?'

'Of course. He's an old friend.'

'Was his visit cleared, sir?'

'No, he just showed up.'

'He'll have to come with us, sir.' At least the guard had the decency to sound regretful.

'Oh, come on, lads. I'm going out of my mind in here. I've got no television, not even a radio… Half an hour.'

The guards looked at one another and started whispering.

The Doctor scanned the room. An idea had hit him. An officer's cap and baton were hanging next to the door. He snatched them up, huffed and coughed and guffawed, giving it as much Lethbridge-Stewart-on-a-wet-Monday-morning as he could muster.

'Quite right, Captain, quite right. These men are only carrying out their orders.'

He planted the cap on his head and took a step forward. Just enough shadow to do the trick...

'Quite right, men. Quite right.'

The guards looked confused. O'Brien grinned, the penny dropping.

'Well, thank you for dropping in... uh... General.'

The two guards snapped to attention.

A sly smile flickered between the Doctor and O'Brien.

'You see what sort of staff car they give me?' He waved the baton imperiously into the light. 'Damned cutbacks.'

The guards were floundering.

'Uh, sorry, sir. We never realised...'

'Half an hour, guys...' O'Brien chipped in.

'Uh... yes, sir. Whatever you say, sir.'

'At ease, lads,' O'Brien grinned as he closed the door.

'I wanted to say that,' said the Doctor.

My dear Cody,

As I am writing this, I know that unless we can prevent it, Ace has at most another twelve hours to live. I am forced to visit Winnerton Flats, so I leave Ace in your care. I beg you, find her by any means possible – I am sure Miss Hawks will help. Get Ace to the TARDIS. Tell her it's where we left it, in the basement of St Thomas's Hospital on Lambeth Palace Road. I'm afraid the way in will be guarded, but it is the only place I feel sure Ace can find refuge.

I shall return as soon as I can.

My deepest thanks,

The Doctor

And then an odd sort of seal.

Rita had waited two long, agonising hours before she opened the envelope the Doctor had left with her. She had stationed herself at McBride's office and waited. He still hadn't returned.

The Doctor had said they had little time.

And he'd wanted her to open it anyway, if anything happened to McBride...

She was a little disappointed by the contents, but instantly sensed the urgency of the note. The girl had to be found.

She scribbled something to McBride on the bottom of the note, placed it back in the envelope, and put the envelope on McBride's desk.

Then she headed for the door.

McBride, however, was a long way from his desk. He was flat on the floor in Mullen's hospital room, drunk. Mullen was above him on the bed, drunk.

At some stage he'd hit the liquor store, passing the bottles up through Mullen's window to avoid the prying eyes of nurses. He hadn't moved for the past hour.

'They've been like it all afternoon, doctor.' The nurse outside the door sounded anxious. McBride and Mullen started to giggle.

'They've been noisy, disruptive, told me to… "something" off. We should call the police.'

'I am the bloody police!' shouted Mullen. 'Now do as I told you and f– '

'So I haven't gone mad then!' The young pilot sounded relieved and angry. 'They told me I'd imagined it. I'd had some sort of breakdown after Tom Kneale died. They haven't let me out of here since.'

'Oh, you're quite sane, Captain. And this is definitely the first time we've met.'

'Definitely.'

'Then I can confirm you have an absolute double lying in a hospital in London. He'd been in a rocket crash.'

O'Brien slumped into a chair, dumbstruck. 'They even had me seeing a shrink.'

'A psychiatrist?'

'He came down from Harley Street – to help me through the trauma of the crash. He said I was in a delusional state – that I felt guilty that Tom had died and not me. You see, I'd almost gone in his place. He had a bit of a cold, but he still wanted to go. In the end we flipped a coin.'

'Your psychiatrist suggested that you'd imagined hearing yourself on the radio.'

'Yup.'

'What else has he said to you?' For some reason the Doctor was getting goose-pimples.

'Nothing much. He's old. A bit doolally himself, if you ask me. I do most of the talking. To be honest, I make a lot of stuff up. Glad of the company, you see. I think he knows, but he indulges me. He seems to spend more time with Drakefell than me – but then Drakefell really needs it.'

'Yes… I'll be having a word with Dr Drakefell,' the Doctor murmured.

'Doctor, what's going on? Who's this guy pretending to be me? Some kind of Russian plant?'

'No, I'm afraid it's much more serious than that.'

O'Brien looked suddenly wary. 'Hey – should I be talking to you?'

'I'm probably the only person in the whole place who'll tell you the truth…'

O'Brien nodded his head.

'So tell me, what was the launch really all about?'

'Oh…' O'Brien shrugged. 'There were a few experiments we had to carry out, but the biggie was the satellite launch. No one was supposed to know about that.'

'Was it a spy satellite?'

'Oh, yeah. Really advanced. There's a top secret project, been on the go a while. Some new technology… I don't know much about it. But the rocket had some weird new piloting mechanisms. It was like learning from scratch. And the satellite was like nothing even the Yanks had developed. They loved it. They jumped on it.'

'Something went wrong, though, didn't it?'

'The rocket exploded. It was huge – it sent all our meters off the scale. Took the satellite with it. Had to be a Soviet missile.'

'But they found no trace of one.'

'No.'

'And the Waverider?'

'Crashed in the sea. How it survived I can't imagine.'

'I see… Now tell me, did you lose radio contact with Colonel Kneale at all?'

'Just after the explosion, yes. For quite a few minutes.'

'And whose voice was coming through when contact was re-established?'

He hesitated. 'It was kind of hard to say at first – the signal was a mess, but… No, if I'm honest, I knew right away. It was mine, all the way down.' He shook his head in bafflement.

There was a knock at the door.

'Captain O'Brien?'

'That's Drakefell,' O'Brien whispered to the Doctor. 'No jam for supper now.'

'Would you open the door, please?'

'Go on,' the Doctor said. 'I need to talk to him anyway.'

O'Brien opened the door. Beyond it stood Drakefell, puffing nervously at a thin cigar that had gone out. At his back were half a dozen soldiers.

'You know the rules, Captain. No unauthorised visitors on site. The same rules for you as for everyone else.'

'Everyone else is allowed to leave the goddamn grounds! I can't go beyond my garden wall!'

'Would you ask your visitor to step outside, please?'

'With pleasure!' The Doctor sprang forward, hat doffed, hand extended. 'You're Dr Drakefell. I recognise you from the television.'

'The question is, who are you?' Drakefell retorted. 'And what are you doing here?'

'Well, actually, I came to see you.'

Rita crept up to the little pink cottage on the outskirts of Kennington, just as she had when she had photographed Ace and her hunky friend delivering their package. She'd been quite unable to sit and wait. She knew they had to find the girl, and this was one of only two leads they had – one of two places they knew she'd been.

Rita figured that maybe, if the girl had accidentally butted in on some Russian spy ring, maybe they'd snatched her.

She slipped through the undergrowth and peered in through a window. Just an ordinary cottage. Rather quaint. A bit old-fashioned.

'Can I help you?'

Rita spun round. The old lady she had photographed taking the package. She was smiling helpfully.

'I was looking for someone. A young woman.'

'Well, I'm afraid there's only me here, and I haven't been young in a very long time.'

'She was here with a young guy. He was delivering a package.'

The woman looked thoughtful.

'Yes… Yes, I vaguely recall… I'm afraid I didn't speak to her.' She seemed to gather herself. 'Would you like to come in for a cup of tea?'

Rita knew she shouldn't. To the best of her knowledge this old lady was a Russian courier. She couldn't resist it.

'Yes,' she said, 'that would be nice.'

She was ushered through into a low-ceilinged, uneven-walled, thoroughly charming living room. A hand-knitted blanket covered the back of the old settee, a massive oak dresser hunched under heavy beams filling one wall. China cups and horse-brasses lined a sturdy, if uneven, wooden staircase rising from the far end. A vase of chrysanthemums on the windowsill. Dead quaint.

'May I know your name?' the old woman said.

'Uh... Jane Smith,' said Rita, scanning the room. No obvious signs of the girl... that weird jacket she wore...

'Emily Desmond,' the old woman said. 'Miss.'

Where might they be keeping the girl? Upstairs.

'It's a lovely place you have here.'

'It's small, but it suits me. Do have a seat.'

The old woman bustled through a doorway. Maybe Rita could slip up now.

'China or Indian?' she called back.

'I'm sorry?'

'The tea.'

The words barely registered with Rita. She felt a sudden, hot shudder. Her eyesight blurred for a second.

'The tea, dear. Are you all right in there?'

'Yes... I'm fine,' said Rita.

She sat down anyway. She was covered in cold sweat. She tried to recall what her host had asked.

'Uh, the tea... just the normal kind will do fine.' Rita couldn't understand the Brits' obsession with the stuff. Tea was tea.

The girl...

Unsteadily Rita got to her feet and poked her head around the kitchen door.

'Can I use your bathroom?'

The kitchen was empty. Emily was gone.

She had to take this chance. Rita hurried back across the living room and up the stairs. What was the girl's name...?

'Uh... Ace? Are you up here? It's OK, I'm sort of with your friend, the Doctor...'

Silence. Three doors.

She opened each. Three bedrooms. All empty. Tiny cupboards. Nowhere to stash a prisoner. There wasn't even an attic space – this floor rose unceilinged up to the thatched roof-beams.

Maybe they'd killed her – the Doctor had said she was going to be shot. Rita swallowed hard.

There was a newspaper on a little table in the third bedroom. The *Herald*. Rita glanced down at the headline.

ROYAL FAMILY RETURN FROM TRIUMPHANT EMPIRE TOUR
*Today the King and Queen and Princesses Elizabeth and Margaret
returned from the final leg of their Grand Imperial Tour to be
greeted by rapturous crowds at Southampton.* HMY Britannia *made
the journey from India in record time –*

Rita was puzzled. The King had been dead eight years. One of the
two princesses was now Queen in her own right. But the paper felt
new. It was dated 26 November 1959.

The day before yesterday.

'Just… Doctor.'

'Yes.'

Drakefell sighed.

'Don't make things difficult, please.'

'I'd say things were already difficult, wouldn't you?'

They were facing one another across the desk in Drakefell's office,
which had once, in the house's grand old days, clearly been a broom
cupboard. The Doctor was flanked by two soldiers.

'Send the soldiers away, Dr Drakefell,' the Doctor said, low and pur-
poseful. 'You and I need to talk before things become any more difficult.'

Drakefell was sweating. His hands clutched and unclutched at his
sides.

'Or I could just come out with it in front of them.'

'All right! You men… go, uh, dismissed.'

The soldiers smirked and left.

'All right, I've done what you wanted – now tell me what you have
to say.'

'Where is the rocket?'

'What? You're here to answer me!'

'The world is in terrible danger, Dr Drakefell.'

'You think I don't know that?' Drakefell exploded. 'The whole
damned planet on the brink of nuclear war, and all because…'

He sank into his chair.

'All right,' the Doctor replied calmly, 'at least tell me who was piloting
it.'

Drakefell gave him a haggard look.

'It was Colonel Thomas Kneale, wasn't it? At least on the way up.
And Davey O'Brien on the way down. Very odd.'

Drakefell was trembling. His mouth moved slightly, but no sound came out.

At last – 'Please…' he whispered.

'Something very bad happened when you launched that rocket,' the Doctor continued. 'And I'm not talking about the Russians.'

'Well, what in Jeee-zuzz name have we got here?' a voice boomed behind the Doctor. He spun round to see an enormous American soldier – a five-star general, no less – filling the doorway.

Drakefell was on his feet.

'General Crawhammer, this man was found –'

'I know, Drakefell. Snoopin' round Davey O'Brien. So what have you got outta him?'

'Well… he calls himself the Doctor.'

'You mean you ain't even learned his name? Jeez, Drakefell!'

The general turned and stomped out.

'Bring him,' he barked.

Two soldiers – American soldiers – marched in and grabbed the Doctor by both arms and dragged him into the corridor. He cast a final glance back at the deathly pale Drakefell, staring paralysed after him.

'You too, Drakefell!' Crawhammer bellowed. 'I'm gonna show you how it's done.'

He flung open an ornate door into a plush, thickly carpeted room with huge, high windows and chandeliers, and stomped in.

'Dora!' the general barked into the air. 'Get me Bill Hark on the phone.'

The Doctor was pushed in after him. Drakefell followed, then the guards, closing the door behind them.

'Very nice, General… What was the name again?'

'Crawhammer.'

'It suits you. So what was this, the ballroom?'

'The small dining room, I'm told,' the general replied. 'Now it's my office. This is where we do the talking in comfort. If that's the way you want to play it.'

'I see,' said the Doctor. 'And suppose I don't? Where then, the cellar?'

'Something like that,' the American replied. 'So tell me – what are you doing here?'

'I came to find out exactly what happened to the Waverider.'

'You should know. It was your Commie puppetmasters who brought it down.'

'Why do you say that?'

'Hey – I ask. You answer.'

'Is it because you have nothing in your formidable arsenal capable of creating an explosion of the magnitude your instruments recorded? Well, let me tell you – neither have the Russians.'

Crawhammer took a step forward.

'Who then? The Chinese?'

'No,' said the Doctor, clipped and losing patience. 'Not the Chinese. General, the destruction of your rocket was caused by a rare and violent exothermic reaction of a type that cannot, at this time and on this planet, be generated.'

'What's this crap?' asked Crawhammer warily.

'What are you saying?' said Drakefell, suddenly stepping forward.

'That something – and I need to find out what – created a reaction capable of crossing certain... trans-dimensional absolutes. Colonel Kneale's craft – what was left of it – was sucked into the rift and almost certainly vaporised, I'm sorry to say. But something came through from the other side.'

'The other rocket...'

'Damn it, Drakefell!' Crawhammer shouted. 'He's supposed to tell us!'

The door opened and a young woman's head popped around it.

'Dr Hark on the telephone for you, sir.'

Crawhammer snatched up the phone from his desk.

'Hark!... Yeah, that's right. The X-ray, yeah... The radiographer – well put him on!'

The Doctor was starting to feel uneasy.

'Yeah, can you describe him?' Crawhammer bellowed into the phone. 'Yeah... Yeah...'

He slammed the phone down and started to pace slowly around the Doctor, all the time staring at him with what seemed to be a mixture of awe and revulsion.

'Drakefell, get out,' he said. Drakefell slipped dutifully away...

'So you're the goddamn Russkie augment...' Crawhammer said to the Doctor with something approaching respect in his voice. 'How do they do it?'

'I'm afraid you've lost me,' said the Doctor.

'Grab him, boys!'

The two soldiers closed in, again gripping his arms.

Crawhammer opened a drawer in his desk and took out a Bowie knife. He strode across and jabbed it into the Doctor's stomach. The tip pressed painfully, just short of breaking the skin.

Slowly the general drew the knife upward. The Doctor's pullover was sliced in two. The buttons pinged off his shirt.

Crawhammer snicked the last button off at the neck, then drew the Doctor's shirt aside. He pressed the knife-point against the left side of his chest, then the right.

'Two hearts… We've been dreamin' about something like you.'

He started to chuckle, and ran the knife up and down the Doctor's breastbone.

'So guess what, boy? We're gonna go right on and open you up!'

Chapter Eight

Rita looked at her watch.

4.35. Had she really been here that long? The woman could come back at any time.

She had to find out more. She licked her lips and scanned the living room. Where to start... She didn't really know what to do – this was the sort of thing she'd hired McBride for.

Papers, documents – anything like that... She crossed to the big old dresser and heaved on its single drawer. It was locked. So were the cupboard doors beneath. She tried the kitchen cupboards, and pulled on a door leading from the kitchen. Locked. So was the back door.

It was a strange kind of lock – Rita had never seen one like it, and she couldn't open it.

Suddenly struck by a nasty thought, she went back and tried the front door. That was also locked, and also with a sleek, impenetrable mechanism.

She went to the front window. Same story. She was a prisoner.

For the first time she noticed the smell of flowers in the room. She was standing over the vase of chrysanthemums. Their fragrance gently wafted upward, lingering longingly at the edge of the senses.

She shook her head to clear it.

She picked up a wooden footstool and hurled it with all her strength at the window, then dived out of the path of the stool as it ricocheted back off the undamaged panes. All she'd done was knock over the vase. She picked it up, and gathered the flowers together, smelling them as she did so.

There was no water. The vase was completely dry.

She put a flower to her nose – the smell really was wonderful – then ran her fingers over a petal.

She tugged. The flower bent but the petal wouldn't break. It felt...

She put the flowers down and picked up the newspaper. She tried to tear off a corner. It wouldn't tear. She held a page in the fire. It wouldn't burn.

It was fake. The flowers were fake. This whole place was fake. It was too perfect – from the crackling of the logs to the pendulous ticking of the big, boxy old clock in the corner.

Nearly two. She looked at her watch again. 4.40. She remembered the time she'd got here – just past 1.30. Her watch had gained nearly three hours since she wound it this morning.

She didn't know what was happening, and she didn't know what to do. And for all she knew, Ace was already dead.

In fact, Ace was having the time of her life. She'd spent the evening eating burgers with Jimmy in Soho. He was quiet, shy, almost dreamy. And a hunk. After they'd eaten they'd had a drink in The Ship on Wardour Street. Years from now Ace and her friends would get chucked out of here for being under age.

She couldn't remember how long it had been since she had been completely independent of the Doctor – usually she was either running alongside him or desperately searching for him.

She felt truly relaxed for the first time in years.

They passed the cinema she'd visited the day before, and Ace told Jimmy about the film.

'I don't go to the movies much,' he'd replied.

'What do you do?'

He'd shrugged. 'Work, I guess. Look at the animals…'

'What about mates?'

Jimmy shrugged. 'I keep myself to myself. I got one good buddy. Works in the reptile house. He got me the job. I'd like you to meet him.'

'What about girlfriends?' asked Ace, fishing.

He shrugged again and blushed.

They'd strolled across Regent's Park in the dark and into the zoo. His room was amazing – a stone bunker underneath the primate house, simply furnished with a single mattress, a rug and a lamp, a trunk in the corner and a picture of a silver Porsche on the wall. Apart from that the room was bare. The window was set high, a dark slit against the ceiling.

Jimmy had been a perfect gentleman that night. He'd kissed her hand and gone to sleep on the rug, insisting that she take the mattress.

When, briefly, she awoke around dawn he was next to her – fully clothed – curled up and fast asleep. The smells and sounds of the wakening zoo wafted in on the sunshine, and Ace drifted back to sleep and dreamed of riding bareback through the Serengeti with Jimmy.

She'd woken later to find a pot of coffee and a note – he'd got the afternoon off. She wandered about the zoo all morning in a sort of daze, hoping for glimpses of Jimmy. The morning was bright and wonderful, and unbearably long.

The Doctor's cell was not uncomfortable – it had hitherto been a bedroom – but he couldn't relax with the two guards stationed in there with him. There were another two outside the door, and one on the balcony outside the window. They obviously considered him important.

He'd had one visitor – an American major called Bill Collins – who'd asked if he had everything he needed.

'Not really, you've locked me up,' the Doctor replied. 'And your General Crawhammer is planning to have me dissected.'

Major Collins had looked uneasy.

'Why isn't there a British officer in charge?'

'We run the show now,' he had replied. 'Are you a Soviet augment?'

'I don't even know what a Soviet augment is,' the Doctor had replied. 'But I can only surmise… you're meddling in something very dangerous. Not that that's anything new, of course…'

The major had gone, assuring the Doctor that Crawhammer wouldn't actually wield the knife. An hour later the guards received an order and escorted him downstairs, to the cellar.

There a team of men in white gowns and surgical masks had taken over, while the guards stood behind them with their guns aimed at him. In silence, and ignoring his howls of protest, they had weighed him, taken his pulse, temperature and blood pressure, taken a blood sample, X-rayed him thoroughly and listened incessantly to the beating of his two hearts.

Now he lay strapped to an operating table, wearing a hospital gown and feeling woozy from a needle someone had stuck in him. The room was empty.

The doors swung. Major Collins.

'I never thought he'd do it.'

'You must stop him! This isn't just about me! We're all in terrible danger!'

'The general's got clearance from the top – and your government's not complaining. They're on a war footing – no one gives a damn about the little stuff now.'

'I do,' said the Doctor. 'Particularly when I'm the little stuff in question. I'm not a Soviet spy, you know.'

Collins looked uncomfortable.

'You're an unauthorised presence in a top security military base on the brink of a war.'

'All right,' said the Doctor. 'If you can't do anything else, at least get a message to a man in London for me. His name is Cody McBride. Tell him I failed, and tell him to take refuge with Ace in the TARDIS. Will you remember this? And also, if you will, tell Miss Rita Hawks. She's a journalist. An American.'

'You know Rita? I know Rita.'

The doors swung again and Crawhammer entered.

'Major Collins, ain't you got anywhere to be?'

'Yes, sir!' Collins shouted in instant response.

'Then be there.'

'Yes, sir!'

And he marched from the room.

Crawhammer rubbed his hands together. Behind him the brotherhood of the white masks was filing silently back in.

'So, Mr Augment…'

'You can't do this…' the Doctor hissed. 'It's against every international law and protocol.'

'So sue me. Mr Augmentski, we're gonna find out exactly what they done to you. We already know they changed your blood… But you know what puzzles us… No artificial components. We knew you bastards had an augmentation programme going, but this… whew!'

'You're insane…'

'War's a whole nest o' hornets, boy.'

'We're not at war yet.'

'Oh, we will be. You Reds screwed with us once too often. When you downed that spaceship you screwed with me! You know, back home where I come from we lynch Commies… But hey, that's Alabama fer ya. Yup, I'm a God-fearin' son o' the South, and we don't take no bullsheeet from no one.'

'If you really fear God, ask yourself why you're condemning His creation to nuclear Armageddon.'

'Why, 'cos I know God's on our side,' Crawhammer beamed.

Rita had searched the house from top to bottom. She hadn't found much. A packet of 'self-seal envelopes' that she'd practically taken her tongue off experimenting with, strangely shaped electric sockets in the walls…

She hadn't found a way out. None of the windows were going to break.

Eventually she'd gone to the refrigerator and made herself a beef sandwich, then another. She was still hungry.

Then Emily returned, as she had presumably departed, through the kitchen door, slipping the key into her cardigan pocket.

'I'm so sorry to have kept you. I'm glad you helped yourself.'

'Little Old Lady, what the hell's going on here?' shouted Rita.

'I don't know what you mean, dear.'

'The flowers…'

'Yes?'

'They're not real.'

'No. I'm allergic to the real thing.'

'And the newspaper… all that crap about the late King and India still being in the Empire. Is this what you feed back into Russia? Propaganda? Is this what the Russians think?'

'Propaganda? Oh, dear me no.' She might have been buying stamps, so light was the old woman's tone. 'A mere novelty, I'm afraid. A gift for my bachelor cousin. I'm afraid he does rather live in the past. Doesn't really approve of a woman on the throne. I tease him…'

'What did you do with the girl?'

'Oh, yes, the girl. I told you, I barely glimpsed her. She's probably off with her young gentleman friend. They did rather seem to me to be stepping out together.'

'OK, I'm going,' said Rita. 'Open the door.'

'I'm afraid I can't do that,' she replied. 'No, you must stay here.'

'Look, I don't want to hit an old lady, but you've got me so spooked, I swear to God I will. Give me the key.'

'I'm sorry, dear. Would you like that tea now?'

'Right!'

Rita lunged forward, aiming for the pocket where she knew the old woman –

Her hands closed on air and she stumbled forward, hitting the wall. The old woman had twisted, or sidestepped or something…

Rita charged again. This time Emily caught her by the upper arms, stopping her dead. She was applying no painful pressure, but Rita was held immobile. Smiling benignly Emily raised her off her feet. She kicked out, finding only air – the old woman was now holding her with arms outstretched, horizontal. Rita doubted many men could do that for longer than a minute, but this old crone appeared not to feel it.

'Please don't struggle, dear,' she said. 'You'll hurt yourself.'

'OK!'

Rita was gently lowered to the floor.

'How d'you do that?'

'Oh, I'm quite spry for my age.'

Emily had turned around and was arranging the teacups. Rita picked up a wooden kitchen chair and swung it with all her strength into the back of the old woman's neck. The chair splintered. Emily turned slowly.

'That hurt, you know,' she said, then sighed. 'I can understand why you're upset. When I was your age I used to want to come and go as I pleased too.'

She opened the cupboard under the old sink and took out a brush.

'Excuse me while I clean this up.'

There was the sound of a key in the front door.

'That will be my cousin now.' She grinned wickedly. 'I'll get him to do it.'

The kitchen door opened. Rita spun round. It was him – Dumont-Smith.

'Hello, dear,' the old woman said. 'Had a nice day?'

'So-so,' Dumont-Smith replied. 'It's time.'

Rita was aware of a flash of movement behind her, and a sharp pain in her neck.

Then everything plunged into dizzying blackness.

'Don't struggle, Mr Augment.'

General Eaglewhatsit's voice was indistinct now. The Doctor's vision was a blur.

'I protest...' he slurred.

One of the white masks came up, wheeling a machine. In his hand was clutched a black rubber face-mask.

'He's nearly out.'

'Then start a-cuttin', doc!'

White Mask put a scalpel to rest on the Doctor's breastbone. Through his haze it felt razor-cold.

'It's almost tempting to start before we put him out properly. Test his response to pain. Shame we gave him the pre-med, really.'

A distant door opened and a white blur approached the table. There was a whisper, then a cry from White Mask, who appeared to crumple to the floor.

'Gee, Hark…' the general grunted. 'Tough break…'

Sustained cries of anguish from White Mask receding into the distance. The door swung.

'Goddamn it!' shouted Crawhammer and stamped from the room. The other white masks followed in slow procession.

The Doctor waited. The corridors beyond the doors became quiet.

He was practically asleep.

'Are you awake?'

He felt a pair of hands shaking his shoulders, and forced his eyes open. Someone was unstrapping his restraints. He was being sat upright.

'Drink this.'

A cup of something hot was pressed into his hands and guided to his mouth.

'Black coffee, very strong.'

The Doctor gulped it down.

'Best I could do, I'm afraid. I guess one of the medics could find something among this lot to perk you up…'

An American…

'You want another? There's not much time.'

Major Collins.

'How did you stop them?'

'I got a bogus message through to Hark, the surgeon.' He grinned. 'Told him his wife and kids had been killed in a car crash.'

'Very inventive.' The Doctor tried unsteadily to sit up. 'You should go into counter-intelligence.'

'They're the ones who got us into this mess. Ours, theirs, yours…'

'Mine?'

'The Brits.'

'I'm from Gallifrey.'

'You're French?'

'No – never mind…'

The Doctor shook his head to clear it and got to his feet from the operating table.

'I've got to get out of here…'

He scanned the room, wishing he was more awake.

'There!'

He pointed to a row of narrow windows under the ceiling in one of the cellar walls.

'You'll never squeeze through those!'

'Oh, you'd be surprised what I can squeeze through when I've got a demented general and his pet surgeon at my back. Would you give me a leg up please?'

The cold, wet November afternoon hit the Doctor like a bucket of water as he slithered through the narrow gap onto overlong, sodden grass. His operation gown was soaked. Major Collins bundled his clothes after him.

'I'll stay put till I hear Crawhammer coming back, then I'll have to sound the alarm,' the Major said. 'Keep low, move fast and head for the trees on your left. The wall's just beyond them.'

'Thank you,' said the Doctor. He set off in the direction the major had indicated, waited a moment and doubled back. He had no intention of leaving without seeing the rocket.

He knew Major Collins would never tell him where it was, but Drakefell might. The man was at the end of his tether and desperate to unburden himself.

The Doctor scurried up a low rise and lay flat on the top. Below him lay the house, half a ruin, and beyond it he could just make out the ranks of red-brick outhouses with corrugated tin roofs. Laboratories, workshops, probably dormitories, the Doctor surmised.

He saw no chance of getting back to Drakefell's office. He'd have to wait until he came out.

The sound of the alarm put paid to that idea. Suddenly there were troops swarming out of the house, out of the barrack blocks. He retreated down the rise, backwards on his belly, away from the house. There was little cover. He strained to glimpse the trees Major Collins had advised him to make for. He could no longer see them.

He was desperately tired. He struggled to keep his vision in focus. Human chemical preparations rarely agreed with him - most were positively dangerous.

Running along the bottom of the slope was a high, thick, well-groomed hedge, with what seemed to be a break in it - presumably a gate. He decided to make a run for it.

Gathering up his clothes, he sprinted erratically towards the gate - actually just an abrupt, straight gap in the hedge - and hurled himself through it.

He crashed into another, equally high hedge and sank to the ground. He was in a narrow, dead straight canyon.

No – there were further gaps in the inner wall.

'He went into the maze, Sarge!'

A maze! He was in a maze!

The Doctor hauled himself to his feet, smiling. If only he could remember…

He darted to the end of the path, where it turned ninety degrees to the left, and waited.

'Well, get in there after him.'

The soldiers filed in.

'There he is!'

The Doctor hared up the path to the third opening and waited for them to round the corner.

'There he is! Stop or we'll shoot!'

But he was off again, counting, waiting. The first thing he had to do was get an overall impression of the shape of the maze. He hoped it was a classical maze – properly symmetrical – or he was in trouble.

He was leading them in. He sprinted off again as they rounded the latest bend.

'Right,' someone shouted. 'Cooper, you stay here! The rest of you, come on.'

The Doctor rubbed his hands. They were splitting up – even better.

For ten minutes he led the brave troop into utter confusion. He admired the sergeant's untiring resourcefulness as he deployed men at various junctions, thinning out his troop until he was alone. The Doctor then simply danced through the maze, luring the sentinels from their posts and losing them anew.

The old Gallifreyan Labyrinth Game. It had been centuries…

Of course, the object wasn't just to get your opponents lost, but to control their movements thereafter. By positioning them carefully, and getting them accustomed to making certain turns, it was possible to send them anywhere in the maze. The probabilities could hold up for a remarkably long time. He had the whole platoon on an outward spiral, dancing past one another, unseen around a single bend or behind a single hedge, with almost balletic precision. They were heading inevitably for the exit.

Their shouts to one another were becoming increasingly pointless. At last the sergeant shouted 'Every man for himself! Just try and find your way out, boys. We've lost him!'

The Doctor smiled. Sign of a misspent youth. At one time there had been a labyrinth on every street corner, even in the Panopticon.

He was desperately tired. His vision was beginning to swim. The game had taken reserves of concentration he didn't have.

He made for the centre of the maze. They wouldn't reach him there. He was about to enter the neat circle of grass when he heard a voice.

'What can I do?'

It was Drakefell. He sitting on the bench at the centre of the little round lawn at the heart of the maze. He was pale and shaking. His knees were drawn up to his chin – his feet off the floor – and he was hugging them to himself and rocking slightly back and forth. A young woman was sitting next to him.

'They've brought the rocket here. Two days ago. Now they want me to inspect it. I can't. I know what I'm going to find there...'

He lit a trembling cigarette.

'It's all been for nothing, Sarah. What have I done?'

A sudden sob wrenched through his body.

The Doctor remained motionless, still largely concealed by the maze wall, watching and listening. Drakefell was facing half-away from him.

'I've destroyed everything. We're about to blow ourselves to pieces... I've got to tell someone. I can't carry this any more. It wasn't the Russians who blew up the satellite – it was me.'

Chapter Nine

'It started a long time ago… during the war. I worked for a chemical company – just an ordinary young industrial chemist making synthetic rubber. I confess I couldn't have fought even if my job hadn't kept me out. The war terrified me. I was in London during the Blitz.

'Like everyone else, when the bombing started I went down into the tube station. Chancery Lane. You could still hear the thump of bombs above. Sometimes they'd be loud and the platform would shake. Dust would fall from the ceiling.'

Drakefell laughed bitterly.

'The Blitz spirit never did much for me. There was never a moment when I wasn't terrified… And then, one night – ' he drew a ragged breath, '– one night there was something else. Something came out of the tunnels. Giant men in silver armour – hideously strong. They ordered us into the tunnels – marched us for miles. Those who resisted were shot with weapons I'd never seen the like of. In the end they…'

He swallowed hard.

'They herded us into a room full of machines, and they… started to put people in them… Started to… operate on them. Change them. One old man… an air warden, bit of a busybody… I'll never forget…'

He suddenly flinched.

'And a baby! Oh, God…'

He was breathing rapidly, hyperventilating, almost. The woman placed a comforting hand on his shoulder.

'I hid… crawled back into the tunnels in the confusion that followed. They found me there the next day. I was nearly hit by a train. I had nightmares for two years.

'I was on sick leave until after the war. I was put on lithium, and… I suppose I managed to pretty much convince myself that it had all been a dream – although I haven't been down a tube station since.

'Then there was this story. Two men – a policeman and an American – started making a lot of noise about giant silver men left inactive in the sewers during the war. No one took much notice – except me. I was petrified, but I had to know. I asked around – scientists are terrible gossips – listened to every rumour, and eventually heard what I dreaded to hear. They'd found the giant men, and they'd started some hush-hush military research programme into them. They called it the Augmentation Programme.'

He suddenly laughed.

'Codenamed Operation Tinman, after the Wizard of Oz.'

He laughed again.

'We're off to see the wizard…' he sang tunelessly.

He sniffed and wiped his nose with his sleeve.

'What was I saying? The Augmentation Programme – yes… Well, I didn't find it all out at once, but I learned it was all to do with getting synthetic body parts to respond to the commands of a central nervous system. So I changed my area of specialisation – I studied, changed jobs, edged myself closer to this big secret. And eventually I got in.'

Drakefell wiped his forehead. He was sweating heavily.

'We were based at London Zoo.' He smiled. 'No one knew. I was there six years. I didn't like what we were doing – I even did a bit of wrecking, on the quiet – but we didn't seem to be getting very far anyway. We dismantled every one of the silver men, but all we got out of it – well, for me at least, it was the pleasure of seeing those things ripped apart.

'The Yanks weren't that interested at the time. It's all nuclear payload with them – or it was…

'And then one night… something happened. We'd been to a party – it had been someone's birthday – and ended up back at the lab – at the zoo. We'd all had a skinful – made a hell of a mess of the lab – and I'd fallen asleep in a corner. Well, I woke up hours later, alone, still drunk. For some reason I made a feeble attempt to tidy up, and I stumbled across a piece of equipment I hadn't seen before. For some reason the sight of it made me instantly nauseous. I threw up. It wasn't the booze –'

He grinned again.

'Part of it was the booze…'

Then his face fell.

'Then I touched it,' he whispered. 'And I was there again! Underground! And the silver men were there, pushing us into the darkness!

'I ran from the lab, found my way home and collapsed. That night the dreams returned.'

He rose to his feet and put his hands over his mouth in an attempt to control his breathing.

'I went sick. I faked glandular fever – I knew they'd put me in the nut-house if they knew the truth. And the thing – I had it sent off into storage.

'Over the next few months I got better and applied for a transfer to the British Rocket Group. They needed a project director, and with my experience of high security work I got the job. We were working on the Hermes project.'

He started to chuckle.

'Oh, I thought it would be that easy. What a fool! I thought it would just let me go. There was some sort of breakthrough at the zoo. The optics boys had come up with something new, and the Americans had suddenly got all excited. They put pressure on the government, and what had been a civilian missile project suddenly became part of the Cold War. They wanted us to launch a satellite. Very advanced and very secret.

'The Soviets had put Sputnik up in '57. The Yanks put Explorer up… shot monkeys into space… Poor sods. Herding them into machines…'

He shuddered.

'But Sputnik and Explorer had really just been floating tin footballs. They didn't actually *do* very much… This was something different. They reckoned the zoo boys had come up with some kind of camera capable of reading a newspaper from space. Can you believe that? They wanted to put up a satellite that no one knew about. And they wanted us to launch it. We were putting various bits of climate-testing and experimental equipment up there anyway – everyone knew that. This would just appear to be another piece of harmless space research, and it would be sending the news hot off the press from Moscow.'

He laughed grimly.

'Not that I cared. 'Cause guess what? The dreams were back! They'd closed down the operation at the zoo and moved it out here – including the stuff from the warehouses in Kew. That damned… thing – my nightmare machine – had followed me.

'Well, I knew I couldn't get rid of it – it would never let me. So I decided to send it where it could never come back. Into space…

'It was pretty much the same size and weight as the optical equipment going into the satellite. So after the final checks I came back to the lab and took it all out – smashed into pieces. And in its place I put the thing. The nightmare machine.'

He shook his head slowly.

'I've doomed us all.'

Drakefell seemed to lose his strength. He toppled forward, stumbling from the little hillock. The Doctor sprang forward and caught him by the shoulders, steadying him.

Drakefell stared at him as if he were the Devil himself, and twisted from his grasp.

'Who are you?' the woman challenged.

'You…!' Drakefell bellowed. 'What are you doing here?'

'I need to get to the rocket, Dr Drakefell.'

Drakefell hesitated.

'It's not from this world, Dr Drakefell. It's from another reality, and that's very bad. I need to find out what it's doing here.'

Drakefell looked uncertain.

Somewhere behind the Doctor a twig snapped. There was a rustle of privet. A shadow flashed through a gap in the hedge.

There was someone else in here with them.

The Doctor darted back into the maze. A heel vanished ahead of him. He plunged after it. He had to concentrate – he was in as bad a state as Drakefell on whatever these psychopaths had put into him. He desperately wanted to sleep.

Shaking himself, he plunged after the eavesdropper, around another bend, then another.

A dead end. Impossible. Where had the figure gone? The Doctor turned to retrace his steps to the centre – then realised that he was lost. He'd lost his bearings – he didn't know where in the maze he was. Who on Earth could have done this to him?

It took him over an hour to find his way out, by which time he was close to collapse. It was a different entrance to the maze. He looked around. In the distance, under the trees, was the stone lodge. Captain O'Brien would help him…

He staggered in the direction of the trees, and got about five hundred yards before his legs buckled under him and he sank face down onto the wet grass.

Jimmy was late. He came bounding up to Ace, mumbling apologies and smiling shyly.

'Had to take a bath,' he drawled. 'You know, working in a zoo…'

She grinned. 'You smell great.'

He looked great too, blue jeans, white T-shirt that clung to his pecs, running his hand through his still-wet, tousled blond hair.

'Let's get outa here,' he said, resting an easy hand on her shoulder as they set off.

They caught the bus to Oxford Street, where she gawped again in horror at the fashions on display. Did young people really used to dress like this?

The weather was good to them. They skipped ahead of the rain, crossed the river on foot and strolled along the South Bank. It was run-down – empty warehouses where later there would be theatres and bars.

They climbed down some slippery stone steps onto the wet banks of the Thames. The river was low, enabling them to walk out as far as St Paul's. They drew patterns in the muddy shingle with a piece of driftwood. Jimmy drew a big heart and wrote both their names. Ace added the year – London 1959.

'Shame it'll be washed away,' she said.

Everything seemed so transient nowadays. She and the Doctor never stayed long in any one place.

'You know what?' said Jimmy. 'I've got an idea.'

He grabbed her by the hand and started running for the nearest steps.

'What?' she called.

'Wait,' he said.

They bounded back up to street level.

'There!'

He dragged her across a road and into a pub.

'Is this it?' she laughed. 'A pub.'

'Nah, this is just Dutch courage,' said Jimmy, catching the barman's eye.

An hour later they staggered out onto the street, drunk and laughing. It was getting dark. Jimmy put his arm round her and she hugged his torso as they walked. She didn't want this to end.

She felt comfortable with Jimmy. He was shy – she'd hardly got anything out of him about his life – though he'd talked passionately about the zoo, and affectionately about the animals. She was grateful that he hadn't asked her anything about her life. He'd think she was barmy.

'Here we go.'

They were outside a tattooist's parlour.

Ace grinned a loopy grin. 'You're kidding…'

Jimmy drew her to him and kissed her on the lips.

She let herself be led through the narrow doorway into the shop beyond.

She knew what Jimmy had in mind. ACE, JIMMY, LONDON 1959. In ribbons over a heart. Corny but irresistible. And something permanent in her life.

'Right,' said a greasy youth smoking a roll-up, 'who's first?'

The first thing Rita was aware of was a harsh light shining directly into her face.

'So this is her...'

'Yes, sir.' Dumont-Smith. His tone was respectful.

'Oh, and well done about the rocket,' the voice said.

Dumont-Smith made ostentatious noises of modesty. He really was grovelling.

'It was him, sir. He's a remarkable man. Quite unique.'

'Hardly that,' said the voice in authority. 'Are you trying to flatter me?'

The man's tone was arch – both teasing and knowing. More sycophantic noises from Dumont-Smith.

'Now, wake her, please,' the voice said.

'I am awake,' Rita slurred. She was sprawled on the settee, but found it difficult to move.

'Ah, then may I ask how you are, my dear?'

His tone was friendly. Like an old vicar.

'Must go...' she mumbled, trying to get up from the settee. Her limbs felt like lead. She gave up and slumped.

'No, no, you must rest,' the voice said.

Rita could just about make out a slender figure silhouetted against the harsh light.

'Find the girl...'

'Is that why you came here? You were looking for a girl...'

Rita managed a vague nod. 'Friend of McBride's.'

'The American detective, sir,' Dumont-Smith intervened.

'I know,' the voice said languidly. 'I know. Why did you think the girl was here?'

'Followed her – with the stud.'

'I think she means the younger American, sir. Our courier. The actor chappie...'

'Yes, yes. Let the woman speak, for heaven's sake.'

'They're going to kill her.'

'Who are?'

'Don't know… Space/time pollution.'

'What did you say?'

'The ants. Criss-cross… pollision… pol… collision…'

'This is unsatisfactory,' the voice snapped. 'How much of that stuff did you put into her?'

'Uh, the standard dose, sir.'

'I have no idea what that means.'

'Uh, no sir. It, uh, all happened rather quickly. She put up a struggle.'

'The standard dose for them or for us?' the voice asked with thinning patience.

'Um… For us, I suppose.'

'She's barely conscious. We'll have to wait until she comes round. I must go. I'll send someone to look after her and have her brought to me.'

'What shall we do with her until then, sir?'

'Keep her here. She has already said enough. They know.'

The figure receded. Rita was sure Dumont-Smith bowed. But then she started to black out again.

'How's your arm?' Ace asked.

'Stings a bit,' said Jimmy, but it's a nice pain. How's your shoulder?'

'Same,' smiled Ace.

They had strolled back through a capital closing for the day and opening up for the night. Jimmy had a key to the zoo. They slipped in, to darkness, and a single, pale light.

'Ted's still here…' murmured Jimmy. 'He sells toffee-apples. Want a toffee-apple?'

Ace suddenly realised the butterflies in her stomach weren't just in anticipation of the night to come. She was starving. They skipped over to the little booth.

'Got any left, Ted?' Jimmy asked.

'Two,' said Ted. 'You're lucky.'

Ace hadn't had one of these in years. She wolfed it down as they walked back to Jimmy's underground room.

When they got there they kissed again, longer and harder this time, and Jimmy slipped Ace's jacket from her shoulders, then his own. She peeled his T-shirt away, and he hers, and they collapsed on the mattress, Jimmy's face moving down her neck and shoulders as she clutched at his back, her eyes closing.

Chapter Ten

It was already dark when Cody McBride came to on his friend's floor. His head felt foul. So did his stomach. He struggled to remember what they'd done.

Above him Mullen snored with the gale.

The doctor – only a young houseman, it seemed the bigwig was away – had agreed to let them sleep it off when they'd threatened him with the contents of Mullen's bedpan.

McBride struggled to his feet, wrapped his coat around his shoulders and crept out into the corridor and into the street. It was five o'clock. The whole day gone.

He felt bad – the Doc had sounded pretty desperate – but so was Mullen. Mullen had needed him there and then.

He hoped the Doc was being lucky. Ace had been a good kid… back in the war. Judging by the Doc's appearance, he speculated that Ace might not have changed either. He'd always thought she kinda liked him. He found himself sucking in his paunch, until he realised it hurt too much. What would she think of him now, nearly twenty years older?

He disappeared into the underground.

At about the same time, a lone figure was standing in McBride's office – bony fingers thoughtfully tapping the Doctor's note – with Rita's addendum – against cracked, slightly smiling lips. Old, pale eyes stared coldly at their own warped reflection in the whisky decanter.

Twenty minutes later the same figure said goodbye to Miles Dumont-Smith in a café across the road and watched him depart. Five minutes after that he watched a very green-looking Cody McBride return to his office, then emerge again, letter in hand, looking even greener. The man took a delicate sip of tea and blinked a blink of slow satisfaction, staring after McBride as he strode off up the road trying to hail a taxi.

Smiling, the man returned to his crossword.

Six across. Five letters. 'He hocks his freedom and joins the ranks

102

guarding castle, church and throne.'

He picked up his pen and started to fill in the blanks.

The Doctor came to in surprising comfort. He was in a clean, warm bed, and Davey O'Brien was sitting beside him, reading a book.

'Good afternoon, Captain,' said the Doctor.

'Oh, you're awake - good,' grinned the young pilot. 'I was getting bored. I saw you fall. The rozzers were here at the time. Luckily none of them thought to look out of the window. Anyway, they searched and left again. Haven't been back since.'

'How long have I been asleep?'

'Only about four hours, but I've never seen anyone so spark out, even on Paddy's Night. What were you on?'

'Many of the concoctions you create on this planet disagree with me,' muttered the Doctor. 'Four hours is far too long. I must find that rocket. It's here somewhere. I must get up.'

'I'll leave you to it,' said O'Brien. 'I sorted you out a new shirt and pullover. Yours were goners... and I didn't think you'd want to go to town in your operation gown.'

He left, closing the door behind him.

A minute and a half later the Doctor bounded down O'Brien's stairs.

'Hey,' the young captain grinned, 'not bad.'

A decent white linen shirt and a rather smart sleeveless pullover - fawn, with a broad band of vague pattern running around the middle of it.

'You have impeccable taste, Captain.'

'You're a pretty nifty dresser for a guy your age, Doc. You want something to eat?'

'No time, no time.'

The Doctor stared out the window, as if willing the rocket to reveal itself.

And then it did.

'Captain O'Brien - '

'You've probably got me busted for espionage. You might as well call me Davey.'

'Davey, those birds, over the wood, do they always behave like that?'

They were flocking and swooping, circling, diving over the dense forest canopy.

'A couple of weeks ago they started. It built up over a few days.' He blushed. 'I, uh, spend a lot of time looking out of the window, you know?'

'Pigeons, mostly… even the odd gull. Scavengers. The sort of birds that flock around human activity.

'As far as I know it's just an old oak wood.'

'Shall we go and find out?'

Rita paced the bedroom with a headache. She'd thrown all the available furniture at the window in vain. The door, of course, was locked.

The house was silent. She was pretty sure she'd been left alone.

She really was starving.

She had to get out somehow. She didn't know what she'd stumbled across – she vaguely remembered a bright light and a man asking her questions. She had no doubt now that she'd stumbled into some Russian spy cell.

She looked about the room for an idea. There was nothing. Nothing she could use to jemmy open the door, nothing that might break through the impenetrable glass.

She had to get help. She tugged the hand-knitted bedspread off the bed. She could hang it in the window and…

And what? Folks would see a quilt in the window and call the cops?

She could write a message on something…

With what? All her stuff was downstairs.

She let out a sob of frustration – she was no good in situations like this.

'Then again,' she said to herself, 'it's not exactly the sort of thing you prepare for.'

There wasn't even an attic she could rummage in – there were always old kitchen knives in attics. Maybe even tools. She looked bitterly up at the high, open roof-space – massive beams and the heavy old thatch lying on top.

What would McBride do?

The thatch. Surely they wouldn't have reinforced that.

She struggled to assemble her thoughts. First, she had to get up there, and she felt far from steady.

She heaved the bed onto its side and dragged the big old iron frame into the corner of the room, leaning it against two walls to make a triangle. The frame was broken – she could see where one of the corner-struts had broken away – and woefully unsteady, but she managed to scramble up onto the bed frame's edge. She could reach the rafters now.

She gripped the nearest of the huge, horizontal beams, wrapping both arms around it, and somehow managed to scramble onto it. Holding on with one hand, she pushed at the thatch where it met the wall.

She should have known. It weighed a ton. She started picking at it, scanning, and tore a nail quite painfully.

Hopeless. She needed some kind of tool. A pick…

A broken iron strut…

Leaning down from her beam she levered the strut back and forth until it had snapped entirely from the frame then, turning to the giant bird's nest above her head, she started to dig.

It was already night among the huge oak trees that clustered together to the south of Winnerton Manor. The Doctor and Davey O'Brien were in every sense groping in the dark.

The Doctor was thinking about Ace. She might be dead by now. He'd brought her here, and in doing so brought about the very thing he was trying to stop – her death. One of time's playful little eddies.

He'd taken a terrifyingly irresponsible decision in coming here – deliberately acting with knowledge of future events in order to change those events. There were reasons his people had laws of time.

He stumbled.

'We should have brought a torch,' he griped.

'Haven't got one,' O'Brien replied. 'I asked for one, but it never came. I don't suppose they want me snooping around at night.'

The Doctor peered about him into the gloom.

'I can't help feeling I'm being watched.'

'Woods are like that in the dark. Ignore it.'

'I don't mean just here. I mean everywhere. Ever since I came here. Even when I'm quite alone, I know there's still someone watching.'

'Spies, you mean?'

'No…'

Who had been in the maze with himself and Drakefell? And how had whoever it was managed to lose him?

'Hold it,' O'Brien hissed.

There was a light ahead of them. It was moving.

'Slowly,' the Doctor whispered. 'Quietly.'

The light bobbed and weaved, vanishing behind trees, then reappearing, always further off. Occasionally it would dip sharply and vanish, as if whoever was holding it had fallen.

'He's going at a bit of a lick,' O'Brien whispered. 'Come on.'

He pushed forward, thrusting aside the branches of bushes and young trees.

'Reminds me of Korea,' he whispered.

The Doctor trotted after him.

The ground soon turned boggy. Water lapped around their ankles, then their knees, slowing their progress. The light was getting away from them. The land rose again and began to dry out, but they were soon pushing though dense brambles that were taller than the Doctor, and which snagged and coiled incessantly around their clothes.

'Got to hand it to them,' said O'Brien, 'they picked a damned good hiding place.'

'Mmm,' was the Doctor's only response. They had been walking for nearly an hour, and he suspected they were lost.

'Best foot forward,' said O'Brien.

The Doctor put his best foot forward and the next moment felt the ground crumbling away beneath it and the forest spring up to attack him. He fell, and landed hard on his ankle, which buckled in sudden agony under him.

'You OK?' O'Brien asked.

The Doctor was sprawled at the bottom of a shallow gully. Gingerly he picked himself up and tested his weight on the throbbing ankle. It would have to do.

'I think we're here,' said O'Brien as the Doctor scrambled out of his hole. 'Look.'

Ahead of them the trees gave way to a clearing and a chain-link fence, easily ten feet tall and surmounted with barbed wire.

The moon was out, and as they approached the clearing, the Doctor began to make out some detail of the darkness behind the fence. A single large grey building – a hangar – dominated the clearing. Smaller brick outhouses clustered around its huge walls, as if frightened of the impenetrable wood.

A road had been cut through the trees on the far side. A wide road. They began skirting the fence. The place seemed deserted.

'No guards,' said the Doctor. 'Odd.'

'Perhaps he sent them away,' O'Brien replied. 'Look over there.'

Ahead of them Drakefell was standing at the gate, staring up at the hangar. The gate was open.

'He is still in charge here,' O'Brien replied. 'On paper, at least.'

Drakefell didn't look as if he was in charge of anything much. He was wearing only his pyjamas and slippers, now sodden and caked with mud and grime.

'Poor man,' whispered the Doctor.

They limped up to the stricken scientist.

'There are no silver giants in there, I can promise you that,' said the Doctor gently.

'I'll tell you what's in there,' said Drakefell. 'Nightmares. Being too scared to go to sleep, keeping yourself awake for days... I can never get rid of it. No matter what I do, it finds me. It comes back to me and it all starts again.'

'This piece of equipment,' the Doctor said slowly, 'your... nightmare machine... can you describe it?'

'It wasn't much to look at. A short silver cylinder, solid, which was quite badly charred... three thick, black tubes coming off it at the base, going into a sort of metal disk, about a foot and a half in diameter. Odd – there was always frost on the disk. And the frost was always cold, but the disk never was. Even in the middle of summer – frost.'

'Vasser Dust,' said the Doctor.

'What?'

'A waste bi-product of time travel. It has telepathic qualities... Please go on.'

Drakefell was shaking his head slowly. 'It was nothing I recognised, and I thought I knew all the Augmentation Programme's junk inside out.'

'Nothing I recognise,' said O'Brien. 'Doc?'

'I'm afraid I do,' said the Doctor.

He fell into a thoughtful silence, staring up at the huge green hangar.

'So are you going to tell us what's going on, Doc?' asked O'Brien.

'Loose ends, Captain. I've been shockingly negligent.'

He turned to Drakefell. 'I'm going in,' he said. 'I think you should come with me.'

'You don't understand,' snarled Drakefell. 'No one else has seen it!'

Drakefell was growing agitated. He smoothed his pyjamas over and over to calm himself down.

'What have you seen, Dr Drakefell? What do you think is in that ship?'

Drakefell stopped stroking and looked at the Doctor – a long, curious, slightly skew-eyed stare. O'Brien took a step forward.

'It's all right,' said the Doctor calmly. 'Dr Drakefell…'

Drakefell struggled for the word.

'Strangeness,' he said at last. 'That's the only way… Awful… horrible strangeness.'

His eyes widened as he warmed to his theme.

'You know the way as a child there's something about spiders. So strange… they're repellent.'

He suddenly lowered his head and drew his arms in tight around his torso.

'I've seen it,' he said quietly. 'And it's something I can't even think about. Alien – horribly, hideously alien – formless… it… went on forever… And lifeless yet… seething, somehow… It didn't feel like it belonged in this universe.'

'It didn't,' said the Doctor quietly. 'Congratulations, Dr Drakefell, you have caught a glimpse of what all scientists long to see. The webs that bind the Multiverse, the boundless nothingness of the vortex, where everything exists in potential. When you touched the Vasser Dust the circuit sensed a bond between you. A common experience. The Cybermen. And so it opened itself to you. When you touched the Dust you looked outside space/time, Dr Drakefell. Frightening, isn't it? It's not for the human mind, I can assure you. Not yet, anyway.'

The Doctor paused.

Drakefell took a step towards the gate, then stopped, holding the fence for support.

'I can't…' he groaned. 'But I must. I promised…'

The Doctor swung to face Drakefell, a dark intensity in his eyes.

'Who was in the maze with us, Dr Drakefell?'

'What?'

Drakefell seemed startled by the question.

'Who were you talking to in the maze?'

'No one. A friend. He… helps me. He listens… He's a psychiatrist, all right?'

'Not old Hopkins?' O'Brien blurted out. 'The shrink you assigned me. You're wasting your time with him. I've never got a word of sense out of him.'

'No,' said the Doctor darkly. 'But I'll wager he's got a very great deal out of you. Shall we go in?'

Ace lay on her back and looked up at the concrete ceiling. She thought *she* lived with few creature comforts, but this place was Spartan. However, at this moment it seemed to Ace the most comfortable place on Earth, as she lay on the mattress, just a sheet covering her. Next to her Jimmy, also naked, lay still and watched her. She cuddled up close to him and he put a muscular arm around her and squeezed.

'I never want to leave here,' Ace purred.

For the first time in days her thoughts strayed to the Doctor. She wondered how he would react to Jimmy? Would they get on? Would the Doctor feel awkward, crowded out. And how would Jimmy take to her strange alien friend? She couldn't see Jimmy ever understanding a word the Doctor said.

Would he let Jimmy travel with them aboard the TARDIS? Would Jimmy want to? Would the Doctor force her to choose between them? And how would she choose?

It was inevitable she'd fall in love one day.

Was she in love? That was stupid – she'd only known him two days – but she couldn't remember when she'd felt so happy. Relaxed.

Safe.

Safety wasn't in great supply with the Doctor. And she loved all that, but she'd had years of living on raw adrenalin, and sometimes she didn't notice how tiring it was.

It had been good for them, spending some time outside each other's company. Whatever the Doctor was up to was his business. He'd probably make a mess of it without her, but he'd chosen not to let her in on his little secret, so he could sort his own mess out.

Was she in love? They'd got themselves tattooed. That was more serious than an engagement.

She couldn't leave the Doctor – never – but right now the prospect of ever tearing herself away from Jimmy's warmth was almost unbearable.

The Doctor had had something on his mind. That was obvious. She shouldn't have been so quick to react.

He'd put a tracking device on her!

'Hey, babe, what you thinking?'

Ace shrugged.

'About my friend. I should really go and make sure he's all right.'

'How about makin' sure I'm all right?'

Jimmy grinned and poked a playful tongue out.

'Again already?' Ace grinned.

'Hey, you know what they say about us cowboys…'

And with that he rolled on top of her, kissing her neck, and all further thought of leaving was banished.

'Strewth!'

Even half-destroyed, the ship was spectacular. Shaped rather like a teardrop – or a finless, tailless fish.

'Well, it's not one of ours,' said O'Brien. 'And the Yanks haven't got anything like this either. And it's certainly not the Waverider.'

'It seems to think it is,' said the Doctor.

'WAVERIDER' was emblazoned across the charred hull of the craft.

'Odd, isn't it?'

Much of the fuselage had been burned away, and a good deal of what was left was torn and twisted. The craft's spine seemed to have snapped – a series of cranes, straps and huge wedges were holding the thing together.

'Is Dr Drakefell not joining us?' asked the Doctor.

'Nope. Keeps saying he has to do it... but he won't.'

'Ah, well... You might have to give me a hand, Davey. I rather injured myself during our nature ramble.'

Immediately O'Brien hoisted the Doctor high into the air and deposited him in what presumably was the entry-hatch. The Doctor clambered inside.

The craft was compact, sleek and well designed, and bathed in a soft light that seemed to have no discernible source. No space around the pilot's chair was wasted, yet the ship was elegantly and ergonomically designed so that movement within its confines was fluid and easy.

O'Brien dropped through the hatch and let out an awed whistle.

'I've never seen anything like this. I wouldn't even know how to start the windscreen wipers.'

The Doctor was barely listening. He was looking for something.

'Aha! Found it.'

He lowered himself into a painful squat over a flat metal plate, about six inches by four, set into the deck.

'Do you know what this is, Davey?'

'Not a clue. The ashtray?'

'It's a dimension stabiliser. Or rather, in this case, a dimension de-stabiliser. It's what he used to get here.'

'The guy who's supposed to be me?'

'Yes. He used it to bore a tunnel through the walls of reality itself.'

'Hang on, I thought you said the explosion did that when the ship – our ship – blew up.'

'From our side, yes. Reality is a funny thing, Davey.'

'No kidding,' said O'Brien, looking around him.

'Have you even considered what might have happened if, say, the day your father first met your mother at the County Fair he'd decided to stay at home and do the gardening instead? No Davey O'Brien. The world turns on the tiniest of axes, Davey.'

'The flip of a coin,' said O'Brien sombrely.

'Quite. Now suppose I told you that there was another universe – many, in fact – where your father did stay at home gardening, and one where he went to the show and met somebody else first, and one where you won the toss and went up in the Waverider. Your alter ego, the chap who piloted this – perhaps he won the toss. There are infinite parallel universes, some of which – the ones closest to our own, are similar to ours in almost every detail. I can perfectly believe that this ship was sent up on a mission identical in spirit to your own. What *they* did deliberately happened *here* by accident – that's the only real difference.'

O'Brien puffed out his cheeks.

'It's all quite a lot to take in. I thought one world was chaos enough – now you say there are... millions.'

'And more,' said the Doctor. 'But they should never be crossed – not in this way, at least. Dimension stabilisers were developed to repair damage to the time lines, not inflict it.'

He used to carry one in the TARDIS...

'Do you have a screwdriver on you by any chance?'

O'Brien rummaged in his pocket.

'Swiss Army knife,' he said sheepishly, handing it to the Doctor. 'Twenty-four blades. It's about all they'll let me have.'

'I used to have something similar,' said the Doctor, flicking through the assorted blades. 'Just a bit more hi-tech.'

He squinted at the plate he was trying to detach from its housing.

'Strange screw-heads...'

He flicked again through the blades, thrust one into a narrow slot and twisted. He repeated the procedure five times, then held the little knife aloft, admiring.

'What is this blade for?' he asked.

'I'm not sure,' said O'Brien. 'I think it's the one for taking stones out of horses' hooves.'

There was a creaking on the fuselage above their heads. They both craned about to see Drakefell standing at the edge of the hatch, watching them.

'Well done, Dr Drakefell,' said the Doctor. 'You see? Not all that monstrously alien.'

He lifted the dimension stabiliser from its base. Its underside was a thick knot of cables and wires that plumbed the machine into the guts of the ship.

'Hopefully with this I can repair the damage to the time lines before it's too late,' he said.

The Doctor tugged lightly at a wire. This was delicate and dangerous work. He had to isolate the little machine from the massive power supply that drove it, and that took up about a third of the ship. Any power surges would blow the hanger sky-high.

There was a sequence to this. If he could remember it...

'What if you can't?' Drakefell asked.

'The holes will expand... more will appear. The fabric of space/time will start to unravel and the universes will bleed into each other. I've already encountered a swarm of giant ants.'

'Giant ants?' queried O'Brien.

'Yes,' said the Doctor, tugging at a stubborn cable. 'Giant ants. Size as an absolute concept has no meaning between dimensions. Some universes would fit in your pocket.'

'My God,' said Drakefell hoarsely. 'What you're saying is I could have brought about the end of Creation... everything.'

'Oh, I doubt it will be that bad,' said the Doctor. 'Not now that I've got my hands on this.'

He patted the dimension stabiliser like a not-entirely-to-be-trusted-with-your-fingers dog.

'And as for the Waverider, I shouldn't entirely blame yourself. After all, we still don't know for certain what caused the explosion.'

'Well, obviously it was my tampering.'

'Except that Captain O'Brien here informed me that the explosion began on the ship, just after the satellite was launched. The satellite was just caught in the blast. I suspect that you weren't the only saboteur, Dr Drakefell.'

'What do you mean?'

'Well, surely the best way to disguise this satellite would be to surround it with as much debris as possible. A very small bomb would blow the Waverider apart.

'But the satellite was destroyed.'

'Yes – and when the blast hit your little package it triggered a much bigger explosion. I suspect the bomb went off too early. Unfortunate, really. Nothing to do but cover your tracks and make some political capital by blaming the Russians.'

'Crawhammer…'

A sound behind them caused the three men to turn suddenly. Major Collins was sliding through the ship's entry-hatch. He had his gun in his hand.

'Well, I'll be… What the hell is going on here?'

'Major Collins,' the Doctor smiled. 'I can assure you there's no need for the gun.'

'Did you lose your way, mister?' Collins said. 'I freed you from custody to save your neck!'

He shook his head in self-disgust.

'All my counter-intelligence training and you took me in.'

The Doctor took a step towards him.

'Stay where you are,' Collins barked. 'I'm within my rights to shoot you on the spot.'

Chapter Eleven

Why, with petrol still being rationed, was there always so much goddamn traffic in this town? It took Cody McBride two hours to make the journey from St Paul's to Regent's Park. The zoo – it was the only other lead they had on Ace.

It was closing by the time he arrived, which suited him. It was already dark. He strolled among the cages, trying to look casual, watching all around him. He was used to this. Divorce cases – affairs – always involved trailing people around the goddamn zoo.

The attendants were asking people to make their way to the gate. McBride slipped into the shadows next to the primate house and kept moving – close to walls, low to the ground, away from light. The few visitors left were thinning out. A few keepers trotted back and forth with buckets and brooms. Apart from the noises of the animals, it was quiet.

This was all backwards. He was running about trying to solve a crime that hadn't taken place yet. It struck him that he'd accepted the Doctor's claim – that Ace was going to be fatally shot – with barely a raised eyebrow. How did the Doctor know? It hadn't occurred to McBride to query his strange statement.

How much did he really know about the Doctor, or Ace for that matter? They'd turned up in his office one day during the Blitz, claiming that aliens had landed. And it turned out to be true. The Doctor had dragged both him and Mullen into a war within a war, with an enemy more soullessly destructive than the Nazis. And then he'd vanished as suddenly as he arrived.

And now he was back. And there were Russian spies everywhere and giant ants in Nine Elms.

McBride lit a sly cigarette, shielding the match with his coat, and the glowing tip with his hand. He smiled to himself. He'd had too many lost dogs to find recently. The Doc was back.

He set off to comb the dim grounds once more.

* * *

'Just one of the keepers having a fag. Everyone else has gone.'

Ace retreated from the high-set window that looked out onto the zoo at ground level. She attempted to disentangle herself from the mangled bed-sheet, which was wrapped around her otherwise naked body like an over-enthusiastic toga. She spun in a circle, twisting to unwrap herself from its coils, and let it fall to the floor as Jimmy lay before her, smiling, watching her. She started to gather up her clothes.

'I've really got to go,' she said. 'There's something I've got to sort out.'

To tell the truth she didn't really know where to start. She'd run from the Doctor in haste, and had no real idea where to find him. She supposed she'd just head back towards the TARDIS and hope he did the same.

'Aww…'

'I'll come back later.'

'I want you now.'

Jimmy rolled onto his side and pulled her back onto the bed, nuzzling her belly as she tried to dress.

'Later – we've been in here hours. I'm starving. All I've eaten is that toffee-apple.'

Ace scrambled free of his embrace and continued pulling her clothes on. Jimmy seemed to reach a decision and followed suit. He was dressed before she was.

Ace grabbed him in a bear-hug and planted a deep, wet kiss on his mouth, then made for the door.

Suddenly Jimmy darted in front of her, blocking her way.

'Jimmy…' He didn't move. 'Get out of the way.'

Ace tried to push past him but he blocked her again, and thrust her back into the room.

This was ceasing to be funny.

'Look, are you going to let me out?'

'No,' snarled Jimmy, suddenly agitated. 'I know your game.'

'What?'

'I even saw the badge on your jacket.'

'What badge?'

'Your goddamn Commie red star. I know you're working for them.'

'Working for who?' Ace didn't know what he was talking about.

'The Russians! I didn't want to believe it…'

'I'm not working for the Russians! I'm not working for anybody! Let me out!'

She pushed forward, trying to dislodge him. He thrust her back hard.

She tripped on the edge of the mattress and her head slammed into the wall. She sank back onto the bed, dazed.

Jimmy couldn't look at her.

'You're flamin' barmy…' she said.

Without another word the American broke from the room, slamming the door behind him.

Ace could hear the key turning in the lock.

She couldn't believe this…

'You really expect me to believe that crock?'

Things weren't going the Doctor's way at Winnerton Flats. Major Collins didn't seem in a receptive mood.

'Listen to him, Collins!' Drakefell yelled. 'It sounds insane but he might actually be telling the truth.'

He took a step forward. Collins raised his gun.

'I don't care,' said Collins. 'It's not my job to ponder the great unknown – it's my job to round up unauthorised personnel.'

'I'm authorised,' said Drakefell.

O'Brien looked him up and down. Mud-caked dressing-gown, one filthy slipper, one bare foot, pieces of twig in his hair.

'I'm sorry, but you've been categorised a security risk, Director. The general's been watching you. He thinks you're cracking up.'

'He hasn't the right – '

'Look, buddy,' Collins said, not unkindly, 'like it or not, this is in the hands of the US military now. You just present the public front to the Brits.'

'I haven't got time for this,' grumbled the Doctor, and turned his thoughts once more to the dimension stabiliser.

'Stand away from that machine,' Collins shouted.

The Doctor ignored him.

'You're all under arrest on suspicion of espionage.'

Outside they could hear the roar of vehicles and shouts of soldiers.

'Come on, Bill,' Davey O'Brien ejaculated. 'You know the Russkies haven't got anything like this – look at it!'

A great rolling metallic rumble as the huge hangar doors were opened. Then an English voice shouted out. 'Major Collins…'

'That's Major Graham. He's the most senior English officer left here. It's out of my hands now,' said Collins. 'This is still technically a British operation.'

O'Brien sniffed disdainfully.

'Situation's under control in here!' Collins shouted. 'Intruders! I'm bringing them out!'

He gestured with his gun.

'You heard me, move.'

The Doctor turned away.

'Not without this,' he said, turning his back to Collins and dropping into a squat over the dimension stabiliser.

'I don't think you realise the gravity of your situation!' Collins barked. 'Espionage is – '

He never finished the sentence. Outside there was a sudden, dull explosion, followed by two more. Machine-gun fire. Shouting.

The Doctor peered through a tear in the wreck's fuselage. Through the vast, open front of the hangar he could see troops scattering for cover amid clouds of billowing smoke. And running towards them out of the forest and through the gate, machine-guns blazing, were perhaps a dozen figures dressed in tough black fatigues. Commandos.

'Oh, dear,' the Doctor said. 'We seem to be under attack.'

It took Rita two hours to make enough of a hole in the thatch for her to drag herself through. Then, clinging to a drainpipe to slow her descent, she more or less slid down to the ground.

She was exhausted, hungry and she stank, but at least she was free. The road, flanked by high, neat hedges, stretched out ahead of her. She set off into the dark. It was a nice night – more like late summer than the end of November.

The first thing she did was put some distance between herself and the cottage. She headed for where she thought Kennington tube station ought to be.

She didn't have any money. It had all been in her bag. She looked a state, covered in three hundred-year-old dust, grime and thatch. She'd have to blag it.

Looking like this? Who was she kidding?

Telephone… She'd call McBride, reverse the charges.

She looked about for a kiosk and noticed for the first time that, apart from the moon and stars, there was no light to be seen. The cottage must have been further out than she thought. No sign of a phone. She trudged on.

The hedges gave way to buildings. Still no telephone kiosk. And still no light. Must be a power cut.

Crossing a main road, she was almost knocked down by a taxi.

She hadn't heard it coming – it had come from nowhere.

It screeched to a halt and the driver got out.

'Sorry, love,' he said.'Didn't see you there.You all right?'

Rita scrambled to her feet.

'I need help. I need to get to Grant Street. It's off behind St Paul's. I've been locked in a cottage by Russian agents. They drugged me, they interrogated me…'

The driver chuckled.

'Russian agents, eh?'

'Will you help me? I've got no money.'

'Oh, I get it. Hop in then.'

Rita couldn't believe her luck. She scrambled in.

'And next time,' the driver said, starting the engine, 'remember you're in England now.You don't need no silly sob story.'

He chuckled.

'The Russians! You should do your homework love. They're our friends.Your first visit, is it?'

'Uh, no,' said Rita.

'It must be bloody marvellous for you lot,' the driver said, 'coming over here. Another world.'

'I'd hardly call it marvellous,' said Rita.

'Well, you're about the only one,' said the driver. 'You run about with your little cameras, always wanting to use the phone…'

'Can you stop at a phone?' Rita chipped in. 'I need to call someone.'

'See what I mean? This is England, love! It's only you lot use them. There's hardly any left.'

'What?'

'We've got no use for them, 'ave we?'

'Excuse me? Are we still talking about the same thing?'

The driver suddenly swerved, and Rita was practically thrown from the seat.

'Maniac!' the driver yelled out of the window.

For the first time Rita noticed how fast they were going. Then to her horror she realised that the taxi had no lights on.

'Hey, what happened to your lights!?' she yelled.

The driver sighed and threw a switch.

Bright headlights lit up the road in front. The road was thronging with traffic – all of it driving in darkness, and all of it going at colossal speed.

The driver killed the lights again.

'That's a ten quid fine if a copper caught me,' he said.

'What, for driving with your lights on at night?'

'Confuses the animals and birds,' said the driver.

Rita shook her head vigorously. Obviously whatever drug Dumont-Smith and his friends had given her was still in her system. It was confusing her. Either that or she'd got into a car with a maniac.

'Gettin' busy, love,' said the driver. 'You'd best belt up.'

'What? Oh.' Rita fumbled for the safety-belt.

Just in time. The driver hauled the wheel hard around to the right, and Rita felt herself thrown in the opposite direction. He swerved again, one hand on the wheel, the other out of the window making a rude gesture. Rita was thrown the other way.

'Sorry about that, love,' the driver said, then promptly did it again.

'Why don't you slow down, for God's sake!' she yelled.

'No need,' the driver said. 'We never crash.'

Cody McBride had covered the zoo three times and found nothing. The place was deserted now. It gave him the creeps. It was a still night, and the smell of the animals was heavy in the air. Behind shadowy glass and bars he could hear their constant muted roar, their calls, their sleep, their nocturnal rituals. He switched on his flashlight. Unlikely to be discovered now.

A sudden shriek made him spin around, his light darting across the darkness, finding two black eyes staring at him. A row of sharp grinning teeth. He leapt back with a cry.

He drew a deep breath. It was just an ugly baboon or something. He was back at the monkey house. Square one.

Nothing for it, it'd have to be breaking and entering. Not the ape house though – no fear. His torchlight found the small mammals' enclosure. That was more the sort of thing he had in mind. He strode to the door and tested it. Pretty solid. No problem. He fished his jemmy from inside his coat and thrust it between door and jam.

The door was tough. The wood splintered slowly, loudly protesting McBride's every heave on the iron bar. He stopped, breathless.

'Hello…'

A voice. A girl.

'Is anybody there? I'm locked in.'

It was coming from the primate house. His torch found a row of cellar windows set at ground level, partly obscured by grass. The voice was coming from one of them.

'Ace? Is that you?'

'Who's that?'

'McBride. Cody.'

'Cody McBride? Bloody Nora, that's a turn-up! Can you get me out?'

'Just give me a minute…'

He edged his way along the wall, searching by torchlight for a door. He found one by accident, set back in the wall, out of the way down a short flight of steps which were almost wholly hidden by long grass. In fact it was the steps he found first, when the ground suddenly vanished from under him. He picked himself up and looked at the grey double doors. Once again he hefted his jemmy.

The door gave easily. He was in a low-ceilinged stone corridor, windowless, with doors at regular intervals.

'Ace…!' he called.

'McBride!'

He was at a crossroads. It was difficult to tell exactly where Ace was calling from. Left, he was pretty sure.

'Keep talking, Ace!'

'I don't know what to say.'

McBride grinned.

'Tell me how you come to be locked up in a monkey-house.'

'A bloke locked me in here. He's… well, I suppose you could say he's my bloke.'

'I thought that was me, babe.'

Ace laughed. McBride could hear her clearly through the door. He'd found her.

'Stand back,' he said. 'I'm gonna force the door.' McBride had no time for the subtler arts of burglary.

The door splintered and swung. And there was Ace, exactly the same as the last time they'd met. Nineteen years ago. Unchanged.

She rushed from the room, arms and grin wide, then stopped. Her smile slipped a bit.

'Cody,' she said with forced lightness.

Nineteen years…

'I know,' grunted McBride. 'I got old. Whaddaya expect? It's what people do around here.'

Ace smiled warmly now, and hugged him.

'It's good to see you again, Cody,' she said with genuine emotion. 'Did the Doctor send you?'

'Kinda,' said McBride. 'He reckons you're in big trouble. Someone's out to shoot you.'

'Me?' spluttered Ace. 'Why?'

'Let's just get out of here, shall we?' said McBride. 'This place always gives me the creeps.'

'You ain't going anywhere!'

A lazy Texan drawl echoed down the stone passageway.

'What's this, the Seventh Cavalry?'

A man was strolling up to them. He looked tough. He was carrying a machete.

He looked familiar. Fresh, open face, dirty blond tousled hair... he looked American.

'Jimmy – you can't keep us here!' Ace yelled. 'What do you want anyway?'

'I'm just doin' my job,' the newcomer said.

He was American. Jimmy...

Then it dawned on McBride.

'You're James Dean,' said McBride. 'The movie star. You're supposed to be dead.'

'Wrong, fella,' said the matinee idol with the machete. 'You're the one's supposed to be dead.'

Suddenly he swung the machete in a broad, swift, lethal arc. McBride lurched out of its path, feeling it slice the air beside him. He swung again, and again. McBride could do nothing but dance unevenly backwards, hoping to keep his footing.

At least he was leading this psycho away from Ace.

His attacker – James Dean, or whoever the hell he was – was playing with him, grinning and jibing.

'This what you like is it, Joe? They train you up for this, Russkie-boy?'

The blade sliced through McBride's coat.

Worse – he'd hit a dead end. He'd run out of corridor. His back was against a brick wall.

His mind raced – the blade swung down – McBride fumbled, raised a flailing arm, his jemmy clutched in a white fist. Metal kranged on metal. Blade and jemmy shuddered with the impact. McBride felt the shock wave judder through him, down his spine. A shard flew from the blade past McBride's face and sliced into the wall...

His attacker raised the blade again.

There was a sort of raucous bellow.

And from nowhere a chair – a heavy, metal-framed waiting-room chair – arced overhead and came crashing down on the handsome blond head.

Ace.

'You're out of your tree, Jimmy,' Ace snarled as the attacker crumpled. 'You should be locked up.'

Neatly she kicked the dropped machete under a big wooden cabinet that stood against the wall.

'Oh, and you're dumped.'

The hunched figure looked up at them both with something dark and red oozing between his teeth.

'Tough break, Jimmy,' McBride sneered.

Then Jimmy made his move.

He surged upward, a fist pistoning out, not at McBride, but Ace.

'Bitch!' he spat as he connected with her face. McBride winced – he could hear bone breaking. He saw Ace go down, senseless,

Before he could react Jimmy had turned and was charging him like an enraged elephant, slamming him into a wall, pushing the breath from him.

Jimmy grabbed at McBride's wrist, pinning his jemmy arm uselessly, twisting, bending, working the iron lever from his grip. With his free hand McBride pounded his assailant's face and torso, but to little effect. This guy was tough, and McBride was forty-seven.

He still knew a few good moves though...

He pushed away from the wall, bringing his knee up hard between Jimmy's legs. Jimmy let out a groan and staggered back, doubled up.

'Mister, you're a dead man,' he hissed.

McBride needed to get his breath back, and needed to make sure Ace was all right. She hadn't moved from where she had fallen.

He shouldn't have taken his attention off Jimmy. He felt the butt of his own jemmy driving into his guts. He struggled for breath. A punch to the face. Again he was staggering backwards. His vision blurred and clouded with blood.

He turned and tried to run, to lead the maniac away from Ace. Clutching at the wall, he skidded into an unlit corridor which ended in a set of double doors. He yanked at them – please...

They opened freely, towards him. Behind them, he was facing the bars of a cage.

The end of the corridor, immediately beyond the doors, was caged off.

He turned. Jimmy slammed into him, iron jemmy held in both hands, pressing on McBride's throat, crushing him against the bars.

He couldn't breathe. His arms flailed uselessly, clutching at Jimmy, clutching at the bars, the doors, anything.

They closed on a button. A big, wall-mounted, bakelite button, which sank beneath McBride's hand. There was a rattling, whirring sound, and McBride felt the bars juddering against his back. They were moving. They were being raised.

He staggered back into the darkness beyond and fell.

Jimmy was still in the doorway. He hit the button again, and the cage wall crashed back down, trapping McBride.

He was laughing now.

'Well?' demanded McBride. 'What's so goddamn funny?'

'You'll see,' said Jimmy, grinning. 'You'll see.'

And with that he turned and sauntered off down the corridor, whistling.

'Hey, wait – ' He couldn't just go. 'Hey, bud… Jimmy, whatever your name is – '

Jimmy rounded a corner, vanishing from McBride's sight.

'Jimmy!' the prisoner yelled. Then, 'Ace?'

He couldn't see her from his cage. There was no sound to break the silence.

The Doctor had to hand it to the troops, British and American, they seemed to be holding their own – the attackers had yet to penetrate the hangar. The air was thick with smoke. Gunfire punctured the night.

A group of four soldiers had holed up inside, succeeding in closing the vast hangar doors under heavy fire. Three privates and a young lieutenant. Hotly they debated what to do, whilst taking pot-shots through the windows.

'Right,' said Major Collins aboard the wrecked Waverider, 'everybody off the ship. Down into the hangar.'

Nobody moved. Drakefell was on his knees next to the Doctor, trying to help him safely uncouple the dimension stabiliser. O'Brien hovered uncertainly between the Doctor and Collins.

'Didn't you hear what I said?'

'Bill,' said O'Brien. 'Sir – I'm no damned Commie. You know that. And if we're under attack, I'm not going to stand by just because I'm supposed to be under arrest. I'm a soldier, sir.'

Collins stared hard at him, smiled grimly and patted O'Brien roughly on the shoulder.

'OK, you two – '

'Major,' the Doctor cut in, 'might I suggest you go and fight your battle and leave us to do this intricate and frankly rather dangerous work in peace?'

Collins looked as if he was ready to shoot the Doctor there and then.

'Watch them,' he said to O'Brien. 'Don't let them take anything off the ship. I'm going to find out what's happening.'

He scrambled up through the hatch and down the tattered fuselage.

'Nearly there,' said the Doctor.

He turned to O'Brien.

'Davey,' he said. 'I'm going to need to get this out of here somehow.'

O'Brien looked troubled.

'I can't begin to stress how important it is.'

'In for a penny, in for a pound, I suppose. I deserve to get shot – and if I survive this lot, that's probably what they'll do to me. What did you have in mind?'

'Wait until the soldiers are fully engaged down below and take advantage of the confusion of battle. Major Collins trusts you. You will have to get it away. We will follow as quickly as we can.'

'Now hold on, Doc... you heard what I said to Collins. I'm a soldier. We're attacked, I stay and fight.'

'You'll make brigadier one day with thinking like that,' said the Doctor dryly. 'Captain, the fabric of the dimensions is splitting, and this is the only piece of equipment on the planet that is capable of repairing it. Without this machine we're lost.'

They were interrupted by Major Collins's noisy entry through the hatch.

'What's happening, sir?' O'Brien asked.

'Seems there's about a dozen o' them,' said Collins. 'They just came out of the woods. Straight-ahead charge – smoke bombs, grenades, tracer, and I'd say they've got some kind of special night-vision goggles. They're well armed and well trained and fast. Special Forces, obviously. Up against them we're about twenty in total, and carrying only light arms. They were just out looking for him.'

The Doctor smiled apologetically.

'They've cut the road off... we're trying to get reinforcements, but they're jamming our radio. A couple of men got out through the fence and into the woods. They should be able to raise the alarm.'

'If they ever get out of the forest,' mused the Doctor, rubbing his ankle. It was swelling badly now, and he feared to put any weight on it. Another reason he needed Davey O'Brien.

'But even then,' Collins continued, 'there are maybe another fifteen, twenty troops in the compound and that's it.'

'Against a dozen Russians?' O'Brien chortled. 'No sweat!'

'You haven't seen the way this lot fight,' said Collins. 'I've never seen anything like it. They've got most of our men pinned down in the outbuildings. Caught them by surprise, moved like lightning.'

His final words were drowned by a sickening bang that echoed around the big metal building. It shook. Several panes in the glass roof broke and fell in. There was a hot blast of air, and the shrieking, shuddering, grating of torn metal. The mighty hangar doors lay twisted, all but torn from their hinges. The enemy swarmed in.

McBride's eyes were starting to get used to the blackness. Either that, or they were starting to play tricks on him. Vague shapes emerged, then vanished again in uncertainty. He'd spent enough time snooping around in the pitch black to know the eye plays tricks, but the ear? He was sure he could hear the faintest of noises.

He was beginning to think he wasn't alone in the darkness. He groped along the wall for a light switch. It was big, the room. Huge. And it stank.

His hand closed on a hefty switch and he threw it.

Nothing. The darkness continued unabated. Obviously not the light switch. He fumbled on.

Then he stopped. Just for a second a dull flicker of light, a spark, had faintly and briefly penetrated the darkness, somewhere up at ceiling level. There was another. A momentary low, electrical buzzing. He could detect a whiff of ozone in the air.

More than that, the still of the room seemed to have been stirred. He was certain now he could hear something. Slight movement. The rustle of fur.

The room really did reek.

McBride's blood chilled. He was locked in with one of the animals. He froze – he didn't know what to do.

Keep still… don't make any sound.

Hell, animals could see in the dark. They could smell him. He was already lunch.

He definitely heard something now. The hollow clatter of cheap metal, somewhere up around the ceiling, a brief, harsh electrical buzz, and a momentary faint red glow above him.

And something else. There was more in here than just him and some faulty wiring: A huge bulk was shifting, scraping along the floor, yawning.

That settled it. Whatever was in here was massive. He had to find a way out.

The hums and pops overhead were more frequent now. There were more sparks too. And more definite sounds of animal movement. Whatever was in here, there was more than one of them...

He stopped. His legs were up against something soft. Warm. Breathing. It turned over and stretched itself – a huge arm buffeting the side of McBride's head, knocking him to his knees.

It was an ape. A big one.

It stood up. There was a sort of crack from the ceiling, and a shower of sparks that briefly lit the beast's face. A gorilla.

McBride could smell the ozone again, even against the rank, stale animal miasma that surrounded him. It reminded him of the Underground trains. Electricity.

The animal tossed its head and drew itself up to its full height. Another cascade of sparks.

McBride scuttled away from the beast, away from the walls and into the black maw of the huge enclosure. He wasn't sure where the door was any more – even if he knew how to open the cage from the inside.

There were more electrical exchanges above his head – they seemed to be happening all the time now, all around the room. And there was more movement – a slow, hesitant stirring all around him. Giant shadows were shuffling slowly all around him, as if in a monstrous, slow, silent dance. They seemed barely aware of him. He edged around the sounds, constantly moving to avoid the invisible giants. More than once he bumped into a wall of coarse fur and muscle.

More than once he gashed his legs against something hard and sharp. There seemed to be a lot of machinery lying about.

The ragged hum of electricity was constant now, and a constant fine rain of sparks fell from above. He could just about make out a regular pattern in the flashes of light.

There was some sort of electrical grid covering the whole ceiling.

He sensed movement, a disturbance of the air, heard a deep, wet snuffling sound, and ducked as something heavy, cold and metallic swung through the air, clipping the side of his head. He reeled, and fell once again.

The animals were moving the machinery about. Not playing with it, not throwing it around or pulling it apart. Moving it with quiet precision.

A massive, dark silhouette moved across the gentle downpour of sparks. It towered over him, then swooped downward. McBride rolled. He was aware of something sharp slicing the air – a pole, with some sort of blade, like a scythe – and clanging off the concrete floor only inches away from him.

These apes had weapons...

He dashed a falling spark from his hair. The staccato light from the overhead firework display was becoming sufficient to see by – just. He squinted to make sense of the mass of indistinct, flickering shapes that surrounded him.

There were apes of all types here – chimps, orang-utans – but...

He felt dizzy. His stomach lurched and buckled. These apes had been horribly altered. The machinery was attached to their bodies. Rubber tubes erupted from fissures in their skin. Boxy metal limbs and probosces had been grafted to their torsos. He could make out a gorilla with half its face erupting with tubes and wires, one huge, artificial eye and an ill-fitting metal cranium.

It brought a sickening kaleidoscope of memories spinning back to McBride. The Blitz, the last time he'd set eyes on the Doc. An electronics factory where people were turned into Cybermen.

So he and Mullen had been right. In spite of all the denials, they had been working on this stuff. He looked around him in pity and disgust. Compared to the monstrous efficiency of the silver giants, this looked wretchedly crude. They seemed to be getting power from the ceiling grid. Each primate had a bulky back-plate, and each back-plate had a pole extending upward from it, around which cables snaked upward to a long, thin metal plate – the blade of the scythe. Whenever an ape stood upright the plate would make contact with the grid.

It was just like the goddamn dodgems at the fair.

He let out a brief, high, hysterical laugh and was suddenly sick.

Rita had never been so frightened in her life. She was clinging to her seat, sweating, cold as the taxi swerved through the night.

The cab driver talked continuously, but she heard none of it. This was worse than any damned roller-coaster she'd ever been on.

At last she felt them slowing down.

'Now don't get me wrong, I'm not a racialist or nothing...' The driver was still talking, oblivious to her terror. 'But it's not what we want. There's too many of us over here as it is. And we're... different.

Anyone can see that. We're more advanced.'

'What?' Rita tried to concentrate.

'And I'm sorry, but we don't want to end up with a Western saloon bar on every street corner and the whole country smelling of hamburgers.'

'I'm sorry...' Rita was utterly confused.

'You lot,' the cabby said. 'Since the war, coming over 'ere. And it's no good trying to slip in the back door neither – I hear you're all trying to get into India now. Well, they won't wear it neither, I can tell you.'

He came to a halt.

'Anyway, we're here,' he said.

Instinctively she reached into a pocket, and her fingers closed on some crumpled paper. Two fivers...

'Oh, here!' she said with relief.

'I told you, Calamity Jane, it's free. You're in England now.' He spoke as if he was talking to a backward child. 'You lot just don't get it, do you? Yankee see, Yankee do. Go on...'

Rita clambered out of the taxi, which pulled smoothly away. She hoped it was just the drugs...

There was a light on in McBride's office. Good. She went up to the door and banged on it. She heard footsteps coming down the stairs.

'McBride, it's me!'

The door opened.

'What you want?'

She was looking at a fat Chinese guy in a vest and pyjama bottoms.

'Uh... Cody McBride.'

'No. Wrong address.'

He started to close the door.

'Wait a minute,' said Rita. 'This is his office, goddamn it!'

'Not office! This restaurant!'

He gestured with an angry arm to Rita's right, then slammed the door.

Rita could see it now. The unlit shop-front had changed. It was a Chinese restaurant.

The End of the World. It had obviously been there for years.

Chapter Twelve

The hangar had become a shooting gallery. All but one of the unfortunate soldiers now lay dead on the ground. They had been brave and had actually driven the attackers back on their first assault. The second time they hadn't been so lucky.

The sole survivor of their ranks was scrambling on his back up the side of the ship, alongside Collins and O'Brien. All three were dragging ammunition boxes and extra weapons with them, and all were firing repeatedly down at their pursuers.

The Doctor watched through a tear in the hull as they retreated.

'They've got some sort of bullet-proof clothing,' O'Brien shouted. 'They just don't go down!'

The three men tumbled through the hatch.

'Right,' said Collins, 'we re-arm properly and we break out.'

'Where to?' the young soldier from below howled. 'If we move from here, we're dead! You saw what they did down there. That was three of them.'

'At ease, Private Stubbs,' Collins growled. 'We're sitting ducks in here. They can pick us off when they like.'

'We're just about finished here,' said the Doctor, uncoupling the final connection. He mopped his brow with his handkerchief. 'It's safe now. Thank you, Dr Drakefell.'

O'Brien was chain-feeding ammunition into the guns they'd managed to rescue from the chaos below.

'That thing had better be worth it,' he muttered to the Doctor.

'Oh, it is,' said the Doctor. 'Now, what can I do to help?'

'Too late!' Collins shouted. 'Here they come.'

The commandos were swarming up the sides of the ship like spiders. They moved with shocking speed. The soldiers responded with clip after clip of ammo. Private Stubbs blasted one of them from the hull. He fell to the concrete floor, got up and renewed the assault.

'I wish they wouldn't keep doing that,' said O'Brien. 'Heads up!'

The first of the commandos was coming through the hatch. Collins and O'Brien opened fire. They could see their bullets hitting him.

They drove him back like punches, but none of them broke through his clothing. He unholstered his gun.

'Everybody down!' yelled Collins. He barrelled forward and careered into the intruder. Collins had a knife in his hand. He drove it at the commando's stomach. It slammed his tunic, but didn't penetrate. The commando swung, tossing Collins effortlessly, and hard, into the ship's bulkhead. Collins sank, sack-like, to the deck.

Before the commando could raise his gun again O'Brien had opened fire. Stubbs followed suit.

'Try to drive him back out of the hatch!' shouted the Doctor over the gunfire.

He had an idea. He scrambled past the gunfight and tugged free a panel beneath the pilot's seat. Lights winked and terminals opened enticingly. He looked at the chaos of wires erupting from the bulkhead where the dimension stabiliser had resided and wondered how easy it actually was, even with his undisputed genius, to find a needle in a haystack.

In the event it was surprisingly simple. Some basic reprogramming, three relevant terminals, three (out of umpteen thousand) relevant wires, and that was that.

The commando was retreating up through the hatch. O'Brien was making to follow him.

'No!' the Doctor shouted. 'Everyone stay where they are!'

He plugged in the wires and pushed a button.

There was an explosion from outside the ship. The commando was flying through the air. Smoke appeared to be wafting from his clothes. He landed on the concrete with a dull crunch.

The commandos milled about, shouting to each other. The Doctor's brow creased in puzzlement.

'Russian,' said Collins. 'Happy now?'

The Doctor shook his head.

'I really can't explain that,' he said.

'What did you do to Flash Gordon out there?' asked O'Brien.

'Electrified the hull,' said the Doctor. 'I'm afraid we can't go out while it's on.'

'That's impossible,' said Drakefell. 'I read the reports. They tried all that – current, magnetism, every chemical you can name – nothing reacted to it. It was completely inert.'

'It's one of the intelligent metals,' said the Doctor.

'What do you mean?'

'It can adapt its physical and chemical properties to suit different situations.'

'You mean it became conductive...'

'Because I told it to, yes.'

The Doctor smiled.

'I shouldn't worry, Dr Drakefell,' he said reassuringly, 'intelligent metals won't be invented here for another two hundred years. Now I really think we should check on our friend.'

They'd almost forgotten Collins.

'I'm all right,' he grunted as they clustered around him.

He dragged himself to his feet, wincing.

'Bust a couple of ribs, I reckon,' he said. 'Still... how're we doing?'

'We have a temporary reprieve,' said the Doctor.

The commandos seemed to have withdrawn to cover.

'I need to get the dimension stabiliser to safety,' said the Doctor. 'That's more important than anything.'

'Damned if I'll put a machine before lives,' Collins barked. 'We're gonna get ourselves to safety. The machine'll just have to take its chances. How long'll the power last? I thought the ship was dead.'

'She is. This is the outboard power supply for the dimension stabiliser. Much bigger. It should last... a billion billion years if we're lucky.'

'So we've got that long to figure out what to do,' Collins grunted. 'Great.'

'It's not the power failing I'm worried about,' said the Doctor. 'It's just that I'm rather gambling on our enemies' intentions here.'

'What do you mean?' the major growled.

'Well, it all depends what they want to do with the ship,' said the Doctor.

Collins shook his head.

'Whether they want it back, or – '

An explosion of gunfire settled the matter. It ripped through the broken ship, punching fist-sized holes in the fuselage. The Waverider rocked and juddered on its flimsy supports.

' – not!' finished the Doctor, jumping for cover.

'They'd let a ship like this go?' O'Brien sounded almost hurt.

'I fear so,' said the Doctor. 'I dare say their shops are bursting with dimension stabilisers.'

There was a much bigger explosion. The whole structure lurched to one side, sending everyone tumbling.

'They certainly won't let it fall into our hands,' shouted the Doctor above the din.

It was more than the tortured superstructure could bear. The deafening screech of ripping metal told them that. Suddenly the deck was at forty-five degrees. The ship lurched again.

Collins was sliding towards a great gash in the hull. The lethal, live outer skin of the ship lay beyond.

The Doctor threw himself across the swaying, buckling deck towards the pilot's station, grasping at his hasty wiring job, yanking the cables free as Collins slid through the tear.

He saw the dimension stabiliser, with minute slowness, start to slide away towards a chasm in the hull from which flames were starting to appear. He sprang out and made a grab for the machine, but his ankle buckled beneath him and he keeled over. He crashed into what, had the ship been upright, would have been a wall alcove, and struggled to right himself.

There was a hissing sound and he felt something pass in front of his face.

He couldn't move. He could see his friends but suddenly could hear nothing. He tried to call out...

He couldn't breathe.

He started to struggle.

'Emergency evacuation in ten seconds,' a calm female voice said.

It was a transparent panel, holding him in. He was in some sort of escape module.

The air supply wasn't working.

'Disengaging locking mechanisms.'

He didn't want to escape! He could still see the dimension stabiliser inching towards destruction.

'Engaging primary thrusters.'

His eyes caught Drakefell's. The project director looked anguished, petrified. He threw the Doctor a glance of desperation and despair and dived towards the machine. He clasped his arms around it and vanished with it into the dark crack.

The next thing the Doctor was aware of was a screaming in his ears and the walls of the hangar blurring towards him. The pod hit the glass roof at a suicidally oblique angle, missing the wall by inches. The glass scattered, and blue light drenched him.

No controls... The Doctor was suffocating. In desperation he kicked and thumped the side-panels of the craft.

To his relief he felt the gentle whisper of breathable air. He gulped it down.

There was a rumbling from somewhere far below, and an orange fireball belched up from the forest, dwarfing the trees, shaking his little craft. The end of the Waverider.

He had failed. All he had to show for his efforts was that – a colossal fireball consuming friends and hope.

He thought about Ace. He was certain now he couldn't save her. He knew who was going to kill her. He knew why he'd lost control of events so badly, why everything was collapsing into chaos.

One man.

One frail, polite, elderly gent, with a mind more dangerous than a nuclear device. By human standards – and he was only human – his intelligence far outstripped any other known to the Doctor. The last time they had met he had tried to add Cyber technology to the already lethal cocktail of the Second World War. Single-handed he had deceived the Doctor, British Intelligence – even the Third Reich.[5]

And all motivated by an insatiable, all-consuming curiosity. He considered the world, its people, history and future to be little more than his own personal chemistry set.

Drakefell had confirmed it. The Doctor had instantly recognised Drakefell's 'nightmare machine'. It was the lode-circuit from a crude time machine, piloted here by Cybermen nearly twenty years ago.

The devious old fiend had used it to escape the Doctor, and the Doctor had let him. He should have been scattered across time along with the machine. The Doctor had been so certain...

He swallowed hard. He had given that geriatric Lord of Chaos a time machine...

The Doctor's little craft shuddered slightly and changed its course. It seemed happy to pilot itself. There were no controls that the Doctor could see. They were over London now.

He was down there somewhere, waiting for Ace.

Her face was raw and swollen. She could feel where her nose and lips had bled and the blood had dried. Ace awoke from insensibility into a world of pain.

She was cramped and in darkness, curled in a ball on a cold stone floor. Walls hemmed her on three sides, a door on the fourth.

[5] See *Doctor Who: Illegal Alien*

He'd put her in a bloody cupboard. Furious, she kicked out at the door and didn't stop until the lock gave and she tumbled out into the corridor.

'Now you jus' better stop doin' that.'

Jimmy was approaching in a not very straight line. A half-smile, half-sneer played about his mouth. He looked drunk.

'Why won't you jus' stay put?' he chided. ''Stead o' smashin' all our doors down. What'm I gonna do with you now, missy?'

'Where's McBride?' Ace snarled.

'Oh, you wanna go see your private dick? OK, fine by me. Let's go!'

He grabbed Ace by the wrist and hauled her to her feet.

'You're dogmeat for this mate,' she spat. 'You'll wish you'd never been born. When the Doctor gets here – geddoff me!'

He ignored her protests and dragged her along the empty corridor. There at the end of it was the cage.

'McBride!' she called. 'Cody!'

'Ace?'

'You want to go in there with lover boy, huh?'

'No,' McBride yelled. 'There's something in here, Ace!'

Jimmy let out a whoop. 'Somebody turned the monkeys on!'

The place was aglow with flickering orange light. Ace could see huge, indistinct figures shambling about. From somewhere in their midst McBride was calling. 'I'll try and get to you – hang on!'

Jimmy threw Ace against the bars.

'I was gonna give these to you last night,' he drawled, 'but I figured it would spoil the surprise.'

He clamped a metal manacle around her wrist and pushed her arm through the bars.

'Now hold still, willya?'

Handcuffs.

The other bracelet snapped closed. Ace pulled back hard. The linking chain clunked against the cage.

'Why are you doing this, Jimmy?' Ace demanded. 'What am I supposed to have done?'

'Aww babe…' Jimmy drawled, 'you know I love ya, dontcha…'

He nuzzled up close and tried to kiss her. He reeked of booze. Ace tore her head away.

'Take your goddamn hands off her!'

McBride slammed against the other side of the bars.

'Yeah,' Jimmy sneered. 'What you gonna do, Mr Private Dick?'

'Let me out of here and I'll show you.'

Jimmy smiled.

'Ain't the monkeys cute?' he said. 'You wanna see them play?'

He opened what looked like a fuse box on the wall. Behind it was a row of large knobs and dials. He turned a knob.

'They ain't barely woke up yet,' he said. 'You wait.'

And with that he shambled off, fumbling for a cigarette.

Ace tore against her chain.

'Wait!' she shouted.

Jimmy didn't look back. He just raised a hand and wiggled his fingers.

'You OK, kid?' McBride asked.

'Yeah. You?'

'So far, but I don't like what's happenin' in here.'

They were apes... Ace could see that now. Fitted with...

The ceiling suddenly erupted in a violent shower of sparks, lighting up the room.

It seemed to agitate the apes. A chorus of squeals and shrieks struck up.

'Can you get me out of these cuffs?' Ace shouted above the din.

McBride tugged at the chain.

'Careful! Those are my hands in there.'

'Sorry, kid. These are tricky...'

The apes were screaming now. A fight had broken out. A gorilla with grafted-on arms like metal coffins was squaring up against what seemed to be a square-ish knot of struts and wires on twin caterpillar tracks, and surmounted by two shrieking baboon heads, set lopsidedly next to each other. The gorilla pounced. The other thing – which seemed to have a single metal arm on each of its four sides – spun on its tracks, using its arms like flails, catching the gorilla in the chest and sending it flying straight towards them.

'Cody!'

McBride dived to one side as the massive ape crashed into the wall beside him.

The thing on the tracks closed in. The other apes followed, jumping and howling.

'You got to get out of there!'

'You don't say, kid,' said McBride from the floor.

The baboon-thing made a grab for the gorilla. The gorilla slipped under its lunge and closed its arms around its foe, and with a deep

135

grunt lifted it off the floor. Its twin heads screamed at one another. The gorilla pivoted and threw the thing hard.

'Cody!'

McBride rolled away into the shadows as the monster landed, cracking the concrete.

Ace was desperate. She tugged vainly at her handcuffs. She glanced at the electrical box on the wall, much too far away...

There was a noise from somewhere far off up the corridor, she was sure.

'Help!' Ace yelled, hoping she could be heard over the din.

Ace craned her neck around. Someone was coming, moving slowly down the dim corridor.

'Help! My friend is locked in there!'

She recognised the uniform of a zoo-keeper.

'Hang on,' she called to McBride. 'Someone's coming.'

She craned again.

'Hurry up!' she called.

He was old – probably going as fast as he could.

The primate fight raged on behind the cage door. She could no longer see McBride.

'Oh, dear,' a soft old voice said. 'We are in a pickle, aren't we?'

Ace's blood froze. Her head reeled. She recognised the voice.

'You!'

George Limb.

'I suppose it would be facile to ask how you are,' he said.

It couldn't be...

'The Doctor said you were dead. Scattered through time.'

'I'm afraid even the Doctor can't be right all the time,' he said.

Of all the people she'd met on her travels with the Doctor, all the enemies they'd fought, she hated George Limb more than any of them.

It was because she'd taken to the old man so warmly at first. He'd wound her round his little finger – not just her, the Doctor too. Then he'd betrayed them without a second thought to the Nazis.

It wasn't that he was evil, he just... didn't care.

'I have a key for those,' he said. 'Somewhere.'

He fumbled in a pocket of his zoo-keeper's jacket.

'Here we are.'

He reached up with an unsteady hand and undid one of her manacles. In an instant Ace sprang away from the bars and spun around, tensed, ready to fight.

The old man turned slowly. It was him. A bit older, a bit frailer, but definitely George Limb. He was pointing a pistol at her.

'When did you turn into Johnny Morris?'

'I'm sorry, my dear,' said Limb. 'I don't understand the reference.'

He cocked the trigger.

'You gonna use that?' Ace said, trying to sound contemptuous, angry at the uncertainty in her voice.

'I'm afraid I have no choice, my dear,' said Limb. 'The Doctor expects it of me.'

He appeared to hesitate.

'I don't suppose this will make things any easier for you, but you have affected my young friend Jimmy quite profoundly.'

'He's got a funny way of showing it,' Ace spat.

'He is behaving like a drunken brute at the moment because he is in pain. His sense of duty and patriotism is in conflict with his heart.'

'He's off his rocker - but hanging around with you, I'm not surprised.'

'I really am sorry about this, you know,' said Limb.

The last thought to strike Ace was what McBride had said. Her lover - Jimmy - was James Dean…

Then all she was aware of was a sudden explosion of noise and pain, instantly extinguished.

Less than an hour later George Limb and a sobbing Jimmy dumped Ace's body, wrapped in a sack, off Blackfriars Bridge in the rain. Late the next day it was washed up at Wapping, taken to a mortuary and labelled Jane Doe.

PART THREE

Chapter Thirteen

Police have admitted they are 'baffled' by the body of a mysterious young woman which was discovered yesterday washed up by the Thames at Wapping Old Stairs. The woman, whom police have so far failed to identify, is estimated to be in her late teens or early twenties, but who she is remains a mystery.

A London River Police spokesman described the woman as aged about eighteen, with long brown hair and 'tomboyish' in appearance.

'On first sight we thought it was a young man,' said Inspector Clements. 'She was wearing a short black jacket and American army-style combat trousers and boots.'

He went on to describe the gruesome manner of her death.

'She was shot in the face. There was massive damage, which has made her unusually difficult to identify. It was a particularly brutal and sadistic crime.'

He went on to reveal one clue to her identity. 'She had a tattoo on her back, and from that we believe she had the unusual name – or nickname – of 'Ace'. That is the name found tattooed on her shoulder, linked by a heart to someone called Jimmy. Attempts to locate this Jimmy have so far failed.'

One theory is that she was a street-walker who picked up the wrong client or offended her overlord. Said Inspector Parks, 'Her body displayed signs of recent sexual activity.'

He appealed for anyone who might know the identity of the girl to come forward and (continues on page 17)

Cody McBride kicked angrily at the old newspaper that tangled around his leg. The wind carried it off again. It sailed listlessly among gravestones before disappearing into the dark line of trees beyond.

A thin, sharp skein of sleet blew suddenly against McBride's face, stinging his cuts. He had three broken ribs and a whole mess of bruises and lacerations running the length of his body. He'd been lucky to escape the primate house with his life.

Luckier than Ace.

He had watched in horror from across the caged room as George Limb, that terrible old man, had shot Ace in the head. He'd tried desperately to scramble around the warring, shrieking ape things to reach the bars, shouting himself hoarse.

His progress was slow – other apes were now beginning to fight. One leapt over him on a single, huge metallic arm. A metal jaw, vicious with pointed steel teeth, bit into the plate-metal neck of a gorilla, which had what looked like a deep-sea diver's helmet for a head.

He had crawled frantically forward. His shouts were lost in the chaos. Limb didn't even notice him. The old man had shuffled out, instructing a silent, shaking Jimmy to bag the body and wash up the blood.

'Turn out her pockets,' he said. 'I think her – ah – personal effects will be of more use to me than to the police. And for heaven's sake, turn the primates off. They're not toys, you know!'

By the time McBride reached the bars Jimmy was struggling to get Ace – what was left of her – into a huge canvas sack.

'You goddamn son of a bitch murderer!'

McBride had hammered on the bars.

Jimmy looked pale and rattled. He didn't reply. He'd started to shove at Ace's body.

'She was a goddamn kid! Look at her!'

Jimmy knotted the top of the sack roughly.

'You shuddup!' he suddenly yelled. 'You don't know zip! You don't know what she done!'

'You been listening to George Limb? He'd sell his own mother down the river! Probably did!'

'I owe George my life!' Jimmy snarled.

'So you helped him kill a girl!'

'You just shut your mouth!' Jimmy shouted. He swung towards the wall-mounted controls and twisted. With a triumphant leer he started backing away from the bars, watching expectantly.

The roof above McBride exploded in cascading light. Sparks drenched him.

Screams of rage and pain filled the stone room. The creatures started thrashing wildly, tearing and biting at themselves and each other. Something huge hurled itself against the bars. McBride stumbled away once more.

Where to go? The whole cage was dancing with pain. He dodged and ducked wildly – there was nowhere.

Then it happened. Something careered into his chest, knocking him off his feet, and landed hard on top of him. It writhed and buckled, a huge arm – jointed metal plates, trapped beneath the thing's bulk – scraped and twisted, crashing into McBride's chest as he tried to roll out from beneath the monster. He staggered to his feet, his chest crumpling with blinding pain. The other arm sailed through the air like a windmill blade, gashing him from head to foot, sending him to the floor once more.

He felt himself blacking out. Breathing was difficult and agonising. He had to stay awake or he was dead. He heard the trundle of metal tracks on stone – the twin-headed abomination on caterpillar tracks was rolling slowly, blindly towards him. The heads were shrieking and biting at each other. One had lost an eye, the other was bleeding heavily from a livid gash in its skull.

Gritting his teeth, he rolled out of its path.

The room swam. This was it…

The creatures seemed to be moving in slow-motion now.

No, they *were* slowing. They were stopping.

The ceiling was growing dim – and suddenly the place was flooded with electric light. A tutting George Limb was picking his way among the half-slumbering monstrosities.

'Jimmy…' he hissed with exasperation.

McBride had lain motionless and watched as Limb worked his way to the far side of the room.

The cage door was open…

Agonisingly McBride began to drag himself towards it, hoping the noise and slow twitching of the dying ape-machines would conceal his movement.

He had to speed up – the old man was coming back. He was carrying a mop and bucket.

'If you want a job done properly…' Limb muttered.

McBride's hand closed gladly on a metal bar. He dragged himself forward and crawled through into the corridor.

He was crawling through Ace's blood…

Horrified beyond pain, he had lurched to his feet and run from the hellish dungeon into the sunlight.

* * *

'Even in the midst of life, we are in death...'

McBride had heard the spiel often in the past. It went with the job. But this was indescribably worse. He'd been there. He should have saved her. The Doc had trusted him...

He'd managed somehow to get himself to a hospital – lucky not to have punctured a lung – then had discharged himself prematurely and gone straight to the cops. They'd checked out the zoo, then had suddenly gone quiet. Polite, regretful, blank in response to McBride's enquiries. McBride knew when he was being stonewalled. It was the Cyber thing all over again. A cover-up.

Then the body had turned up. That had caught them on the hop – it made a bit of a splash in the papers before they could squash it.

There couldn't even have been an autopsy. It was all too quick. They just wanted the whole thing out of the way.

Dead and buried. McBride almost laughed.

He'd tried unsuccessfully to find Rita – he was going to raise a holy stink about this. That was when the Doctor had appeared, silently, like a ghost, pale and drawn, old-looking, and told him no.

That was all he'd said: no. He'd told him when the funeral was, then left, and McBride hadn't seen him until just now when he'd turned up at the graveside.

He looked at the strange little man. He seemed even smaller. Shrunken by his loss...

He hadn't yet met McBride's eyes.

The vicar finished his recitation and leaned towards McBride and the Doctor.

'Would you like to throw the earth now?'

They each had a handful of earth. Solemnly they let it fall, first the Doctor, then McBride. The earth rattled hollowly off the lid of the coffin.

Apart from the two of them, the vicar and some professional bearers, there was no one else around the sad little grave, though a policeman lurked some distance away beneath the trees.

'Thank you, gentlemen,' the vicar said. 'My deepest condolences. I shall leave you alone now.'

'Thank you,' the Doctor croaked.

The vicar smiled sympathetically and shuffled off.

'I'm sorry, Doc. I failed,' McBride said.

'The fault is mine, Cody,' the little man said in a quiet, hollow voice. 'I did a terrible thing bringing her here. I found her body, you see.

In the future. I found out the point in time where it was to happen and brought her back here. I didn't want this hanging over her... or me. I was sure I could prevent it.'

He shook his head slowly. The pair began to walk from the lonely graveside.

'Did you know there are laws of time?' the Doctor asked.

'Yeah?' McBride could barely follow all this.

'And I broke them. I came here with prior knowledge of future events, intending to change things, and in doing so I've helped make them happen. Time won't be tricked, Cody.'

'It was George Limb, Doc!'

'I know.'

'I saw him do it – I couldn't stop him. He had this big flunky – sounds mad, but I'd swear it was James Dean...' McBride shrugged. '... and he –'

'James Dean?' the Doctor interrupted, suddenly sharp-sounding.

'The movie star. He was killed in a car crash back in '55. This guy was a dead ringer for him. Tough, too.'

McBride's hand rested lightly on his bandaged ribs.

The Doctor stopped walking.

'This situation gets worse by the minute, Cody. I half feared as much.'

'What?'

'James Dean. It appears I'm not the only one who's been messing around with time.'

Chapter Fourteen

'What in the name of Jesus has been going on here?'

General Crawhammer sucked furiously on the fat stump of a cigar. He was at the zoo, beneath the primate house, surveying a scene of stomach-churning carnage. Next to the general, Bill Collins swallowed hard.

There were ten or so people about – police, army, government. A man passed, looking green, with a clipboard. Crawhammer grabbed him by the collar.

'I ordered this place shut down! Those things broken up – or killed, or whatever… What happened?'

'I don't know, General,' the man spluttered. 'The place should have been gutted and sealed. There must have been some sort of a mix-up in the office. Oh, dear…'

The man pressed a handkerchief to his mouth and closed his eyes.

Crawhammer pushed him away.

'Always the goddamn paperwork with the Brits,' he barked to Collins. 'Every time there's a screw-up – count on it. Too much of the stuff, that's the trouble.'

He dropped his cigar butt into a puddle of blood veined with engine oil.

'Collins, get some of our boys in here.' He scowled about the little assembly. 'They'll know what to do. They know what gutting means. Now what about this murdered girl?'

A man tapped Bill Collins on the shoulder

'She's – ah – been dealt with. Inspector Hamilton, Special Branch.'

He flashed his badge. No need – he looked like an English cop.

'We tried to get hold of you earlier, General.'

'Just flew in,' Crawhammer snapped.

Collins suppressed a smile. The general had been touching down in Washington at the time of the Russian raid, and had been personally informed about it by a furious President Eisenhower.

'Nothing's been touched,' the policeman said.

Crawhammer hunkered down, eyeballing the cop, his lips drawn back across his gleaming, crocodile teeth.

'Does no one in this country get it?' he whispered. '*I want this place destroyed!*'

They returned to Winnerton Flats in the general's staff car in silence. He'd been in a thunderous mood since he touched down. Strike that – since the ship blew up. He'd received Collins's report on the raid in icy silence.

'So tell me one thing, Major,' he'd said after a suitable pause. 'How come you're not dead?'

'Sir?'

'If this was such a rerun of the goddamn Alamo, how come none of my men have got more 'n a scratch or two between them? What were you all doing out there? Were you on a goddamn Easter egg hunt?'

'I can't explain it, sir. I was hit…'

He'd felt the impact, felt a cold shock through his whole body, and woken up in the sick bay in the bed next to O'Brien. Apart from some impact bruises, he was fine. So was everyone else.

So they'd combed the grounds and found no bullets – except their own – no cartridges, no sign that the Russians – or the ship – had ever been there.

'The president wants me to report back personally,' Crawhammer had fumed, 'and that's what I got to tell him. Super-fast soldiers with advanced stun weapons.'

'I don't think you should underestimate these men,' Collins had urged. 'I tell you sir, they outclassed us big time. If they'd been shooting to kill…'

'At least they got Drakefell.'

Drakefell hadn't been seen since the raid, and Crawhammer had taken to consoling himself with the fact.

'Goddamn welcome to the fruitcake sonofabitch.'

The traffic thinned quickly as they sped out of London, the silence broken only by Crawhammer's constant urging the driver to put his foot down.

'When I find out who ballsed up at the zoo they're gonna wish they were digging Commie coal in Siberia.'

'I think it's more important to find out who's been using the place, sir.'

'We know who, Collins. Goddamn Reds! Cells of them, everywhere. Even under London Zoo!'

Crawhammer let out a long, tired sigh.

'I'm used to fightin' enemies I can see, Major. A uniform. Or at least some slitty eyes or a funny accent… All this spy stuff… War should be fought by men face to face. Or at least firing missiles at each other… And now what are we doing? Turning gorillas into walking tanks…'

'I never liked the monkey experiments, sir.'

'Maybe I'm just getting old, Major. War's a shitty job. Always has been, always will be. Fifty-five million people died in the last war. You know that, Collins?'

'No, sir.'

'It could have been less if things had been done differently. Deals made with other Nazi leaders, maybe. The Jews saved… Maybe we didn't have to go to war at all.'

'Sir?' This didn't sound like Crawhammer.

'But there's one thing war teaches you, and that's you never, ever blink in the face of an enemy. You get me? It's a staring contest, and you better not blink, cos you know damn well ol' Adolf won't, or Joe Stalin, or Mao Tse-tung.'

He spat the chairman's name.

'That's why fifty-five million people died, Collins – cos we didn't blink.'

'And… that's why we experiment on monkeys, sir…'

Crawhammer rapped Collins's shoulder proudly.

'That's why we experiment on monkeys, son.'

McBride drained a bottle of whisky. His office was thick with tobacco smoke. He'd been drinking since they returned from the funeral. So had the Doctor. Most of the time they'd sat in silence.

'I didn't think you drank, Doc.'

'I don't,' said the Doctor. 'Not usually, but then this isn't a very usual day.'

'You're hitting that stuff pretty hard. If you're not used to it, you're in for a heck of a time.'

'It doesn't really affect me,' said the Doctor. 'My anatomy is some-what different from yours.'

'So why're you drinking it?' McBride asked.

The Doctor shrugged. 'Just being sociable, really,' he said, and slumped back into silence.

'There's… something you don't know, Doc,' McBride said after a while, 'but I think maybe you should. That James Dean guy… him 'n' Ace were kinda… having relations…'

The Doctor nodded slowly. 'She was sleeping with a man who doesn't exist. A ghost. The one thing I didn't check Ace's body for was Vasser Dust.'

'I just thought… I guess Ace'd have told you herself if she…'

His voice tailed off and he sniffed slightly.

'Thank you, Cody.'

McBride jumped to his feet.

'Damn it, why don't we do something, Doc?'

The Doctor looked sadly up at him.

'I should never have come here, Cody.'

'Yeah, you said already. But seeing as how you are here…'

'I closed the door on my own temporal trap.'

McBride hadn't understood this sober. Now, drunk, he thought he understood perfectly.

'So… you came here in your crazy blue box to stop Ace getting shot.'

'Yes.'

'So… why not get back in your blue box and go round again?'

'And dig myself in deeper. You can't constantly intercept time like that. There would be chaos. The time lines would collapse. No, my only course of action is to leave before I do any more damage.'

'Aw, c'mon, Doc… Sure, you're down on yourself now…'

'You don't understand. I really, really shouldn't be here at this time, in this reality. The more I interact with it, the more I tangle things up. The walls are already damaged.'

'But didn't you say Limb had a time machine too?'

'He did the last time we met.'

'So maybe it's him that's messed things up, not you.'

'Oh, I'm sure he's at least as guilty as I am, but that's not the point. Even by trying stop him – even by talking to you now – I'm contaminating this reality. I'm trapped by the paradox I created. Do I try to solve the problem and risk making it worse, or do I withdraw and try to minimise the damage? I don't know, Cody. The temporal variables are too imponderable. I'm too deeply entangled to see the way.'

'So Limb's just going to get away with it.'

'Haven't you heard anything?'

'And what about Rita? We still ain't heard a word! You just gonna walk away from her?'

'I'm sorry, Cody…'

The Doctor rose to his feet.

'Perhaps it's time I was on my way. I truly wish our reunion had been under better circumstances, my friend.'

'Yeah,' McBride grunted.

The Doctor smiled and shuffled towards the door.

'You know, Doc... wherever she is, I hope Ace ain't watchin' right now,' McBride said, loudly and levelly. 'Cos if anyone did to you what Limb did to her she'd hunt them down. You know she would! How can you just walk away like this and call yourself her friend? And without that, all this cosmos crap of yours means squat. You hear me?'

The Doctor stopped. He took a deep breath and turned.

'Alexander the Great,' he said.

'What?'

'Gordium... Little town in Asia... Tricky sort of knot thing on a plough. Along comes Alexander – '

' – and cuts it through with his sword,' McBride interjected. 'I remember that.'

'Exactly,' said the Doctor. 'I wonder if you're descended from him?'

'Uh, what did I do?' McBride felt lost as usual. The whisky didn't help.

'Cut through an insoluble problem. Reduced it to a human level. We'd better start work, Cody.'

'That's better, Doc!'

'Perhaps it is, Cody.' The Doctor smiled. 'Or perhaps I've just condemned the cosmos to oblivion.'

McBride grinned.

'Tough call, Doc.'

'Cody, remind me to have more chats with you about dimensional paradox. You have a very stimulating outlook. Now, I suggest we start with Rita. When did you last see her?'

'Miss... You can't stay in there forever, miss.'

Rita reclined back on the most comfortable bed she had ever slept in and ignored them. She could make them go away, she was sure, just by ignoring them, but she'd locked the door and pushed a wardrobe in front of it anyway.

At first things had been confusing, frightening. The speed of the traffic, the details. The money, for one. Her money had been refused everywhere. It had caused much amusement, and the likeness to Princess Elizabeth was impressive, but everyone doubted the King would be much pleased. People were friendlier than usual, which was nice. Everyone seemed to think she was a bit dim, and more than once she caught the word 'American' mouthed in voiceless sympathy.

She had spent the first night and the next as a guest of the Wongs, the elderly owners of The End of the World Chinese restaurant. They spoke barely a word of English, but had seen the state she was in and ushered her inside. They'd given her food and a bed, and some bitter black concoction that Mrs Wong insisted she drink.

She felt better the next day, and staying above a restaurant had its perks. She hung about the kitchens like a stray cat, being fed titbits. She discovered to her amusement that the Brits in the restaurant were being conned. Their food was cooked separately – or, at least, unboxed and sloshed in a wok for ten seconds. It was all fake. Pre-packed.

Mrs Wong insisted Rita eat the same food as the family and any Chinese diners.

After her second night with the Wongs it was time to go. She'd imposed enough, though they seemed distraught to see her leave. Mr Wong had given her a five pound note – or some shiny imitation of one. And there was the old King – looking even older, but still on his throne.

'You go to embassy,' were the Wongs' parting words of pidgin-English. 'Not good here. Go home.'

So home was where she'd gone – Putney – or almost.

She thought about McBride's office. What if she got to her flat and it wasn't there? She couldn't bear that. She decided to check out the paper instead.

Not far, on a normal road. This was a racetrack, as much by day as by night. She didn't know which was worse, hearing things whooshing past at night or seeing them by day. And not just the traffic – the pedestrians too.

It had to be the drugs the Commies had given her. She felt fine. The air was refreshing and clean – a slightly post-storm tang to it, Rita thought. But everything – even leaving aside the traffic – felt wrong…

She saw the sign above the door of a doctor's surgery, edged along the pavement and went in.

'Excuse me, I think I was given some drugs and I'm getting hallucinations,' she said to the receptionist. 'Like the traffic going really fast. And everything looks a bit funny…'

The receptionist and a colleague exchanged a sympathetic glance.

'You're… American, aren't you?'

'Yes, I am.'

'You're not… one of us.'

'Hey, I'm just a normal American and I think I'm going out of my mind! I want someone to help me!' Rita wailed.

A door opened and a man came out.

'Is everything all right?'

'She's American, doctor.'

'I see…'

The man leaned forward slightly and put a hand on Rita's shoulder.

'I'm afraid there's nothing we can do for you here,' he said loudly and slowly. 'You should go to your embassy. They can arrange your passage home.'

'Thanks for nothing,' Rita snapped, and stumbled back onto the street.

Her office shouldn't be far, if it was there at all. She decided a bus would be her best bet. She spotted a stop and waited. Almost immediately a red blur became a bus in front of her. She stepped forward and felt the sudden impact of ten or more people slamming into her as if fired from a cannon. She went down, under the bus, trampled.

Someone hauled her to her feet.

'Thanks,' she said. 'Goddamn rush hour.'

'Are you American?' he rescuer said.

'Yeah…' she said cautiously. She was beginning to sense a general lack of enthusiasm for her countrymen.

'D'you take Americans?' the man asked the driver.

The driver shook his head. 'More 'n my job's worth,' he said. 'Too dangerous. Look what just happened.'

'They shouldn't be over here,' someone else chipped in to murmurs of agreement.

'Get a taxi, love,' her knight errant advised. 'It's safer for you.'

Rita walked. She kept close to the walls, avoiding both vehicles and speed-walkers. Annoyingly, every few yards she'd come up against a pedestrian, just standing there, back to the wall, not moving.

Insane and rude.

She stopped outside the Rose and Crown – reassuringly, wonderfully, there. She stumbled inside.

The beer, unlike the money with which she paid for it, was definitely real. She gulped down her pint.

'Is Ted about?' she asked.

'Ted?'

'Ted Lovell, the landlord.'

'I'm the landlord, miss,' said the man behind the bar.

'You must know Ted. He was here before the first war. Bombed out in both wars – a Zeppelin raid in the first.'

'She's right about the Zeppelin,' an old voice croaked from the corner. 'I remember it. But she weren't hit in the last war.'

'Sure she was,' said Rita. 'I saw the photographs. It was a V2 raid, right at the end, '44 or '45.'

There was general chuckling around the bar.

'Where'd you learn your history, love?' chirped a girl with too much make-up on.

'What d'you mean?'

'War was over by '43, weren't it?'

'That's right,' one of the men confirmed. 'Paras stormed Berlin late '42. By '43 it was just mopping up in the East.'

'The Russians liberated Berlin in 1945.'

This caused uproar.

'The Russians!'

'American,' someone whispered to someone else.

'Hey, why's everyone got it in for the USA all of a sudden? What we ever do to you?'

'Tried to give us rock 'n' roll,' someone grunted. More laughter.

'And anyway, if the Yanks went who'd protect you from the Commies?'

'What's she talking about?' someone whispered.

'The Reds! The Russians!'

'What is it with you and the Russians?'

'What's she saying?'

A little cluster was forming around her.

'She doesn't like the Russians, Tom.'

'Goddamn it, who does? We hate them and they hate us! Where've you been for the last twelve years?'

'Obviously not watching the same news programmes as you, love.'

'Forget it,' said Rita. 'Gimme a sandwich.'

'Sorry, love. Got nothing for you. Don't get many of your lot in here.'

'What about those?' Rita queried, pointing to a rack of what looked like ham and cheese salad, drying slightly under glass.

''Fraid they're not for you.'

'Why not? They're for sale.'

152

The landlord – so called – smiled awkwardly. 'You serious?'

'Yeah…' How bad could they be?

'Leave it out, love. There's our food and your food, you know that. And we don't keep any of your food. Savvy?'

'More to be pitied, really,' some old bag opined from an alcove.

Rita left. It was all getting a bit surreal again.

She wasn't going to let it get to her. She was going to stick to her plan.

Another two racetrack crossings, and Rita turned into Furnish Alley – and there it was – the sign she'd prayed for. The *London Inquisitor*, shining above an open door.

Not the same sign they usually had, but what the hey…

She went in. Different decor. Smarter. A lot classier.

'Rita!'

A familiar voice. George Pryke, her editor.

He was wearing a pink cravat and beret.

She didn't care – she hurried forward, smiling.

'At last!' he said, and kissed the air about a foot from each of her cheeks. 'We were beginning to worry about you.'

'Sorry,' said Rita. 'You won't believe the week I've had.'

'Tell me about it, love. How's the dashing Hugo?'

'What?'

'Hugo – never mind. God, look at the state of you. Was it rough out there?'

'Rough's not the word.'

'Aah,' George 'the Spike' Pryke cooed. 'It's not fair. It's too hard on you. It'll drive you all away, those that are left.'

His eye caught the clock.

'God, is that the time? I've got to run, love. If I'm late again, it'll be no pudding from his nibs for a week. Uh, here's your bumf.'

'Bumf?'

'For the big do! You're with Murphy.'

George Pryke handed her a brown envelope, then kissed the air again and swept out. Rita could have sworn he left a lingering trail of perfume.

That was when it hit her. She was dreaming. The scraps of reality, the weird details… She'd never before dreamed so lucidly or so long – maybe she was still out under the Russian drugs.

Or was that part of the dream too?

Then she had another thought. If this was a dream, and she was aware of the fact, she could surely control it. Whatever was in the envelope – she could make it something good.

She tore it open.

A press pass – nice photo of her – some big three-day fashion do at the Savoy. Accommodation included.

'Miss... We're going to break down the door...'

Rita wished they'd go away. She heard a new voice – a woman's.

'What kind of a hotel do you call this?'

Harsh, American.

'I'm sorry, madam, but she... well, she had an authentic reservation and identification and she did look remarkably like you.'

'I can't believe I'm standing here having this conversation in a corridor outside a locked hotel room.'

There was a banging on the door.

'Get out here, you little bitch!'

Rita shuddered. There was something about the voice that went through her.

The man was talking peace – and quiet. 'If madam wouldn't mind,' he said. 'So as not to disturb the other guests.'

'Well, how the hell you gonna bust the door in without disturbing the guests?'

'Well, I had rather hoped to avoid actually having to, as it were...'

Rita tried to ignore them and get back to enjoying her dream.

She'd gotten away with it for a night, at least. She'd bathed for hours, clambered over the huge bed, ordered lavishly on room service, eaten, drunk... She cleaned out the mini-bar, ate until her belly hurt, and within minutes she was hungry again.

And weak. She hadn't felt full since leaving the Wongs.

OK, follow the logic of the dream...

She went out and got a Chinese. Once again she was asked if she was American. If anything it made the Chinese more attentive. She was made to sit with a huddle of Chinese, rather than with the rest of the diners.

'Why you no go home?' she was asked more than once.

'Why don't you go home?' she countered.

'You think we want to stay here?' came the reply. 'We stay because we can't go home.'

She'd returned to the room. They had a TV by the bed, a ridiculous amount of channels… She found one doing just movies – some old classics, which she loved, and some she'd obviously missed. Tomorrow she was supposed to start covering an event she'd never heard of in a place she'd never heard of, but tonight the dream was hers.

She tried to think hard about Alan Ladd.

And now some American harpy was at the door, baying for her blood.

Rita heard her stomp off, snarling about getting the police. What a bitch…

She supposed it was time to go. She rose from the bed, dressed (she'd had the hotel launder her clothes) and heaved the wardrobe back into its place.

'I'm coming out now,' she called, unlocking the door.

Two flunkies were ringing their hands in front of her.

'This is a most unfortunate instance – ' one began.

'Yeah, shove it,' Rita replied and marched proudly out.

Chapter Fifteen

'Dr Hopkins, thank you for agreeing to see me.'

'Always a pleasure, Edward. Have a seat and tell me how you are.'

Edward Drakefell took a deep breath. 'I did it.'

'You…'

'Confronted it, like you said. I went aboard the ship.'

'Well done, Edward.'

Drakefell shook his head slowly.

'It was remarkable. The Doctor – I told you about him – he explained a few of the principles to me, and it's terrifying.'

'I should love you to tell me.'

'Damage to the fabric of space/time. When we sent the rocket up…'

Drakefell paused. He was becoming agitated.

'There, there, Edward,' his psychiatrist said. 'Sit down, do. And pray don't alarm yourself. This Doctor sounds like something of a prankster to me. Damage to the fabric of space/time indeed! I fear we will have to concern ourselves more immediately with our Russian friends, don't you?'

Drakefell rummaged in his baggy briefcase.

'I wish the Doctor was here,' he complained. 'He could have explained it. I wish you could have met him.'

'You speak as if…'

'I don't think he made it off the ship.'

'Something happened to the ship?'

'I shouldn't tell you this, it's highly classified.'

'Come now, Edward.'

'The Russians attacked. Blew it up. Not a trace left.'

'Indeed?'

'You won't hear a thing about it on the news, of course. The place is in turmoil.'

'Blew it up. That is unfortunate.'

Drakefell fished again into his briefcase and pulled out a large, flat metallic box.

'I managed to save this. The Doctor seemed to think it was vitally important. Something about repairing the damage.'

'Did he, indeed?'

'I don't know what to do with it. I can't keep it. It reminds me of...'

'Yes, yes, don't worry. Leave it with me.'

'I know I should have given it to General Crawhammer, but...'

'Edward, I don't think you should even mention this. Least of all to the military.'

'But what should we do?'

'I must think about this. Leave it with me. I shall call you when I have mulled things over.'

'Thank you, Dr Hopkins. You've taken a weight off my mind.'

'That's my job, Edward. I'll see you to the door.'

George Limb watched as his patient scurried down the street, glancing anxiously around him. Poor man. He genuinely felt sorry for him. Drakefell had a fine mind, but his physicist's insight into the cosmic vastness filled him with more terror than wonder. Limb hoped his rather improvised psychiatry wasn't doing too much damage. He had become fond of Drakefell, he noted with a little surprise.

With his sleeve Limb wiped a smudge from the gold nameplate next to the door. Dr John Hopkins. Had to keep the place up for the old boy. As far as his Harley Street neighbours were concerned, he, George Limb, was just standing in for John Hopkins, who was spending six months mountaineering.

He smiled, knowing how dangerous the Alps could be.

He returned to his consulting room, picked up the telephone and dialled.

'Mr Dumont-Smith, please... Tell him it's George.'

He tapped his long fingers in a spider pattern on the desk until he heard Dumont-Smith's voice.

'Hello?'

'Miles? George. What happened?'

'What?'

'The ship, Miles. I told you to prepare a contingency plan to snatch the thing in the event that I couldn't gain access by other means. The next thing I hear, it's been blown to smithereens. What went wrong?'

'This need not concern you, George.'

'Why couldn't you wait? I'd practically won Drakefell over.'

'Regrettably, I don't take orders from you, George.'

'Well, I hope no damn fool *ordered* the ship to be blown up.'

Dumont-Smith paused.

'I don't believe it. Do those cretins in the Kremlin realise what they've destroyed? I handed you the most advanced piece of technology either of us has ever encountered... and you blow it up. Now I must insist that if I am to continue working with you, you take no more such steps without consulting me.'

'Where are you calling me from?'

George Limb licked his lips.

'A telephone kiosk. I have had to vacate the zoo rather hurriedly.'

'There is work for you to do. We believe that a component from the ship survived the attack. It must be found.'

'And destroyed, I suppose. You imbeciles! This isn't just another weapon. It is remarkable.'

'We are relying on you, George.'

'Well, naturally I will see what I can do. Describe the component.'

'It has a flat case of grey metal and eight rows of rectangular silver buttons.'

The old man glanced at Drakefell's unexpected gift and smiled.

'I can't promise you anything,' he lied, 'but I shall see what I can do, Miles.'

'Time is of the essence, George.'

'Yes, yes. Good day, Miles.'

'Wait. Where will you –'

But George Limb had hung up.

The door opened and Jimmy entered with a tray.

'I brung you some tea, George.'

'Thank you, Jimmy. Dear boy. Put it here.'

George Limb took a sip, and turned his attention to the curious grey box. Jimmy made a lovely cup of tea... On reflection, things hadn't turned out too badly.

'No one in, Doc.'

The Doctor was peering down at a small metal gizmo. It looked like a Geiger counter to McBride.

'Try a window.'

'What does that thing do, anyway?'

'It scans for minute traces of Vasser Dust.'

'And that's important?'

'Trans-dimensional contamination. Signs of reality-jumping.'

The Doctor fiddled with a knob.

'I hope it's working.'

McBride tested a window. The wood was quite rotten. It forced easily.

'OK, here goes, Doc...'

The Doctor was still tinkering with his new toy. McBride hauled himself painfully through the window. He hoped to God he didn't have to do any more fighting.

One of those cute old English places that his mother had collected pictures of. They'd always looked fake to him, but there you go...

The room smelt musty. In a vase on the far windowsill a bunch of wilted flowers sagged against a grey sky.

The Doctor scrambled through the window after him and landed on his rump on the floor.

'I was gonna open the door for you, Doc.'

'No, I like to do a little breaking and entering from time to time. Just to keep my hand in.'

'Looks like there's no one in, Doc. I'll check upstairs.'

'I'm getting a signal,' said the Doctor. He moved towards the kitchen. 'This way, no...'

He turned around.

'It's much stronger over here. I think it's a second signal...'

'What does that mean, Doc?'

'It means we should get out of here, Cody.' The Doctor's voice was low and deep with menace. 'Right away.'

There was a sudden screaming, tearing sound, which battered McBride's eardrums, and an icy, blasting wind. He spun around, reaching for his gun.

Something was cutting through the wall of the cottage. A great gash was ripping its way up the massive stone slabs, opening them up like you'd open a can of beans with a knife.

A pair of black claws was slashing at the breach, widening it, pulverising the stone like it was pumice. More claws appeared up the crack – dozens of claws, clattering against each other, jostling and snapping.

Not claws – mandibles. Two jointed black legs pushed through the crack and skittered against the stone.

It was those ants again. Dozens of them by the look of it.

'Doc...'

'Out of the kitchen window, I suggest.'

They darted into the kitchen. The window was tiny. McBride tugged at the door.

'Locked.'

He banged his fist against it.

'What now, Doc?'

There was a sickening pop from the living room as a single ant shot like a cork from a bottle into the room and landed with a thud. It was nearly a foot long.

Others followed, larger still, slashing at the stone wall with their jaws, widening the gap. Forget dozens – there were hundreds. Like before, they moved slowly. Unlike before, this was a full-on invasion.

'The window we came in by,' said the Doctor.

But how? The floor was already swarming with ants. McBride slammed the door in front of them as the first of the ants decided to explore in this direction.

The Doctor spun around and scanned the kitchen shelves. All sorts of herbs sat in jars.

'Doc?'

'Aha!'

The Doctor lifted down a big glass jar full of glistening white crystals, unscrewed the lid and sniffed.

'TNT?'

'Sugar.'

He opened the larder door.

'And honey. Oh, and a fresh jam roly-poly. Excellent! Arm yourself, Cody.'

'Have you lost your mind, Doc?'

The Doctor edged past McBride and up to the door. They could hear the clatter of chitin against the heavy oak.

'I used to play a decent game of cricket,' said the Doctor, hefting the sugar jar, 'back when I was younger... Now I want you to open the door carefully, just enough to give me a throwing line. And be prepared to slam it shut with all your strength if I yell.'

'OK.'

McBride inched the door open, his legs planted, his shoulder braced for any sudden impact. It came. The door slammed into him. A score of black legs thrashed about in the opening, whipping his legs.

The Doctor threw.

'Now!'

There was a sound of smashing glass from the living room. McBride hurled his weight against the door. So did the Doctor. It slammed into the legs of the ants, causing a sort of clicking shriek to rise from them.

'Again,' said the Doctor. 'Ease it open.'

The Doctor stepped back and picked up another missile. McBride took the weight with a groan. His ribs were ripped with pain.

The Doctor threw again and again. Cakes, jars, a bowl of over-ripe plums.

It was working. The ants were retreating from them, crashing and piling over one another to get to the feast.

The way to the window was clear.

'After you, Cody,' said the Doctor.

McBride sprinted across the room and almost dived through the window. As he picked himself up from the grass, his ribcage wishing it had never been born, the Doctor tumbled on top of him.

They got to their feet, breathless.

'What now?'

'We've got to keep them inside the house.'

'Oy! You two!'

The voice was accompanied by the irregular splutterings of a motor. A police constable was drawing up to them on a motorbike.

'I seen that! You're nicked, the pair of ya. Breakin' an' enterin'.'

'There's a perfectly simple explanation,' said the Doctor. 'We were searching for a friend, then a breach opened in the walls of reality and a swarm of giant ants came through. We're trying to work out what to do about it.'

'All right, Jack Benny, you can keep your comedy routine for the station. Come on.'

The Doctor tapped the glass of the open window, smiling sadly. The constable looked into the room. He turned pale.

'I'm afraid I'm telling the truth,' the Doctor said.

The constable swallowed hard, then turned on his heels and ran.

'I was rather hoping he might have helped us. Oh, well...'

'So how're we gonna keep those things in there? You saw how they ripped that wall apart.'

'There was a dimension breach in the space occupied by the wall. The ants only had to punch their way through a thin layer of stone. It would take them a very long time to get through the walls, or even those heavy doors. No – it's the windows I'm worried about.'

He closed their exit window and wedged it with a stone.

'Where are they coming from, Doc?'

'Another reality, Cody. A slightly larger one, it would seem.'

'Is it some kinda invasion?'

'No,' said the Doctor. 'It's just bad luck. This cottage is the bridge. The dimension walls are thin here. They've been worn away, like an old blanket. Holes are appearing.'

'And?'

'And it would appear that at the spot that corresponds to this in whatever reality is on the other side of the hole, there is an ant's nest.'

'An ant's nest. Shame we haven't got a giant kettle.'

'Watch out!'

Behind McBride a pane of glass shattered and a pair of black tentacles emerged. Legs sought for a purchase and a sectional black body bit and butted its way through the pane. McBride scrabbled for his gun, pushed it up against the black shell and pumped two rounds into it. There was a splattering of viscera, a shriek, and the thing tumbled back into the room.

More were advancing. McBride fired off another round.

'I ain't got bullets for all o' them, Doc,' he called. 'You better think of something.'

Footsteps hammered on the tarmac, approaching the battered blue police-box. Hands scrabbled at its faded doors, clawing for a purchase.

The door groaned and shuddered, but didn't give.

A pause. Heavy, ragged breathing.

Then a key was slid into the lock.

The door opened easily onto a pool of darkness. An arm swung inside, groping around, finally closing on the black bakelite telephone. The hand snatched it from its trestle.

'Tango One Two to Charlie Oscar…'

'Charlie Oscar receiving.'

'Five six eight Stevens here. I'm in Kennington. Fentiman Road. Requesting assistance. I think this is one for the army…'

'Nearly there…'

McBride pressed his face against the tiny, newly broken window and reached as far as he could into the room.

Behind him the Doctor revved the engine of the vanishing policeman's motorbike and stared hard at the door as if willing it to open.

'Nearly…'

He was working blind and trying not to think of the two-inch mandibles snapping and probing just a foot below his arm. He felt the rasping brush of a swaying antenna, its hairs like thorns – and his hand closed on the door-latch.

'Got it!'

He unlatched the door and stepped back.

'You'll have to force it open,' said the Doctor from his saddle. He revved the engine again.

He had a funny look in his eyes. McBride was afraid he might actually ride the thing into the seething mass.

McBride pushed against the door, fighting the resistance of the ants. They paused, disorientated by the daylight.

'Ace would have loved this,' said the Doctor in a voice that mingled sadness and anger, then, with surprising elegance, he swung himself from the bike's saddle, gunned the gas and let it fly forward, through the door and into the cottage.

''Ere! What you doin'?'

The police constable was pounding, breathless, towards them.

'Now please, Cody,' said the Doctor.

McBride aimed his pistol at the bike's gas tank and fired. The force of the blast slammed the door on them.

'Whew,' said McBride. 'What now?'

'We wait,' the Doctor muttered, scowling. 'Make sure none of them get out.'

'What... you... done to my bike?'

The policeman was struggling for air. He staggered to the window and peered inside at the burning wreck.

'We kinda had no choice,' said McBride.

'I had to go and phone for back-up,' the constable said in a small voice. 'The radio was out on my bike. I was gonna get it repaired tomorrow...'

The cottage caught quickly – wooden furniture, wooden staircase and then the thatch at the top.

The ants – there must have been thousands by now – were burning too, fighting, flailing, with nowhere to run. The thick walls held the ants and the flames and, though the windows blew out, the doors were holding.

McBride fired into the head of an ant that had reached the burning window-ledge. It jerked back into the flames. He'd used up all his bullets.

'Er, lads...!'

McBride sprinted around to the back of the house, where there were fewer and smaller windows.

An ant was squeezing itself through a space hardly bigger than itself.

With a grunt, Constable Stevens swung his truncheon into the creature's head. It landed with a crunch, but the ant kept coming.

Stevens was hitting it repeatedly now, McBride suspected working off his anger about the bike.

The Doctor had remained silent throughout, staring into the flames, whose light danced accusingly in his sad eyes. McBride sensed he was thinking about Ace.

He'd tried to strike up a conversation.

'Funny, I used to pour gasoline on ants when I was a kid back home. Miracle I didn't burn the block down. It just feels... a bit weird. I mean, I know they're just ants, but when they're that big it kinda feels like they're... you know... proper animals. Like... dogs or cats or something.'

'I've destroyed planets,' the Doctor whispered, still staring deep into the macabre bonfire.

The light was starting to fade, and the flaming cottage to glow against the dark. Somehow McBride was reminded of a film he'd seen. A Viking funeral. A flaming ship sailing over the horizon, bearing away a fallen hero.

More fitting than that shabby affair in East London in the rain. He sensed the Doctor was thinking something similar.

McBride swallowed and sniffed.

'See ya, kid,' he whispered.

'There's nothing coming out of there, believe you me!'

Stevens was scurrying around the blackened and billowing cottage towards them.

'You should have seen the things go up!'

He looked at his watch.

'Fire brigade should have been here by now,' he said. 'What'll we tell 'em? I mean, we can't exactly ask 'em *not* to fight the fire...'

There was a sound of approaching vehicles.

Not fire-engines, trucks. Army trucks. Two of them, and an American staff car.

Soldiers jumped from the trucks and raised their weapons. Others fanned out around them.

'Nobody move!' an officer shouted. 'Raise your hands!'

'Make up your mind,' muttered McBride.

The Doctor didn't move. He didn't even seem to hear. Slowly McBride lifted his hands over his head.

'It's all right, sir,' Stevens piped up. 'The situation's been brought under control.'

'Shut up!' the soldier barked.

The door of the staff car opened and a figure emerged. McBride recognised him – Hark, the smoothie surgeon who was so keen on cutting up his friends.

'Any of these, sir?'

Dr Hark smiled and pointed at the Doctor.

'Him.'

Immediately three soldiers closed around the Doctor. His arms were forced behind his back and locked in handcuffs. He struggled, but didn't say a word. Even when they produced a cloth bag, put it over his head and tightened it at the neck, he didn't make a sound.

McBride sprang forward, fists tightening, only to receive, out of nowhere, a blow that sent him reeling. A rifle-butt to the side of the head. Lights flashed, he staggered and fell, his head swam. Through the haze he could see the Doctor being led away to the staff car. He looked like a man trussed up for the gallows.

Chapter Sixteen

For most of the journey the Doctor said nothing, nor did his captor sitting next to him, nor the two soldiers sitting in the front.

Eventually his captor broke the silence.

'I'm sorry we had to be so rough with you. It's just… Doctor, isn't it?'

His disembodied voice sounded muffled inside the Doctor's sweaty, dark hood. He didn't reply.

'But we had to stop you running. You're very important to us.'

The voice paused. Though blind, the Doctor could feel the weight of his captor's gaze.

'You're a miracle. You are, quite literally, beyond my wildest dreams. I do hope you won't try to escape again. I look forward to talking to you far more than I look forward to the… surgical procedures I must carry out.'

'Just cut me open,' the Doctor said at last. 'I doubt I would have anything to say to you, and I know you have nothing to say to me.'

'Nearly there, sir,' said a voice from the front.

The staff car slowed.

'St Thomas's Hospital,' said the Doctor. 'You wasted your time with the hood.'

'Remarkable.'

'Not if you concentrate. Besides, I had a sneaking suspicion you were bringing me here. This is where all the top secret research is done, isn't it?'

The Doctor felt the hood being lifted from his head.

'How do you do,' his captor said. 'I am Dr William Hark. Please, call me Bill.'

The car drew inside the gates.

'Marvellous hospital,' said Hark.

'Obscenely used,' the Doctor spat.

He was escorted inside by the soldiers, and taken up several flights of stairs to a huge, empty ward, where his handcuffs were removed. The soldiers left.

'You have the freedom of this floor,' said Hark. 'The top floor.

I shouldn't try to escape, the windows are barred and there's a guard on each side of every door with orders to shoot if you try anything. Remember, we can still learn a lot from you dead.'

He left, and the Doctor slumped back onto one of the beds.

The anger he had felt earlier at Ace's fate was less acute now, the sadness greater. And the uncertainty. He felt the tangle of the time lines around him, leading him deeper into their appalling net. Was he making things better or worse? He looked around him. Worse, by the look of things.

'Doc?'

His head snapped around, and he smiled.

'Davey...'

Davey O'Brien, in a pair of striped pyjamas.

'You escaped the attack then. Good.'

'We all did, Doc. It was weird - no-one had anything but a few bruises. I spent a day in sick-bay, then they sent me here.'

He looked around and shuddered. 'Gives me the willies, this place.'

'Yes,' said the Doctor. 'I've been here before. Are we the only, uh, patients?'

'There's an old chappie in the next ward. They keep him sedated. I've never got two words that made sense out of him, poor sod.'

'Why did they bring you here?'

'Don't know. They keep doing tests on me - blood tests, word association tests, ink blots... I think it must be some kind of military nut-house. Maybe I cheesed my shrink off.'

'Yes,' said the Doctor slowly. 'Dr Hopkins, wasn't it? Would you describe him?'

O'Brien shrugged.

'Old feller, slight, thinning grey hair, very gentle voice. Funny, sort of, slow way of blinking...'

'George Limb,' said the Doctor. 'Everything leads to him, whatever it is he's up to.'

O'Brien raised the transistor radio he was carrying.

'I found this under one of the beds - the neatest thing.'

The Doctor frowned. Sony Walkman, circa 1980. It was Ace's. She must have dropped it when they were first here. Its radio crackled quietly in O'Brien's hand.

'What's been happening, Doc? No-one told me anything after the crash. I just heard they're accusing Khruschev of acts of sabotage - they're not saying exactly what, of course -'

The Doctor let out a sigh of exasperation.

'– and Khruschev's accusing us of cooking up warmongering propaganda.'

'And if I can't get anyone to listen to me, this planet is going to blunder into another global orgy of destruction!'

A male nurse passed through the ward.

'I need to talk to Dr Hark,' the Doctor muttered. 'Excuse me…'

'Yes?' The nurse smiled, but kept on walking.

'He'll be going to give the old boy his pills,' whispered O'Brien.

The Doctor trotted off after the nurse, past the guards into the next, identical, ward. Again, there was only one patient, in bed, propped half-upright on pillows.

'I need to see Dr Hark,' he said.

'The doctor will be doing his late rounds in an hour or so.'

'I don't have an hour or so.' The Doctor sounded petulant.

He watched as the nurse popped a pill into the old man's sagging mouth and tried to hold a cup of water to his lips.

'Come on,' the nurse said gently. 'I know they catch… There's a good chap…'

He closed the old man's mouth and strode out, smiling at the Doctor as he passed. Immediately the Doctor went up to the old man and, slipping his arms behind the man's back, flexed sharply with his fingers. The old man hiccupped and the pill popped up.

'Diazedrine,' muttered the Doctor. A powerful sedative. He popped it into his pocket.

'Uh,' the old man mumbled. 'Uh…'

The Doctor stared deep into the old man's eyes. They were half-lidded, vacant and unfocused. Only then did the Doctor recognize him. Chief Inspector Mullen.

He looked years older, thin and pale.

'Hello again, old friend,' the Doctor whispered sadly. 'I'm going to try and sort things out if I can.'

He didn't know how. The formerly doughty policeman looked too frail to move. An escape attempt with him was out of the question.

'Ah yes, you two are old friends, I take it.'

Hark was back.

'What have you done to him?' the Doctor snarled.

'Really, nothing,' Hark replied. 'He's just… given up. I think he wants to die.'

'Then why don't you release him?'

'He knows too much, Doctor. We treat him comfortably.'

'You're keeping him sedated and waiting for him to die!'

'Oh come, come. I find this all rather sanctimonious. If it wasn't for programmes like ours, you yourself wouldn't exist.'

'What exactly is it that you think I am?'

'You're a marvel of genetic engineering. Two hearts, a blood type that contains antibodies that I have never before seen… Who made you?'

'You're wrong,' said the Doctor. 'Nobody made me. I'm not an augmented human being – the conceit of it!'

'Then what?'

'I am an alien,' said the Doctor. 'I come from a planet called Gallifrey in the galaxy Kasterborous, 29,000 light years from here.'

He could see Hark weighing this up. Hark smiled slightly.

'A little green man from Mars…' His smile broadened. 'Yes, I suppose it would have to be a fairly bizarre cover story to explain your physiognomy. I'm sorry, but 29,000 light years? I know genetic manipulation is theoretically possible, but travel over that distance… I would like to believe you, really.'

He glanced at his watch.

'They will be around to feed you soon,' he said. 'Try to make yourself comfortable.'

'All right,' said the Doctor. 'I'll tell you what you want to hear. I was made out of slugs and snails and puppy dogs' tails in a laboratory underneath Moscow. I am the next generation of Russian spy, of Russian soldier. And the West doesn't have a prayer!'

Hard had sat back on one of the empty beds.

'Incredible…' he whispered.

'Impossible!' snapped the Doctor. 'Do you believe the Russians could build a living being like me?'

'We've… had access to one of your comrades. Him we understand – a man-machine hybrid. Tremendously sophisticated, but the sort of thing we've been working on ourselves. And I've been shown inside your rocket – remarkable.'

'Yes, and that wasn't built by the Russians either! Why won't anybody listen to me? The world is about to slip into a nuclear war over a complete misunderstanding!'

Hark continued to stare at him. He shook his head.

'All right,' said the Doctor, 'if you believe that I and the ship are constructs of Russian technology, then surely you must realise that you can't win any war against us. Peace is your only hope. You must take me to the authorities. Please!'

Hark smiled again.

'Not our only hope, I believe,' said Hark.

'What do you mean?'

'I believe General Crawhammer has a plan to stop you in your tracks. Then, given time, we'll catch up with you, believe me.'

'What plan?' spat the Doctor. 'The only thing that could stop –'

He looked hard at Hark.

'A nuclear first strike. That would be the only way...'

'Indeed,' said Hark. 'That would be my guess.'

The Doctor let out a long sigh.

'And you approve?'

'What I think makes no difference,' said Hark. 'Unless I can come up with a valid alternative... If you were to co-operate with me, think how many lives might be spared. But if not... who knows what might happen?'

'Are you a family man, Dr Hark?'

'Certainly am, Doctor. Wife and two beautiful daughters.' He fished a photo from his pocket. 'That was last summer in Broadstairs.'

'Lovely,' said the Doctor. 'Do you really want them to grow up in a nuclear desert? Assuming they aren't among the millions who are vaporised when the things fall? The Soviets will respond to any first strike, you know.'

Hark's face darkened. 'I lost my family in the Blitz, Doctor. All of them. My mother and father, two sisters and a brother. Grandparents too. I was away at medical school, studying to save lives, while they were being slaughtered.'

He sounded momentarily angry, then steely.

'I've got a new family now, Doctor, and no enemy's going to take them from me.'

He gazed deep into the Doctor's eyes.

'What are you?' he snarled. 'I'll get to the bottom of you, rest assured. Even if I have to cut out every organ in your body.'

He strode out. The Doctor turned his attention back to Mullen. He looked close to death. His blankets were raised on some sort of frame over the space where his legs ought to be.

He wouldn't be here if not for the Doctor's intervention at the bomb-site. Had not he and McBride blundered in there, dragging the walls of reality behind them...

Mullen's head lolled in the Doctor's direction. His eyes flickered slightly, his tongue moved slowly and uncertainly about his open, drooling mouth. He tried to formulate a word…

'Don't… Don't make me…' It was barely a whisper. 'Don't make me…'

His head slumped again and his eyes closed.

'Has he said anything to you?'

The Doctor hadn't heard O'Brien enter.

'You were right: he's heavily sedated. He's a friend of mine. His name is Joe Mullen.'

'Shee… I'm sorry, Doc.'

'So am I,' said the Doctor.

'They'll be in to feed him pretty soon. It's heartbreaking to watch. I'd come away if I were you.'

The Doctor followed O'Brien back into the other ward.

'How often does he have his pills?' asked the Doctor.

'Four times a day.'

'They must be very mild doses. Probably afraid he'll die, which is ironic – it's this place that's killing him.'

He lowered his voice.

I want you to do something for me, Davey.'

'Sure, Doc.'

'I want you to make sure he doesn't take his next medication. Just keep an eye on the nurse and be quick. A sharpish tap between the shoulder-blades should be enough if you're quick, or failing that a couple of fingers down his throat.'

O'Brien winced.

'If we're to get him out of here, he'll at least have to be awake.'

'What are you going to do?'

'Find a means of escape,' said the Doctor. 'First I must have a proper look round, try and formulate a plan. Come with me, you can be my tour guide.'

The Doctor peered out at the darkening sky, slyly testing the window's strength. The glass was reinforced with wire, the frames metal, sunk deep into the brickwork, and beyond the Doctor could see a grid of iron bars. He exited the ward, O'Brien at his heel, and looked down the broad stone staircase. A pair of guards on every landing.

He passed into a further ward, empty, guarded like the others.

There was no guard at the far end, and no door. The room ended in a painted metal hatchway. The Doctor touched it, then withdrew his hand.

'What's this?' he asked quietly.

'Furnace,' said O'Brien. 'Just a big old chimney – a chute down to a furnace. This part of the building's ancient. They don't care if you look – there's no escaping that way.'

The Doctor opened the hatch, peered in and coughed. It was hot in there and choked with rising, billowing clouds of smoke. A deep, dark pool of red glowed far below him.

Above him the shaft rose a good fifteen feet into darkness.

'It's too dark to see now,' said O'Brien, 'but there's a metal grille at the top.'

'Sssh!' the Doctor suddenly hissed. 'Listen.'

Dimly, over the muted roar of the furnace below, the Doctor could hear another sound, less even… Dull clanging thuds, like mallet blows somewhere overhead. And something else. A sort of howling, crying, almost animal in its despair.

'What is that? Stick your head in here.'

Instead O'Brien drew back from the hatch.

'Something wrong, Davey?'

O'Brien shook his head. 'I'm OK,' he said, but still ventured no nearer.

Behind them the guard was being relieved. The newcomer sipped at a steaming mug and called to them.

'You won't get out that way guys.'

The Doctor strolled over to the guard. 'No, I don't suppose we will.' He fixed the guard's eye, locked his gaze.

'But if I had to leave, you could help me, couldn't you?' the Doctor said, his voice imperceptibly slowing and deepening as he rummaged for his pocket watch.

The guard smiled. 'So you could go running back to Russia? Guess again, buster.'

The Doctor smiled thinly. This one at least wouldn't succumb to hypnotism. He guessed that none of the guards would.

He released the watch. His fingers brushed against something small. His smile broadened. In the darkness of his pocket he began to crush Mullen's sedative pill between his thumb and forefinger.

'How long have you been posted in London?' the Doctor asked.

'Long enough,' the guard replied.

'Where are you from originally?'

'Wisconsin, why?'

'Just making conversation,' said the Doctor. 'Good day – oops!'

His hand brushed against the side of the guard's coffee cup, causing it to splash. The Doctor steadied the cup.

'Clumsy of me,' he apologised. 'I'll leave you in peace.'

And with that he strode back across the landing to his own ward. He glanced back to see O'Brien following him and the guard watching, sipping at his coffee. He beamed back at him, and at the two stair-guards.

Back in the Doctor's empty ward he sat on his bed and fiddled with his shoelaces.

'What now?' O'Brien asked.

'We wait for the powder I slipped into his coffee to take effect. It's Inspector Mullen's medication. It might take up to an hour.'

O'Brien grinned.

'And what then?'

'I'm going up the chimney.'

'There's practically nothing to hold on to,' said O'Brien. 'And that fire down below. And I told you – the top is barred.'

'I'm not aiming to escape – not yet. Dr Hark told me that we were on the top floor. Judging by the height of the chimney, and by the noises I heard in there, he lied.'

'Just pipework clanging,' said O'Brien. 'That and the wind.'

He sensed O'Brien flinching.

'What is it, Davey?'

'Nothing.' He sounded stressed.

'Nothing?'

'What do you think makes those sounds, Doc?'

'A human being in pain,' said the Doctor.

'They go through me,' O'Brien whispered, shuddering again. 'It's like someone's walking on my grave.'

Rita was beginning to doubt her dream theory. It felt too real. It was too consistent.

So she must be mad. She didn't know what to do.

She decided to seek refuge in Regent's Park. Surely there would be fewer people there. She tried to keep to side-streets and alleys, away from the main, terrifying throng of racing people and cars. When she had to venture onto a main road she hugged the wall like grim death. Those infuriating pedestrians – the ones who insisted on just standing

motionless on the pavements, their backs pressed against the walls –
actually provided her with some shelter from the torrent of passers-by,
which never quite touched them. She found they generally moved
on after ten minutes or so, rejoining the throng and allowing her to
gain another few yards of wall before having to wait again. It was a
slow business, but safe.

She had made Bloomsbury Way before she heard the voice.

'Rita! Rita Hawks!'

She spun around. A woman of about her own age was standing
behind her, smiling broadly.

'It is you, isn't it? Stella Williams – don't you remember? We were in
college together.'

Rita remembered.

'Stella!'

She felt boundlessly glad to have run into this dimly remembered
acquaintance. She gave her a sudden hug.

'How've you been?'

'Oh, very well,' said Stella. 'Of course – who isn't nowadays? But what
about you? You've become a bit of a celebrity!'

'Me?'

'Top reporter for the *Daily Briefing*...'

'You read that?'

'Don't be modest – who doesn't?'

Rita shook her head. The *Briefing* was a low-circulation rag.

Stella was still smiling fondly.

'Rita Hawks...' she said again, then checked herself. 'Of course, it's
not Hawks any more, is it? Didn't I read you'd married a handsome
millionaire?'

'I did?'

'Well, if not a millionaire, he certainly wasn't poor. I suppose that
made it easier for you to stay over here.'

'Stella – what's going on?'

'What do you mean?'

'This place. I mean... We went to college together, yeah?'

'Of course.'

'Night school in Bromley. It closed when the war broke out.'

'Yes.'

'And since then?'

'Well, I'm married too... He's an accountant. We've two lovely
children. A boy and a girl – they're away at school.'

Rita shook her head impatiently. She didn't know what she was trying to say.

'And… what about me? Is this the first time we've met since then?'

'Definitely,' said Stella. 'I've seen you on television of course, and in the papers. I was so proud of you.'

'Stella… why is everyone so down on the Americans?'

Stella opened her eyes wide with horror.

'Oh, not you, darling,' she gushed. 'Everyone adores you! It's just… the others. Well, most of them… they just come across as so… backward. And not just in – you know – the obvious way.'

'But what about the Western alliance? The great transatlantic bond? Roosevelt and Churchill…'

Stella's face clouded. 'You really shouldn't mention that name, you know,' she said.

'Churchill?' Rita exclaimed. 'Why the hell not? He's a goddamn hero!'

'Rita, I really do think that's in poor taste. It's… been interesting seeing you again, but you really must excuse me.'

'Sure,' said Rita, still puzzled. What had she said?

She expected Stella to be swept up in the people-flow. Instead she smoothed down her dress, straightened her shoulders and placed her back against the brick wall.

Rita's eyes narrowed. There was a minute, electrical-sounding hum, and Stella twitched slightly. Rita peered at the wall behind her. In the tiny space between Stella's hair and the brickwork, Rita could just discern two needle-thin metal prongs extending from the wall.

She swallowed dryly and felt instantly sick. They looked for all the world like they were penetrating the back of Stella's skull.

Chapter Seventeen

Edward Drakefell hadn't left his Islington flat since his return from Harley Street. He hadn't left his front room, to be more accurate. He'd repeatedly tried to call Dr Hopkins, but had only got his rude American assistant. He hadn't eaten or washed or done anything except sit on the floor with the curtains closed and watch the television, listen to the World Service and comb and re-comb the pages of every national newspaper. The situation was deteriorating fast. Details of a Russian attack on a 'top secret Anglo-American research facility' (though nothing about the ship) had been released to the press. Parliament was in all-night session and there was mounting pressure on the prime minister to address the nation.

But it was worse than that. For years Drakefell had nurtured a suspicion – no, it wasn't much more than a vague feeling really – that some unseen hand was guiding the world towards a dark future.

He'd felt that ever since the dark days of the Blitz. They hadn't won the last war, they'd survived it. They'd clung on by their fingernails until the next time, and now that time had come. They'd lost their tenuous grip.

He recalled the Doctor's dire warning. Cosmic chaos. But to Drakefell it seemed only natural. He saw it every day in the nature of his work, in the results of experiments. He watched stars collapse. He recorded events so huge that all the warheads on the planet going off at the same time wouldn't even be a pinprick in comparison.

He had lived in fear all his life. He'd been drawn to it. Why else had he gone to work at the primate house?

The doorbell rang.

Drakefell ignored it. He'd been expecting a visit – he hadn't reported back to Winnerton Flats since the Russian attack. He turned the television and radio down and curled up in a ball in a corner of the room to wait for them to go away.

But they didn't.

He heard a sharp crack as the front door splintered. Two people, a man in his fifties and an elderly woman, both smartly dressed, walked towards him.

'Stop…' he stammered. 'That is, can I help you? Did the general send you?'

The man reached forward, grabbed his wrists and jerked him to his feet. Drakefell struggled, but he couldn't begin to break the man's grip.

The woman was shining some sort of a torch onto his hands. It didn't give out any light as such, but made the palms of his hands and his fingers glow with a silvery sheen.

'He's been in contact with it,' she said.

'Where is the dimensional stabiliser?' the man demanded.

'I don't know what you're talking about,' Drakefell pleaded.

The woman began opening cupboards, effortlessly upending furniture, tearing the carpet up.

'I can crush your hands,' said the man, increasing the pressure of his grip until Drakefell cried out. 'Where is it?'

'Harley Street!' Drakefell cried. 'With my psychiatrist!'

His assailants looked at each other.

'What number?' said the man.

'Fourteen!'

'Name?'

'Dr John Hopkins.'

'Describe him' the woman cut in.

'He's old,' whimpered Drakefell. 'In his eighties. Frail-looking. I don't know…'

'It seems our friend has been holding out on us,' the man said, suddenly releasing his grip.

Drakefell collapsed onto the carpet and was sick. Without another word the man and the woman left.

The guard was asleep.

'Keep an eye on him,' whispered the Doctor.

He had a screwdriver in his hand and was poking away at one of the barred metal headboards on the beds.

'What are you doing?' O'Brien whispered.

'I'm hoping to build myself a sort of ladder,' the Doctor replied, removing struts from the headboard and laying them quietly in a row on the bed.

'A ladder? How? Where?'

'Inside the chimney.'

When the Doctor had finished he gathered up the struts, crossed to the furnace-hatch and opened it. It was hotter now than before. The shaft was thicker with smoke, the subterranean glow brighter and fiercer.

The Doctor eased one of the struts into the brick cylinder and jammed it against the curving brickwork just below the level of the hatch, driving its ends into the old, soot-blackened mortar, wedging it in place. He placed another, higher and further around the wall.

He'd have to do the rest as he went. Gingerly he squeezed himself into the hole, arms first, head and shoulders, then, gripping at his makeshift rungs, he hauled his entire body through.

'Close the hatch, Davey,' he whispered, 'then wake the guard. Then make yourself scarce. Go and sleep in one of the other wards.'

'I don't like this,' the young captain replied. 'How'll you get out up there if the hatch is closed? Assuming there's a hatch up there at all... You'll be stuck in there.'

'I'll be fine. I shouldn't be long. Close the hatch.'

O'Brien did as he was told. The Doctor was locked in.

The strut he was standing on groaned and shifted slightly. Six floors below him the fire raged.

He jammed a third, higher strut into place, hauled himself up, then a fourth...

He was practically blind from the smoke. The heat billowed upward in painful waves. He tested his weight against another rung and began hauling himself up, only for it to twist from the wall in a shower of mortar, jerk from the Doctor's hand and fall clattering into the furnace six storeys below.

The Doctor was unbalanced. He felt his foot slipping on the metal bar. He slammed against the wall and tried to steady himself, his fingers taut in the brickwork's ungenerous cracks.

Slowly he continued his upward task, until, six struts up, his head drew level with another hatchway.

He barely saw it, so thick was the smoke. A human would be unconscious by now and fast approaching death. He didn't feel too well himself.

He probed at the crack around the door with his one remaining strut. He hoped for some small crack, some misalignment, some purchase that he could perhaps jemmy the door off.

The door fitted perfectly. His tool slipped at once from the narrowest of cracks, not once but continually, until finally it twisted and tore itself from his grasp and bounced and spun and fell into the furnace far below.

Now he really was stuck. And it was getting hotter, and even his adaptable lungs were starting to give out. The soles of his shoes were starting to melt.

He closed his eyes and tried to be still, to slow his breathing down, down…

As his own breath fell shallow and silent, he became aware of the other.

Beyond the hatch, in the room, a slow, steady sobbing.

The Doctor's eyes snapped open. The fumes must be making him slow. He banged on the hatch with his fist.

'Hello,' he called. 'Is anybody in there? I seem to have become stuck in the chimney. Can you let me out, please?'

The sobbing stopped.

'Hello,' the Doctor called again. 'I'm afraid I may suffocate if you don't let me out. I won't hurt you. I think I know who you are, and where you come from. I think we've met before, briefly.'

The Doctor waited, tense, listening. Suddenly there was a sort of groaning, whirring sound, followed by a series of heavy and irregular footsteps and the occasional clang of metal.

The hatch opened and a face peered in at him.

'Have we met before?'

'Yes, Captain O'Brien, we have.'

The Doctor was shocked at the face that confronted him. How unlike the Davey O'Brien he had just left. This one – his other-dimensional self – looked drawn, terrified, his eyes wide, red and rimless. He wore a tattered dressing-gown that was too big for his shrunken frame, and his hair was falling out in clumps.

He hadn't even been like this when the Doctor had last seen him – just after his ship had come down, that first day when he and Ace had materialised here.

O'Brien's hands closed about his shoulders and he felt himself being lifted to safety. They were in a smallish room with stone walls, no windows and a heavily reinforced door.

O'Brien seemed to find the task effortless. He paused for a moment, the Doctor held high, then set him down as smoothly as a machine.

The Doctor reached out a hand and drew back the sleeve of O'Brien's old dressing-gown.

Beneath the uppermost layer of skin, from the wrists upwards, the

Doctor could see an astonishing network of tiny wires ascending his emaciated arm.

O'Brien drew back.

'Is that all you came here for? To stare at the freak? Is this some sort of damned experiment again? Leave me alone!'

'Please excuse me,' said the Doctor. 'That is the most elegant bio-mechanical interface I think I have ever seen. May I ask, what is your primary motor force? Some form of micro-hydraulics?'

'You know,' said O'Brien, surprised. 'The others, they puzzle, they guess.'

'I'm not from these parts,' said the Doctor. 'Any more than you are.'

'They don't know how to feed me properly,' said O'Brien.

'I imagine you have some sort of biochemical/electrical storage system.'

O'Brien nodded. 'Two vents in the back of my skull. You can't just plug me into the damned mains!'

'Is that what they do?'

O'Brien nodded. 'My hydraulics are still working – they can convert and use raw electricity – but my flesh is wasting. Rotting on me!'

He drew his robe apart slightly at the neck. His torso was an even more elaborate filigree of intersecting wires. The effect might have been beautiful were it not for the great, hungry hollows in his flesh, and the patchwork of purple lesions and open sores that covered him.

'My body is dead but I remain alive, a prisoner of these savages!'

'Why can't you escape?' the Doctor asked. 'If your hydraulics are still working. I've felt your strength.'

O'Brien shook his gaunt head.

'You don't understand. When my ship crashed I damaged my legs. These... barbarians... tried to repair them.'

He let his robe fall to the floor.

The Doctor closed his eyes for a moment in shock and sympathy.

'This is what they did to me.'

From the waist down O'Brien was a mess of metal plates and boxes, rubber tubes snaking in and out of them, industrial pistons, bolts and rivets.

He took a clumsy step forward, hissing and clonking, holding the wall for support.

'The operations...' he whispered. 'So many of them. Sometimes the pain's so bad I howl like a bloody animal.'

'If I can, I will help you,' said the Doctor. 'But first you must tell me what you were doing when you crashed.'

'High atmosphere engineering work,' said O'Brien. 'We were building a bridge.'

'A bridge...'

'A trans-dimensional bridge. We'd never tried it before. They'd had some success with smaller relays, but this was something new.'

The Doctor was open-mouthed.

'You tried to force a permanent, stable breach between dimensions...'

'I'd opened the breach... everything was going smoothly, then there was an explosion from somewhere...'

'From the other side,' said the Doctor. 'This side. You were sucked through the breach.'

'I guessed that,' said O'Brien.

'But why?' said the Doctor. 'Aren't your people aware of the dangers of such an experiment?'

'The P.M. himself told us it was safe,' said O'Brien. 'Said it was vital to the security of the realm.'

The Doctor's face creased in thought. He barely heard O'Brien's voice – the other O'Brien – echoing ghostly from the furnace.

'Doc,' he called. 'You up there? You've been rumbled.'

The Doctor's head snapped round with a sudden, horrified realisation. Davey's voice was getting louder and less reverberant. He was climbing the shaft.

'Davey, don't –'

Too late. Davey O'Brien's soot-stained head appeared in the open hatchway. He started to haul himself through.

He hadn't yet noticed the third party in the room. He freed himself from the hatch and started dusting himself down, coughing.

'Neat ladder, Doc.'

'Davey –'

O'Brien had seen. He froze, staring into the face of his hideous *Doppelgänger*.

'So it's true,' he croaked. 'I knew, even from the sound of the voice in the stack.'

He let out a short, bitter laugh. 'Davey O'Brien, meet Davey O'Brien.'

'I know it's hard to take in,' said the Doctor gently. 'There are infinite numbers of us out there – of every one of us. All us, but all different, with different fates and fortunes. We just don't normally get to meet them.'

'What happened to him?' O'Brien whispered.

'Your people did this to me!' his alter ego spat. 'They're killing me with their ignorance and savagery!'

'Why did you come up here, Davey?' the Doctor suddenly asked.

'God, yes...' O'Brien struggled to reassemble his thoughts. 'They're on to you, Doc. They're searching the whole floor.'

The Doctor looked around the room. The door resembled that of a bank vault.

'So we're trapped,' he said.

'We should be safe up here for a while,' said O'Brien. 'I've left the hatch so it looks shut until you get right up to it. They won't think of the chimney just yet.'

There was a coughing scuffling in the shaft. The Doctor shot O'Brien a sceptical glance. O'Brien tensed himself, fists clenched.

A pair of feet appeared in the hatchway, swung and slipped and tried to find something solid. The rest of the man followed. O'Brien sprang forward, arms swinging.

'Wait!' the Doctor shouted, jumping forward. 'It's all right, I know him.'

'You sure?'

'His name's Cody McBride. He's here to help us.'

'Hey Doc,' said a very sooty McBride. 'How's –' He suddenly stopped, then – 'Jesus, what's that?'

'This,' said the Doctor, a little embarrassed, 'is Captain Davey O'Brien. And so is this. It's a long story.'

'No time, Doc,' said McBride. 'We gotta go. This is a breakout.'

'Which way?'

'The way I came in. The Santa Claus way.'

'Is there no other way?' the Doctor asked, looking at the half-human O'Brien. 'I'd like to take our friend here.'

'We can't go down,' said his human double. 'All the guards are out. Your friend started coming round off his medication. Attacked Hark. Snatched a scalpel from his own pocket and tried to kill him. Gutsy sod – I never realised they'd taken his legs.'

'What happened to him?' the Doctor asked.

'He's back under sedation. Hark guessed what you'd done and started looking for you.'

'Hang on,' McBride interrupted. 'Are you saying that Mullen's here?'

The Doctor nodded his head.

'Where?'

'One floor beneath us. He's very frail, I'm afraid. I don't think we can safely move him, and certainly not in these circumstances.'

'So you're saying we should leave him with these bastards?'

'For a short time, yes. I don't think the inspector is in any imminent danger. He's been no use to them since he got sick. They're just keeping him sedated and waiting for him to die.'

'We can't leave him, Doc...'

'Then what do you propose we do? Go down there and try to shoot our way out while someone pushes Mullen in a wheelchair?'

The Doctor laid a hand on McBride's filthy sleeve.

'We will come back, Cody.'

He turned his gaze to the young, dying pilot from another dimension.

'For both of you.'

A knotted rope hung down the shaft. O'Brien (the able-bodied one), McBride and the Doctor had little difficulty making the ascent. The first thing that the Doctor saw was a hulking figure silhouetted in the moonlight, a pair of bolt-cutters slung over one shoulder. The grille that had covered the top of the stack was now peeled back like the lid of a tin.

'Careful, the roof's slippery,' said McBride as the Doctor steadied himself.

'Here,' said the stranger, extending an arm to the Doctor. The moonlight caught his face, and the Doctor recognised him.

'Mr Dean, I believe,' he said dryly. 'A truly immortal actor.'

He swept aside the proffered arm.

'I can manage, thank you,' he said.

Then, 'Cody, what's going on?'

'Let's get off this roof first, Doc, then I'll explain everything, OK?'

One by one, using the knotted rope, they lowered themselves over the edge of the roof.

'Now just drop down onto that there fire escape,' said the late James Dean.

From there it was easy – down the steep metal stairs and landings to the ground.

A car was waiting there, its lights off, its engine running.

'Cody –'

'Doc...'

'All right.'

The Doctor squeezed into the back seat with McBride, O'Brien and James Dean.

The car roared away.

There was a woman at the wheel.

'Right, back to Harley Street,' she said. The Doctor recognised her voice – Drakefell's companion in the maze.

'You again. This is a surprise.'

'Oh, I love an adventure,' she beamed at him in her rear-view mirror. 'And I'll do anything for Uncle George!'

The sixth figure in the car, the front-seat passenger, a man in a worn-out tweed hat, craned his neck around.

'You can't imagine how much I have looked forward to this, Doctor,' he said, 'or how I have enjoyed our little game of cat and mouse.'

'Limb,' the Doctor snarled.

He looked accusingly from one to another of them, then fixed on McBride, who was staring into his lap.

'Cody?'

'Sorry, Doc,' McBride mumbled. 'The way he explained it to me it didn't seem like I had any choice.'

Chapter Eighteen

'Well?' demanded the Doctor. 'Grateful as I am to you, I feel I require an explanation. Cody?'

The car was bearing them swiftly and powerfully north through the darkness of London.

'Well, he got you out, didn't he?' McBride knew he sounded defensive. Guilty. 'After they took you and my head stopped spinning, I went back to the office. Those two were waiting for me – Limb and the girl. He offered to help me free you. What was I supposed to say? He came up with the plan, got hold of the building blueprints, he even thought of a greased magnet for unlatching those iron furnace doors from the inside.'

'But why? This is the question.'

'I think you should listen to him, Doc,' said McBride.

'Thank you, Mr McBride,' George Limb cut in. 'Please let me assure you of my good faith and noble purpose. I want your help to stop a nuclear war.'

They eventually stopped outside a big house in Islington, long since turned into flats. The Doctor marched up to the front door, flanked by Limb and Jimmy. The Doctor rang the bell and they waited.

'Are you sure this is the right address?' the Doctor snapped.

'I am certain,' said George Limb. 'Ring again.'

'Wait,' said the Doctor, pressing his hand against the front door. It swung inward on its hinges.

The Doctor strode into the darkness.

'Dr Drakefell,' he called, but got no answer.

There was a sobbing sound coming from behind a door. The Doctor opened it. Drakefell was lying on his side, curled up on the bathroom floor.

The Doctor immediately dropped into a squat beside him.

'Dr Drakefell, are you all right?'

Drakefell didn't seem to recognise him. His mouth moved but no words emerged.

'Edward, my dear chap…'

At the sound of Limb's voice Drakefell's face contorted into a snarl.

'You lied!' he suddenly shouted. 'They were here!'

'Who was here?' the Doctor demanded.

'The Russians! They wanted the device from the ship! He's betrayed us!' His voice tailed away to a whisper. 'I've betrayed us…'

'You managed to rescue the dimensional stabiliser. Good! Where is it?'

But Drakefell had lapsed back into silence. He could only stare at George Limb. The Doctor too turned towards the old man.

'The device is quite safe, Doctor. They won't find it. Though I daresay they will turn my lovely new home upside down.'

'Where is it?'

'All in good time, Doctor.'

'Why will no one listen to me?' the Doctor shouted. 'We have no time left!'

Rita awoke in Regent's Park from a nightmare dream of brain-drilling on the roofs of careering buses. She was cramped and shivering.

All thoughts of dreams, all thoughts of Communist plots had by now vanished from Rita's head. Seeing Stella… *plugged in* like that…

She'd seen *Invasion of the Body Snatchers* not long ago. She'd heard the Doctor and McBride mentioning aliens. That had to be it. Everybody'd been taken over.

Except the Americans and the Chinese… Maybe they had some natural immunity. She remembered at the end of the movie the Body Snatchers won.

She didn't know what to do. She wished she could find the Doctor and McBride.

She didn't know how long she'd walked for. It had been dark for hours when she'd fetched up here, more by luck than judgement.

She'd squeezed through a gap between the massive hedge and ornamental gate, dog tired, and gone to sleep in a bush.

The park was cold and damp, though quite beautiful in the milky light of dawn. She crawled around the dripping bush and stumbled over what she thought was a log, until it moved.

She screamed. The log became a bundle of rags, that made some attempt to assemble itself into a person.

'What you want?' the figure spat.

It was a tramp. An old man. The first she'd seen, Rita realized, since the world had gone mad.

'Easy, old feller,' she said. 'I'm not gonna hurt you.'

'American,' the tramp grunted.

'Uh, yeah,' said Rita. Boy, was she getting tired of this.

The old man smiled.

'Like to go to America,' he said sadly. 'Should've gone. Could've. A lot did. But I stayed. It's all mad now.'

Rita felt a wave of pity for the smelly old man.

'What happened to you, old-timer?' she asked gently.

'Wouldn't have the implants,' he muttered. 'Wouldn't have the bloody implants.'

He sank back to the ground, wriggled a bit and then went back to his slumbers.

It took Rita a moment to snap out of her reverie. Suddenly she too wanted to be back in the States. However backward these weird auto-people seemed to think her country, she wanted it more than anything.

She dusted herself down and set off across the park. It was promising to be a warm, bright day. She saw a young couple, arm in arm, strolling towards her. Strolling, not careering at her at breakneck speed. The sight filled her with a surge of relief and gladness.

Other people started to appear. Old people. Families. Almost all appeared, for once, to be living life at a normal pace. She heard a distant church-bell ringing. It must be Sunday.

She knew she had to start getting some answers, but for the moment all she wanted to do was bathe in this unexpected languid normality. She strolled across the park to the zoo and peered through the railings into the wolf cage.

'Howdy fellas,' she said. 'Long time no see.' She smiled, struck by a sudden thought. 'Hey,' she said, 'guess what. I can't get out of the park either. I'm just like you.'

And we're both a long way from home, she thought, turning away and striking out for the nearest bench.

They had remained at Edward Drakefell's flat just long enough for the Doctor to clean the grime of the escape from his body and climb into one of Edward Drakefell's suits. Cody McBride had baulked when he heard where he was going.

Now Jimmy was driving the Doctor and Limb straight into the heart of government.

'So tell me...' said the Doctor.

The pair were sitting in the back seat. George Limb raised an eyebrow.

'Well, it's rather difficult to know where to start.'

'Why did you go to all this trouble to lure me here? That's all Ace was, a lure.'

'Of course, but one I knew you couldn't resist.'

'But why?'

'I needed to smoke you out! I knew – or feared – that you were close. I'd seen Ace at the zoo, do you see? I must admit it gave me quite a shock. I have important business afoot at the moment – I couldn't afford to have you suddenly popping up over my shoulder, Doctor. I had to think on my feet. I told Jimmy to befriend her, which gave me a little time to think. I didn't resolve to kill her until the following day.'

'It wasn't necessary.'

'Well, perhaps not, but you see, I wasn't sure where you were. Or when, more to the point. I had to lay a trail, to be certain you would come. I had to send out a larger signal. One that would endure, one that you would surely come across at some point in your doubtless extraordinary travels.'

'Ace's death.'

'I fear so. It afforded me no pleasure, Doctor, please believe me. I was always fond of the young lady. She had great spirit.'

'You're unspeakable, Limb,' the Doctor hissed.

'Oh, Doctor, please be assured I intend to right the wrong I have done to your young friend. Just as soon as I get Betty back.'

'I beg your pardon?'

'Ah,' Limb smiled, 'the Cybermen's time machine.'

'Betty.'

'That's what I call her.'

'Infantile,' jeered the Doctor. 'It's just a mode of transport, and a dangerous one at that.'

'Well, I must admit I thought I was going to die the first time, when I made my escape from Jersey. It was rather like the Big Dipper... But I ended up, somewhat disappointingly, in London in 1954. A jump of a mere thirteen years. I dreamt of seeing mighty vessels charting a course to distant suns. Instead I got petrol rationing.'

'You were lucky to survive,' said the Doctor.

'You're too pessimistic, Doctor. Betty's fine once you get to know her. I poked around in her for a while, trying to work out what was what, then I took the plunge. She does have some frustrating limitations, though. I could never seem to get back any further than my point of departure in late 1940.'

'Correct,' said the Doctor.

'And she always insists on bringing me straight back here after every journey. To the point at which I first arrived.'

'When you were *poking around* you must have switched the lodecircuit on,' said the Doctor. 'It's possible it's been on ever since.'

'And, try as I might, I can't seem to get any further forward than 1962. And I've only managed to get that far once.'

'It's a banger! It's only capable of short hops, and then you were lucky.'

'But it was so frustrating, Doctor. 1962 is a tantalising time. The austerity of the war is finally lifting. Young people seem to be coming into their own. There's something quite tangible in the air. There's a very interesting young musical group performing in Liverpool…'

'I've met them,' said the Doctor dryly.

'You know Burt Swanley and the Debonnaires?' Limb sounded impressed.

'Er, no,' said the Doctor. 'Go on.'

'Well, we… had a lot of jolly outings, Betty and I. Time is such a wonderful playground, Doctor.'

The Doctor felt his muscles tense and his nostrils flare.

'What have you been doing?' he hissed.

'Experiencing history, Doctor. More than that! Changing history!'

The Doctor buried his head in his hands. 'You fool!'

'Oh, only in small ways at first. Like saving young Jimmy. A life ruined by success, then given a second chance. And betting.'

'Betting?'

'I needed an income, Doctor. And it's not really gambling when you've a time machine, is it?'

The Doctor scowled.

'I'm going to dismantle that time machine,' he growled.

'I'm afraid you will have to be patient, Doctor.'

'Why? Where is it?'

'Under some trees in the cemetery where poor Ace was laid to rest, two days in the future. You see, there was one more journey I had to make. Unfortunately a component had burned out on her a year or two ago.'

'The lode-circuit.'

'So it would appear. I was working at the zoo by now, and had copies of all the keys and codes to the primate research labs. I took the circuit to the workshop one night after the project people had gone home. I was trying to repair it when the whole research team – nearly thirty of them – burst in, drunk as lords. I was forced to make a surreptitious exit without the component. When I returned the place was a wreck and I couldn't find it anywhere.'

'Drakefell took it.'

'Yes, I confess I hadn't expected that. It took me a long time to get Drakefell to open up to me, and by then the blessed thing was destroyed. But in the meantime Betty seemed to be running normally, and I had to take the risk. I was resolved to carry out my plan.'

'To dig Ace up and plant clues on her body for me to find. You're obscene, Limb.'

'Oh, I intend to put it all right again,' said Limb. 'Just as soon as we, as it were, catch up with ourselves. You see, I returned from the graveside but the machine did not. It's still there, three days hence.'

'You can't just "put it all right", Mr Limb. It doesn't work like that. Ace is dead.'

'And yet isn't that exactly what you came here to do?'

'I was acting from selfish motives. I wanted to create the illusion that Ace was still alive. It was terribly wrong of me.'

'I'm not sure that I understand,' said Limb.

'Of course you don't understand! You don't understand any of this, and yet still you play these dangerous, dangerous games with time! You can't undo what you've done – ever! You can go back and stop yourself pulling the trigger, but you don't change what happened – you can only change your position with respect to what happened! Somewhere out there, though you can't see it from this perspective on reality, you will for ever more be shooting Ace in the head and dumping her corpse in the Thames! Somewhere out there the last thing she will see is you, pulling that trigger! It's unalterable!'

'I see...'

Limb rubbed his chin thoughtfully.

'Oh, but it's worse than that,' the Doctor snarled. 'Much, much worse! Infinitely worse!'

'Do tell me,' said Limb. 'I am keen to learn.'

'Every point in space/time has endless variations. It's an infinitely branching tree, filling the vortex. These are not mere potential realities, they are actualities. They exist. And more are created every time consciousness interacts with the physical world. An infinite rate of expansion. The vortex is packed, Mr Limb.'

'Fascinating…'

'The whole system is finely balanced. You and I have upset that balance.'

'Really? How?'

'When someone intercepts a specific time line with the intention of altering known events this creates whole new chains of actualities. The vortex becomes overfilled. The realities become too dense. The walls that separate them become worn. Damaged. Sometimes they can even break.'

'Oh, dear.'

'It's happening, Mr Limb. I've already experienced some localised effects. And if I can't stop it, the results could be cataclysmic.'

'I see,' said George Limb, with the hint of smile and a faraway look in his eyes. 'Fascinating.'

Cody McBride had been left behind in Islington, along with Davey O'Brien and Sarah Eyles, with instructions to take care of Drakefell. While Sarah tended to the patient and O'Brien snoozed, McBride bathed and reflected. It was always the same with George Limb – suddenly you were left not knowing whose side you were on – whose side anybody was on.

McBride's ribs burned while the rest of his body ached dully. He crawled out of the bath to find that Sarah had made up a bed for him on the settee. He was far too tired and far too sore to be gentlemanly – he crawled under the blankets and for a fitful hour tried to sleep, before getting up again.

'Tea?' offered Sarah.

'Uh, yeah,' said McBride.

'Edward's sleeping now,' she said. 'I think he was glad to see me. I work for him, you know.'

'So what's the set-up here?' McBride challenged. ''Cos it stinks to me.'

'What do you mean?' the girl queried.

'You and your Dutch uncle.'

'Sorry?'

'How much do you really know about him?'

'Uncle George? I've known him my whole life.'

'Yeah, but how much do you know about him? What's he told you about all this?'

'Perhaps you should ask him that.'

'I'm asking you. C'mon, I climbed down the goddamn chimney for you, didn't I?'

Sarah Eyles smiled.

'All right,' she said. 'Well, I suppose you'd call him a sort of secret agent. The government are worried about potential security leaks high up in weapons research, and Uncle George is keeping an eye on some people they're particularly worried about. Hence all the psychiatrist stuff.'

'And where do you fit into all this?'

'Well, I suppose you could say he recruited me.'

McBride sucked in his cheeks.

'Well, I tell you babe, *my* Uncle George used to tell me stories like that around Thanksgiving and I believed every one o' them. But then again, I was only eight.'

'Did *your* Uncle George bring Winston Churchill to your ninth birthday party?'

'Uh, not that I recall, no.'

'He always worked close to the government. During the war they sent him overseas.'

'Jersey?'

'Poland and Russia. He stayed behind Soviet lines after the Cold War started, but they uncovered him and he spent the next six years in a Russian prison camp.'

McBride snorted. 'He looks good for a Russian prisoner. In fact, he hardly looks a day older that when I ran across him during the war.' He laughed out loud. 'George Limb in a gulag? He'd be running the country inside of a year.'

'It's not funny. I thought he was dead. Killed in the Blitz. He just vanished, you see? Overseas.' She lowered her head. 'I lost both my parents a fortnight later.'

'I'm sorry,' said McBride.

'I had no family… then they let him out. The Russians. I'd never been so happy. That was nearly a year ago now.'

'Look… I gotta tell ya kid – it's tough, but… I know stuff about George Limb that'd make your hair stand on end. You know he killed a girl? He shot her in the face.'

Sarah Eyles scowled.

'That's wicked!' she said. 'I don't believe that for a second!'

She turned and marched out of the door.

'Try to get some sleep,' she said icily, not looking back.

The traffic was heavy for a Sunday morning. The day was fine and people clearly wanted to make the most of it. The Doctor couldn't blame them – they sensed there might not be many more of them.

He was slumped in the seat, propped up on his elbows, his chin sunk on his fists.

'I defeated you once, you know,' said Limb.

'Mmm?' the Doctor mumbled.

'I went back to London just after the Blitz ended, located the Cybermen in the sewers. By then, you see, I knew from Inspector Mullen and Mr McBride's heroic little protest that they were there. So it was easy to nip back a few years, dig them out and get on to my old friends in government.'

'Mr Churchill.'

'Oh, Winnie was a disappointment. But there were plenty of others who were prepared to listen. Our old friend Major Lazonby got his dream, albeit posthumously. We built our Cyberarmy. We overran Hitler's Europe within a year. I was a hero!'

'I'm surprised you left.'

'Wanderlust,' said Limb wistfully. 'And homesickness. You see, I'd remade the acquaintance of my dear goddaughter by then – I should say my goddaughter and my great-niece – and she is the joy of my life.'

'And Edward Drakefell's secretary.'

'Ah yes, Edward.'

Limb smiled again.

'You still haven't told me why you're doing all this,' said the Doctor, 'though I can guess. Trying to develop some form of Cyber-technology on primates, posing as a psychiatrist, weaving your nasty little spells around Dr Drakefell. And then there's your acquaintance with Mr Dumont-Smith.'

'Ah...'

'You've been up to your old tricks again, haven't you? Passing secrets, carrying tales, setting one side against another. Can you deny that this war you're so keen for me to avert is partly of your creation?'

'Of course I don't deny it,' Limb exclaimed. 'Doctor, I fully intended to start a nuclear war.'

Chapter Nineteen

'D'you think there'll be a war?'

Sarah Eyles had found Cody McBride walking in the overgrown garden behind Drakefell's flat.

'I dunno,' said McBride. 'Nah – not if I know the Doc.'

'I like your friend the Doctor,' said Sarah. 'He reminds me a lot of a younger Uncle George.'

'Believe me, they're nothing like each other,' said McBride.

'You don't know Uncle George,' said Sarah plaintively. 'He's a wonderful man. He's kind, clever...'

'Oh, he's clever all right,' said McBride. He was recalling their first meeting with George Limb, at his house in Belsize Park, back in '41. He'd certainly charmed Ace. And the Doctor. McBride had mistrusted the old man from the start.

'They've been giving instructions on the radio for what to do if there's a nuclear attack.'

'Duck and cover,' snorted McBride.

'Yes,' said Sarah hollowly.

McBride watched as she sniffed at an overgrown rose bush. It made a pretty picture.

'Why are you so set against Uncle George anyway?' she asked. 'Where did you hear he shot someone?'

McBride hesitated. What was the point?

'Ah, it's nothing, I guess,' he lied.

He saw a rose crumble as Sarah's lips brushed its petals. It was late in the year – the bush was already dying.

'All this...' Sarah said. 'It could all be gone in seconds. Us too...'

She shuddered.

'Nah,' said McBride, smiling grimly. 'Not if we duck and cover.'

They were stuck outside Trafalgar Square. A bus had broken down. Jimmy jammed his palm against the horn and swore. The Doctor rapped his fingers impatiently against the dashboard.

'I zipped about through time a lot,' said George Limb. 'Sometimes watching, sometimes meddling, I admit... You know, I feel quite responsible, knowing what I now know, Doctor. I was always so scrupulous, do you see? One would never leave one's litter strewn about the countryside after a jolly good ramble, would one? And yet you tell me that is precisely what I have done, haven't I?'

'Litter,' grunted the Doctor.

'Yes... You see, I always went back and put things right again. Stopped myself at the crucial moment, as it were... Quite intriguing, meeting one's other selves...'

'Overrated,' grunted the Doctor.

'But in my case, terribly illuminating.' Limb stared hard at the Doctor. 'How many beings in the cosmos, Doctor, get to witness in advance their own demise? Many, do you suppose?'

The Doctor straightened in his chair.

'I have seen it, Doctor. Many times. I stumbled upon it by accident at first. It shocked me.'

'Why?' asked the Doctor. 'We all die.'

'Not like this.' George Limb shuddered. 'Time has an alarming sense of caprice, do you not think?'

'Undoubtedly.'

'In the end,' said Limb, 'it seems I am destined to pay for my past meddling in a most appropriate way. I helped open the bottle and – as it were – let out the Cyber genie. And it would seem that I myself am destined to become a victim of the Cyber process.'

'As you say, appropriate,' said the Doctor.'

'Naturally, I used my runabout to try and alter things. It never worked. Whatever I did, however I interfered with the pattern of events, the end result was always broadly the same.' He shuddered again. 'I say broadly, Doctor... I have seen some truly hideous manifestations of the Cyber process.'

He was agitated. His breathing sounded fast and irregular.

'Nothing I did worked,' he said. 'In the end it was always... those machines. So I intervened more heavy-handedly, but still I couldn't change a thing. I began to realise that it would take an event of cataclysmic proportions to do so.'

'A nuclear war.'

'Precisely.'

'You know, it's one of time's great ironies,' said the Doctor, 'however we reckless time-travellers might succeed in altering the world around us, we can never alter our own destiny. You might by your interference win an incalculable fortune – but if you are destined to live out your life in poverty, that – somehow – is what will happen. You're at the eye of the storm, Mr Limb. When all is in chaos around you, you are untouched.'

'Oh dear,' said Limb. 'And I'd gone to so much effort.'

'I can see that,' snapped the Doctor. 'You've woven your usual tangled web. Tell me, how did you ensnare Edward Drakefell?'

'Oh, Edward,' said George Limb, with what sounded like fondness in his voice. 'Well, you see, having decided that time-hopping wasn't going to solve my dilemma, I set about finding out just how far Cyber research in this reality was progressing. Mr McBride and your police inspector friend helped, with their little publicity splash. Apart from that I had to work entirely from media sources. All my old contacts were gone, do you see? They were all either dead or in prison or too old to remember their own names. News reports on television and radio, the newspapers… they were all I had. Luckily I was used to reading between the lines of government announcements, official denials and so forth – I used to write the blessed things… Do you know, it's what they don't say that is often most revealing? Well, in any event I finally located the focus of the research, at London Zoo. They were experimenting on primates. I got a job as a lowly assistant keeper in the reptile house – little more than a sweeper-up, really. I swept and I observed. It was there that I first noticed Dr Drakefell, though I'm glad to say he failed to notice me. He seemed… interesting to me. Nervy… Brilliant, but curiously unsure of himself. I had no particular use for him at the time, of course…'

George Limb yawned.

'Do forgive me, Doctor. It has been a long day.'

'Go on,' said the Doctor sharply.

'Very well… The research programme began very shakily, and I must admit I did my utmost at first to ensure it remained that way. The whole area was off-limits to us keepers, but remarkably none of the locks had been changed. Gaining entry was easy, though to my disappointment there was precious little to see. They made very poor progress until I began surreptitiously nudging them in the right direction. I would sneak in at night and alter figures in their computing engine.'

'Accelerate allied military capability to a point where the Soviet Union became so alarmed –'

'– that they would respond with all means at their disposal,' Limb interrupted. 'That was my plan, yes. Although, curiously, the Russians already knew something was afoot. It was they who contacted me. Heaven knows how they found me.'

'I assume you're referring to Miles Dumont-Smith,' said the Doctor.

'Yes. A man of little insight or competence,' said Limb. 'Just a party apparatchik beneath his expensive suit.'

'You're wrong,' said the Doctor.

'Really?'

'Later,' snapped the Doctor. 'Carry on.'

Limb paused for a moment, registering his polite overlooking of the Doctor's brusqueness, then continued.

'By this time Drakefell had left the augmentation project, and I must admit I had rather dismissed him from my mind. The Americans were starting to take a serious interest in the project – particularly in the field of Cyber optics.'

'Oh yes, the spy satellite.'

'Indeed. They started to move people and equipment to Winnerton Flats. I observed from a distance, and was delighted to see that Dr Drakefell was appointed director. It was at this time that I began to cultivate his acquaintance. Ironic – I had no notion that he had Betty's lode-circuit.

'Drakefell seemed… focused, one might say. Obsessive, even. A man driven by his work. They launched the rocket…'

'And it apparently crashed.'

'Yes,' said Limb. 'Or so everyone claimed. But by then I knew Drakefell well enough to see that he was covering something up. The old nervousness returned. He clearly was no better at handling pressure here than he had been at the zoo.'

'So in order to draw the truth out of him, you set yourself up as his psychiatrist.'

'Oh, I did more than that, Doctor. I pushed him to the point of nervous collapse. I increased the pressure on him. I gave Miss Hawks a tip-off – anonymously of course – that the official statements about the rocket launch were untrue. I set her upon her investigation. I even recommended that she hire a private eye.'

'Cody McBride.'

'I couldn't resist it, Doctor.'

'But it did you no good, did it? The ship was still destroyed before you could get your grubby little fingers on it.'

'It took me a long time to get the truth out of Drakefell. He was terrified. I persuaded him to take my dear Sarah on as his personal assistant – she was an immense help to me, but still I was unable to penetrate the ship.'

'It was you listening in the maze at Winnerton Flats, wasn't it?'

'Ah, the maze!' Limb smiled. 'Delightful, our little chase. You know, I devised a very similar sort of game when I was a lad. I used to go to Hampton Court a lot.' He chortled. 'I would get my chums terribly lost. I can't have played that game in seventy years, Doctor.'

Rita basked and dozed until the sun warmed the day. She watched some toddlers play – they looked just like normal tots, stumbling, crying, laughing. She saw a young couple practically making out on the grass, and raised her eyes. You didn't see that in public every day.

An elderly couple sat alongside her and spread a white handkerchief on the bench between them. The woman reached into a bag and pulled out and unwrapped a packet of sandwiches. Some cake followed, wrapped in greaseproof paper, and a Thermos flask.

She sidled closer, a vague plan forming in her mind.

'Good morning,' she said. 'They look nice.'

'Good morning,' each of them replied. Then, from the woman, 'Elevenses. Would you like one, dear?'

'Oh, my dear,' the old man interjected, ' I don't think the young lady… That is… Forgive me for asking my dear, but you're not… American, are you?'

Rita smiled.

'Heck no,' she said. 'I, uh, spent a lot of time out there. Studying them. Funny little folk.'

'Oh, please forgive me,' said the old man. 'Would you like a sandwich?'

'Thanks,' said Rita, taking one and biting into it. Cucumber.

Sort of. It was just like the food at the hotel.

'Funny,' she said. 'Food never really fills you up, does it?'

The old man looked at her in surprise.

'Well, of course not,' the old man said. 'We vent everything we need.'

She'd half-suspected as much. Stella had been… filling up, just like at a gas station.

'Personally I wonder why we even bother,' the old man continued.

'No, you don't,' the old woman chided. 'You love our picnics.'

She turned to Rita.

'Well, I could never give up eating,' she said. 'I would miss it terribly. But I agree – it's not quite the same any more…'

'How long has it been now?' asked Rita.

'Well, we weren't done until '53,' the old woman said. 'We didn't fancy it.'

The old man looked embarrassed.

'*She* didn't fancy it,' he corrected. 'Half of Europe was done before I could persuade her.'

'Well…' said the old woman. 'I just… didn't fancy the idea, at my age.'

'Bet you're glad you did, though,' said her husband. 'Can you imagine what it must be like out there for monkeys?'

'Stan,' the old woman scolded. 'You shouldn't call them that.'

'Her sister,' Stan confided. 'Her and her husband. His fault – always a crank. Big Churchill man.'

'Stan, he was not!'

'Wouldn't have it done. Went to America. Maybe you met them when you were out there.'

He harrumphed a short laugh.

'He's just showing off,' the woman said. 'Are you going home to watch the speech, dear?'

Rita hesitated. Careful…

'I'm not sure yet,' she said.

'We're going to Trafalgar Square. Come with us if you like.'

'Sure,' said Rita. 'I fancy a stroll.'

Trafalgar Square seemed unusually crowded with people. Jimmy honked and struggled to navigate the car between the crowds and out into Whitehall. Crawhammer hadn't been very hard to trace – he was almost a celebrity in these dark hours.

'What made you change your mind?' asked the Doctor?

'I'm sorry…?' Limb queried.

'About starting a war.'

'Oh, I sensed larger events in the wind, Doctor. Alien technology… the fact that you had appeared… it gave me grounds to hope that there might be another way to avoid my fate. I don't relish the prospect of nuclear war, you know.'

'I wish I knew what was going on,' said the Doctor. 'I don't suppose there's a radio in here.'

'A wireless… no.'

'No…' said the Doctor, then slapped himself on the forehead. 'Or rather yes, there is.'

He lifted Ace's Walkman from his pocket and, ostentatiously keeping it out of Limb's view, put the headphones on and fiddled with the dial. A sombre, resolute voice emerged from the static.

'We interrupt this programme with a live newsflash.'

It was odd. Stan and Elsie seemed just like any other English pensioners, but Rita had seen through Stan's thinning pate the two tiny metal-lined holes that sank like fang-marks into the back of his skull.

'So you looking forward to the speech?' Rita asked, fishing again.

'Of course,' Elsie replied. 'Aren't you?'

'Must be something important,' said Stan. 'Middle of a Sunday.'

They reached Trafalgar Square without incident. Everyone seemed relaxed and friendly. No one was in a hurry. 'All Things Bright and Beautiful' wafted through the doors of St Martin-in-the-Fields.

As distant Big Ben sounded eleven o'clock, the church fell silent and the congregation flooded out and down the great stone steps of the church. There was suddenly frenzied movement all around Rita – people poured into the square from all sides. She felt the crowd pushing her away from her elderly friends, sweeping her into the square. She stumbled and went down next to one of the lions, and cowered against its massive stone plinth.

A voice boomed out across the square, somewhere over Rita's head.

'We now take you live to the Ministry of Augmentation, where the prime minister is about to speak. The prime minister.'

Instantly the hubbub in the square was stilled. Everyone stood motionless and silent, facing towards the source of the voice.

Another voice took over, sage and old, powerful and reassuring.

'Citizens of the British Empire...'

'How much longer do we have to stay here?' McBride demanded, slouching into Drakefell's lounge. 'The screwball's still asleep. I gave him a coupla sleeping pills –'

'Sssshl' hissed Sarah Eyles. She was staring at the TV. 'It's the prime minister.'

' *– government and I, in close concert with our American allies, yesterday demanded of the Soviet government in Moscow certain explanations, undertakings and assurances with regard to the recent escalation of aggression towards this country, beginning with the shooting down of our Waverider rocket and culminating in the* *recent attack by Russian forces on British soil. It is now my duty to tell you that Mr Khrushchev's government has responded by issuing a blanket denial of any wrongdoing and by accusing Her Majesty's government of fabricating the incidents.'*

'Old Macmillan's shovelling it on,' said McBride, perching on the settee next to Sarah.

'We're too late, aren't we?' she suddenly said. 'The Doctor and Uncle George – they never made it.'

McBride felt Sarah grab his arm and draw him close to her. He put an arm round her and held her tight.

'Another war,' she whispered. 'I lost everyone in the last one. Everyone except Uncle George...'

McBride held her tighter. He didn't know what to say.

' *– a threat to our freedom and our way of life, indeed to our very survival, but one that we can and shall overcome.'*

Rita struggled to her feet. She recognised the voice – but she was sure it wasn't Harold Macmillan. She gasped – for the first time she noticed the huge glass screen that covered the front of Admiralty Arch. It was the biggest TV set Rita had ever seen. The face of the speaker filled the screen. It *wasn't* Harold Macmillan. It was the man from the cottage – the man who had appeared to interrogate her.

'It is a threat we have prepared for over many years, and a threat we are more than ready to deal with. BEHOLD MY WORKS, YE MIGHTY, AND TREMBLE!'

There was a whooshing in the air all around Rita. She covered her ears and craned her neck skyward. Planes – weird-looking craft – were flying in from all sides. Something was happening overhead. A cracking, booming sound, like the sky tearing open...

A great gash of light pouring into the sky from... somewhere else.

Rita could see, dotted around the giant gash, machines of some kind. They must be huge...

The ships, the planes, were flying into the light in their dozens, being swallowed whole and endlessly.

'It seems we are too late, Mr Limb,' the Doctor said. 'Even now –'

He was interrupted by a sound. An explosion – a boom that shook the car and cracked the windows.

'Holy sweet Mother of God...' whispered Jimmy. 'What is *that*?'

The sky was a rip of white light, almost from end to end, through which flying craft by the dozen were pouring. Some fanned out and jetted away in different directions. Others swooped low over the streets. Explosive projectiles raked over the heads of pedestrians, who began to panic and run, trampling each other, fighting.

And then, from the ships, came men, descending as if on invisible parachutes, soldiers, black- and khaki-clad, heavily armed with weapons of lethal sophistication. Just like at the hangar, but on an immeasurably greater scale.

One landed on the road in front of them. Jimmy fumbled beneath the dashboard and pulled out a pistol.

The Doctor laid a restraining finger on the boy's shoulder. The soldier spun round in a lightning blur, his rifle pointed directly at them.

'I suggest we raise our hands,' the Doctor said.

'Never to a Russian!' spat Jimmy.

'Look at the markings on his sleeve, young man,' said the Doctor testily.

'What?'

'Three feathers,' cut in George Limb, puzzled. 'The Welsh Guards.'

'Nobody would listen to me,' wailed the Doctor. 'Everybody was so convinced it had to be the Russians. The Russians are about the only innocent parties in all this. They know next to nothing about what's going on.' You've been passing secrets to a far more formidable foe, Mr Limb. Now you have crossed them, and I suspect have caused them to bring forward their invasion plans.'

'Who, Doctor?' said Limb urgently.

'The British, Mr Limb. The British.'

PART FOUR

Chapter Twenty

'Citizens of London, brave and loyal soldiers, lay down your arms! We do not come to wage war upon you, but rather to save you from war. You stand upon the brink of nuclear Armageddon, brought about by nothing other than your own fear of shadows.

'We are not Russians and we are not Communists. We are British. We are your brothers, and we come in friendship.

'Allow me to introduce myself. My name is George Limb, and it is my honour and privilege to serve as prime minister of the United Kingdom of Great Britain and Ireland and of His Majesty's colonies and dominions overseas. The Britain that I serve is not this one, but another, existing invisibly alongside this one. It is a Britain that has conquered disease, conquered poverty and achieved lasting, secure peace. These are the gifts we bring to you. I say again, lay down your arms. We bring only peace!'

Half a dozen black-and-white screens went blank, fading to static. The Doctor, Limb and Jimmy had abandoned their car and were huddled in front of a small television and radio shop off Trafalgar Square. The soldier had lost interest once Jimmy had fumbled the gun, and they had bolted from the car.

All around the Doctor could hear car horns and gunfire, the screams of hundreds of people. The sky was lit by the flickering from the energy tear, and troops dropped like black snowflakes onto the streets of London.

He stared carefully at the lined face of George Limb. For a man who had just learned that the people he was working for were from an alternative reality and who had just been confronted with an alternative version of himself *from* that reality, he was remarkably calm.

Limb blinked slowly. That long, languid blink that made him seem almost reptile-like. The Doctor shivered. He could almost see the man's mind at work, plotting, scheming, taking in everything that was playing out before him and analysing it, working out how best to use it to his advantage. He turned away from the flickering television sets and smiled at the Doctor.

'Ah, well, at least I was outwitted by someone whose intellect I respect. My... other self seems to have done remarkably well for himself...'

The Doctor felt a wave of anger.

'Whereas you appear to have made a monumental mistake.'

Limb frowned. 'Oh, come now, Doctor, I think that you are being a little unfair. I will admit that I was unprepared for the fact that my Russian friends were in fact nothing of the sort, but the overall effect isn't spoiled by that fact. No, this adds a certain... balance to the proceedings. Yes...' Limb pursed his lips and nodded. 'Yes, I have to say that I find this development quite... amusing...'

'Amusing?'

The Doctor grasped Limb by the arm of his jacket and spun him roughly to face the shattered street.

'Look around and tell me what you see is amusing!'

People were running blindly, unable and unwilling to comprehend what they were seeing. The huge flickering tear in the sky cast long dancing shadows across the streets, a noise like a giant crisp bag being rustled echoing across the rooftops. Vast needle-pointed aircraft hung like barrage balloons over the city, searchlights blazing down, lighting up the rain and sweeping across the terrified crowds. Small triple-winged fighters swooped though the searchlight beams, droning like bees. The sky was thick with parachutes, wave after wave of troops landing on the streets of London.

The Doctor turned on Limb his eyes blazing.

'These people have been through a war already, seen their city destroyed, struggled and sacrificed to get their lives back to some semblance of normality. They should be shopping for Christmas presents, spending time with their loved ones, not running for their lives again. No one can possibly benefit from this!'

'So where do you propose we go now?'

'South,' said the Doctor.

'On foot?' Limb asked.

The traffic was at a standstill, abandoned by terrified drivers and passengers.

'Unless you have any better suggestions.'

'Well, we could always take the Underground.'

* * *

General Crawhammer gripped the pearl handle of his Smith and Wesson automatic and pumped round after round into the line of men advancing along Lambeth Palace Road.

Major Bill Collins shook his head in disbelief. The general actually seemed to be enjoying himself. When the tear had opened up in the sky the general had been as awestruck as the rest of them, but as soon as the first troops had appeared, as soon as he had had the first glimpse of an enemy that needed fighting, he had been nothing short of magnificent. He'd rallied the few troops in the Ministry of Defence building and tried desperately to round up more support. No telephone or radio set was working.

'Goddamn Reds jamming 'em!'

He'd dismissed the bizarre claims they'd heard on the radio out of hand.

'Commie propaganda, Collins! They're tryin' to confuse us.'

Collins had led a small reconnaissance group onto the roof. The skies across London were full of descending paratroops. Ships hung in dark clusters like storm clouds. They had all the city's barracks pinned down.

'Why don't the Limeys fight back?' Crawhammer had growled. 'We're no use here. Collins, get the chopper fired up.'

And so had followed the most terrifying ride of Bill Collins's life. The pair and their pilot had taken off from Horseguards' Parade, keeping below the roof-line, skimming the tops of snarled-up, stationary, mostly abandoned cars. Most of the drivers were simply running.

'You ever fly down the Grand Canyon, Collins?'

'Yes, sir. But we weren't being shot at.'

Miraculously, they'd made the hospital in one piece, actually flying underneath Westminster Bridge to keep out of sight of a sleek grey wedge of a ship that hovered silently nearby.

'I need men I can rely on,' Crawhammer had insisted. 'My boys.'

Besides, there was an armoury in the hospital basement.

The men were way ahead of them and they'd landed to a volley of heavy machine-gun fire. Just in time. A group of heavily armed enemy soldiers had launched a fast and furious attack on the main hospital gates.

The general was standing on one of the brick gateposts now, firing his revolver at the retreating foe and letting out the occasional whoop. They were driving them back.

The thunder of their gunfire subsided as the invaders sought cover.
'Well done, General.'

Collins and Crawhammer spun around at the same time. The Doctor
was standing behind them. 'But I'm afraid it won't hold them off for
long.'

'OK mister, what'll Ivan do next?'

'Didn't you hear the broadcast, General? They're not Russian.'

'Commie propaganda. Lessen the culture shock.'

The Doctor sighed. 'Why won't you trust me, General? I'm the only
person here who knows what is going on, and I'm offering to share
that knowledge with you. Free, gratis and without your having to stick
probes into me or cut bits out of me.'

Crawhammer stuck a half-smoked cigar butt between his jaws and
chewed slowly on it, scowling at the Doctor.

'OK,' he said. 'Shoot.'

There wasn't time. There was a squeal of brakes and a huge white
van tore down the road towards the gates. Crawhammer's pocket
army spun, machine-guns raised. The Doctor threw himself forward,
knocking Collins's gun out of the way with his umbrella.

'No! Wait, wait!'

'Goddamn it!' Crawhammer bellowed. 'Get him out of there!'

Collins reached for the Doctor's collar, but his hands closed on
empty air. The Doctor danced through the line of soldiers and stood
defiantly in front of the van. 'I hardly think that an invading army from
another dimension is going to be using a removal van with 'London
Zoo' painted on the side to mount a major offensive, do you, General?'

The throaty diesel rumble of the truck cut out suddenly and the van
door creaked open. A very nervous-looking Cody McBride peered out,
hands raised.

'Jeez. Not quite the reception I had in mind.'

The Doctor beamed at him. 'Cody, what a pleasant surprise!'

The passenger door opened and Davey O'Brien got out. 'And Captain
O'Brien!' the Doctor beamed.

Crawhammer pushed through his troops. 'O'Brien!' he barked. 'What
the hell's goin' on?'

'Ah, General Crawhammer,' the Doctor chirped, 'I'd like you to
meet a friend of mine, Cody McBride, private investigator. Cody, this is
General Crawhammer of the American military.'

Collins had to stifle a laugh. The general looked as though he was
going to explode.

'And what in the name of God is Cody McBride, private investigator doing here?'

The Doctor cocked his head on one side. 'Yes, I did rather think that I'd asked you pair to stay with Drakefell and Sarah?'

McBride looked awkward. 'We sort of had an idea, Doc. Reinforcements. O'Brien guessed you'd come here, seeing as all the regular barracks are pinned down.'

'Not quite my reasoning, but I'm very glad to see you both, nonetheless.'

'What about these reinforcements?' Crawhammer barked. 'What have you got in there, sonny? The Mounties?'

The Doctor tapped his lips with his umbrella. 'I rather think that Mr McBride has brought us something more useful than that.'

Captain Frank Williams of the Imperial Welsh Guards raised his thermal imaging binoculars and scanned the street ahead. Fires flared brightly though the viewfinder and the device whined softly as the software compensated for the high levels.

Williams frowned. He had been expecting resistance, but there was seemingly nothing. For fifteen minutes they had been holed in the lobby of the hospital by a torrent of gunfire, then suddenly, nothing.

He lowered the binoculars and waved his men forward. They were jumpy and on edge. He couldn't blame them. The world they had dropped into was a mirror image of their own – and about as alien as they could possibly have imagined. Oh, the structure was the same, the buildings, the layout, but there was a feeling that was wrong, an atmosphere.

And a smell.

That had been the first thing that had hit Williams as they had come through the gate. This world smelt different. It smelt warm, organic. Animal smells and vegetable decomposition. They had been told about it at the briefing: all his troops knew what to expect, but the reality of it was almost overpowering. They had been offered additional augmentation before the mission. Nasal filters or full artificial replacement. Williams was beginning to regret turning it down.

A scuffle from the darkness brought his mind sharply back into focus. He took a deep breath and sent a 'spread out' pulse to his squad, wincing at the pain in his temple. He'd have to see the MASH unit when they had secured the city: some of his circuitry hadn't liked the trip through the gate.

Williams tightened his grip on the butt of his gun, tensing a muscle to unlock the safety catch. He could hear something echoing in the gloom of the entrance lobby. He concentrated. It sounded like breathing, and the animal smell that pervaded everything was stronger here, muskier.

The three soldiers at his shoulder were tense, watching him, waiting for orders. He indicated the staircase with the barrel of his gun. 'Wallace, Trim, you take the staircase. Evans you're with me.'

Stooping low he darted through the deserted reception, Private Evans close behind him. Swinging double doors loomed in front of them. Evans eased them open gently. 'Nothing, sir.'

Williams shook his head. Something was wrong. Why had they been held back so ferociously only to suddenly be allowed this freedom? He turned to where Corporal Wallace and Private Trim were approaching the stairs in time to see something huge drop from the first-floor landing.

Trim didn't stand a chance. The thing landed squarely on his shoulders, the crack as his back broke echoing around the lobby like a gunshot. Wallace barely had time to raise his gun before he was clubbed to the floor.

The thing threw back its head and bellowed with rage. Williams's jaw dropped. It was a gorilla. A gorilla with huge metal hands, its head a tangle of wires and cables.

'Jesus.' Evans was shaking his head. 'They've got augments, Captain'. They've got bloody augments.'

The gorilla swung its massive head towards them, bared rows of vicious steel teeth, and bellowed. Other creatures' voices joined the clamour. Primates of all shapes and sizes erupted into the entrance way, screaming at the soldiers, bounding down the central staircase. Williams could hear gunfire echoing throughout the building, the cries of men and the howls and shrieks of the animals. Evans brought his gun up and unleashed a barrage of bullets. He was screaming something in Welsh. Williams could barely hear him above the din. The implants in his skull were swamping him with data, all of his squads trying to report in at once. He reeled, staggering and crashing onto his knees. Evans caught him by the arm. 'Captain, we've got to get out of here! NOW!'

Williams forced himself to concentrate, trying to channel the data as they had trained him to. 'Sir?' Evans was shaking him. The babble in his head started to subside. He looked up at Evans and nodded. 'I'm OK, Private, I'm all right.'

Williams's eyes widened with horror as a semi-mechanical monstrosity loomed out of the shadows. Private Evans barely had time to turn before the ape ripped his head off.

Williams dived to one side as blood-soaked paws crashed into the floor, shattering tiles like glass. He rolled and came up firing, the stream of bullets practically cutting the ape in two. It crashed to the floor, foam gushing from its chest unit, blood and hydraulic fluid spraying everywhere.

The young captain desperately sent out a pulse. Withdraw and regroup. Withdraw and regroup. He wiped the blood from his eyes. He could see the doorway across the reception hall, if he could just make it outside.

He tensed augmented muscles and threw himself forward. Five metres, four metres, three metres.

Something caught him across the midriff with a blow that sent him skidding across the floor. He crashed into a wall, struggling to draw breath. Huge shapes were converging on him. He scrabbled frantically for his gun, oblivious to the shards of glass that lacerated his fingers. His hand closed on something cold and metallic. He looked down to see crude metallic fingers grasping his own. There was a wrenching pain as he was hauled to his feet. The creature that had caught him was scrutinising the circuitry in his arm, poking at him with clumsy artificial fingers.

All around him were apes of different sizes and shapes, each of them uniquely and crudely augmented. Steel teeth loomed closer and closer, hot animal breath wafting over him. Williams's final thought was a sudden memory of a visit to the zoo when he had been five, then everything went mercifully black.

The Doctor winced at the sounds of gunfire and screams that echoed from elsewhere in the building. The enemy had broken through and were driving the soldiers back.

McBride caught his eye and gave a weak smile.

'It's not like we have a lot of choice, Doc.'

The Doctor shook his head and turned back to his task. The baboon stretched out on the bed was inert, the thin metal rod that acted as its power collector dismantled. Wires and cables curled inelegantly from the back of its skull.

A door crashed open and Captain O'Brien entered. Behind him Jimmy struggled into the room, staggering under the weight of the heavy car battery clasped to his chest.

'Where do you want this one?' asked O'Brien.

'Oh, here, please.' Limb scurried forward, a screwdriver clasped in his hand.

Jimmy let the battery drop onto a hospital trolley with a clatter.

Limb frowned. 'Is that it?'

'We're clearing out all the cars we can find. The general's not going to touch any of the army vehicles though.'

'Oh, what a shame.' Limb pouted like a disappointed child. 'We've still got so many of our friends to revive.' A sudden thought struck him. 'Is there still a battery in the van that you and Mr McBride... appropriated?'

O'Brien nodded. 'I think so.'

'Then we'll have that one too, please, Captain.'

'Hey, I might need that!' McBride looked concerned. 'You guys may not have noticed but London ain't exactly the most fun place to be at the moment! Having a vehicle that still runs might be an advantage.'

'You'll be leaving with us, McBride, don't worry about that.'

O'Brien tapped the breathless Jimmy on the shoulder. 'Come on, soldier. Battery for Mr Limb.'

'Great.' McBride watched them go and lit a cigarette. 'Suddenly we're workin' for the military again. And there was me thinking I was nicely independent.'

'Oh really, Mr McBride,' Limb tutted, 'we all have to make sacrifices in wartime you know.' He peered down at the tangle of wires. 'Now then, Doctor, let's see if we can get another of our simian allies running about under his own power shall we?'

'Do you have to enjoy this quite so much?' snapped the Doctor.

Limb stared accusingly at him. 'I seem to remember that this particular solution was yours...'

'Yes, I know...' The Doctor snatched the screwdriver from Limb and started making the modifications that were needed to get the augmented apes running on battery power.

McBride and Jimmy had arrived with thirty of the augmented apes in the back of the truck. He and O'Brien had driven to the zoo, hot-wired a truck and loaded as many of the big apes as they could into the back.

The Doctor had converted a ward up on the third floor into a makeshift surgery, the inert bodies of the apes stretched out on the stark metal-framed beds. It was a bizarre sight. Apes of all shapes and sizes lying in neat rows, limbs tangling across clean linen sheets, the

Doctor and Limb scurrying around them like consultants. It had only been when he had started a careful examination of the Cyberprimates that he had realised what a dangerous and crude experiment they had been. All of the augmentations had been designed to run on static electricity, the apes fitted with power collectors like obscene dodgem cars. It had been a simple matter to convert them to run off battery power; vehicle batteries had seemed like the obvious choice. They were plentiful, they would last a considerable length of time and the apes were perfectly capable of carrying the weight.

What the Doctor hadn't counted on was the awesome savagery of the creatures once they were revived. His eyes flicked to the twisted shape lying in the corner of the room and the smaller body laid out on a stretcher next to it. The first ape that they had revived, and the first victim of that folly – one of Crawhammer's men, his throat ripped out before he could even scream. It had only been Bill Collins and his submachine gun that had prevented a massacre. After that they had revived the primates once they were outside the room, watching as they shambled off down the stairwell. An indiscriminate weapon.

The Doctor closed his eyes and took a deep breath. For the moment he had no better ideas. He needed a breathing space and the apes were providing it. It would at least give the invading troops something to think about. No, at the moment his problem was Crawhammer. The general had nuclear blood-lust in his eyes and the Doctor was frightened. History was tearing itself apart at the seams and he was right at the epicentre. Things would have been difficult and dangerous at the best of times, but with Limb here they were almost unmanageable. The Earth as he knew it was in danger of ending here in the 1950s, and the shockwave was liable to fracture the entire web of time.

Aware of Limb watching him, he tightened a connection and wiped his hands on the lapels of his borrowed suit. 'This one's ready.'

'Right, Doc.' McBride stubbed out his cigarette and pulled on a set of thick gloves. He, O'Brien and two of the soldiers heaved the baboon off the bed and dragged it across the linoleum towards the door.

The Doctor watched as they manhandled the brute into the corridor, unwinding a length of twine that led to the creature's chest as they did so. That had been the Doctor's suggestion, a switch that they could activate remotely, like pulling the pin on a grenade... or a can of Nitro Nine. The Doctor smiled humourlessly. He doubted that Ace would approve of his methods. Or his allies.

With the ape safely locked out in the corridor, McBride pulled on the twine. There was a second's silence, then a savage roar. The doors shook violently. Then there was silence.

McBride let out a deep breath. 'They never wake up in a good mood, do they?'

'Would you if you had that much ironmongery strapped to you?' O'Brien crossed to the remaining apes. 'Which one do you want next, Doctor?'

Limb scurried over. 'Now, let's see what we have to choose from. Another gorilla, I think, they seem very effective.'

The door at the other end of the ward crashed open and Bill Collins staggered in, another battery in his arms. Limb clapped his hands.

'Immaculate timing, Major. On the table if you please.'

Collins let the heavy lead acid battery crash onto the trolley. 'Crawhammer wants to see you, Doctor.'

The Doctor scowled. 'I'm busy, Major Collins.'

'I'm sure that Mr Limb can cope without you for a few minutes.' The major's hand dropped imperceptibly towards the butt of his pistol.

McBride hurried over to the Doctor's side. 'Look, Doc, I'm sure we can get things moving along without you for this one. Best keep the general happy, eh?'

The Doctor smiled at McBride. 'Thank you, Cody. Looking after my best interests as always.'

He sighed and made a half-hearted attempt to brush the dirt from his jacket.

'All right, Major Collins, lead on.' He shot a look at Limb. 'You can manage without me, I trust?'

Limb smiled slowly. 'Oh yes, thank you. We'll do very nicely without you.'

McBride watched as Major Collins escorted the Doctor away. The Doc was worried, and that made McBride worried. Crawhammer was up to something, and McBride didn't trust the big southern general as far as he could throw one of these gorillas.

He looked down at the sleeping ape, his stomach churning at the ugly tubes and bolts that wound in and out of the creature's flesh. It had been nearly twenty years since he had seen anything like this. Twenty years since the Doctor had stepped into his life and shown him things that had haunted his nightmares ever since. Now the Doctor was back and the nightmares were real again, but this time they were home-grown. No silver aliens to deal with. Just people, stirred up by the Doctor and Limb. Two dangerous, powerful little boys.

McBride shook his head. Ace dead, Rita missing, Mullen crippled.

Mullen, who could have whipped his ass if had ever come to a straight fight, was lying in a hospital bed upstairs with no legs, waiting for people to turn him into this. He clenched his fists.

It wasn't fair. He wasn't a young man any more. During the war it had almost been exciting; now it just made him sick. Sick and scared.

'You OK?' Davey O'Brien was looking at him.

McBride nodded. 'Just thinking about ants.'

'Ants?'

'Yeah. Did you ever used to stir them up when you were a kid? The black and the reds?'

'Sure.'

McBride nodded across to where Limb was working on the battery. 'Well, he and the Doc have stirred 'em up good this time. With a very big stick.'

As if on cue, Limb turned and smiled that sickly old man smile of his.

'I'm ready for that one now, if you don't mind, Mr McBride.'

McBride almost laughed. With his screwdriver poised, Limb looked like some crazy dentist – a mad scientist. O'Brien called over two of the soldiers and between the four of them they heaved the comatose gorilla onto the tiny bed. Limb patted the gorilla's chest.

'My, you are a big strong boy, aren't you?'

Leaning over the table he began to connect the gorilla to the battery.

O'Brien slumped into a chair, offering McBride a cigarette. 'You know what bothers me, McBride?'

McBride flicked his lighter into life and shook his head.

'The red ants always used to win.' said Davey O'Brien.

The Doctor followed Major Collins down the long, darkened wards of the hospital. From outside he could hear the distant crackle of the dimensional tear and the screams of frightened Londoners. Visible through the tall windows, the strange flickering light lit up the brooding November sky, sending dancing shadows across the thick pile of the carpet. A Christmas tree, strewn with elegant silver baubles, scattered reflections of the dancing energy across the sterile green walls and high ceilings of the sombre old building. If it wasn't for the screams and the gunfire, it would be almost magical; a fairytale Christmas in London.

All around him American soldiers, rifles clasped tightly in their hands, snapped smartly to attention as they passed, but the Doctor could see the suspicion in their faces. The fear. He represented everything that they had been taught to hate. Something different, something unknown. A Russkie. An augment. A little green man from outer space. Limb couldn't have chosen a worse time in history. A time of massive distrust and paranoia, when the two most powerful countries on Earth had access to appallingly powerful weapons, and neither had the wisdom or understanding to realise what they could unleash.

The Doctor sighed. If only Limb had managed to make it another twenty years in the Cybermen's time machine, then there might have been a chance. The Brigadier might be pig-headed and set in his ways, but he was like a Sunday school teacher compared to Crawhammer.

The Doctor glanced at the young major by his side. Despite his youth, there was something very reassuring and confident about the tall American. In many ways he reminded the Doctor of a young Lethbridge-Stewart. There was a level-headedness about him more common in a man twice his age. Certainly he had Crawhammer's trust. The Doctor had no doubt that the major would follow the general's orders to the letter; the problem was he wasn't sure how dangerous those orders were going to be.

'Do you trust the general, Major?'

Collins said nothing.

'Will you follow your instructions like a good soldier even if it means the destruction of everything that you hold dear?'

Collins stopped. 'Look, Doctor,' there was strain in the major's face. 'I don't know what to believe any more. I'd rather you'd never arrived at all. I wish you'd stayed on Mars or Venus or wherever. You talk about aliens and time travel and other dimensions, and a whole barrel of other weird crap. I'm a soldier. I'm from Oregon.'

'And you were trained to fight Communists.'

'Yes.'

'No questions, no uncertainty.'

'No. A simple choice.'

'The world laid out in red and white...'

The major's face flushed with anger. 'Have you ever seen the effects of a nuclear blast, Doctor? Have you ever seen what it can do to a city?'

'Oh, yes,' the Doctor's face was grave.

Collins stared at him. 'I was out on Bikini Atoll last year; with a military survey team assessing the damage to the environment. Do you know that the sand had turned to glass, the trees to stone?'

The Doctor met his gaze, his steel grey eyes sombre and reflective. He remembered standing on a world burnt up by nuclear holocaust, the forests petrified, the soil turned to ash, the people mutated. It had followed him for the rest of his life.

'I know what you mean, Major.'

'It can't happen again, Doctor.'

The Doctor shrugged. 'Right now, anything could happen.'

Collins straightened his uniform jacket and nodded towards an office door at the end of the corridor.

'The general is waiting for you, Doctor.'

Chapter Twenty-one

Cody McBride dragged hard on a cigarette. Limb had given him a break – they were running out of monkeys anyway – rather than have him smoke where there was a risk of explosion. He'd chain-smoked his way through almost an entire packet. He listened to Crawhammer's muffled, distant bellow. Obviously the Doctor wasn't winning the general over. McBride swore he could see, twenty yards down the corridor, the office door rattling.

He was thinking about Mullen – he was in here somewhere. Mullen was the reason he'd come here: finding the Doc had given McBride new heart, but had sidetracked him. McBride wanted to go and find Mullen.

There was a sudden commotion from the other end of the corridor. A soldier was running from the direction of their workshop, shouting.

'He's gone!'

McBride crawled to his feet. 'Who's gone?'

'The old man!'

'Go get the Doctor – the guy who's arguing with the general.'

He didn't wait for any debate, but sprinted to the end of the work-shop corridor, drawing his gun. He peered around and moved towards the doors. There was no sound and no movement.

He decided, 'To hell with it', and burst through the doors, both hands on the butt of the gun.

The ward was a mess. Beds were on their sides, electrical equipment and glass strewn across the floor. Bodies of the remaining apes littered the floor, but of Limb there was no sign.

'O'Brien?'

McBride could see the captain slumped over a chair on the far side of the ward. He stirred at the sound of McBride's voice and tried to haul himself upright, but instantly slid back to the floor clutching his head.

'Jeez. How long have I been out?'

'Search me,' said McBride. 'I've been gone half an hour…'

He spun as the big double doors crashed open and a dozen troops pushed into the room, Crawhammer towering over them. The little figure of the Doctor pushed through them and hurried over.

'Cody. Are you OK? What happened?' The Doctor pulled a paisley handkerchief from his pocket and dabbed delicately at O'Brien's scalp.

'We couldn't stop him, sir,' O'Brien said to Crawhammer. 'He and the ape just took off. Knocked me cold as I tried to stop them.'

Crawhammer strode across the devastated room. 'What in God's name...?'

'The old man and the American kid. Gone, sir,' said O'Brien. 'They went out of the window. Carried by one of the apes.'

'One of the apes?' Crawhammer bellowed. 'You mean he can control it? How in the name of holy hell's he managed that? These things don't respond to a quiet word and a handful of nuts!'

'Ultrasonics, I daresay,' said the Doctor. 'Control on a very basic level. Still, at the moment anything that helps him helps us.'

McBride was puzzled.

'I don't get it.'

'It was George Limb's move,' said the Doctor, smiling slightly. 'I was waiting for him to make it. I hadn't expected the ape... I'm sorry about that. One of you could have been seriously hurt.'

O'Brien tried to smile through the pain of his pounding head. 'No problem, Doc.'

'And now it's my move,' the Doctor said.

He turned to McBride.

'Hold on there one minute, boy,' boomed Crawhammer. The Doctor ignored him.

'Come on, Cody.'

He turned to leave, but Crawhammer stepped into his path. 'No one's goin' anywhere.'

The Doctor's eyes flashed with anger. 'I don't have time for this, General!'

He ducked under the big general's arms and made for the door. In one smooth movement Crawhammer spun and pulled one of his pearl-handled revolvers from its holster.

'I said no one is goin' anywhere.' He pulled back the hammer of the gun with his thumb. There was a sharp click. The room went deathly quiet. McBride held his breath.

The Doctor turned slowly, staring levelly down the barrel of the gun.

'You know, General, I once spent a summer in Louisiana, on a ranch that bred racehorses. I met a little girl there called Ellie Jane. She used to make necklaces out of wild flowers, help her mother stir sugar into the home-made lemonade and she was very proud of her grandfather.'

The Doctor took a step towards Crawhammer, his face dimly reflected in the lenses of the general's sunglasses.

'She told me that her grandfather was big and strong and kind, and had helped her build a doll's house the previous summer. He had been a soldier a long time ago, but he didn't talk about that much. She said that he was too old to play with her now, but always sat on the porch when she was out in the fields to keep an eye on her. He used to sit in an old creaky chair and carve little toys out of bits of mangrove wood.

'Ellie was named after her grandmother, but she'd died the previous year. Her grandfather wasn't sad, though, because he said that they had had so many good years together, and that he had seen so much death that it didn't frighten him any more. Now he was happy just to sit and watch life go by, carving his toys and watching his granddaughter.'

The Doctor took another step towards Crawhammer. The muzzle of the gun was almost against his forehead. McBride's heart was pounding.

'The events that are unfolding around us are a mistake, General, a mistake compounded by things that I have done and things that George Limb has done. If you shoot me now, then it ends here, for me, for you, for everything. I join my friend Ace as a statistic, a casualty of war, another corpse amongst the millions that will litter these streets. If you shoot me now, then within hours the bombs will start falling and everything will be gone. Past, present, future. Gone. Not just in this dimension, but in millions of others.

Crawhammer's gun didn't waver.

'George Limb is the catalyst, the linchpin that all this chaos is revolving about. He is my responsibility. I'm the one who gave him the tools to unravel history and I'm the one who has to stop him.'

The Doctor turned and began walking calmly across the ward. In the doorway he stopped and turned back to the general. 'You should go to Louisiana, General. It's very beautiful in the summer.'

Then he was gone.

The Doctor was halfway down the stairwell when McBride caught up with him.

'Hey, Doc, wait up.'

The Doctor turned and looked quizzically at him. McBride was pale and sweating. 'You gotta remember that I'm not a young man any more, Doc. Stunts like that do nothing for my heart...'

He leant against the wall, breathing heavily. 'So did your meeting with General Custer go badly?'

The Doctor looked grave. 'He's a brave man, and resourceful... but he has a disturbing sense of mission, and that's very dangerous.'

He shook his head as if to clear it and started back down the stairs. McBride hurried after him.

'Where we goin'?'

'The TARDIS. There are a few things that I need if I'm going to catch up with Mr Limb.'

'Your box of tricks? You mean it's here?'

The Doctor nodded. 'In the basement.' .

'Hang on a minute,' McBride caught the Doctor by the sleeve. 'The basement's going to be crawling with these soldiers from another dimension, not to mention half a dozen bad-tempered battery-operated monkeys that we've just released down there.'

The Doctor patted the pockets of his borrowed jacket. 'And I'm right out of bananas. Come along, Cody.'

As the Doctor trotted down the stairs, McBride pulled a packet of Lucky Strikes out of his trenchcoat and lit one up. He took a deep lungful and shook his head. 'And I thought these were going to kill me.'

Crawhammer chomped on his cigar and scowled at Bill Collins. 'Well?'

'The task force is ready, sir. I've armed them with everything we've got.'

'And the chopper?'

'Ready to go, sir.'

'You realise we'll probably be shot down, Major.'

'Yes, sir.'

'We jus' gotta pray to good God the assault will be enough to throw 'em off.'

He didn't sound convinced.

'It's not much,' he said, 'but it's all we got.'

Suddenly there was a screaming in the air. Crawhammer drew his gun and strode to the window.

'It's the RAF!' someone shouted. Somebody else whooped.

'Nice to know someone out there has their shit together,' said Crawhammer.

There were cheers as a sleek grey airship, armed to the teeth was brought down by a Lightning jet. Nice move. Other planes were strafing the ground. A line of bullets tore through the window.

'Down!' Collins shouted, hitting the deck.

Peering up, he could see the enemy being driven back. Crawhammer stood, unmoved, at his position.

'This is it,' he said. 'Roll out the assault group. Fire up the chopper.'

McBride clamped his hands over his ears and tried to shut out the whoops and howls of the apes, the roar of planes and the clatter of machine-gun fire. Beside him crouched the Doctor, his face a mask of concern. The two of them were crammed into a storage cupboard on the ground floor, hunched amongst piles of folded bed-sheets and crisp, clean-smelling nurses' uniforms.

Getting down the stairwell had been a nightmare, the hospital was cold and dark and the jungle sounds of the augmented apes had made McBride's skin crawl. At every floor the Doctor had peered cautiously onto the landing before tiptoeing over to the next flight of stairs, and at every floor McBride had been waiting for two hundred pounds of augmented ape to come crashing through the doors and tear them to pieces.

The evidence of the augments' savagery had been strewn everywhere. Twisted, torn corpses lying in pools of congealing blood, absurdly young faces frozen in expressions of sheer horror.

At the first corpse they had found the Doctor had stopped, hands running expertly over the delicate tracery of wires and filaments that tattooed the skin of these soldiers from another dimension. After that he had ignored them, his face unreadable, those steel-grey eyes darting from shadow to shadow as he led McBride into the guts of the hospital.

As they had stepped into the ground-floor reception, a sudden scrape of metal on metal had made McBride jump. The place had been a mess, chairs and papers scattered everywhere, the only light coming from the street lamps outside, and the Christmas tree in one corner. The flashing of the fairy lights had sent shadows dancing and moving across the room, making it impossible to see clearly. As McBride's foot had brushed against something soft and heavy, he had been quite glad of that fact. The two of them had started nervously across the reception hall when the scraping noise had come again. Waving for McBride to stay put, the Doctor had started to tiptoe forward when the gorilla had reared up in front of them.

The Doctor wasn't a big man at the best of times, but confronted by the towering ape, he looked like a midget. For a second, Time Lord and gorilla had stared at each other in surprise, and then, with a shattering roar, the primate had brought its augmented fist slamming down onto the linoleum floor sending the Doctor tumbling backwards and cannoning into McBride.

All sense of stealth abandoned, the two of them had hurled themselves back towards the stairs. McBride had felt the ground shudder beneath his feet as the gorilla pounded its chest in fury. He could hardly draw breath, the pain from his ribs lancing through him with every jarring step.

At the foot of the stairs the Doctor had skidded to a halt, McBride almost tripping over him. Down the stairwell had come another ape, a vicious-looking baboon, its features stitched and twisted, the harsh silver metal of its augmentation battle-scarred and leaking hydraulic fluid. Startled, its lips curled back in an angry snarl. McBride had seen his frightened face reflected in the gleaming silver teeth and at that moment had realised that he was as close to death as he had ever been.

The baboon had started barking angrily, lashing out at them with a crude club. McBride had felt the bile rise in his throat as he realised what the club was – the lower half of a human leg, an army boot still tightly laced to it. From behind them had come an angry growl.

Baboon and gorilla had thrown themselves together, each screaming with fury. McBride and the Doctor had ducked and weaved as the two apes clubbed at each other with massive paws. Sparks flew from the heavy car batteries that powered then.

A glancing blow had sent McBride sprawling, stars dancing before his eyes. He had heard the Doctor bellowing his name, the roar of the apes, and then suddenly, deafeningly, the clatter of a heavy machine-gun.

Through streaming eyes, McBride had seen the heavy double doors across the reception area swing open and surprised soldiers spill out. Almost immediately, the ape had turned on them, tearing the guns from their hands and clubbing them down.

A firm hand had caught McBride by the collar and pulled him to his feet, pushing him forward through the doors. Head reeling, he had been bundled down the corridor and into a cupboard, the Doctor slamming the door behind them. Now they sat, waiting for the noise of battle to subside. McBride was under no illusions as to who was going to win that battle. The troops were well trained and well equipped, but they were no match for the augmented apes. The Doctor knew it too, McBride could see it in his eyes.

There was another burst of gunfire, then a scream as something heavy crashed against the cupboard door. There was the barking roar of one of the augments, deafening in the confined space. McBride screwed up his eyes and muttered a prayer under his breath, waiting for the door to burst open and huge mechanical hands to drag them from their hiding place.

Suddenly there was silence, unexpected and shocking.

McBride squinted out from between his fingers. The Doctor had one ear pressed to the door, his brow furrowed as he strained to hear what was going on outside. All McBride could hear was his heart pounding in his chest.

The Doctor shot McBride a sideways glance and reached tentatively for the door handle. McBride wanted to scream at him not to, to leave the door shut, for them to stay here safe amongst the clean bedlinen, but his throat was dry and all he could manage was a strangled croak.

With a soft click the door opened and McBride nearly cried out as something slumped backwards into the cupboard, landing heavily on the floor between them. A look of weary resignation flickered over the Doctor's face as he stared down at the mangled body of the soldier, then, with a deep sigh, he peered out into the corridor.

McBride strained to see past him. The corridor was empty save for the shattered remains of a hospital trolley. Distant barked orders drifted from somewhere far off in the building.

The Doctor scampered across the blood-slick floor and gently eased open the double doors that led to the reception area. Head cocked on one side, he paused for a moment, listening, then waved McBride over. The only sound was the steady, sonorous tick of the large, inelegant clock above the reception desk.

Pressing a finger to his lips, the Doctor caught hold of McBride's hand and the two of them picked their way through the shattered reception and down the stairs to the basement. McBride had to stifle a laugh. A forty-seven-year-old man being led by the hand like a frightened toddler. He remembered another cold November night, a long time ago in another country, his father leading him down the stairs to the basement and telling him that the dark was nothing to be frightened of and that monsters existed only in books.

McBride was older and wiser now. His father was gone and the monsters were real.

The Doctor pushed open the basement door and McBride looked apprehensively into the gloomy corridors, childish fears hovering at the back of his mind.

'Do you go out of your way to find dark, empty, scary places to land, Doc, or is it just a knack?' he whispered.

'You'd have preferred it if I'd landed at the reception desk and made an appointment, perhaps?'

'Yeah? I could have coped with that – bright lights, nice receptionist to talk to, a couple of nurses...'

'I'll try and do better next time. This way.'

Keeping a wary eye on the pipework that hung low from the ceiling, the Doctor padded softly down a side passage and pushed open a grubby wooden door marked BOILER ROOM. McBride could see the dark blue shape of the Doctor's ship, his TARDIS, nestling amongst the tangle of pipes and dials.

The Doctor slipped a delicate chain from around his neck and slid a key into the lock. There was a click as the police-box door swung inwards, and a shaft of warm yellow light sent long shadows chasing across the basement floor.

With his childhood bogeymen looming from every one of those shadows, McBride vanished gratefully into the light.

Chapter Twenty-two

The TARDIS was as impressive as McBride had remembered, the vast, gleaming control centre peppered with softly glowing indentations, the huge many-sided console that dominated the room twinkling with thousands of tiny lights, as if the Doctor was celebrating his own Christmas, decorating the control room with some vast, technological Christmas tree.

The whole place was bathed in a warm glow, the low background hum soothing and settling. McBride felt himself relax for the first time in what felt like days, and was suddenly aware of how tired and hungry he was.

The Doctor brushed past him and pulled at a large red lever. The massive double doors swung smoothly shut.

'Don't want any unexpected simian company now, do we?' The Doctor started dancing around the console, prodding and poking at controls. McBride lowered himself into a high-backed leather chair, wincing at the pain from his screaming ribs. 'Don't suppose this spaceship of yours has a hot tub?'

The Doctor looked at him quizzically, 'Well, yes, as a matter of fact it does...'

McBride gave a snorting laugh. 'Of course it does. Stupid of me.'

The Doctor started prodding at buttons on the central console.

'What are you doing, Doc?'

'Tracking George Limb,' said the Doctor. 'The tracer that I put on Ace...' He went quiet for a moment then, rather forcedly, brightened. 'I slipped it inside the lining of his jacket.'

The Doctor took a deep breath. 'There's a few things that I need to get, Cody. You just rest there a moment. I won't be long.'

Shrugging out of his borrowed suit jacket, the Doctor crossed the control room and vanished into the bowels of his ship. Cody McBride closed his eyes and let the warm calmness of the time ship wash over him.

In seconds he was asleep.

* * *

McBride was woken from a dream of cybernetic ants and giant gorillas by someone shaking him gently by the shoulder. The Doctor was standing over him, smiling.

'No time to let you sleep, Cody. I'm sorry. I thought this might help.'

McBride took the mug that the Doctor was holding. Strong black coffee, but with a whiff of something else. He took a sip and blinked hard. There was a generous slug of something strong in there.

'Jeez, Doc. What did you put in here? Rocket fuel?'

The Doctor's smile widened.

'Something like that.'

McBride hauled himself up in the chair. The Doctor was dressed once again in his usual clothes; checked trousers, dark jacket and that absurd tank top covered in question marks that he seemed to think was fashionable. McBride rubbed at his eyes and took another sip of his coffee. There was something different about the Doctor now, a spring in his step that hadn't been there before. It was as if returning to the TARDIS had given him a boost, revitalised him in some way. There was an energy about him, a determination in those grey eyes of his, the sense of something... alien. McBride felt goose bumps run down his spine.

They were about to start playing the endgame.

McBride could feel his system being jolted back to life by whatever the Doctor had slipped in his coffee. Feeling better than he had in days, McBride looked across to where the little Time Lord was hovering by the control console. He hauled himself out of his chair, drained the remainder of his coffee and crossed to the Doctor's side.

'What's up, Doc?'

'He's going to Kennington. To the cottage. He's going to cross over. Oh, the arrogance of the man. Right, Cody, time to get going.'

McBride shuffled awkwardly.

'I ain't goin' with you, Doc.'

The Doctor turned and peered at him. 'Well, if you'd rather stay here... Dimension jumping can be... disorientating.'

'Hey – I'm no coward!' McBride felt himself reddening under the gaze of those brilliant grey eyes.

'I didn't say you were,' said the Doctor gently.

'It's just...' McBride took a deep breath. 'It's just that you've lost your friend and I don't want to lose mine. Mullen's alone, Doctor. He's alone and trapped up there and until now I've not come up with any way of saving him, but now...'

'Now that you know that the TARDIS is here you think that you can.'

McBride nodded. 'I've been figurin' out ways of getting him out of this hospital and keep coming up with zip. But I don't have to get him out of the hospital. I just have to get him down here.'

The Doctor raised an eyebrow. 'Is that all?'

'Oh hell, Doc, I know I've got these extra-dimensional guys and cybernetic monkeys to get by, not to mention avoiding getting fried to a crisp by Crawhammer and his missiles, but it's a chance and I've got to take it... if you'll let me.'

'I'll send the TARDIS back on an automatic relay. You won't even realise it's gone.'

The Doctor solemnly lifted the TARDIS key from around his neck and held it out.

'Don't let the general get his hands on this, whatever you do.'

McBride took it. 'Thanks, Doctor. I owe you one...'

The Doctor nodded, slowly. 'You're a brave man, Cody McBride. Ace would have been proud of you.'

He pulled at the large red control handle and, with a low drone, the double doors of the time machine swung open.

McBride scratched at his chin. 'Just don't wind up in any giant ants' nests...'

The Doctor pulled a bottle of ant powder from his jacket pocket. 'Always prepared.'

With a sort of half-wave, McBride stepped back out into the boiler room. The doors swung shut behind him. There was a godawful trumpeting sound and the blue box seemed to flicker for a second, then the silence and stillness returned. McBride stared at the elegant filigree key in the palm of his hand.

'You'd better damn well appreciate this, Mullen.'

Snow had settled on the charred remains of the chocolate-box cottage. The Doctor was crouched by the side of the road examining the body of a young policeman. He could barely have been more than twenty-one years old, his neck twisted at an unnatural angle, blood staining the perfect white of the snow.

The Doctor reached out and closed the policeman's eyes, angry and frustrated. In all his lives he had never met anyone with such a casual disregard for life as George Limb. The frail old man seemed to kill without remorse, without compunction, reducing lives to statistics, pawns in some sick chess game, weighing up their usefulness to his plans, then using them or casting them aside.

He looked back towards London. From here the dimensional tear was like a huge jagged crescent in the night sky, making the lights of the city look pale and muted. The quiet of the night was punctuated by harsh whiplash cracks of energy.

The Doctor straightened. This game had gone on long enough. It was time to take control, to put things right. He crunched up the snow-covered pathway to the cottage and pushed open the front door.

The cottage was gutted, a tangled mess of burnt furniture and timbers, crumbling brickwork and charred linen. In the centre of the room were the twisted remains of the police motorcycle, and everywhere were the curled and blackened bodies of the ants. The roof was gone and snow was dusting the burnt surfaces, turning the inside of the cottage into a nightmarish monochrome landscape.

The Doctor picked his way gingerly through the ruins, grimacing at the acrid smell that hung in the air. There was a clear trail through the snow and ash. Three sets of footprints, two small, one large. Limb, Jimmy and their primate bodyguard.

The tracks led through the ruined house to what had once been a back parlour. The Doctor peered cautiously through the remains of the doorway. Somehow this room had been partially saved from the fire. Blackened shreds of what had once been floral curtains waved in the cold night air, a tall parlour palm – miraculously untouched by the flames, its leaves frosted with ice – stood by a shattered window.

In the middle of the room the tracks stopped. A large circle had been melted through the snow, revealing blackened floorboards. The Doctor knelt down and pressed his hand to the floor. It was warm – and the boards were loose.

He lifted first one board, then another. Below him an array of lights blinked rhythmically. He ran his fingertips across a row of buttons, smiled and keyed in a simple sequence.

There was a sudden discordant wailing, and the air shimmered for a moment. Suddenly the Doctor felt flooded with warmth. The snow vanished, the smell of acrid smoke cleared – and the cottage sat around him, bright and clean, pristine, with no sign that there had ever been a fire.

'Now, let's see…' the Doctor muttered, and hit another button.

Everything shimmered and changed again. He was in a harshly lit underground bunker. He hit another button…

Now he was in the middle of a large, elegant conference room. Huge, sombre portraits lined the wood-panelled walls, an elaborate crystal chandelier hung from the ceiling. At the end of the room were tall shuttered windows. Footfalls echoing on the polished wooden floor, the Doctor crossed the room and eased one of the shutters open.

Below him London stretched out along Whitehall, but not the London that he knew so well. All the landmarks were there, the skyline was so nearly familiar, but there was something not quite right about it, as if someone had taken a photograph of the city and photocopied it over and over again, losing definition with every generation.

Below him people flickered through the rain-slick streets like hummingbirds, cars were little more than blurs of light on the roads. Overhead the night sky was dominated by the huge energy tear – airships and gyrocopters hovering around it like bees.

The Doctor gave a deep sigh. He remembered another Christmas, many years ago, when he had stared out across another carbon copy of London, looked at another unfamiliar sky and watched helplessly as people struggled to survive by abandoning all their humanity. Earth's fate had always been irrevocably linked with that of its twin. There had always been the possibility that Earth would follow the evolutionary path of Mondas, that humanity would surrender flesh and blood to cold, gleaming technology. George Limb had forced that evolutionary path. His endless tinkering had thrown up time line after time line, endless alternatives running side by side through history, each of them playing out to a different conclusion, each of them fundamentally, irrevocably wrong.

On the surface everything in this reality seemed so clean and orderly. The people improved – faster and stronger than they were before. The augmentation on the corpses that the Doctor had examined back in the hospital had been elegant and delicate, but ultimately he feared it was the first step that led to an inevitable destiny, to the human beings of this world becoming a new race of Cybermen.

He had been helpless to save the people of Mondas...

He was about to turn away from the window when something caught his eye in the street. Amongst the flickering streams of pedestrians there was a slow-moving shape, a figure struggling through the drifting snow.

Frowning, the Doctor pulled a pair of opera glasses from his jacket pocket, struggling to focus through the blur of people and traffic.

A weary, haggard face swam into view.

The Doctor let the glasses drop in surprise.
'Rita..?'

Rita stared up at the imposing grey façade of the Ministry of Augmentation. All around her was the constant buzz of super-fast conversation, the blur of lights as traffic flashed before her.

She could almost shut it out, now. Almost. Her eyes were streaming from trying to keep up with the lightning-quick people around her, her head pounded from the constant babble. She had stopped trying to dodge out of people's way. Now they just surged around her, as if she was a rock in a riverbed. She caught the occasional word. Snatches of conversation, insults, pity.

In the end it was the snowflakes that had saved her. The snowflakes that had stopped her wanting to step out screaming into the tide of traffic. In all the world it seemed as if they were the only things moving slower than her. If she concentrated on their gentle fluttering paths, then everything seemed all right. Everything fell into place. Focused her.

It had been the broadcast that had finally given Rita a goal. The face of the so-called prime minister staring sternly out from one of the huge city television screens. A face that she now clearly remembered looming over her in the cottage.

A link back to her own reality. That was the spur she needed.

She had stumbled through the cheering crowds, out of Trafalgar Square and up Whitehall. The Ministry of Augmentation was lit up like a beacon, floodlit and festooned with Christmas lights. She had no idea what she was going to do once she got there. Improvise, she told herself. She'd bluffed her way into more important places than this before.

Now that she was standing outside the huge old building, though, she felt her confidence starting to fade away. Press and photographers were milling at the foot of the steps. Policemen stood in imposing ranks outside the huge, elegant doors.

Rita looked down at her snow-sodden clothes. She wasn't exactly looking her best. Certainly not in a fit state to bat her eyelashes at the cops. Assuming that she could bat her eyelashes fast enough in this crazy, whirling world.

'You pick a great time to try and get back home, girl.' She muttered under her breath. 'Wait until the damn country goes to war and then try and get in to see the prime minister.'

Brushing some of the snow from her shoulders, she pushed her way to a zebra crossing, flinching as the cars snapped to a halt, their radiators perfectly lined up on either side of the black-and-white strip. Ignoring the curious glances of the drivers behind their windshields, she scurried across the road, tucking into the shadow of the great grey building. Lights burned bright and warm behind the netted windows; vague shadowed figures flitted past open doors.

Rita threw a glance towards the main entrance. Policemen were pushing the crowd of photographers back onto the sidewalk. One of them peered over to where she huddled against the wall. Rita pulled her collar up and pushed herself into the crowd of Christmas shoppers, ignoring their complaints and letting herself be carried along in the tide.

Stupid. What did she think she was going to do? Climb in one of the windows and hope that nobody noticed her?

Out of sight of the policemen, she extricated herself from the bustling crowds, slipping between the shadowed pillars of Whitehall. The wind was starting to bite through her now and she pulled her coat tight around her, cursing her taste in skirts, shoes and fishnets. She blew into her hands, trying to coax some life back into her fingers.

'Jeez, I wish more people smoked in this screwed-up city.'

A coughing laugh made her jump. She could make out a figure huddled against one of the pillars.

'I'd offer you one of mine, but this is me last one.'

A pinprick of orange light flared up in the darkness for a moment and Rita caught the whiff of tobacco as the wind whipped the smoke past her. She squinted at the silhouetted shape.

'Do you make a habit of scaring the crap out of people, or do you just save it for Christmas?'

'No, most of the time I just scare the crap out of myself.'

A tousled figure emerged from between the pillars, pulling the last lungfuls of smoke from the stub of a cigarette. Rita took a nervous step backwards as the man flicked the butt into the snow. He was thin, in his forties, maybe his fifties, his hair thinning, his clothes just a little on the wrong side of shabby. He peered at her curiously.

'You're not from round here, are you?'

'No,' she replied. 'I'm an Eskimo.'

'Course you are. I should have guessed, what with the high heels and the fishnets an' everything.'

'You sayin' Eskimos can't be well dressed?'

'I'm saying that Eskimos' teeth don't chatter when they talk. You American?'

Rita felt her hackles rising. 'Look, I've just about had enough of people saying, "Are you American?" in that tone of voice. Have you got a problem with where I'm from?'

'Nope.' The man shrugged. 'Explains why you're here, that's all...'

'So why am I here?'

'Same reason as me, I guess.' The man nodded at a small doorway tucked amid the grandiose stonework of the ministry, a single white spotlight making the snow on the step glisten. 'Last three Christmases I've come here, smoked myself hoarse amongst these pillars and tried to make the same decision.'

'What decision?'

'Same one as I guess you're trying to make. Do I become like them?' He peered past her at the oblivious crowd that raced beyond the pillars, his face sad and pale. 'Do you take the generous Christmas offer of the Ministry of Augmentation, the St Nicolas farthing?'

He pulled a copper coin from the pocket of his shabby jacket and stared at it solemnly. 'I've always said that I'd never do it, always stuck to my guns, told myself that I'd die human, no tubes an' bits of metal in me, but...'

'But...?' Rita stared at him, puzzled.

'It gets harder every year. Every street has more energy points than before, everything gets geared up for a faster pace of life, everyone around you becomes a blur, leaves you behind.' He looked at Rita with hollow eyes. 'Do you know that the houses they are building now don't even have kitchens, that they're trying to phase out food shops from the high streets altogether.' He shrugged. 'I've got to live here to work, and if I stay, then I've got to adapt.'

'You mean – ' Rita's voice was low '– sockets in the back of your head, wires under your skin?'

The little man nodded. 'Last three years I've thought about it, last three years I've scared myself sick and walked away, but now...' He toyed with the coin in the palm of his hand. 'Every year they hand out the St Nicolas farthing in Covent Garden. If you takes it, then there's tax breaks, and notes made on your papers, and better work opportunities...'

'If you allow them to do the... augmentation.'

'Oh, I know that it's not top-level work. Cosmetically, I mean.' He smiled sympathetically at Rita. 'And if I was as pretty as you, then I'd be having second thoughts too, but this year...' He gripped the coin tight in his fist and turned towards the small door with its single spotlight. 'This year I don't think that I've got any choice. I need the work before I run out of...'

'Energy?'

The man laughed again, humourlessly. 'Energy. Right.' He took a deep breath. 'No point putting it off any longer...'

'What's your name?'

'My name?'

'Yes.' Rita flashed him her most brilliant smile. 'I just wanted to know your name, that's all.'

'Sid... Sid Napley.'

'Then I'm really sorry, Sid.' said Rita

He looked at her, puzzled. 'For what?'

'For this...'

Rita put all her strength into a punch that caught the little man on the tip of his jaw. He spun around, his face a mask of surprise and crashed into the snow with a wet thump.

'Jeez...' Rita clutched at her knuckles, gasping at the pain. 'That always looked easier in the movies.'

Napley lay at her feet, flat out on his back, arms outstretched. Rita suddenly remembered a winter in Maine with a favourite cousin. The two of them used to fall back into the powder-soft snow and make angel shapes. Napley didn't look much like an angel now. The bruise was already starting to come out on his jaw, and his breath was ragged in his throat.

Ignoring her throbbing hand, Rita caught the little man under the arms and hauled him into the shadows, leaning him gently against one of the pillars. His fist was still clamped tightly around the St Nicolas farthing. Rita prised his fingers apart and held the coin up to the light. Words were crudely inscribed around the tarnished copper edge.

'Embracing the future through technology.'

Rita shook her head and stared down at the unconscious body of Sid Napley. 'It's a future that you're better off without, Sid, trust me. That jaw of yours may ache a bit over Christmas, but you'll thank me for it one day.'

Rita pulled Napley's jacket tight around him and buttoned it, then stood, brushing the snow from her coat, and scurried over to the inconspicuous little doorway. A small, expensive-looking plaque was screwed to the door, emblazoned with a symbol – a stylised baby held in a mechanical hand. Suddenly feeling sick, Rita gripped the St Nicolas farthing tightly, took a deep breath and pushed the door open.

She stepped into a small, dreary office, stiflingly hot after the bitter November night. Posters endorsing the benefits of augmentation peppered the walls, a sad tree strewn with threadbare tinsel failed miserably to create a festive atmosphere.

At the far side of the room a bored-looking man sat at a counter, flicking through a magazine. Rita crossed to the desk. The man half glanced at her.

'Office opens again first week in January. Application forms are in the rack by the door.'

'I was told to come here with this.' Rita placed the coin on the counter.

The man gave a weary sigh, closed his magazine and took the coin, turning it over and over in his hand.

'It's genuine. Honest.' Rita felt a surge of panic.

'Of course it's genuine. No one in their right mind is going to try and bluff their way in here.'

The man peered up at Rita, frowning slightly.

'You don't look the usual type.'

Rita shrugged. 'American.'

The man nodded, as if that explained everything. He dropped the coin into a metal box on the desk, handed her a thick form and indicated a door on the far wall.

'Take a seat in the waiting room and fill out the form.'

He pressed a button under the counter. There was a strident buzz and the door swung open.

'You coin-takers always leave it late. This is the last intake tonight and some of us have families to go to, Christmas to celebrate.'

Rita could hear the contempt in his voice. No wonder Napley had been having second thoughts. She gritted her teeth and forced a smile. 'Thank you.'

The man grunted and turned back to his magazine. Heart pounding, Rita stepped into the waiting room.

Two dozen pairs of eyes swung in her direction. Rita had to choke back a sob. Never had she seen people with such despair in their faces. They sat in neat ranks on stark metal chairs; weary, dishevelled men, frightened women and children. Stainless steel hospital trolleys lined up near a set of heavy double doors, posters with stark warnings about the dangers of falsifying forms dominated the room. Nothing was done to soften the harsh reality of what was about to happen to these people.

A noise made Rita start. In one corner a young girl tried desperately to get her baby to stop crying. Rita had a sudden vision of that baby grasped in a huge mechanical claw and felt a wave of anger. This was wrong. It was sad, and pathetic and *wrong*.

Tears blurred her vision. Throwing her sheaf of papers to one side, she crossed the waiting room and hauled open the heavy doors. Someone caught hold of her arm, shouting something about waiting her turn. Rita pulled herself free and stumbled blindly into the corridor beyond. She had no plan, no carefully thought-out strategy for finding her way out of here. She just wanted to get away from this strange and twisted world. She wanted to get back to her own world, her own Christmas. A world where flowers had smell and food had taste and people didn't have to be turned into machines in order to survive the winter.

Someone suddenly caught hold of her. She nearly screamed but a hand slipped over her mouth, cutting off the sound. Panic welled up inside her and she started to kick and punch at her attacker. There was a sudden firm pressure on her forehead, then everything went calm and quiet.

She felt her eyes closing.

When she opened them again the Doctor was peering at her, concern in his face. He gave a little half smile, grey eyes twinkling.

'What's a nice girl like you doing in an alternative reality like this?'

The short one – Bure – lit another cigarette with shaking hands and stared out at the flickering energy tear that hung over London like an electric curtain.

'I just don't understand why we couldn't go with them, that's all.'

Hark – the boss – looked up from his desk in irritation. 'Because the work is here, everything we have worked on. Every note, every file. You would have us abandon all that?'

'No. No, I suppose not.'

'Your enthusiasm is overwhelming.'

'I'd just feel a lot happier at Winnerton Flats, that's all,' snapped Bure.

'And I'd feel a lot safer if they hadn't let the Doctor go.' Hark rubbed at the scar on his arm where Chief Inspector Mullen had stabbed him. 'I could use a little scalpel work at the moment.'

'What about those apes? You saw what they could do.'

'Primitive experiments. Hardly capable of stopping bullets. The general should have mopped them all up on his way out. By now they'll all be dead.'

Hark looked over at where his flunky was hovering in the window. 'Oh, for heaven's sake, sit down, man! I tell you there's nothing to worry about. The general has left some of his best men looking after us. He knows the value of what we do.'

'Are you sure about that?' Cody McBride stepped from the shadows of the doorway where he'd been lurking, an army service revolver in his hands.

Bure dropped his cigarette. 'Oh, my God...'

Hark leaned back in his chair, watching McBride with an amused smile. 'Well, well, our enterprising private detective. And what can we do for you?'

'A little prescription, Doc. Nothing much. There's a friend of mine in a ward downstairs. I'd like you to get him a wheelchair, and I'd like you to wake him up.'

'Ah, our unfortunate Inspector Mullen.'

'Chief Inspector.'

Hark nodded. 'As you wish. *Chief* Inspector Mullen. And may I ask where you think you are going to take him? It would be dangerous to move him. He's a very sick man.'

'No, I think you're the sick one around here.' McBride's face was stern. 'And if you don't do what I say, then I'm gonna do some surgery of my own and put a hole in that nasty little skull of yours.'

Bure gripped Hark by the shoulders. 'See, I told you we should have gone!' he stammered. 'How did he get past the guards? Crawhammer's best, you said!'

Hark shrugged him off angrily.

'My colleague is a little over-emotional, but he does have a point, Mr McBride. You do seem to have got up here with remarkable ease.'

McBride shrugged. 'What can I say? Crawhammer's men seem to have the most childlike trust in military authority.'

'But you *have* no military authority, McBride.'

'Yeah, and isn't that a bitch? Fortunately, I have friends in high places.'

With the gun still trained on Hark's forehead, McBride called back over his shoulder.

'How we doin' out there, Davey?'

Davey O'Brien appeared, breathless and sweating, a machine gun slung over one shoulder. 'I've got him into the chair, but he's not a happy bunny. I really hope you know what you're doing, McBride.'

Hark raised a quizzical eyebrow. 'Captain O'Brien? I thought that you would have left with the general.'

'That's what the general thought, too.' said O'Brien. 'Unfortunately he's American army whereas I'm RAF, so I don't take orders from him.'

'He was very useful in getting us past Crawhammer's best, though.' A trace of a smile flickered over McBride's face. 'And my buddy here tends to give most of his orders with the butt of his gun, but then he does have kind of a personal perspective on our little situation...'

'What are you going to do with us? What is it that you want?' Bure was white with fear.

'I told you,' said McBride. 'I want you to wake up Mullen, and then you, me, the Chief Inspector and the O'Brien twins are going to go for a little walk.'

'You'll never get out of here, you know.' Hark's smile had faded, his face shadowed and stern. 'You'll never escape.'

'Well, now, here's a thing.' McBride brought the gun closer to Hark's face. 'I've got myself a bit of a plan, and once you've revived Mullen for me, then all I need from you is the key to the elevator at the end of the hall.'

'I don't know what you mean.'

'Come on, Doc. I've been running about all day, being shot at by the Welsh Guards and jumped on by monkeys and all this time there's been an elevator. Problem is that it's a staff elevator and it needs a key. So I started wondering, "who would use the staff elevator", and you know what answer I came up with? Doctors. You're a doctor, so you must have a key.'

'I really don't know what you're talking about.'

'No?' McBride pulled the hammer back on the revolver. 'Because if that's true, then I really don't know why I need you.'

'You need me to revive Mr Mullen.'

'Nah, not really. I'm sure that your stooge here is capable of giving him the, uh, shot.'

He pressed the barrel of the revolver against the bridge of Hark's nose.

'Give me the key.'

Hark reached into the pocket of his white lab coat and pulled out a small silver key. McBride took it and threw it over to O'Brien.

'Davey, why don't you get your, uh, twin – take Shorty here – and get down to the basement. I'll be right behind you.'

'McBride, you might need a hand.'I'm not sure...'

'I can handle this goon. Besides, your other half might not be the best thing for Mullen to see at the moment. He's sort of got a bit of a thing about cybernetics.'

O'Brien nodded. 'All right. Be careful.' He pointed his rifle at Bure. 'You, come with me.'

A trembling Bure scampered past McBride, throwing a terrified look at Hark as he passed. Hark didn't even glance at him.

McBride took a deep breath and pulled the gun away from Hark's face. 'Well now, Dr Hark. Time to visit the patient.'

Chapter Twenty-three

'Mullen? Mullen, wake up!'

Chief Inspector Mullen forced apart his crusted eyes and stared into the face of Cody McBride.

'Damn it, McBride,' he groaned. 'You're not the first thing that I want to see when I wake up.'

McBride forced a smile. 'Right now I might be more use to you than some pretty nurse. We're getting out of here, Mullen.'

Mullen tried to laugh, but his throat was too dry and all he managed was a croaking rasp. McBride waved his gun at Hark. 'Get him some water.'

His face like thunder, Hark filled a glass from a jug on the bedside table and handed it to McBride.

'What's he doing here?' growled Mullen.

'Just helping out. Don't worry about him.' McBride raised the glass to Mullen's lips. The big Irishman took a gulping mouthful, water splashing onto his hospital gown.

'Hey, hey. Slow it down there.' McBride tried to wipe some of the spilled water from Mullen's chin with the sleeve of his coat. Mullen batted feebly at his arm.

'Don't you dare go soft on me, McBride.'

There was a distant rattle of gunfire and an echoing howl. Mullen raised a quizzical eyebrow at McBride. 'Why is it that I think things have got a hell of a lot worse whilst I've been asleep?'

'You don't know the half of it.'

Mullen slumped back weakly onto his pillows. 'It's no good, McBride.'

'I mean it. I'm getting you out of here.'

'How, exactly? In case you haven't noticed, this is a bed, not a getaway car, and I'm stuck in it.'

Keeping a careful eye on Hark, McBride pulled a delicate silver chain with a silver shape at the end from his pocket and dangled it in front of Mullen.

'Very pretty, McBride. Christmas decoration or stolen jewellery?'

'TARDIS key,' McBride whispered

Mullen's eyes opened wide. 'TARDIS? You mean...?'

'I mean that the Doc has parked his space machine in the basement.'

'And trusted you with the key? Things must be bad.'

McBride said nothing. The two men stared at each other for long seconds. Then Mullen nodded.

'All right. How do we get there?'

McBride pointed to an ancient wheelchair at the foot of the bed. 'Dr Hark has provided some quality transportation for you.'

'So you get me into this godawful contraption, we get in the lift and you wheel me to the safety of the Doctor's TARDIS, is that it?'

There was another rattle of gunfire from somewhere deep in the hospital.

'It's not going to be quite that straightforward,' said McBride.

'But how did I get here, how did you get here, and where in the name of hell *is* here?'

The Doctor waved frantically for Rita to be quiet, took one final look out into the darkened corridor and closed the office door.

He caught Rita by the arm and led her to a deep leather sofa. She slumped back into it, the Doctor perching on the arm.

'Miss Hawks, I regret not having time to give you a full lecture on multiple universes. For the moment will you just accept that you have been taken through a crack between dimensions, brought to a world that is running parallel with ours, alike but not identical?'

'And this world is trying to invade ours?'

'Yes.'

'And if they succeed, then the universe could be destroyed?'

'Yes.'

'And you are trying to stop it?'

'Yes.'

Rita lowered her head into her hands. 'I so need a drink.'

The Doctor laid a gentle hand on her shoulder. 'And when we get out of here I promise to buy you the finest Manhattan that London has to offer.'

Rita raised her head and smiled at him. 'That's the nicest offer anyone has made me in this whole world.'

'I try my best...'

'How did you know I was trying to get in?'

'I didn't. I was trying to get out. I saw you through the window.'

'But how did you...'

'Recognise you? It wasn't that difficult. You were the only one not trying to break a land speed record. I doubted you'd be hard to track down once I was outside.'

'I thought I'd never see you again.'

The Doctor stared levelly at her. 'I was hardly just going to leave you stranded here, now was I?'

Rita leaned forward and gave him a peck on the cheek. 'Thank you.'

The Doctor looked flustered and embarrassed. He stood up and held out his hand. 'We should go.'

Rita took it and pulled herself out of the couch. 'Where are you going to start looking? I mean, this building is huge, and someone's bound to see us sooner or later.'

The Doctor eased open the office door and peered out into the corridor. 'Act as if you own the place, that usually works. As for Mr Limb, well, I think it would be difficult to remain inconspicuous with an eight-foot cybernetic gorilla in tow.'

Rita's jaw dropped. 'Come again?'

Grunting with effort, McBride and Hark eased Mullen into the wheelchair. McBride slumped back onto the edge of the bed, clutching at his ribs.

'Either you're getting too heavy or I'm getting too old, Mullen.'

'You should be grateful. I've lost a lot of weight recently.'

McBride snorted, then realised what Mullen meant. He felt himself flush. 'Come on, we'd better get going.' He pulled a blanket from the bed and threw it across the big Irishman's lap. 'Davey O'Brien should be waiting for us.'

'Are you sure that the Doctor's going to be happy with all these people knowing about his little conjurer's box?' murmured Mullen.

McBride shuffled uncomfortably. It was true his plan to rescue Mullen had involved far more people than he had expected. Truth be told, he wasn't even sure he could just sit by and watch Hark and his snivelling assistant die if it came to it.

'I'll worry about that later.'

He waved his gun at Hark. 'Right, Doctor. Let's take our patient for a little walk, shall we?'

Scowling, Hark gripped the handles of the wheelchair and started to push Mullen across the ward.

'You're never going to get away with this, McBride. Even if you get past the guards, where are you going to go? London's crawling with Russian soldiers.'

'Why don't you let me do the thinking and you just concentrate on the pushing, eh Doc?'

He followed Hark out into the corridor, and peered across at the lift door. A small arrow pointing down was illuminated. McBride gave a sigh of relief. O'Brien had sent the lift back. 'We might just get away with this,' he murmured under his breath.

Relief turned to puzzlement as the floor started to tremble under McBride's feet.

'What the hell?'

There was a shattering roar and the entire hospital heaved and shook. The air fizzled and crackled, and fingers of blue lightning arced across the ceiling. Shelves collapsed, spilling glass and files across the floor. McBride ducked as light-bulbs exploded, sending shards of glass showering down on them. Hark was curled up in a ball on the floor, whimpering like a child. Mullen cursed as his wheelchair was sent skittering across the corridor and crashed into a wall.

The shuddering subsided and McBride edged over to his friend.

Mullen gave him a long-suffering look. 'And what in the name of all that's holy was that about?'

McBride shook his head. 'I have no idea, but I *really* think it's time to get out of here.'

Kicking debris away from the wheels of the wheelchair, he heaved it away from the wall, backing it across the corridor to the lift. 'I just hope to God that this is still working.'

He stabbed frantically at the buttons. There was a soft chime.

Mullen gave a weak smile. 'Luck of the Irish.'

The doors slid open and two invading soldiers stepped out, futuristic rifles raised.

'Oh, crap,' said McBride.

Rita clung to the Doctor's arm as the shuddering and flickering lighting subsided.

'Hey, since when did they have earthquakes in England?'

'That was no earthquake.' The Doctor's face was grim. 'That was a dimensional tremor. There won't be a part of the multiverse that didn't feel that. It's started.'

'The end of the world?'

'Much worse.'

As if on cue, a long chilling howl rang out through the cavernous corridors of the Ministry of Augmentation. Rita tightened her grip on the Doctor's arm.

'I'm no expert, but did that sound like a frightened gorilla to you?'

The Doctor peered out from under the staircase where they had taken refuge. 'Upstairs I think.'

The two of them padded softly up the thickly carpeted stairs, the Doctor abandoning all attempts at stealth now. Below them the few staff who were still working milled around now, spilling out of offices and chattering nervously. If anything, they were even faster than the people outside. Panic, Rita assumed. She wasn't even sure that they were aware of her and the Doctor.

On the landing the Doctor stopped, holding up his hand. Rita could hear the low murmur of conversation. The Doctor pointed at an open door, a long shaft of light spilling out across the floor. Crumpled shapes cast long shadows on the carpet. Rita peered at them, then realised they were bodies, or parts of bodies, strewn carelessly around like a child would discard toys.

She covered her mouth with her hand. 'Oh, God...'

The Doctor caught hold of her hand and squeezed it. 'Are you going to be all right?'

Rita nodded. 'Yes... Yes, it's just...'

'I know. This will be over soon, I promise.'

Rita took a deep breath, straightened her coat and ran a hand through her tousled hair.

'I'm hardly looking at my best to be meeting the head honcho in this universe.'

The Doctor smiled. 'You look fine. Ready?'

Rita nodded.

The Doctor linked arms with her and the two of them stepped through the door.

'Good evening. I'm the Doctor and this is my friend Rita.'

Two George Limbs looked up in surprise.

'Doctor,' said one.

'What a delightful surprise,' said the other.

A huge gorilla turned towards them and gave a shattering roar.

Rita fainted.

* * *

Davey O'Brien had no trouble getting the sweating, twitching Dr Bure to take him up to the garret in which his tortured other-world counterpart lay dying.

He tried not to look at the creature.

'What do you want?' the dying cyborg said.

His voice – Davey shuddered.

'We've come to get you out,' he replied.

'Why?'

'In case you hadn't noticed, we're under attack. I'm trying to save you.'

'Why?'

'I don't know. But if our positions were reversed, I know you'd have to do the same for me. Us.'

The thing took an awkward step towards him.

'Steady... uh... mate.'

Davey tucked himself under his alter-ego's gaunt, wire-threaded arms and tried to support him as they walked. Bure scuttled along just in front of them.

Davey stopped. He could hear movement. He struggled behind some pipes with his patient. Bure squeezed in behind them. He could see the silhouettes of two enemy troops.

He motioned to his companions to keep silent.

'Over here!' the other O'Brien bellowed with as much strength as he could muster.

McBride stepped out of the hospital into a cold, wet November night, wincing at the shock of the freezing rain. The hospital grounds were awash with other-dimensional troops. Overhead a futuristic Zeppelin hung low and silent.

A searchlight from the airship swept across the car park and McBride saw the rubble and broken glass left by the tremor.

A sharp shove in the small of his back set him stumbling over the wet pavement.

'Hey, bub, watch the coat.'

McBride glanced back at where two soldiers were manhandling Mullen and his wheelchair out of the hospital. The police officer looked pale and old and McBride felt his heart sink. He'd failed. Instead of getting Mullen somewhere safe, he'd dropped him in the middle of something worse.

'Hey, it's all right. I'll take him.' McBride caught hold of the handles of the wheelchair and stared at the soldiers defiantly. He looked around for O'Brien. Perhaps he'd managed to get away...

Hark pushed his way out of the door, protesting loudly.

'I tell you I'm not with these men! I'm a doctor, you have no right –'

McBride gave a wry smile as one of the soldiers clubbed Hark casually over the back of the head and pushed him forward roughly. The three of them were marched over to where a mobile command centre was set up in the middle of the square. One of their escorts saluted smartly.

'Three civilians found in the building, Captain Williams, sir!'

A young man in a captain's uniform raised himself painfully from his chair, supporting himself on an inelegant military crutch. He was badly bruised, one eye so swollen that he could barely open it. His uniform was ripped and McBride could see blood-soaked bandages through the tears. One arm was mangled and twisted, and McBride could see the pain in his face.

Williams regarded the three of them carefully with his good eye. 'Medic. Check out the man in the wheelchair, see how he's doing.'

McBride stepped forward protectively. 'He's lost both legs. He's in a lot of pain.'

'Then if you get out of our way and let our medic take a look at him, perhaps he can help.'

McBride paused for a moment, then nodded. 'Thank you.'

'Don't thank me yet.' Williams snapped. 'Civilians, are you? So you wouldn't know anything about the apes that killed most of my men and beat me to a bloody pulp.'

McBride said nothing.

Williams lowered himself painfully back into his chair. 'No, you wouldn't, would you? Just like you wouldn't know about a heavily armoured group of men who broke out of here an hour ago, and a rogue helicopter that slipped away at the same time.'

McBride shrugged. 'Like you said, we're civilians.'

Williams pulled an odd-looking service revolver from its holster and placed it on the desk in front of him.

'I am in command of a rescue squad. I currently have over a quarter of my men either dead or in a field hospital suffering from wounds inflicted during the battle to secure the area. And now there has been a seismic disturbance, which my technical staff inform me is due to dimensional instability. An advance unit by the Thames has had to ward off an attack by lizard people emerging from an energy tear near

Battersea. A sapper unit working on the bridge has had to destroy a number of heavily armoured robot creatures using blasting explosives.

'Then I guess you've had better days.'

Williams pointed the gun at McBride.

'This city will soon be under martial law, and at the moment I can't think of a single good reason why I shouldn't have you shot.'

'There's a man who calls himself the Doctor,' blurted Hark.

'Shut up,' hissed McBride.

'He's not from here, he's different. Alien.' Hark was babbling now. 'His X-rays were all wrong, a cardiovascular system unlike anything I've ever seen. It was he who set the apes loose. He did the adaptations, he...'

'I said shut up!' McBride swung a right hook at Hark, sending him crashing to the floor. McBride lunged at him but a sharp blow on the back of the head sent him sprawling. He rolled over, groaning, and looked right into the barrel of Williams's gun.

'Sir! Sir, we've got three more of them!'

A breathless squaddie scurried over. 'Found them in the basement, sir.'

A figure was pushed past McBride. Captain Williams stared incredulously. 'O'Brien? Davey O'Brien?'

O'Brien shook himself free from his captors. 'Name, rank and serial number is all you're going to get.'

'Davey, it's me, Frank Williams. Remember?'

O'Brien stood stiffly to attention, staring straight ahead 'O'Brien, D. Captain, Royal Air Force. 262704K, sir.'

The squaddie pointed nervously over his shoulder, 'Er, sir, I think you should see the other one.'

'Other one?' Williams frowned. 'What the devil are you talking about, soldier?'

'The other O'Brien, sir. Over here.'

Williams turned and his jaw dropped.

McBride rubbed his aching head and craned his neck to see. Bure and the O'Brien that had tumbled through from another dimension stood in the rain, a dozen soldiers standing guard around them. As he watched, the young pilot shambled forward, mechanical legs hissing and clanking, pain running in waves across his face with every step that he took. He reached out, pleading. 'Take me home, Frank. For God's sake. Take me home.'

Williams caught him as he tumbled forward. 'Medic! Medic!'

Army doctors darted across the square, taking O'Brien from Williams's arms and lowering him gently onto a stretcher. McBride saw a look of pure horror flicker across the chief medic's face as he examined O'Brien's legs, then the stretcher was whisked away in a blur of motion.

'Who did this?' Williams hissed.

No one answered. Then – 'It was him!' shouted Dr Bure, pointing at his boss Dr Hark. 'I only took orders…'

Hark stepped forward, his voice trembling. 'We did our best. We needed to find out how you worked, how you were built.'

Williams spun, his face a mask of rage, fumbling for his gun. 'You animals! You primitive barbarian butchers!'

The army captain levelled his revolver, his hands shaking with fury. Hark dropped to his knees with a whimper. McBride closed his eyes. He was dazzled anyway.

Tendrils of blue lancing energy tore though the night air, making the rain hiss and boil. The ground heaved and split, and McBride felt himself tumbling backwards. He crashed into O'Brien and the two of them rolled across the pavement. From the hole in the shattered tarmac came the ants, hundreds of them, pouring out into the road like a black tide. Hark barely had time to scream before they were on him, pincers tearing into his flesh. Gunfire tore through the night air as disbelieving soldiers came to their senses. Williams fired round after round into the advancing tide, bellowing orders.

McBride felt someone hauling him to his feet.

'We've got to get out of here!' screamed O'Brien.

'Where's Mullen?' McBride looked around frantically. 'Did you see where they took Mullen?'

'Forget him, he's gone.'

'No, damn it! I'm not going to lose him now!'

McBride struggled to get free from O'Brien's grasp, oblivious to the chaos erupting around him. All he could think of was his friend.

O'Brien suddenly gave a scream of horror. McBride spun. From over the pile of the shattered tarmac appeared two of the ants, antennae twitching. With a high-pitched chirruping, they darted forward. McBride lashed out with his foot, catching one of them in the side of the head and sending it skittering across the rubble. He saw the other one catch O'Brien's arm in its jaws. The young soldier screamed in agony as the ant started to drag him back towards the entrance to its tunnel.

McBride threw himself on the creature's back, kicking and screaming, hammering on the slick black chitin. He was barely slowing it up. O'Brien twisted and spun in the ant's jaws, bellowing with pain. McBride looked around frantically for something that he could use as a weapon.

A length of steel bar jutted out from the shattered pavement. McBride lunged for it, muscles straining as he struggled to pull it from the rubble. The bar shifted a few feet, then jammed. McBride screamed in frustration. O'Brien was hammering at the ant's head with a lump of rock. Blood was pouring from his arm now, shocking against the jet black body of the ant.

McBride put all his strength against the bar. With a grind of steel on stone it came free. Bellowing in rage, McBride brought the bar crashing down with all his might. There was a horrible crack and the ant collapsed down onto the rubble, thick ichor spurting from a deep crack across its back.

Flinging the bar to one side, McBride scrambled over to O'Brien, whipping off his tie and slipping it around the soldier's arm.

'Are you all right?'

O'Brien grimaced as the tie pulled tight. 'Oh yeah, get bitten by giant ants all the time.'

He gripped McBride's arm. 'Thanks...'

'Don't thank me yet.' McBride hauled O'Brien to his feet, his face grave. From over the top of the rubble came another ant, then another and another. A cacophony of chittering filled the air.

'Nice knowing you, McBride.'

A shattering roar drowned out the clatter of the ants and everything was lit up by another sheet of brilliant blue lightning. McBride craned his neck back as a shimmering tear ripped up into the night sky. Through streaming eyes, McBride could see something moving inside the tear, something vast pushing its way though.

A huge boot crashed down, smashing onto the ants. McBride kept leaning back, trying to see the top of whatever had just pushed through the dimensional bridge. A voice like distant thunder boomed out through the rain.

'Gordon Bennet!'

'What the hell is that?' screamed O'Brien.

McBride's jaw dropped as he craned his neck higher and higher. She was huge.

'This is...' he spluttered. 'This is... incredible... this is... Ace...'

Chapter Twenty-four

Bill Collins was disorientated – to say the least. Their flight from the hospital had been gut-wrenching. In the brief ten minutes of chaos wrought by the air-strike they had taken off in the helicopter, dodging down canyon-like streets, almost touching the roofs of abandoned buses, in as much danger of being shot by the RAF as by the enemy. The assault was working – enemy ships were on fire.

As they flew over the river, the pilot had suddenly gone into a dive. An RAF Lightning, its tail on fire, was bearing down on them. They were almost touching the water…

A shadow passed overhead. London Bridge. They were going under it. The roaring of the blades was momentarily multiplied, then was drowned in an explosion that rocked the chopper as it tried to ascend. The jet had slammed into the bridge behind them.

'That's some flyin', boy!' Crawhammer had bellowed.

Collins had struggled to hold his stomach together.

They had landed outside Drakefell's flat in Islington. The lock on the door had been broken. Drakefell and his PA were there – Drakefell in pyjamas and dressing-gown. Crawhammer hadn't even waited for him to dress. He'd bundled Drakefell into the helicopter, ignoring the protests – and then the blows – of Sarah Eyles, and ordered them to fly like hell for Winnerton. They'd left Sarah an angry dot on a receding cityscape.

The journey had been easy – enemy ships were much sparser as they left London, and simple to avoid.

They found the men waiting for orders, cut off from communication and confused.

'I'll give you an order!' Crawhammer had barked. 'Red alert, boys!'

And he had marched into the central control room and opened a set of locked metal doors at the far end. Behind them lay the controls to the ballistic missile system they were developing.

'Major Collins, I want the missiles armed. All of 'em.'

Collins suddenly felt cold. 'Armed with what, sir?'

'Nuclear warheads, Major. It's time to kick ass!'

* * *

'I tell you I'm fine.' Rita scowled at the Doctor and brushed his hand away from the bruise on her forehead. 'I just fell, OK? Fell, not fainted. I'm not the type of girl who faints. Are we clear on that?'

From the other side of the room Jimmy gave a snort of contempt and lit up a cigarette.

Rita shot him a filthy look. 'Shouldn't you be dead or something?'

Jimmy scowled at her and slouched against the wall, blowing a cloud of tobacco smoke into the room.

The Doctor looked across at where George Limb – *his* George Limb – was training a gun on his morning-coated counterpart, who seemed quite unruffled by the experience.

'I did rather imagine you might take it as a compliment, old bean. You must understand, I wanted the best. Someone I could trust.'

And slowly the two of them began to smirk like schoolchildren. Then one of them began to cough and wheeze. The other didn't.

'You should get that chest looked at,' he said. 'I can get someone to look at it for you. You need never be out of breath again.'

Then he turned to the Doctor.

'Is the young lady going to be all right?'

'I think so,' said the Doctor. 'A combination of malnutrition, exhaustion and shock. All obsolete in your England, no doubt.'

'Indeed…'

The prime minister paused and raised a finger to his temple. Slowly he smiled.

'This ought to be amusing… Good evening, General.'

One wall of the room – holographic, it would seem – melted away to reveal an enormous television screen. And on the screen was none other than General Crawhammer.

'Now listen here, you Commie English bastards, or whatever the hell you are, I got a whole bunch of nuuu-cleeeer missiles aimed right into your big shiny crack! Now I'm askin' you politely to get yo' forces back through that hole and close it up. You got ten minutes to decide.'

And the screen went blank.

'How'd I do, Major?'

'Very well, sir.' Bill Collins had believed Crawhammer's ultimatum. But then he knew Crawhammer.

The general had said virtually nothing to him since they had arrived. He had issued orders, stomped around, but explained nothing. Not that much needed explaining. Everywhere was cut off from everywher else by the blanket communications jam. The chain of command would be screwed – they'd never get the birds in the air if they waited for someone to fly to Washington to consult the president.

Winnerton Flats was perhaps the only facility this side of the Pacific that had independent control of its own nuclear arsenal. For developmental purposes, of course.

The general was clearly convinced where his duty lay.

He had stood over Drakefell while the shaking man, looking frail and frightened and clutching his dressing-gown around himself, input the authorisation codes for the usual test-firings. Only the payload was unusual.

Collins was surprised when Crawhammer fetched the camera crew in from outside the base.

'I bet this baby gets through,' he'd grunted. He'd been right.

'What now, sir?' Collins asked.

'We wait and see, Major.'

George Limb, prime minister of Britain and Empire, smiled gently to himself.

'Bluffing, of course,' said his less august double. 'The general is a death or glory man. He would simply have fired the wretched things. No… I sense your hand in this, Doctor, and you would never be so… apocalyptic.'

'Well done,' said the Doctor. 'The rather severe deadline wasn't my idea, however – and it leaves our friend here with a dilemma.'

'Whether or not to trust the general's restraint,' the PM concluded.

'Quite,' said the Doctor.

Time passed. Crawhammer was silent and grim, turning the situation over in his mind.

The Doctor had told him on no account to actually fire the missiles. He hadn't told him what to do if that didn't work.

'Sir…' Bill Collins prompted. The deadline was almost up.

What choice did he have? They didn't know the situation out there, but it couldn't be good. They had to strike back with whatever they had at their disposal.

The Doctor had warned of the consequences. But was enslavement to a perverse and alien ideology worse?

The Doctor had said a lot. He'd talked about an old man in a wheelchair in Louisiana…

Crawhammer dismissed the image from his mind, but it popped straight back.

'Ten minutes, General,' said Collins.

At his sides, Crawhammer clenched his fists until the knuckles whitened.

Inside the Ministry of Augmentation, two identical old men and a Time Lord were wasting precious minutes, while Jimmy and Rita looked on.

'Quite apart from the terrible danger involved in breaching realities,' the Doctor pleaded, 'I can't see what you hope to achieve by this invasion.'

'Living space, Doctor. This planet is now terribly overcrowded – people are born, but nobody dies any more. Interstellar travel, sadly, is still beyond our capability, and the challenge of colonising other planets formidable.'

'So you intend to colonise another Earth. Presumably wiping out its existing population as you go.'

The old man looked sympathetic. Suddenly, in his morning coat and winged collar, he reminded the Doctor of an undertaker.

'It is regrettable,' he said, 'but we must remember that there is an infinity of Earths out there. Some will thrive, some will be obliterated.'

'And you think that excuses what you're doing?' the Doctor hissed.

'I find Liebermann's ideas cast the universe – or should I say multiverse – into an entirely new, much larger moral framework.'

The Doctor closed his eyes and sighed. 'Moral framework.'

'Do I know any Liebermann?' queried the other George Limb.

'A brilliant scientist. His theories of trans-universality have made all this possible.'

'Based, presumably, on our own dear Betty.'

'Indeed. Liebermann is a genius. A European Jew. Perhaps in your world he never made it through the war. Perhaps he merely wandered a different path… Look, would you mind awfully lowering the gun?'

'Yes,' the Doctor acidly cut in, 'I've heard about people threatening to kill themselves, but this is ridiculous.'

'Not as ridiculous as you might think, Doctor.' Limb smiled that lazy smile of his and relaxed his aim slightly. 'As I told you, I've been working towards this moment for many years, tweaking and turning the tides of time in order to avoid a rather unpleasant fate.'

'Trying to avoid your destiny.'

'Destiny seems such a final word. Something that final needs to be thought about carefully, planned for, prepared. One should always have an eye on the future.'

'And you think that this is it? You think this is your future?'

Limb gazed around the plush interior of the office. 'It all seems very nice. He's prime minister, you know. And a great one, it would seem. He has embraced the instrument of his – our – doom and made it serve him and the world.'

'Augmentation.'

'Indeed.' Limb nodded to himself. 'As futures go, this world seems very clean and tidy.'

'Tell that to the poor coots lined up downstairs,' spat Rita.

'Oh, you have it quite wrong, my dear. Those poor people are being helped towards a better way of life.' The prime minister smiled genially. 'We're taking away their disease, their weakness, the burden of frail old age.'

'Ultimately, you risk taking away their free will, their hope, their humanity,' snapped the Doctor.

The prime minister sighed. 'So many of you misunderstand what it is we are trying to do here. Augmentation is the future, a good clean future for us all.'

Limb turned towards the Doctor, his eyes alive with excitement. 'You see, Doctor, all my hard work, all my waiting has given me a chance to make a difference, to find a position in the world where I can put my considerable talents to good use. This is a clean world, a good world. You've seen the way that our own reality is going... Fear, mistrust, the brink of nuclear Armageddon, all of that is gone here.'

'But I've seen where this eventually leads...' the Doctor was pleading now. 'You know nothing of the future, nothing of the horrors that wait for you along this path. However well intentioned this augmentation is, however elegant it may seem here and now, the price will eventually be too high. And that's not all – already our presence is starting to affect the barriers of creation. You've felt the tremors. That is just the beginning. Soon time and space will start to collapse. You would be destroying everything, just to save your own life.' The Doctor held out his hand. 'We can end this. Come back with me, stop this madness before it's too late.'

The visitor shook his head and steadied his aim. 'I'm not going to end up old and alone lying forgotten in an anonymous hospital bed,

Doctor. I'm not going to let them try to save me with their knives and their tubes and their lies. I'm not going to let it happen.'

'And what do you think you're going to do? Shoot him and simply take his place? Purge all those close to you before you're discovered? Quietly have yourself augmented?'

'What an excellent idea, Doctor.'

George Limb turned and fired three shots into the right honourable George Limb's chest.

'What the hell is going on, McBride? Why has everything shrunk?'

Ace's voice boomed. McBride winced.

'Look, I'd love to explain everything to you,' McBride bellowed, 'but we've got a few problems at the moment.'

The huge Ace reached down, flicking at the scurrying ants and scooping up McBride and O'Brien in her gigantic fingers.

'This is too weird. One minute I'm standing alongside you dealing with that creep Williams, the next – *shazam* – there's a great tearing noise and I'm doing my King Kong impression.' She frowned. 'Hey, where's the Professor?'

'Ace, this is going to take a while. In the meantime, will you please get Mullen somewhere safe!'

'Right.' Ace plucked McBride and O'Brien from the palm of her hand and carefully put them down on the roof of a nearby building.

'You two stay here, I won't be long.'

Round her feet the astonished soldiers had started shooting at her. Ace winced.

'Hey stop that! It stings!'

Batting away soldiers and ants with an enormous hand, Ace peered into the makeshift command headquarters looking for Mullen.

McBride gave the incredulous O'Brien a weak smile.

'Lucky for us she turned up, eh?'

O'Brien said nothing.

McBride sighed. 'God knows what the Doc is going to make of all this.'

The right honourable George Limb, prime minister, looked down at the three smoking holes in the fabric of his morning suit. He brushed at the fabric, tutting in irritation.

'My tailor is going to be very unhappy about this.'

Limb stared in astonishment. 'I don't understand...' Hands shaking, he raised the gun and fired again and again.

The Doctor and Rita ducked as bullets ricocheted around the office. The prim minister gave a horrible, humourless smile. 'For a supposedly intelligent man, you really have been extraordinarily stupid.' In one fluid movement he rose from his chair and pushed his desk to one side. The heavy oak table span across the room as if it was made of balsa.

Rita gasped. From the base of the prime minister's jacket a long, heavy electrical cable snaked across the thick pile of the carpet, terminating in a socket near the skirting-board. It dragged behind the prime minister like an obscene tail.

'Do you really think I would permit the rest of this country to reap the benefits of augmentation and not save the best for myself?'

Limb staggered backwards, fumbling with the gun. 'Keep back.'

'Oh, really, George. I'm hardly going to be put off by a few bullets.' He unbuttoned his jacket and flung it open.

With a cry of pure anguish, Limb dropped to his knees.

'Oh my God!' Rita covered her mouth with her hand. The prime minister's body was mechanical. All of it. A complex construct of gleaming steel and chrome, pistons and motors, valves and circuits. Transparent tubes snaked through the metal skeleton, thick hydraulic fluid coursing through them, a bulbous mechanical pump pulsed rhythmically in the centre of the welded ribcage. Most horrific was the head. From just below the collar the flesh was stretched and clamped to the bearings of the neck, livid scars etched into the skin. Bundles of coloured wires twisted round the exposed spine and down into the workings of the mechanised chest. Rita's stomach churned.

With a whir of servos, the old man's head, which sat atop the mechanical monstrosity smiled, reached into the mechanics and flicked a switch in his abdomen. With a low whirr a section of panelled wall slid back, revealing a hidden alcove. Inside the alcove sat a squat silver machine, lights flickering over its surface, a huge gyroscope-like centrepiece whirling and spinning. Relays clicked and clattered as the prime minister spread his arms wide.

'This is the future that we offer.' Lights on the machine pulsed in time with his voice. 'The perfect fusion of man and machine. A wonderful union.'

The Doctor stared sadly at the crumpled figure of Limb on the floor. 'You see, Mr Limb, you cannot escape what time has in store for you. You are the eye of the storm – all the chaos you create cannot touch you. Wherever you turn, this is the inevitable, irrevocable conclusion.'

Tears were rolling down the old man's face.

The prime minister reached out a hand. 'Accept the gift we offer. Don't try and resist us. We will bring our technology to your world, stretch out across the barriers of reality. Soon you will belong to us. You will be like us.'

'No.' Limb hissed through gritted teeth, his face a mask of bitterness and betrayal. 'Never.'

Before the Doctor could stop him, he pulled a boxy device from his pocket, twisting at dials, stabbing at buttons. There was a shrill burble of radio noise. With a shattering roar, the gorilla leapt to its feet, clutching at his head.

'Limb, no!' bellowed the Doctor.

'I created you,' Limb spat at his machine double. 'I can destroy you.' He twisted a control savagely.

Sparks flying from its joints, the gorilla hurled itself across the room, catching the prime minister across the face with a swipe of an enormous paw. His body arced across the room, the cable that connected him to the mainframe trailing behind him like the tail of some absurd kite. Rita scrambled out of the way as the mechanical body crashed against the wall. The machine in the alcove began to chatter animatedly.

The prime minister hauled himself to his feet, the pump in his chest was beating faster now, servos whining and buzzing as he tried to regain his balance.

'Stupid... pointless...'

The voice was unsteady, more mechanical than it was before. Warning lights started to blink inside the skeletal body.

There was a low growl and Rita stared up in horror as the gorilla gathered itself to spring. She threw herself to the floor as it bounded over her. The prime minister gave a high-pitched squawk as the primate crashed into him.

The silver machine was spinning faster and faster. The prime minister's voice was harsh and grating – mechanical.

'RESISTANCE IS FUTILE>'

The gorilla smashed its fists into the cybernetic chest. Sparks flew into the air.

'YOU BELONG TO US>'

The prime minister flailed desperately at the huge ape. Casually it tore one of his arms off. Hydraulic fluid sprayed into the room. There was a muffled explosion from the alcove. Rita cowered as a gout of flame surged into the room.

'YOU WILL BE LIKE US>'

With a savage roar, the gorilla wrenched at the prime minister's head. There was a horrible gurgling scream as it came away from the mechanical body. Electricity arced through the air. With a howl, the gorilla stiffened, its limbs quivering, smoke pouring from its joints. Blue lightning tore through its body. With a choking roar, it collapsed forward over the dismembered body of the prime minister.

Another shattering explosion tore through the room, sending flaming debris showering everywhere. The mainframe was spinning wildly now, repeating the same phrase over and over.

'YOU WILL BE LIKE US> YOU WILL... BE... LIKE US> YOU... YOU WILLBELIKE... UUUUUSS>'

Rita felt someone dragging her to her feet. The Doctor was staring frantically around the room. 'Where's Limb?'

'There!' Through the smoke and flames she could see Jimmy helping Limb to his feet. The old man smiled thinly at the Doctor and pulled the dimensional stabiliser from beneath his shirt.

'No!' The Doctor darted forward but another explosion sent him reeling backwards. Coughing and spluttering, he watched as Jimmy and Limb vanished through the door.

'Come on, Doctor, we've got to get out of here.' Rita was hauling at his arm. 'This entire place is going to go up!'

'But you don't understand.' The Doctor started at Rita with despair in his eyes. 'I know where he's going to go, what he's going to do. He'd gambled everything on this being his perfect solution. Now he's checkmated himself, he has only one move left open to him.'

'So do we, Doc. Get out of here before we get blown sky high!'

'Listen to me!' bellowed the Doctor. 'Limb's got the dimensional stabiliser. He will use it to home in on the time machine. He knows that it's due to appear at Ace's graveside any time now. If he gets hold of that, then he can start this entire cycle all over again, and that would be catastrophic!'

'But there's nothing we can do!' screamed Rita.

'Oh, yes there is,' said the Doctor.

'Sir?'

The atmosphere in the room was tense. Technicians hardly dared breathe. All eyes were on Crawhammer, Bill Collins's included. The general hadn't spoken for what seemed an age. He was staring, motionless, at the static of a monitor screen.

He seemed to stir, lifted the safety-catch from the number-pad that controlled the launch. Four simple digits. His fingers played across the numbers. Collins murmured a silent prayer and thought about his family back home.

'We'll give them another five minutes,' said Crawhammer.

Rita clamped the Doctor's handkerchief to her nose, desperately trying to see what he was doing.

The smoke was choking now, flames starting to lick at the ceiling. The Doctor was crouched on the floor scrabbling at a section of panelling. The voice of the machine had dropped to a low droning howl, barely intelligible.

'What the hell are you doing, Doctor?'

'Finding us a way back home.' The Doctor didn't look round.

'And you think you're going to find one in the wainscoting? I'm not a mouse you know...'

'The PM was connected to the mainframe, yes? Hardwired you might say.'

'So?'

'So he is unlikely to have gone outside this room. But you said that he appeared in our dimension – in the old lady's cottage.'

'Which means there must be a dimensional doorway in here somewhere!' Rita felt a surge of excitement. 'God, Doctor, if you get me out of this in one piece, I might just have to marry you!'

The Doctor raised a quizzical eyebrow at her as a section of wall slid back with a soft whirr.

'Can we discuss that when we're back in our own dimension? I do have the universe to save at the moment.'

'Typical man. No commitment.'

She nodded at the complex controls set into the wall. 'Is this thing OK?'

The Doctor's hands danced over the controls. 'If I can just adjust the settings so that we follow the trail Mr Limb will have left...'

A section of ceiling crashed down behind Rita and a wave of heat rolled over them.

'You can deal with the fine tuning later, Doctor! Just get the damn thing working!'

The Doctor stabbed at a control and the wall began to ripple and soften before them. The Doctor caught hold of Rita's hand. 'Make a wish...'

'I guess it worked for Dorothy...'

Rita shut her eyes tight as the flickering wall of energy engulfed them.

The sudden blast of cold air made Rita gasp. She staggered and almost fell.

The Doctor caught her arm.

'Did it work?' she asked.

'There's no place like home...' said the Doctor.

Tentatively Rita opened her eyes. They were in a graveyard. Grey headstones jutted out from the snow; leafless trees were nothing more than spindly silhouettes against the night sky. Rita shivered.

'And this is no place like home. Why would Limb come here?'

'Because this is where his time machine finally broke down and catapulted him back to his own era. This is the day that he planted the evidence on Ace's body for me to find.' The Doctor's face was grim. 'Look.'

On the far side of the graveyard Rita could see a squat black shape, not unlike an upturned child's spinning top, steaming quietly in the snow.

'So let me see if I've got this straight.' Rita's head was reeling. 'That ... thing... is a time machine.'

'Correct.'

'That George Limb has just used to come from the past.'

'Yes.'

'But it broke and sent him back to where he started.'

'Yes.'

'But Limb has always known the exact time and place when he would catch up with the machine that has been waiting for him in *his* future.'

'Exactly!' The Doctor beamed at her. 'You have an excellent grasp of temporal mechanics!'

'But lousy timing. Look...'

From the trees on the edge of the graveyard Limb and Jimmy were making their way towards the time machine.

'Come on. We've got to get to it before them!' The Doctor hared off across the graveyard. Rita stumbled after him, heels slipping on the wet grass.

Limb looked up in surprise as the Doctor dodged and weaved through the headstones. With a burst of speed that belied his age, he darted forward, pulling open the hatch on the top of the machine.

'George, wait! You don't have to do this,' the Doctor bellowed.

'Too late, Doctor. You can't stop me now,' said Limb.

With a lazy puff of his cigarette, Jimmy pulled a revolver from his pocket. The Doctor skidded to a halt, breathless and panting. He could see Limb connecting the dimensional stabiliser to the instruments in the time machine. In seconds the machine would be working again.

'George, please. Stop this now and I can help you. We can work something out.'

'I don't need your help, Doctor.' Limb didn't look up. 'With this machine operational again I can go back and make a few... tweaks, a few changes. I can avoid that dreadful reality and create a better one.'

He stared through the window of the machine. 'It's only a matter of time.'

The Doctor started forward but Jimmy stepped into his path, the gun pointed directly at the Doctor's head.

'Leave him alone, Doctor.'

'You have no idea what damage he is doing with his meddling, do you?'

Jimmy shrugged. 'It worked out OK for me. I coulda died in a car crash. This seems a damn sight better to me.' He took a long drag on his cigarette. 'Hey, if he creates another reality, I might even end up as president. How about that, eh? An actor as president of the United States.'

'God forbid,' said Rita.

'Do you want to know another alternative that Mr Limb has denied you?' The Doctor's voice was low and dangerous. 'Fatherhood.'

'What?' Jimmy frowned. 'What are you talking about?'

'A father, with a healthy baby daughter.'

'I haven't got any daughter.'

'Jimmy, don't you listen to him.' Limb sounded snappy.

'Ace's baby.' The Doctor's voice didn't waver. 'Did you know that she was pregnant, Jimmy? Did you know that she was carrying your child when he shot her in the head?'

Jimmy shot an anguished look at Limb. 'I...'

The old man was fumbling with the controls, frantic and clumsy.

'Did you!' shouted the Doctor.

Jimmy let the gun drop. 'You're lying. She couldn't have...' Tears were rolling down his cheeks. 'You shouldn't have told me.'

Screaming with anger, he swung the gun towards Limb.

'*You* should have told me!'

'Jimmy! No!'

The Doctor lunged forward as the gun went off. At the same moment Limb activated the time machine.

A piercing shriek tore through the night air. The Doctor saw the bullet slow to a standstill, caught in the temporal field generated by the machine. Jimmy stood, frozen, lips drawn back in a vicious snarl. Rita was caught tumbling backwards, high heels slipping on the ice-slick ground.

All around time was suspended, held in check by the faulty circuits of the Cybermen's time machine. Wave after wave of temporal energy buffeted the Doctor, trying to hold him within its grasp. Inch by inch he forced himself forward. He could see Limb inside the machine, wrestling with the controls, staring incredulously as the Doctor fought against the tides of time.

Suddenly there was a flare and the ground and the air stretched and popped and seemed to collapse, then tumbled back to tranquil normality. The Doctor collided with a spherical ball of energy thrown up around the ship. Jimmy threw himself forward, pounding uselessly against the force field Limb had created.

Rita fell backwards into the snow.

Through the portals of the time machine the Doctor could see Limb blinking in bemusement. Whatever he had managed to do was by luck not design. The man was playing, operating something he didn't understand by pressing every button in sight until something happened. It was like watching a six-year-old trying to drive a car.

With a scream of anger, Jimmy vanished into the night. The Doctor called after him, but the actor was gone.

There was a sudden cry of pain and frustration from the graveyard. The Doctor hurried over to where Rita struggled in the snow. He stretched out a hand and hauled her to her feet.

'What the hell is going on?' She vainly tried to brush the snow from her coat.

The Doctor nodded at the time machine encased in its flickering ball of energy. 'Mr Limb has activated his machine, with limited success.'

'You mean he's failed? We can stop him?'

A shuddering roar shook the ground around them. Rita reached out for the Doctor in alarm.

'No,' said the Doctor. 'I rather think he's made things worse.'

Chapter Twenty-five

Captain Frank Williams punched at the ground in anger and frustration.

The last few hours had seen his entire operation go to hell. First the ambush by primates in the hospital that had left him half dead, then the attack by giant ants, and now a sixty-foot tomboy with a big mouth making a mockery of him and his troops.

From his fallback position on the far side of the square he could see her squashing the ants with her thumb and sending soldiers tumbling as she struggled to reach the prisoner in the wheelchair that they had captured.

He raised his rifle and fired, watching with satisfaction as she grasped at her arm, wincing.

'I'm warning you,' she bellowed.' If you don't stop that, I'm going to stick you all in a big jar with some of these ants.'

Willams tried to concentrate, sending a coms-pulse back to control. He'd heard nothing from them for nearly fifteen minutes now. He winced as static blared in his skull. 'Williams to control. Report please. Report!'

Finally through the static he thought he could hear something. 'Control!'

'BEEEE LIIIIKE UUUSSSS> YOOOOU WILLL> BEEEEEEE>'

He shut down his remote link as the slurred voice threatened to overwhelm him. He was getting reports from all over London about the same problem with control.

The ground heaved abruptly beneath him, sending masonry crashing to the floor.

And then an emergency channel opened itself up. That only happened in the event of a complete systems breakdown. Its signal was clear and brief – Evac Plan Alpha. Total abortion of mission. It was time to leave.

He took a deep breath and confirmed the recall signal. Engage the bridge and evacuate. Retreat.

McBride watched from the rooftops as the energy tear in the sky suddenly flared with light. As he watched, it seemed to pulse and swell.

'Holy mother of God...'

The airships that had been hovering over London since the attack began suddenly wheeling around in the night sky. Searchlights blazing, they shot like arrows into the dimensional breach in a surge of energy.

McBride's head rang as Ace gave a cry of triumph.

'Hey! Can't take it, can you? Well, get lost then!'

Shafts of light started to sweep across the ground, snatching up soldiers and sweeping them into the rift.

Ace cheered and bellowed. McBride could see a small figure clutched in her hand. A small figure in a wheelchair.

He felt a wave of relief wash over him. Ace had got Mullen.

Drakefell was two feet from Armageddon. He felt its power. It soothed him.

Only inches away from Armageddon, General Crawhammer was sweating. His deadline was long past, with no word from the other side of the breach. Crawhammer couldn't do it, Drakefell knew.

But Drakefell could.

All he could think about was the voice that had replied to their broadcast, that had swept across all their loudspeakers at once. The man who had preyed on his madness. His friend. Dr John Hopkins. Or George Limb, or whatever he was called.

And Drakefell's fears and torments had collapsed into a singularity. He represented the sum of Drakefell's fears. The Ministry of Augmentation. The Cyber process that had tormented him for years, writ large across the land. And Limb at its head.

A chance to destroy him. And more – a blow against the brute vastness and endless chaos of the truth...

'They're retreating, sir,' said Bill Collins. 'Look.'

It was true – men were pouring onto the ships, and the ships were streaking off into the breach. Crawhammer let out a heavy breath.

'Thank God,' he said.

Drakefell smiled. He felt bold for the first time in his life.

An end to it.

He pushed forward, shouldering General Crawhammer aside, threw himself at the buttons that held the code that opened up hell, and deftly triggered the sequence.

'Drakefell!' Crawhammer bellowed. 'Get away from there!'

'Too late!' he sang. 'Too late!'

He was vaguely aware of Crawhammer drawing his pistol, aware of the noise, aware that he'd been shot. The last thing he heard was the automated voice of rocket control confirming a successful launch. The warheads were in flight.

The Doctor sat cross-legged in the snow, eyes closed, palms pressed against the crackling ball of energy that flickered around the time machine. Rita watched nervously. The Doctor hadn't moved for a while, and the tremors shaking the graveyard were getting stronger.

'Doctor?' She reached out and tapped him on the shoulder. 'Doctor are you all right?'

The Doctor opened his eyes and stared at her sternly. 'Miss Hawks, I am attempting to break through a temporal force field. It is a complex and delicate operation that requires quiet and a great deal of concentration. Now, if you don't mind...'

Rita backed away. 'OK, OK! Sorry...'

The Doctor took a deep breath and placed his hands back on the force field. Inside the bubble she could see Limb poking at controls, his face as determined as the Doctor's.

Suddenly the ground began to tremble. Rita stared around her as a throaty roar filled the air.

'Doctor...'

'Shhh!'

'No, really Doctor, I think we should go.'

'Not now, Rita!'

'No time to argue, Doctor.'

Grabbing him by the collar of his jacket Rita hauled him backwards across the frozen ground.

Before the Doctor even had time to argue, something huge and silver flashed before him.

The Porsche 550 Spider slammed into the energy bubble at eighty miles an hour. Rita saw Limb throw up his hands in horror as the sports car sliced through the bubble of energy, glancing off the time machine and sending it spinning across the graveyard. Headstones shattered as car and machine tumbled end over end. Rita stared in horror as the Porsche landed on its roof and burst into flames.

The Doctor scrambled to his feet. 'Of course, there is always brute force and ignorance to fall back on.'

The Doctor and Rita picked their way though the shattered graves and burning wreckage to the twisted remains of the two machines.

The sports car was an inferno: there was no way that anyone could possibly have survived. The Doctor waved at Rita to stay back as he approached the blazing wreck. Rita saw him reach down and pluck something from the snow. He came back grave-faced, shaking his head. 'There's nothing we can do...'

Rita glanced over at where the remains of the time machine lay amongst a tangle of brambles. 'And Limb?'

'Let's see, shall we?'

Pulling the brambles aside, the Doctor heaved open the hatch of the battered machine. Limb, bruised and bloodied, stared up at him with baffled eyes.

'I can put it all right you know... in time...'

The Doctor reached inside the machine and tore the dimensional stabiliser free of the old man's hot-wiring.

'I think you've done enough damage.'

There was a distant roaring. Rita could see vapour-trails in the sky, at least two dozen, all blazing skyward, all converging on the shrinking chasm of light in the sky. And there were no enemy craft left to stop them.

'They did it,' the Doctor gasped. 'The idiots! It was just a bluff! I begged Crawhammer...'

He turned to Limb. 'I hope you're satisfied,' he whispered icily.

Limb caught hold of his arm. 'You don't know, Doctor... You don't know how many times I've watched myself die cold and lonely and in pain. You understand that, don't you? I know how I'm going to die, and I can't bear it... There has to be another way.'

'There is.' The Doctor reached into his pocket and pulled out a revolver.

Rita held her breath. That was what the Doctor had plucked from the snow. Jimmy's revolver.

'Your fate is set, Mr Limb, the same as everyone else's. You can try to break free from the clutches of time, but in the end there is no escape. Whatever you do, however many alternatives you create, the end will always be the same. Destiny.'

He handed the old man the revolver.

'This is the only solution I can offer you,' said the Doctor. 'I will stay with you, if you wish.'

'Thank you, Doctor,' said George Limb. 'I would appreciate that – and I imagine you would appreciate knowing that I am actually dead.'

The Doctor smiled mirthlessly, then turned to Rita.

'Why don't you make your way out,' he said gently. 'I'll catch you up.'

Rita flashed the Doctor a shallow smile. She couldn't look at the old man. She turned and limped wearily away towards the exit.

Behind them in the trees she heard a single gunshot. Rita closed her eyes and clenched her fists.

Epilogue

Mama's Bar was alive with the babble of conversation and the beat from the jukebox. The Doctor sat at a table near the window sipping at a glass of red wine, watching the people around him.

Over at the bar McBride was arguing with Mama.

'That's the lousiest excuse I ever heard in my life, McBride,' the big black bar-owner growled. 'Ten years you ain't set foot in the joint, then you roll on in with a story like that.'

'I swear to God it's true!' McBride protested.

'Buuullshiiit,' Mama drawled. 'You always were full of it, McBride.'

The Doctor smiled. Temporal scarring. Anomalies.

Ace, hunched over to avoid cracking her head on the low ceiling, was trying to play pool with O'Brien, while the crowd gawped openly. She was shooting balls like bullets across the table, and like bullets they ricocheted into the crowd.

It had been nearly two days since the dimensional rift had sealed itself – had swallowed the nuclear arsenal – and since then she had been steadily regaining her normal size. At the moment she just topped seven feet and dwarfed the pool table. Mama had joked about keeping her on as a bouncer.

'Hey, Doc...'

McBride was standing next to him.

'Cody.'

McBride slumped into a chair and took a long swig of beer. He nodded over at Ace 'How's she doing?'

'Oh, she'll be back to her usual size by the end of the evening.'

'That's not what I meant. Does she remember anything?'

The Doctor stared at his young companion. 'She remembers everything – or she thinks she does. As far as she's concerned, nothing has changed. She is Ace. The *only* Ace. To all intents and purposes she is the same Ace that she was before, barring one or two small details. She doesn't have a tattoo saying "Ace and Jimmy" on her back, she doesn't like peas and she has trouble remembering what her correct surname is...'

'And she was never shot in the head...'

'No... that rather important detail never happened.'

'And Limb?'

The Doctor suddenly looked oddly drawn.

'I buried him in Ace's grave,' he said, then smiled sadly. 'Time's way of putting things right. One life saved, another taken to balance it.'

'Well, Time might be tidying things up, Doc, but she's being a mite slapdash about how she's doing it.'

The Doctor frowned. 'Oh?'

McBride glanced around the room. 'As far as I remember, this place got hit by a V2 towards the end of the war.'

'Ah...' The Doctor gave a secretive smile. 'Well, I'm sure a few things might be a little out of step with the way they were. Infinite possibilities, remember...'

A figure slipped into the Doctor's view.

'Miss Eyles!' he cried. 'I'm very glad you came.'

Sarah Eyles looked sadly at him. 'I didn't have much else to do,' she said. 'Uncle George... gone. My employer dead...'

'Doctor Drakefell?'

'Apparently General Crawhammer shot him. It was Drakefell who fired the missiles. Crawhammer couldn't bring himself to do it.'

The Doctor blinked and thought about the two men.

'Doctor, what about... the people on the other side of the rift?'

'It must be hellish over there,' said the Doctor gravely. 'But they have an advanced technology, and all the dubious advantages of the Cyber process. I imagine they will bounce back... And how are you?' he asked Sarah gently.

'I'm... a little lost, to be truthful, Doctor.'

'You will come through, Sarah. Your great-uncle –'

'Please –' Sarah interrupted, 'I don't want to know. I want to believe he was loyal and brave and kind. And that in some way he died working for his country, not against it.'

'A part of him did,' said the Doctor. 'I was going to say he was the strongest, brightest, most resourceful human being I believe I have ever met. I'm sure you have inherited his better qualities.'

Sarah smiled.

The Doctor took another sip of wine. 'There are realities out there where the skies are water, the trees are made of air and the people speak in rhyme, realities where...'

'Oi!' Ace lumbered over and tapped the Doctor on the knee. 'What have I told you about getting all poetic? This is meant to be a party, remember?'

She handed him a set of spoons. 'Rita's going to be here any minute and you promised to be the percussion section.'

The Doctor waved his hands at her in irritation. 'Yes, yes, yes!'

Ace loped over to the door and peered out into the night.

McBride grinned. 'It's our Ace all right. As bossy as Rita and twice as sassy.'

The Doctor gave McBride a sideways glance. 'Our Miss Hawks is a very brave lady, with a great deal of affection for you. You could do a lot worse, you know.'

'McBride gave an embarrassed smile. 'Yeah, I know.'

Ace bounded back into the room. 'They're here. Everyone ready?'

Mama snapped off the lights and a giggling hush descended on the little bar.

A shaft of cold light arced across the room as the door swung open. A gruff Irish voice broke the silence.

'For God's sake, woman, there's no one here. You must have got the date wrong.'

'If you're not careful, I'll take you back to the hospital,' said Rita. 'Inspector or no inspector.'

'It's Chief Inspector,' growled Mullen. 'And why the hell is it so dark in here?'

The lights snapped on.

'Surprise!'

Mullen stared in astonishment as the little bar erupted into a chorus of 'For He's A Jolly Good Fellow' accompanied by McBride on the harmonica and the Doctor on the spoons.

As singing gave way to laughter, Mullen glared at McBride. 'Your idea?'

The American held up his hands. 'Hey, nothing to do with me. Rita organised it. I just do what she says.'

'I wish!' said Rita.

'You never do anything that I damn well say,' snorted Mullen.

McBride glanced nervously at his old friend. 'How are the legs?'

Mullen rapped his knuckles against his thigh. There was a metallic clang. 'Doctors say that I'm going to be able to start walking on them in a week or so, but you know what doctors are like. You can never trust 'em.'

'Quite right,' said the Doctor. 'You rarely can.'

'Oh, I don't know...' Ace tapped him on the nose with an oversized finger. 'I do all right by you.'

Mama sauntered over with a glass of Guinness in his hand. 'I thought this might be what you were looking for, Chief.'

'Ah, you're a life-saver and no mistake, Mama.'

'V2 rocket,' Mama scoffed as he passed McBride.

McBride shook his head. 'Guess I musta dreamed it.'

'McBride!' Mullen called. 'There's a poker game out back!'

Mama was pushing Mullen's chair through the crowds. Rita sashayed over and linked arms with McBride. 'So, are you going to buy me a drink or what?'

McBride nodded. 'Whatever the lady wants.' He looked at the Doctor and Ace.

'What about you two?'

The Doctor smiled. They could relax now. Time was repairing itself, and so were his friends' battered imaginations. Ironing out inconsistencies. Mama's was already seeming to McBride as if it had always been here. Human minds could rarely hold temporal pluralities for long.

Except for the late George Limb's, of course.

The Doctor looked quizzically at Ace. 'I think we've done enough racing around for a while. How about we stay here for Christmas, Ace?'

Ace grinned. 'Wicked.'

Acknowledgements

Thanks to:

Sophie and Sylvester
Andy Tucker
Justin Richards
Steve Cole
Miss Sue and Mr Steve
Karen Parks
Paul Dale Smith
Natalie Sedgwick
Moogie
Unta fae 'Tyre, Gub and Charlie – Y.C.C.

About the Authors

ROBERT PERRY and MIKE TUCKER still live on opposite sides of London, both still try to work within the media, and both still fill up any spare time they have by writing scripts and novels.

Their previous contributions to the *Doctor Who* range include the novels *Illegal Alien*, *Matrix*, *Storm Harvest* and *Prime Time*, and the short stories 'Stop the Pigeon' and 'Ace of Hearts' – all featuring the Seventh Doctor and Ace. *Loving the Alien* concludes that story arc.

BBC DOCTOR WHO BOOKS

'EIGHTH DOCTOR' RANGE

DOCTOR WHO: THE NOVEL OF THE FILM by Gary Russell
ISBN 0 563 38000 4
THE EIGHT DOCTORS by Terrance Dicks
ISBN 0 563 40563 5
VAMPIRE SCIENCE by Jonathan Blum and Kate Orman
ISBN 0 563 40566 X
THE BODYSNATCHERS by Mark Morris
ISBN 0 563 40568 6
GENOCIDE by Paul Leonard
ISBN 0 563 40572 4
WAR OF THE DALEKS by John Peel
ISBN 0 563 40573 2
ALIEN BODIES by Lawrence Miles
ISBN 0 563 40577 5
KURSAAL by Peter Anghelides
ISBN 0 563 40578 3
OPTION LOCK by Justin Richards
ISBN 0 563 40583 X
LONGEST DAY by Michael Collier
ISBN 0 563 40581 3
LEGACY OF THE DALEKS by John Peel
ISBN 0 563 40574 0
DREAMSTONE MOON by Paul Leonard
ISBN 0 563 40585 6
SEEING I by Jonathan Blum and Kate Orman
ISBN 0 563 40586 4
PLACEBO EFFECT by Gary Russell
ISBN 0 563 40587 2
VANDERDEKEN'S CHILDREN by Christopher Bulis
ISBN 0 563 40590 2
THE SCARLET EMPRESS by Paul Magrs
ISBN 0 563 40595 3

THE JANUS CONJUNCTION by Trevor Baxendale
ISBN 0 563 40599 6
BELTEMPEST by Jim Mortimore
ISBN 0 563 40593 7
THE FACE EATER by Simon Messingham
ISBN 0 563 55569 6
THE TAINT by Michael Collier
ISBN 0 563 55568 8
DEMONTAGE by Justin Richards
ISBN 0 563 55572 6
REVOLUTION MAN by Paul Leonard
ISBN 0 563 55570 X
DOMINION by Nick Walters
ISBN 0 563 55574 2
UNNATURAL HISTORY by Jonathan Blum and Kate Orman
ISBN 0 563 55576 9
AUTUMN MIST by David A. McIntee
ISBN 0 563 55583 1
INTERFERENCE: BOOK ONE by Lawrence Miles
ISBN 0 563 55580 7
INTERFERENCE: BOOK TWO by Lawrence Miles
ISBN 0 563 55582 3
THE BLUE ANGEL by Paul Magrs and Jeremy Hoad
ISBN 0 563 55581 5
THE TAKING OF PLANET 5
by Simon Bucher-Jones and Mark Clapham
ISBN 0 563 55585 8
FRONTIER WORLDS by Peter Anghelides
ISBN 0 563 55589 0
PARALLEL 59 by Natalie Dallaire and Stephen Cole
ISBN 0 563 555904
THE SHADOWS OF AVALON by Paul Cornell
ISBN 0 563 555882
THE FALL OF YQUATINE by Nick Walters
ISBN 0 563 55594 7
COLDHEART by Trevor Baxendale
ISBN 0 563 55595 5

THE SPACE AGE by Steve Lyons
ISBN 0 563 53800 7
THE BANQUO LEGACY by Andy Lane and Justin Richards
ISBN 0 563 53808 2
THE ANCESTOR CELL by Peter Anghelides and Stephen Cole
ISBN 0 563 53809 0
THE BURNING by Justin Richards
ISBN 0 563 53812 0
CASUALTIES OF WAR by Steve Emmerson
ISBN 0 563 53805 8
THE TURING TEST by Paul Leonard
ISBN 0 563 53806 6
ENDGAME by Terrance Dicks
ISBN 0 563 53802 3
FATHER TIME by Lance Parkin
ISBN 0 563 53810 4
ESCAPE VELOCITY by Colin Brake
ISBN 0 563 53825 2
EARTHWORLD by Jacqueline Rayner
ISBN 0 563 53827 9
VANISHING POINT by Stephen Cole
ISBN 0 563 53829 5
EATER OF WASPS by Trevor Baxendale
ISBN 0 563 53832 5
THE YEAR OF INTELLIGENT TIGERS by Kate Orman
ISBN 0 563 53831 7
THE SLOW EMPIRE by Dave Stone
ISBN 0 563 53835 X
DARK PROGENY by Steve Emmerson
ISBN 0 563 53837 6
THE CITY OF THE DEAD by Lloyd Rose
ISBN 0 563 53839 2
GRIMM REALITY by Simon Bucher-Jones and Kelly Hale
ISBN 0 563 53841 4
THE ADVENTURESS OF HENRIETTA STREET
by Lawrence Miles
ISBN 0 563 53842 2

MAD DOGS AND ENGLISHMEN by Paul Magrs
ISBN 0 563 53845 7
HOPE by Mark Clapham
ISBN 0 563 53846 5
ANACHROPHOBIA by Jonathan Morris
ISBN 0 563 53847 3
TRADING FUTURES by Lance Parkin
ISBN 0 563 53848 1
THE BOOK OF THE STILL by Paul Ebbs
ISBN 0 563 53851 1
THE CROOKED WORLD by Steve Lyons
ISBN 0 563 53856 2
HISTORY 101 by Mags L. Halliday
ISBN 0 563 53854 6
CAMERA OBSCURA by Lloyd Rose
ISBN 0 563 53857 0
TIME ZERO by Justin Richards
ISBN 0 563 53866 X
THE INFINITY RACE by Simon Messingham
ISBN 0 563 53863 5
THE DOMINO EFFECT by David Bishop
ISBN 0 563 53869 4
RECKLESS ENGINEERING by Nick Walters
ISBN 0563 48603 1

'PAST DOCTOR' RANGE

THE DEVIL GOBLINS FROM NEPTUNE
by Keith Topping and Martin Day
ISBN 0 563 40564 3
THE MURDER GAME by Steve Lyons
ISBN 0 563 40565 1
THE ULTIMATE TREASURE by Christopher Bulis
ISBN 0 563 40571 6
BUSINESS UNUSUAL by Gary Russell
ISBN 0 563 40575 9
ILLEGAL ALIEN by Mike Tucker and Robert Perry
ISBN 0 563 40570 8
THE ROUNDHEADS by Mark Gatiss
ISBN 0 563 40576 7
THE FACE OF THE ENEMY by David A. McIntee
ISBN 0 563 40580 5
EYE OF HEAVEN by Jim Mortimore
ISBN 0 563 40567 8
THE WITCH HUNTERS by Steve Lyons
ISBN 0 563 40579 1
THE HOLLOW MEN by Keith Topping and Martin Day
ISBN 0 563 40582 1
CATASTROPHEA by Terrance Dicks
ISBN 0 563 40584 8
MISSION: IMPRACTICAL by David A. McIntee
ISBN 0 563 40592 9
ZETA MAJOR by Simon Messingham
ISBN 0 563 40597 X
DREAMS OF EMPIRE by Justin Richards
ISBN 0 563 40598 8
LAST MAN RUNNING by Chris Boucher
ISBN 0 563 40594 5
MATRIX by Robert Perry and Mike Tucker
ISBN 0 563 40596 1
THE INFINITY DOCTORS by Lance Parkin
ISBN 0 563 40591 0

SALVATION by Steve Lyons
ISBN 0 563 55566 1
THE WAGES OF SIN by David A. McIntee
ISBN 0 563 55567 X
DEEP BLUE by Mark Morris
ISBN 0 563 55571 8
PLAYERS by Terrance Dicks
ISBN 0 563 55573 4
MILLENNIUM SHOCK by Justin Richards
ISBN 0 563 55586 6
STORM HARVEST by Robert Perry and Mike Tucker
ISBN 0 563 55577 7
THE FINAL SANCTION by Steve Lyons
ISBN 0 563 55584 X
CITY AT WORLD'S END by Christopher Bulis
ISBN 0 563 55579 3
DIVIDED LOYALTIES by Gary Russell
ISBN 0 563 55578 5
CORPSE MARKER by Chris Boucher
ISBN 0 563 55575 0
LAST OF THE GADERENE by Mark Gatiss
ISBN 0 563 55587 4
TOMB OF VALDEMAR by Simon Messingham
ISBN 0 563 55591 2
VERDIGRIS by Paul Magrs
ISBN 0 563 55592 0
GRAVE MATTER by Justin Richards
ISBN 0 563 55598 X
HEART OF TARDIS by Dave Stone
ISBN 0 563 55596 3
PRIME TIME by Mike Tucker
ISBN 0 563 55597 1
IMPERIAL MOON by Christopher Bulis
ISBN 0 563 53801 5
FESTIVAL OF DEATH by Jonathan Morris
ISBN 0 563 53803 1

INDEPENDENCE DAY by Peter Darvill-Evans
ISBN 0 563 53804 X
KING OF TERROR by Keith Topping
ISBN 0 563 53802 3
QUANTUM ARCHANGEL by Craig Hinton
ISBN 0 563 53824 4
BUNKER SOLDIERS by Martin Day
ISBN 0 563 53819 8
RAGS by Mick Lewis
ISBN 0 563 53826 0
THE SHADOW IN THE GLASS
by Justin Richards and Stephen Cole
ISBN 0 563 53838 4
ASYLUM by Peter Darvill-Evans
ISBN 0 563 53833 3
SUPERIOR BEINGS by Nick Walters
ISBN 0 563 53830 9
BYZANTIUM! by Keith Topping
ISBN 0 563 53836 8
BULLET TIME by David A. McIntee
ISBN 0 563 53834 1
PSI-ENCE FICTION by Chris Boucher
ISBN 0 563 53814 7
DYING IN THE SUN by Jon de Burgh Miller
ISBN 0 563 53840 6
INSTRUMENTS OF DARKNESS by Gary Russell
ISBN 0 563 53828 7
RELATIVE DEMENTIAS by Mark Michalowski
ISBN 0 563 53844 9
DRIFT by Simon A. Forward
ISBN 0 563 53843 0
PALACE OF THE RED SUN by Christopher Bulis
ISBN 0 563 53849 X
AMORALITY TALE by David Bishop
ISBN 0 563 53850 3
WARMONGER by Terrance Dicks
ISBN 0 563 53852 X

TEN LITTLE ALIENS by Stephen Cole
ISBN 0 563 53853 8
COMBAT ROCK by Mick Lewis
ISBN 0 563 53855 4
THE SUNS OF CARESH by Paul Saint
ISBN 0 563 53858 9
HERITAGE by Dale Smith
ISBN 0 563 53864 3
FEAR OF THE DARK by Trevor Baxendale
ISBN 0 563 53865 1
BLUE BOX by Kate Orman
ISBN 0 563 53859 7

SHORT STORY COLLECTIONS

SHORT TRIPS ed. Stephen Cole ISBN 0 563 40560 0
MORE SHORT TRIPS ed. Stephen Cole ISBN 0 563 55565 3
SHORT TRIPS AND SIDE STEPS
ed. Stephen Cole and Jacqueline Rayner ISBN 0 563 55599 8

The Worlds of Doctor Who

May 2003 – Also this month

From Big Finish Productions:
Creatures of Beauty
by Nicholas Briggs
Featuring the Third Doctor and Jo

Doctor Who Books Telepress
covers, reviews, news & interviews
http://www.bbc.co.uk/cult/doctorwho/books/
telepress

Coming soon from
BBC *Doctor Who* books:

The Last Resort
By Paul Leonard
Published June 2nd 2003
ISBN 0 563 48605 8
Featuring the Eighth Doctor

'I think time and space just fell apart.'

Anji isn't sure, but then it's hard to be sure of anything
now. Good Times Inc. promised a new tourist experience,
with hotels in every major period of human history – but
that kind of arrogance comes with a price, and it's a price
the Doctor doesn't want to pay.

As aliens conquer an alternative Earth, Anji and Fitz race
to find out how to stop Good Times without stopping
time itself – but they find that events are out of control;
they can't even save each other. When the Doctor tries to
help, it gets far worse. At the Last Resort, only Sabbath can
save the day. And then the price gets even higher…

*This is another in the series of continuing adventures
for the Eighth Doctor.*